The Last Man Anthology

Tales of Catastrophe, Disaster, & Woe

Edited by Hunter Liguore

A Sword & Saga Press Book

Sword and Saga Press

THE LAST MAN ANTHOLOGY: TALES OF CATASTROPHE, DISASTER, AND WOE

Edited by Hunter Liguore

Published by Sword and Saga Press, L.L.C.
www.SwordandSagaPress.com
Where the Names of Heroes are Born
Warriors Wanted

"A tribute to Mary Shelly, the mother of science fiction, and her novel, "The Last Man."
"A Sword and Saga Book."
Contents: Tales of Catastrophe, Disaster, and Woe.

ISBN: 978-0-615-38505-1

1. Science Fiction, Worldwide. 2. Science fiction, English. 3. Liguore, Hunter
Library of Congress Control Number: 2010934233
Printed in the United States of America

Praise for *The Last Man Anthology*

In her novel *The Last Man,* the mother of science fiction, Mary Shelley, provided nineteenth century readers with their first taste of catastrophic literature. *The Last Man Anthology* pays tribute to Shelley by showcasing contemporary, catastrophic-themed stories and poems that celebrate her influence on the science fiction genre for the twenty-first century reader.

"The anthology seamlessly interweaves classic tales and fresh new perspectives, page-turning prose and heart-tugging poetry, creating a haunting portrait of an all-too-possible (and not-too-distant) future.

"Within these pages we see a Wellsian view of alien invasion through the innocent eyes of a child and are forced to ponder the paradoxes and perils of time travel and panspermia.

"Page after page the reader finds themselves increasingly faced with the precariousness of our own existence, a philosophical exercise of vital importance in an age which has brought us to the brink of nuclear war as well as to impending shortages of natural resources and environmental devastation."
~Dr. Kristine Larsen, Professor of Physics and Astronomy, Central Connecticut State University.

"There is a dazzling smorgasbord of fiction and poetry here: classic stories about pandemics that kill off whole communities, as well as old and new stories about global warfare, alien conquests and natural disasters. The combination of pieces from different eras is inspired, and sets up a ghostly discussion where writers from the Golden Age of sci-fi speak to 21st-century writers haunted by 9-11 and global warming. This book is exhilarating to read."
~Jean Roberta, English Professor, University of Regina, Canada.

"*The Last Man Anthology* is brilliance at its best from some of the great authors of our time"

"A hauntingly beautiful collection of tales by new and established authors. A definite must-read."

"The Last Man Anthology is brilliance at its best from some of the great authors of our time. From the first moment you open the book until the last tale, you will be whisked away on a dark and dreary journey of catastrophic events, from the alien encounter to nuclear warfare to pretty much the last man standing. Each story is a road map of one possible future for mankind and should be viewed with an open mind—the future is about to start."
~Shelby Patrick, author of *The Fear Within*

"When I first picked up the *Last Man Anthology*, I have to admit I had no real idea what to expect. I'd never read Mary Shelley, only had a vague idea of the storyline behind Frankenstein and no knowledge whatsoever of *The Last Man*. When I finished, I felt like I knew the apocalypse in and out, I felt changed, and was left quietly reflecting on how I felt about humanity and the struggle to survive, about loneliness and how the machinations of the human race might fare after we are gone.

"This anthology gripped me, kept me reading late into the night and left its own marks on me afterward. There are some great stories in *The Last Man anthology*, and not just the ones that are written by established authors—in this anthology, Liguore has assembled a crop of new writers so damn good one could almost cry at their talent. This hauntingly beautiful collection of tales is a definite must-read. No question about that. A solid five out of five stars."
~E. S. Wynn, author of *Pink Carbide*

"Shelley would certainly have a copy of *The Last Man Anthology,"* on her nightstand! Gripped me from the first story, to the last."
~Cyndi Adamo, Librarian, University of Hartford Library.

"Dedication to the illustrious dead.
Shadows, arise and read your fall! Behold
the history of the Last Man."

Mary Shelley, 1826

Table of Contents

Tales of catastrophe, disaster, and woe

A Paradox: Tales of Hope
by
Michael D.C. Drout

This is the way the world ends:

> The breakers beat monotonously at the shores, casting up driftwood. An abandoned seaplane floated beyond the breakers. After a while the breakers caught the seaplane and threw it on the shore with the driftwood. It tilted and fractured a wing. There were shrimp carousing in the breakers, and the whiting that fed on the shrimp, and the shark that munched the whiting and found them admirable, in the sportive brutality of the sea.
> A wind came across the ocean, sweeping with it a pall of fine white ash. The ash fell into the sea and into the breakers. The breakers washed dead shrimp ashore with the driftwood. Then they washed up the whiting. The shark swam out to his deepest waters and brooded in the cold clean currents. He was very hungry that season.[1]

And this is the way the world ends:

> Then the moon came up, quite in her wrong position, very close to the sun, and she also looked red. And at the sight of her the sun began shooting out great flames, like whiskers or snakes of crimson fire, toward her. It is as if he were an octopus trying to draw her to himself in his tentacles. And perhaps he did draw her. At any rate she came to him, slowly at first, but then more and more quickly, till at last his long flames licked round her and the two ran together and become one huge ball like a burning coal. Great lumps of fire came dropping out of it into the sea and clouds of steam rose up.[2]

And this is the way the world ends:

---

[1] Miller, Walter M. *A Canticle for Leibowitz.*
[2] Lewis, C.S. *The Last Battle.* New York: Macmillan, 1956.

There was a sound like that of the gentle closing of a portal as big as the sky, the great door of heaven being closed softly. It was a grand AH-WHOOM.

I opened my eyes—and all the sea was *ice-nine*.

The moist green earth was a blue-white pearl.

The sky darkened. *Borasis*, the sun, became a sickly yellow ball, tiny and cruel.

The sky was filled with worms. The worms were tornadoes.[3]

Or this is the way the world ends:

As the next days passed into weeks, the dignified figure of the Japanese sat in his chair fifty yards away from him, guarding Traven from the blocks. Their magic still filled Traven's reveries, but he now had sufficient strength to rouse himself and forage for food. In the hot sunlight the skin of the Japanese became more and more bleached, and sometimes Traven would wake at night to find the white sepulchral figure sitting there, arms resting at its sides, in the shadows that crossed the concrete floor. At these moments he would often see his wife and son watching him from the dune. As time passed they came closer, and he would sometimes turn to find them only a few yards behind him.

Patiently Traven waited for them to speak to him, thinking of the great blocks whose entrance was guarded by the seated figure of the dead archangel, as the waves broke on the distant shores and the burning bombers fell through his dreams.[4]

Not with a whimper, but with the silence of a man contemplating. Not the entire world, but the world of the one man, the last man.

* * *

How many times the world has ended. In preparing this preface, I started collecting scenes of the ending of the world from science fiction, marginal and famous, classic and

---

[3] Vonnegut, Kurt. *Cat's Cradle*. New York: Dell, 1963.
[4] Ballard, J.G. "The Terminal Beach," In J.G. Ballard, *The Best Short Stories of J.G. Ballard*. New York: Henry Holt, 1995, 244-64.

forgotten. But I soon gave up. There were too many, even of the famous and well-remembered ones. It appears to be a great temptation to end the world when you are a writer, particularly a writer of science fiction. Human minds may be constructed in such a way that they are incapable of imagining themselves not existing, but, it seems, we have no trouble at all imagining the world ending. The end—in fire, or ice, in violent cataclysm or quiet drifting to sleep, in loneliness or mass horror—ever calls with a profound appeal.

Because the worlds being ended are the same worlds that the author has created, there is probably a deep lesson somewhere about the interconnection of creation and destruction, about the makers using their powers to destroy. Perhaps we should read into the fondness for Armageddon a deep-seated death instinct, not for the individual (the death instinct invented by Freud) but for civilization and life itself. Perhaps we should be warned by how easily such fantasies are created, how facile authors are with doomsday, how many the possible endings: maybe there is a deep desire for self-destruction within ourselves and our culture.

Except that in writing the end of the world, nothing is really destroyed at all. The writer's world is there, and the end of the world is there, and it all still exists, the tower and the ruin, the green meadow and the lifeless desert. And the true paradox of world-destruction, of apocalypticism in writing, is that often the art created in the depiction of that destruction is hauntingly beautiful or poignant beyond words: Walter Miller's fine pall of white ash which is, heartbreakingly, all mankind have ever created; J.G. Ballard's crystal prisms swallowing the forest; the inexorable rise of the green wave over J.R.R. Tolkien's Númenor, the million empty cities and terminal beaches and wind-swept deserts that have filled nearly a century of science fiction.

And when you have created something poignant and strangely beautiful (in its own terrifying way), there needs to be someone there to observe it and to report. That person is the last man, who is the author herself, himself: alone, contemplating, reporting, describing, creating, writing the Book of the Dead, saying goodbye and naming the things lost and to be lost, and in so doing, making them be.

* * *

It is a commonplace in bad science fiction criticism—the kind written by critics who read little science fiction—that stories about the end of the world are a particular creation of the post-War era, the nuclear age. Now for the first time, goes the line of reasoning, there really could be an end of the world, and so this technological fact was reflected in fiction.

No doubt there is a kernel of truth in the assertion, and there were indeed many great apocalyptic stories written after Hiroshima and Nagasaki (which occurred exactly 65 years before I wrote this sentence). But Mary Shelley felt the pain and poignancy in the previous century, and 1000 years ago the anonymous Icelandic poet of *Völuspá* wrote of the coming Fimbulwinter, the deaths of gods and men, the sun turning black and the stars falling from the sky. The vision of St John, the Apocalypse, is older still, and before that, going back into the dark, are more stories of the end of the world, from the *Epic of Gilgamesh* to stories lost and forgotten, whispers in the cultural subconscious.

What makes Mary Shelley as prescient in *The Last Man* as she was in *Frankenstein or, the Modern Prometheus* was her understanding that the *real* story, for the readers of science fiction, was not the brute fact of the end of the world but the emotions and intellect of the observer, both inside and outside the story. That the world would end was accepted by millions for generations even if this knowledge was held within the specific religious framework of a Day of Judgment, a *Shoah* or a Calamity: a truth, but in a supernatural context. That physics and inexorable mathematics shows that the sun will eventually expand to destroy the earth, that the heat death of the universe or the Big Crunch is either way the inevitable end even if technology allows humans to spread beyond earth, only moves the knowledge of finality from one epistemological realm to the other. And the distinction is not necessarily as significant as it may seem: medieval Christians believed in the Book of Revelation no less than contemporary readers believe in the book of cosmology and physics, and although we perceive a difference, there is no evidence that they would have.

In J.G. Ballard's "The Voices of Time," a signal from Canes Venatici has been has been received, a series of numbers, each fifty million digits long, each number just one less than the one before it. At the time the series reaches zero, the universe will have ended. The character who explains this to Powers, the dying protagonist, suddenly grips his arm, peers into his eyes, and says:

"You're not alone, Powers, don't think you are. These are the voices of time, and they're all saying good-bye to you."

The death of an individual: the death of the universe. Mary Shelley saw that, in a world of novels and stories, they were the same, and the voices of time were counting down, whether with the inexorable consistency of entropy always increasing, or the surprise of a plague, fire, earthquake, climbing wave, for each man and all men and all their works, would die. But for a writer, the simple portrayal of the physical end was not the real focus, it was only a background—a beautiful, horrifying, meaningful background, but a background nevertheless—against which to place the thoughts and emotions of the last man. Who, in the end, both the writer, who had created the world that was now ending and who was creating that same ending, and the reader, who perceives the final end. Again and again.

* * *

The stories in this collection create worlds as they destroy them. They depict the end of the human race in fire and ice, alien invasion, plague, pollution, nuclear war, cultural evolution. But always there is a viewer, someone to see and describe the end, a character, or a narrator, or, at the very least, the reader reading the writer writing. Humans may have evolved to be unable to imagine their own nonexistence. They easily, and with great vigor and intensity, imagine the end of the world. But even when it is all gone, there is, through the medium of writing, the construction of a reader by the words of the writer, someone to see that end. Even at dying of the earth the strange crabs are seen by the Time Traveler. The Ancient Mariner tells his story to the wedding guest who tells his story to us, time and again. Like a long-buried seed, the story brings to life its reader even at the greatest removes in time and place.

It is possible, even easy, to read stories of the end of the world and the last man as warnings or lessons. Certainly Mary Shelley wanted to express something about the failure of utopian political ideals and both the enlightenment and the sorrow that comes from learning—as humankind so often does—that the abstract model fails in unexpected ways. The Big Bug movies of the 1950s were intended, at least in part, to warn against radiation, nuclear weapons and uncontrolled experiments. Mary Shelley's *Frankenstein* is often—wrongly—described as a cautionary tale, as have been many, many science fiction stories since, and some certainly have been intended to be warnings. Stop doing this, or else... is the message of much bad SF, and even some of the good: not all didactic work is bad, particularly in this genre.

And certainly stories of the end of the world make us, for a moment, better appreciate the world we have, hug our own children tighter when thinking of the little girl clutching her teddy bear in William Woods' story in this volume, the outline of the happy family burnt into the side of the house in Ray Bradbury's "There Will Come Soft Rains." Stories of the end of the world make us think of our own loves (surprisingly, not as frequently of ourselves) and *their* future losses, though we really need only history, not imagination, to remind us of how fragile indeed is everything that seems solid. Stories of the end of the world can certainly frighten us, but no one needs a science fiction writer to imagine a tsunami, a firestorm, the spread of a plague, two airplanes in a cloudless September sky. Imagination, without any help from artistic craft, can take a river overflowing its banks and make the Deluge, a fire in a meadow, Ragnarok. Craft can heighten fear, but it is not necessary for its creation.

Like all well-made artworks, stories of the end of the world and the last man affect us on different levels at the same time—beauty, fear, learning, moralizing—the adrenaline of imagined excitement and the intellectual pleasure of solving a puzzle, the emotion of caring for a protagonist and the pleasure in the play of sound and sense. But amidst all of the complex thoughts and emotions brought about by the stories in this collection, and other stories of the last man, there is something more. That the Ancient Mariner is telling us his story means that he—and more importantly—us, are no longer alone, alone, all all alone (the most terrifying line in all of English poetry) but that someone is listening, someone is reading, someone saw the end and wrote about it, sub-creating (to use Tolkien's word) a new world that had not existed before it was written. When we imagine the last man, we are really imagining the story still going on, the sub-created world and the world outside continuing to have some existence in a mind that is still the mind of our minds, the human consciousness. It may be a false hope, but it is an inescapable one, for to write of the end of the world is to assume that someone will read the writing. In that sense, that circular sense, the end is, shockingly, reassuring. Tales of catastrophe, disaster and woe are, at their heart, like all stories, tales of hope. Someone is listening.

Introduction

Catastrophe, disaster, and woe all have different meanings for different people. Despite our differences, we can recognize when a disaster occurs in the lives of others. Often, it is through catastrophe and disaster that our differences fall to the wayside, and we can cross the bridge, and meet as equals of the human race.

While the immediacy of disaster creates a pandemonium of heartbreak and loss, in the underlying layers, something stronger pushes through. I believe it is hope and the will of the human spirit to persevere that endures through these situations.

I had the opportunity to witness the essence of the human spirit in its finest moment. I was visiting a small town in Massachusetts, known for its arts, education, and its poverty. A homeless man of around fifty, dirt faced, unshaven, greasy hair, and haggard clothes, took a seat at the end of a street bench, where I was reading and listening to a street musician.

The man begged for a cigarette from a passerby. A young kid gave him the one he was smoking. The man sat for a time smoking and listening to the music. It was a warm spring day, with clear skies.

We were in close proximity; enough that as time went on, I noticed him pull out a pocket of change. He searched through mostly pennies to find two clean silver quarters. His whole worth was in his hand, his meal, his possession, his pride. All of what he endured, all the roads he walked had brought him to this moment, and I was a witness.

With two quarters in tow, I watched the homeless man pass the musician and drop the two quarters into the guitar case. He nodded, as if to indicate that he appreciated and approved of the music. Despite being down-trodden in a structured society, one that would put him at the bottom, suddenly he was every man, every person that ever lived through tough times and persevered. He was for that moment just a man who enjoyed the music.

In many ways, disaster is the force that drives people together, to make us look at one another without prejudice or judgment. It is the moment when we have to stop the day-to-day in order to be available to assist another living being that may need a hand.

What is a disaster? It is a sudden event or catastrophe, man-made or natural that causes loss, damage, destruction, devastation, or woe to people, animals, property, the Earth, and more.

Included in this collection is a timeline of disasters for the decade. It is in no way complete, but serves as a reminder of what we've experienced as a collective people. What parts did each of us play in these moments? How did our human spirits persevere? How did we mourn? How did we triumph? We welcome your stories.

During the time that Mary Shelley wrote her novel, "The Last Man," from which this anthology takes its name, she was experiencing her own calamity. Shelley was suffering, and adjusting to the loss of her husband, Percy, who drowned in a sailing accident. It wasn't the first close death she experienced. She had previously mourned the deaths of three of her four children. In 1825, with her last surviving child, Shelley returned to London, and started working on her futuristic novel.

The Last Man tells the story of Lionel Verney, an outsider, who narrates his story of unrequited love, and the eventual extermination of the human race at the hands of a plague. Readers familiar with Shelley's loss will find that Lionel resembles her husband, Percy, and the calamity, one can speculate, is more akin to the loss she was experiencing for her one true love at the time.

But it's important to mention that Shelley's vision was both prophetic and haunting. We've witnessed plagues that have been detrimental, and always have the threat of a super strand virus that could wipe out our civilization. What would our world look like with three quarters of the population buried, or even worse, what if there was only one man, as Shelley described?

The Last Man Anthology is a roadmap to answering this question. What will our future look like amid another century of disaster? At the heart of the collection is the theme of finality—of being last. The collection delivers a myriad of voices across time, boundaries, and continents, and seeks not only to entertain, but to consider what catastrophe, disaster, and woe might look like in a variety of circumstances.

The *Last Man Anthology* is also a record of catastrophe in the past, present and inevitable future. In Shelley's day, plague was the immediate conceivable threat. Included is an excerpt from Jack London's *The Scarlet Plague*, which takes place in the year 2012, and details a plague-ridden *future*.

During the later half of the twentieth century, nuclear war becomes the immediate catastrophe. We include Ray Bradbury's, *There Will Come Soft Rains,* which shows the sorrowful aftermath of a nuclear disaster. C. J. Cherryh brings us "Cassandra," another haunting tale of nuclear warfare.

Moving forward to the present, taking center stage is the preoccupation with overpopulation and reproduction, (*Omega Museum* by Jaleta Clegg and *Origins* by Liz R. F. Coley); alien abduction, (*Arturo* by M. Sullivan and *Teddy and the Last Girl on Brighton Street* by William Wood); terrorism, (*The Last Day of Sanity* by Darryll B. Snyder and *The Paperless Doctrine of 2152* by Aaron M. Wilson); and environmental calamity, (水 by Jack Frey, pronounced "shui," meaning *water*).

But the anthology doesn't stop there. Jacqueline Fedyk takes us to a small town pie baking contest gone wrong in *My Blue Ribbon Pies*; Kodilynn Calhoun shows us the final moments of the last werewolf in *Going Home.* Barry N. Malzberg gives a tragic and authentic look at the last science fiction writer in *Corridors.* Koos Kombuis, once very active in the struggle against apartheid, has the last word, as he takes us to the fringes of the future with the last philosopher in *The Last of the Great Coffee Shop Philosophers.* And these are only a few of the numerous stories and poems that aim to show us a glimpse of our future.

Disaster will continue to strike. Writers will continue to chronicle and record their experiences, real or imagined. We welcome you to partake in our vision, and experience the future, the past—our fragile world.

Hunter Liguore,

Editor-In-Chief
Samhain, 2010

Timeline of Catastrophe, 2000-2010

The following timeline is incomplete, but serves as a record of the immensity of disasters for the current decade across the globe.

2000: Paris, France, Air France Flight 4590 crashes, kills 113, 109 on the plane, four on the ground.
2000: Kentucky, United States, Martin County sludge spill dumps 306 million gallons of sludge in the Tug Fork River.
2000: Mozambique, Africa, floods cover most of the country for five weeks, resulting in 800 deaths, causing devastation for years to come.
2000: Holland, Enschede Factory firework disaster injured 947, killed 23, 2000 homes destroyed, blast felt for 19 miles.

2001: Gujarat, Pakistan, earthquake destroys 400,000 homes, injured 167K, and killed 20-30K.
2001: New York, United States, terror attack on World Trade Center, kills nearly 3000.
2001: Alabama, U.S., No. 5 Mine, explosion, 13 deaths.
2001: China, a series of explosions destroyed four residential buildings, killing 108 people.
2001: Siberia, Russia, Russian Tupolev-154 passenger plane crashed and burst into flames, killing all 145 people aboard.
2001: Algiers, Algeria, Heavy rains caused the worst flooding in two decades; official death toll stood at 651 (701 nationwide).
2001: Lima, Peru, nearly 300 people died in a massive fire that started after someone set off a firecracker.

2002: Lagos, Nigeria, munitions blast kills 600.
2002: Senegal, Africa, ferry Loola sinks off Gambia, results in deaths of 1863 people.
2002: Ayyat, Egypt, 361 people killed in a fire aboard a crowded passenger train. The fire was reportedly started after a gas cylinder used for cooking exploded.
2002: Southern India, brutal heat wave, particularly in Andhra Pradesh State, left more than 600 dead nationwide.
2002: Muamba, Mozambique, 192 people died and 169 more were injured in train crash.

2002: China, torrential rainfall produced floods and mudslides leaving 750 people dead and tens of thousands more homeless.
2003: United States, Space ship Columbia disintegrates over Texas, crew perishes.
2003: Hong Kong, China, SARS epidemic begins in March.
2003: France, heat wave kills over 10,000 in August, with temperatures over 100 F.
2003: SE, Iran, 6.6 magnitude earthquake kills 31,000, injures 30,000, and many more homeless, plus damage to infrastructure.
2003: Bangladesh and Northern India, nearly 400 people perished from cold weather and icy winds in an area where millions of people have no heat, electricity, or warm clothing.
2003: Daegu, South Korea, a subway fire started by an arsonist, raced through two trains, killing at least 189 people and injuring more than 140.

2004: Paraguay, fire breaks out in supermarket claiming the lives of 300 Sunday shoppers.
2004: Darfur, Sudan, WHO Organization reports 70,000 Sudanese dead due to disease and malnutrition.
2004: Indian Ocean Tsunami, started by a mega earthquake under sea, kills over 230,000 and destroys much of the coastal area in Indonesia.
2004: Mecca, Saudi Arabia, 251 pilgrims killed during a stampede at the Hajj pilgrimage.
2004: Eastern coast, Philippines, flash floods and landslides from Typhoon Winnie killed more than 500 people.

2005: Venezuela, South America, jet crash claims the lives of 160.
2005: US, Hurricane Katrina claims the lives of nearly 2000, with 81 billion in damage.
2005: Liaoning province, China, a gas explosion killed 209 miners at the Sunjiawan mine.
2005: Sharm el-Sheikh, Egypt, 88 people killed at an Egyptian resort, when two suicide car bombs collide.
2005: Baghdad, Iraq, 950 pilgrims killed in stampede as they crossed a bridge over the Tigris.

2006: Egypt, ship sinks in Red Sea killing 1400.
2006: Mecca, pilgrimage stampede kills nearly 345.

2006: Java, Indonesia, a 6.3 magnitude earthquake killed more than 5,700 people and destroyed 135,000 homes.
2006: North Korea, severe floods killed 900 people.
2006: Padang, Philippines, Typhoon Durian with winds of 162 miles per hour caused a massive mudslide from Mount Mayon burying more than 500 people under volcanic ash, boulders, and water.

2007: Sao Paulo, Brazil, plane crash kills 200.
2007: Minnesota, United States, a bridge collapses in Minnesota, claims many lives.
2007: Greece, forest fires claim lives of 63.
2007: California, United States, forest fires force 500,000 residents to flee their homes.
2007: Utah, United States, Crandall Canyon Mine collapse, 9 deaths.
2007: Ulyanovskaya, Russia, methane explosion kills 110 people in a coalmine.
2007: Blacksburg, VA, United States, a Virginia Tech student killed 32 fellow students and then himself in the most deadly shooting rampage in U.S. history.
2007: Hunan province, China, a bridge undergoing construction collapsed in southern China, killing 28 people.

2008: Eastern Sichuan, China: Earthquake takes the lives of 87,587, plus destroys much of the surrounding land.
2008: Myanmar, Burma, cyclone claims the lives of 78,000, 56,000 missing.
2008: Spain, 153 killed in plane crash.
2008: China, tainted milk formula kills 3 babies, 6200 made ill.
2008: Simbawi, cholera claims the lives of 1000.
2008: Philippines, a ferry, the *Princess of the Stars*, is struck by Typhoon Fengshen, killing 865 passengers and crew.
2008: Haiti, over 190 students die and over a hundred more are injured when a poorly constructed church-run school collapses on the outskirts of Port-au-Prince.
2008: Russia, 20 people die and 21 more are injured when two compartments of a new Russian nuclear submarine flood with Freon gas during tests.

2009: Melbourne, Australia, bush fires claim the lives of 181.
2009: Mexico, swine flu kills 60.

2009: Italy, quake kills 300.
2009: Southern Sumatra, Indonesia: Earthquake claims the lives of 1117, and injuring 1214, with 181,665 buildings destroyed, and 451K people displaced.
2009: Baghdad, Iraq, a series of car bombs destroys government buildings, at least 121 people dead and 400 wounded.

2010: Haiti, Earthquake estimates 222,570 people killed, 300,000 injured, 1.3 million displaced, 97,000 houses destroyed and 188,000 damaged.
2010: Kazakhstan, Russia, Kyzyl-Agash Dam bursts and floods village, 43 killed, 300 injured, 1000 evacuated.
2010: Rio de Janero, Brazil, floods leave 212 dead, 161 injured, 15,000 homeless.
2010: Salang, Afghanistan, 36 avalanches bury two miles of roads, kills 172, and traps 2,000 travelers.
2010: Gulf of Mexico, United States, British Petroleum oil spill, tons of crude oil covers 2700 miles of ocean.
2010: China, 1500 tons of crude oil spills over 166 miles near the Yellow Sea.
2010: Iceland: Volcanic ash causes economic disaster.
2010: West Virginia, United States, Upper Big Branch Mine explosion, kills 29.
2010: Moscow, Russia, wildfires ravage 450 square miles, 34 dead, thousands homeless.

In loving memory of those who've perished in the Earth's disasters.

The Last Man Anthology:
Tales of Catastrophe, Disaster, & Woe

Snowmelt
by
Lane Ashfeldt

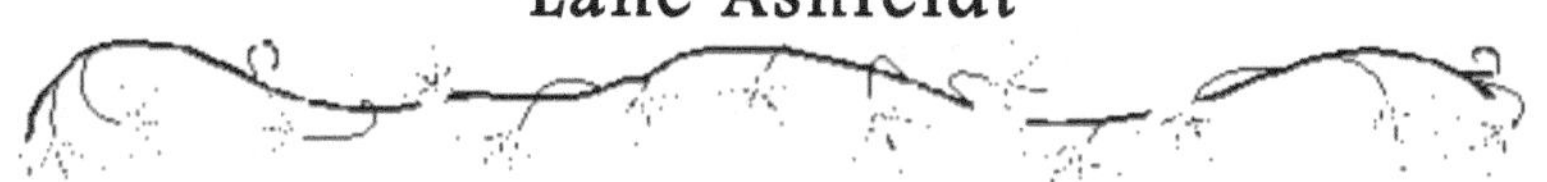

"I had thought such ecstasy dead in me for ever, but the sun of Italy has thawed the frozen stream." -Mary Shelley, "Rambles in Germany and Italy," 1844.

That winter, as snows fell on England and fires raged in Australia, as floods visited both countries, Miss Campbell became convinced the end was near.

She did not say so to neighbors or to people at the library, but this idea was not new to her. For months, she had lived in fear of a plague. Scientists were on the alert for a new contagious disease. It was overdue. The next one to hit would be rapid and deadly, they said. In deference to their opinions she filled two kitchen cupboards with tinned beans and bottled water, enough to survive a month without leaving her attic floor flat. She imagined her neighbors in the event of a quarantine. No "Blitz spirit" for them; they'd be out looting the Tesco Express, the Boots, the Morrisons, even the all-night shop at the garage. When all obvious sources of food and medicine had been exhausted, they would attack each other. Her only chance of survival would be to sit tight with her doors and windows locked.

But what form would this new plague take? Miss Campbell asked herself. The avian flu? Some sort of viral cancer? Perhaps, like the Black Death, it had sneaked in at the back door and was quietly multiplying as it fixed itself on the old, the weak and the young. Mr. Shanahan, a regular at the library, had been hospitalized at Halloween for laser surgery on his eye. By Christmas he was gone. If she ever needed an operation, she would choose day surgery; she did not wish to join the list of superbug victims.

Now, watching the burning bushes and frozen lakes, listening to the signs and portents that issued forth from her television screen, Miss Campbell began to think that the end of the world might after all be precipitated by something other than a plague. By extreme weather, perhaps: melted ice caps, fire and brimstone, a black sun.

She spent the morning boxing atlases and encyclopedias. The building she'd worked in for fifteen years had closed its doors, and they had three days in which to stock the new library. Someone came into the reference room and called out, "Miss Campbell, you here?" She popped her head out from behind the shelf and bumped into Angela from reception.

"Oh! I've a caller asking for the head librarian but Matt's at a conference. He wants to know when we want those PCs set up in HeadSpace—"

"HeadSpace?"

"You know, the new zone for teenagers. He just needs to confirm an installation slot."

Oh yes, the room Matt wouldn't let her order any books for. Some grand scheme of his to "raise the footfall" of young people.

"Very well, I'll speak to him."

She took the phone and confirmed a time on Thursday.

"Excellent. So they'll be up and running ahead of launch?"

Angela smiled at her.

"Indeed."

Miss Campbell found it hard to be enthusiastic. She'd hoped to stay on another eight years at the library, until retirement, but her role was changing so fast. Once, her job had been to share her love of books. Not any more. Books, actual physical books made of paper, were becoming a rarity, something to be tucked away in forgotten corners.

That lunchtime she came across a skip in the library car park filled with old hardbacks. Matt had inquired about stock disposal the other day. "Generally we donate," she said but he frowned and told her, "There are additional costs attached, and we're over budget on the move". She spent her lunch break standing on a chair, reaching into the skip to fish out books worth saving. Then she ferried them down the road to Oxfam. It seemed churlish given how much the council was spending, but Miss Campbell couldn't help it: she was going to miss the old library.

The day of the move coincided with a day's annual leave booked months ago. For weeks, Miss Campbell had looked forward to this trip. She was taking an evening class on the early novel, and a visit to a library of early women's writing was part of her studies.

Fresh snow had fallen and everything looked like a Christmas card. The train traveled back in time as swiftly as it raced through frozen fields and copses, until it came to a station whose platforms held no cafés, only painted wooden shelters and matching footbridges. She finally reached the last stop, the end of the line.

Miss Campbell consulted her map and picked her way down the high street and through the small town, avoiding icy patches and lumps of trodden snow. When she reached the grounds of the house, the whole area was warm and dry. A meadow stretched snow-free and golden into the distance, and a man loaded bales of hay into the loft of a barn as if she'd happened on a small unseasonable patch of summer.

She found her destination, rang the bell, signed in, climbed the uneven wooden steps, and knocked on the library door. A simple room containing books, wooden desks, lamps. A concentrated silence that she longed to bottle and unleash in her own library.

She requested "The Last Man."

It was an early edition bound in three volumes. Leather edged, with marbled covers and a matching box. She slid the books out, noting that in 1826 the name "Mary Shelley" still did not appear. By then, Percy had been dead a few years and her married name might have helped sales, but the credit was to "The Author of Frankenstein." Miss Campbell placed the top book on the foam reader. It fell open to the first page.

"Hear you not the rushing sound of the coming tempest? Do you not behold the clouds open, and destruction lurid and dire pour down on the blasted earth? See you not the thunderbolt fall, and are deafened by the shout of heaven that follows its descent? Feel you not the earth quake and open with agonizing groans, while the air is pregnant with shrieks and wailings—all announcing the last days of man?" —*The Last Man*, by The Author of Frankenstein (Mary Wollstonecraft Shelley), Henry Colburn: London, 1826.

Miss Campbell rose from her seat in alarm. What if this passage from the third volume had revealed itself to her as a warning? A sign. Yes, that was it. The signs were here, but no one could read them. No one wanted to read them.

She hurried to the window, searching for what? A thunderbolt, a quake, a tempest? She half expected to watch the lawn rip asunder, but still it stretched away from the house, green and sunny. She stood at the window as others had stood before her, going back four centuries. Even before the house existed, local thanes had lived in this area, and before them, Romans, drawn by a warmth they missed from the south.

She breathed deeply.

These ancient words, which might have filled her with terror had she read them alone in her flat at night, were not ready to come true just yet.

Miss Campbell returned to her seat, and to her work.

The day passed swiftly, the sun racing across the south lawn to disappear behind the trees. When she looked back as she closed the gate, the last light bathed the house and filled the air around it.

On the walk to the station, the magic of bygone centuries receded. People on the high street did the same kind of thing people in Balham did — bought *naan* bread or *focaccia*, fruit or meat, wine or beer — as they wended their way home. On the train back to the city, the sky closed over, a lid slammed on the world.

Descending the steps into the Underground, Miss Campbell was hit by its rich, dirty stink. Metallic yet animal. A smell she had failed to notice this morning, it had been such a long time since she'd breathed clean air.

That night she settled in front of her 1973 typewriter and began to type. Earlier she had put off this task, because how can you reduce a person to a few pages, a life and its work to five thousand words? Somehow she felt less wary of her subject now. Spurred on by the noisy rattle of the golf ball, she wrote of Mary Shelley's dark loneliness and her struggles as a single parent, of her visions of the end of the world, penned a hundred and fifty years before this typewriter was manufactured and set another century beyond that, in 2073.

"Like Frankenstein and horror," Miss Campbell wrote, "The Last Man was conceived before science fiction was a genre, before others trod accepted paths into this strange new world. Before leaps in time became pedestrian. Mary Shelley's vision of

the future was very different from the one we have today. It had no place for gadgets such as the sonic screwdriver or the improbability drive…"
Miss Campbell typed far into the night, aware and yet unaware of time passing, pausing, rewinding, forwarding.

The following day the computers arrived, and by eleven Miss Campbell was in HeadSpace with the man who had come to install them. Matt, too, was there to see his vision take shape.

"Fantastic, isn't it?"

"I suppose."

"You don't sound so sure."

"It's just, we could fit thousands of books in this space, do you know?"

"And I'm sure you know," he smiled, "that each computer allows its user to view an infinite number of virtual books?"

"No actual books, though."

The man installing the machines looked up and the two men exchanged sympathetic glances. Matt declaimed, as if a small crowd had gathered round to hear him: "What is an actual book? Isn't it quite arbitrary? Engravings, wooden tablets, scrolls, vellum sheets, paper; technology moves on, and we must move with it. Change doesn't have to be a bad thing."

"I like computers. In the library, we use them all the time, to order new books or track returns." A pause while she searched for the right way to put this without appearing confrontational. "But I like books, too. I don't think computers can replace them." She looked up, curious to see how he'd respond, but he was miles away, sending text messages.

At the launch event, she avoided Matt. Easily done. He was busy impressing the local government luminaries who had bankrolled his new library, telling them about the events planned to promote it. They clustered around him, looking even more ironed and dry-cleaned than the librarians, who were at pains to look their best. A champagne reception at work was a rare treat and they were out to enjoy it. Angela followed Miss Campbell's gaze.

"He's such a high flyer, Matt. I wonder, will he still be with us in six months time, or will he have moved on to some other milestone project?"

"Who cares?" said one librarian.

"Fine by me if he goes," said another. "We'll cope without."

"Last week he gave me a lecture on the benefits of change," Miss Campbell said. "I took him at his word. I'm selling my flat and moving out of London."

"Isn't now a bad time to sell?

"Only the worst for thirty years, they say. But I'm not waiting thirty years for the next good time."

There was a rush of questions from her colleagues about where she was moving to, and she told them.

"Oh, not such a long commute," Angela said. "So you'll stay on here? At the library I mean." The look she gave Miss Campbell said, don't do anything foolish, my girl.

"Like Matt says, change can be a good thing. There's a little library out that way that needs a volunteer. I'll love the work, and if all goes well they'll think of me when a paid vacancy comes up."

Half disbelieving, half envious, they raised a toast to her new life and the conversation moved on.

Later Angela took her to one side.

"If you don't mind my saying, I hope you've thought things through. Doesn't pay to be too impulsive, does it?"

Miss Campbell thought of Mary Shelley. Always hard up for money. No wonder, since her men folk were so careless with their finances, but she refused to let money take over. If she had, there'd be less of interest for the modern reader to learn about her. As things stood, the time was ripe for a serious in-depth study, and Miss Campbell thought she might just be the person to undertake it.

"Doesn't the danger lie in entrusting our future to others? Like bankers, I mean. Perhaps, Angela, we should take charge—"

"Don't bring "the recession" into this. I'm thinking of you, is all. You don't want to make things hard on yourself."

Miss Campbell smiled. "I'm thinking of me, too. I'm thinking, *I only have one life and it could end any time.* There are a few things I'd like to do before that happens, do you know?"

The sun tipped her face through the train window and she closed her eyes to focus on its warmth. Already the journey felt familiar. This time she was going south to look for a flat. She had boxed her things in readiness; early that morning a man from Oxfam had come to collect her donation. "Not the kind of stuff people usually give us. Gone off beans, then, have you?"

he asked Miss Campbell as he lifted the crates of tinned food. She smiled. She'd stopped believing there was much point in preparing for a plague or for the end of the world. If it came, it came.

He nodded toward the cardboard boxes. "Those old hardbacks, you'll be wanting them gone too, my love?"

"Oh no," she said. "I'll be needing those."

The train continued south at a leisurely pace. In the sunlight the snow softened and began to dissipate. Brooks and streams, unfrozen, grew brown with snowmelt and brimmed over to lap at fields, their eager ripples forming new and temporary lakes.

Teddy & the Last Girl on Brighton Street
by
William Wood

Hailey peeked out her window at the leaves falling from the sky. The dirt and smoke in the air made her eyes itch and burn. She wiped them with her sleeve and hugged Teddy tight.

Be a big girl, Daddy had said before he went away. *And don't let Teddy cry.*

So far Teddy had cried a little, but Hailey was determined not to cry. She had to set an example.

The string holding the bear's left eye broke yesterday. She'd placed the black, plastic circle on her Polly Pockets nightstand, and asked Daddy if Mommy could fix Teddy when she came home from work. Daddy hadn't answered at first. He hugged her tight, though, and cried a little. When he stopped, he said Mommy was a doctor, and she was very busy helping people at the hospital. She might not be home for a long time. He almost cried again, but Hailey hugged him with all her muscles so he wouldn't. She didn't like Daddy crying.

Most of her ceiling had fallen, burying Teddy and sending cardboard boxes from the attic tumbling down on her along with lumps of fuzzy, pink cotton that made her skin itch. The big fan from the attic that Daddy used to cool the house in the summer lay on her nightstand with bricks and boards from her wall. Hailey had pulled Teddy free of the mess, but she couldn't find his missing eye. She tried to move the fan and the pieces of her wall, but they wouldn't budge. Teddy sat on the floor nearby, waiting patiently, his tan fur and white muzzle coated in gray-white dust. Hailey's lower lip quivered. She'd never find his eye now. The mess was too big.

Her room was getting cold. Every time the evening air howled through the big holes on each side of the window, Hailey hugged Teddy tighter and scrunched down so no one could see her, not even the mean old wind.

I won't let anything hurt you, Daddy had said.

Hailey wished Daddy would come home now. She crawled through chunks of wall, mangled pipes, and busted floorboards to peek out one of the big holes. The street outside was quiet and still. Fog rose from cracks where the road buckled, twisting through the scorched trees along both sides. There was still no sign of Daddy or his big, black car.

Hailey was careful as she leaned forward to see farther up the street. Most of the glass in her window was gone, but the edges still clung to the frame and they were sharp. She didn't want to get cut and make Mommy worry. She was already going to be mad when she saw the house.

Hailey picked her way across her messy room, careful not to snag on the jagged pieces of wood and loose nails that hid under every step. In the kitchen, Daddy's Army friend was sleeping under a piece of the dining room wall. His name was Sergeant. Hailey laughed sometimes because Daddy had so many friends from his work named Sergeant. Red light from the sunset streamed through the open ceiling and the missing wall. She could see straight across the kitchen table into the back yard where her playhouse sat in the crook of the big tree.

Most of the damage to the house had happened before breakfast, a few minutes after the television stopped working and the lights went out. The sky had gotten very bright. A few seconds later, thunder shook the ground so badly that everything started falling, inside and outside. Sergeant had yelled for her to stay put and he would find her. Then more of the house came down and he started screaming things she didn't understand. Daddy had left Sergeant to look after her. Teddy, too. He told her she would be safer at the house than she would be where he was going. He said the aliens didn't care about the little towns, only the big cities and the Army bases where he worked sometimes. Hailey wondered if the aliens looked like the puppets on Sesame Street or if they were the scarier kind like on the Disney Channel.

When Sergeant stopped yelling, he called for help on his radio. Hailey was surprised when no one answered. She'd always watched Sergeant and the other people Daddy worked with when they came to visit. They liked to talk on their radios very much. Sergeant had cried for a little while, too, when no one wanted to talk to him. Then he fell asleep. Hailey didn't even know that Daddy's friends *could* cry, until she heard this one with her own ears. She hadn't known Daddy could cry either. But he did.

Hailey wasn't going to cry, though. She was a big girl.

She sipped at her warm juice box, and hugged Teddy tight in her other arm. Teddy was hard inside since Daddy had fixed him, and warm too. Daddy said Teddy would make sure the aliens didn't hurt her while he was away.

With the refrigerator lying on its side, she could only open the bottom door. The only juice boxes in the bottom were apple and those were okay, but the cherry ones were her favorite. Maybe Sergeant could help her find some when he woke up. She took a juice and closed the door so all of the cold wouldn't get out, just like Daddy always said. Pulling the wrapper from the straw, she poked it into the little hole on top of the box all by herself.

A rumble came from above the house and she jumped. Sometimes the big planes flew so close, roaring and screaming, that they hurt her ears. Each time they passed, she ducked under her Winnie the Pooh blanket with Teddy, and played with the toys in Teddy's backpack, until the scary noises stopped. Daddy flew planes for the Army before he met Mommy. Now he made parts for them so they could stop the bad guys from doing terrible things. Daddy said the aliens were bad guys. He said when the aliens landed on the Moon, they wanted the whole Earth for themselves, and didn't want to share. Hailey didn't think they were very nice. Daddy told her not to worry though, because he and Uncle Sam were going to work together, and stop the monsters until they went away.

Hailey couldn't remember Uncle Sam, but he must be really nice if he was going to help Daddy stop the monsters. Maybe Uncle Sam was like Uncle Derrick. Uncle Derrick always brought presents when he came to visit. Last Christmas he gave Hailey her best friend in the whole wide world—Teddy.

Hailey picked at the loose threads where Teddy missing eye should have been. Poor bear, but he was very brave.

She could hear Daddy's voice in her head. *You're my little angel. Teddy will make sure the bad guys can't hurt you.*

The ground shook and the air squeezed her head as thunder boomed all around. Somewhere nearby, glass shattered. Hailey crouched beneath the window. Soft ringing, like the hand bells Mommy played at church sometimes, filled the air. Whoever was playing *these* bells didn't know how, though, because they sounded awful. Last week, she'd been running around the altar while Mommy and her friends practiced. She bumped into a table and knocked a box full of extra bells to the floor. The ringing outside now reminded her of the noise they made when they hit the floor. The sound was getting louder. Hailey stood still, holding Teddy so his one eye rose above the window seal. When Teddy didn't get scared, Hailey pulled herself up too.

Teddy thought the machine moving down the street looked like a big, shiny egg, but Hailey had seen one before. She held a finger up to her lips and shook her head at Teddy. Hundreds of arms like metal snakes twitched and waved from the egg, picking up pieces of broken cars and houses, and then casting them aside. Hailey ducked as far as she could, but was still able to see out the window. Her body shook from the cold. Teddy was trying to help by making the hard part inside his body even warmer. He was a good bear. This egg looked like the one Sergeant had been watching on the television show when the walls fell. A flattened ball balanced all lopsided on another silver ball. A swarm of metal bugs flitted around the egg, each shining a narrow cone of white light, like flying flashlights. The lights flew in close to the egg and then far away, over and over, making the alien machine look like it was breathing.

The *whoop-whoop* of Old Mr. McGillicutty's car alarm sliced through the evening air startling Hailey. Beams of light from the bugs fanned around, glinting off the car's pretty red paint. The egg stopped moving, and the ringing faded away. Some of the bugs flew away from the rest and surrounded the car. They squealed, like a million hungry babies. Hailey clamped her hands to her ears and dropped to her knees, landing on Teddy because he fell first.

Tears formed in her eyes. She was sure Teddy was going to cry. Then the screeching stopped and the soft ringing returned. Old Mr. McGillicutty's car was gone, replaced by a steaming mound of gray and black.

Hailey had heard Daddy talking to Sergeant about the aliens before he left in the big black car. The alien machines did that to *our* machines. To people, too. They took them apart into pieces too small to see.

A tear ran down Hailey's face and she bit her lip.

I won't let them do that to you, Daddy said. *Ever.*

She snuffled in a breath and leaned through the opening. The swarm of bugs moved in and out from the rolling egg, as it continued down the street. They didn't even slow down at the red sign at the corner.

Never a cop around when you need one, Daddy always said.

Hailey turned and inched through the pieces of her pretty, pink ceiling fan and the toppled bureau full of her winter clothes. Her foot slipped on the soft stuffing from one of Mommy's new throw pillows. She landed hard on her knee, stirring up dust, and sending a box of Legos raining to the floor. A sharp pain stabbed at her right palm. She squealed before she could cover her mouth with her hand.

She looked at the small black object stuck to her hand. It was Teddy's eye!

She slipped the eye into her pocket and crawled back into the kitchen. Sergeant was still sleeping so she moved next to the refrigerator, and tugged at the lower door, letting it flop downward. She looked over her shoulder. Sergeant hadn't stirred, not even a little bit. His hat had fallen from his head now and one eye, opened wide, stared at the ceiling. Hailey opened her mouth to ask if he was awake now, but stopped.

A single beam of light moved down the hallway.

Hailey scrambled under the hanging refrigerator door, clutching Teddy close. Her body shook like she was freezing cold. She wanted to scream for Daddy and Mommy, but she turned to Teddy instead. Teddy wanted her to stay quiet. He told her he would protect her. Squeezing Teddy one last time, she rolled her friend from under the refrigerator.

Bright light moved into the kitchen, bathing Teddy for long seconds as Hailey held her breath. The scary white light grew brighter and the air shivered around her with a whine that made her teeth hurt. The smell of rotten meat spilled under the refrigerator. Hailey gagged, biting her hand to stop the scream that was building inside.

The light died, turned away, and took the whine along, as it buzzed away into the evening. She pressed her face to the floor. Teddy lay in the middle of the kitchen. She crawled out of her cave and lifted Teddy gently from the floor. He was a good bear and wasn't mad at her for sending him out to fight the alien bug.

Sergeant was gone, his body replaced with a hissing, popping, mound of oil and dirt.

She felt around inside the refrigerator for another juice box. Only two left. She took one, glanced back at the pile of dirt, and took the other. Dumping the small toys from Teddy's backpack, she squeezed the two boxes inside and closed the flap.

Hailey found her jacket under the front door and pulled it on. She couldn't zip it up, but hopefully wouldn't catch cold. Mommy would be proud of her for thinking like a big girl. She walked across the toppled kitchen wall, and jumped off the edge onto the lawn. When she got to the sidewalk, she looked up, a flash of lightning drawing her eye. More leaves fell from high in the sky, smoke spreading out behind them as they dropped to the ground far away. A few days before Daddy left, Hailey had been helping to rake leaves and fill the big bags for the trash man. Daddy had said then that autumn was almost over—that winter was coming fast.

Hailey stepped over Mommy's pretty hand-painted mailbox into the road. The side of the box was crumpled and burned but she could still make out the address, just like Daddy and Mommy had made her learn in case she ever got lost. *127 BRIGHTON.* Holding Teddy's paw tightly in her hand, she faced the direction that Uncle Sam's big, black car had taken Daddy. She held her finger to her lips to remind the bear not to cry and looked back at the barren trees in front of all the fallen walls of her house. Snow drifted from the sky, gray snow that smeared on her skin instead of melting. Maybe winter had already come.

Hailey heard the ringing of bells.

An egg machine turned the corner ahead and rolled in her direction, hundreds of lights sweeping over her as the swarm of bugs swirled through the air. Hailey turned to run. The other egg rolled back through the stop sign.

Hailey couldn't move. She missed Mommy. She wanted Daddy to come back. Her body trembled and she dropped to the ground, burying her face in Teddy's fur. He was so, so warm.

I'll never let them hurt you, Angel.

Tears flowed down Hailey's face and in a flash of light, Teddy became the sun.

The End of the Beginning
by George Moore

The End of This Beginning
Some say the world will end in fire; some say in ice.
Robert Frost, "Fire and Ice"

Will they still be saying this follows that
when the Stelliferous era fades to black, degenerates
into nothing but a hole, or is nothing too much

when everything is squeezed into a final, sweet
singularity? And is a hole a metaphor for something
we simply do not know? No space left

to roam, no highways where the bike can kick
into high, and flatten out the desert loneliness
no space at all but a knot of curved Einsteinian

bubble, the next phase, the one we don't see
a wealth of new beginnings in a hundred odd dimensions,
a crack loud enough to stop whatever we are doing.

The Paperless Doctrine of 2152
by
Aaron M. Wilson

1.

Mr. North felt sadly conflicted as he ducked out of the cold Minneapolis wind and into the last bookstore in the Global Village. Vintage WWIV American propaganda covered the walls. Twenty-foot shelves and open boxes of books made the aisles narrow and almost impassable. Price tags hung from book corners like the beginnings of complex spider webs. A tabby cat, curled up in a leather chair, peeked out from under a paw. Mr. North sighed, breathing in the musty tang of aged paper and cloth. Not a tall man, but he could reach the top shelves without the aid of a ladder. He brushed his finger across one of the shelves, picking up enough dust to make his Mark Twain-styled moustache twitch before sneezing.

Waste, Mr. North thought, all waste. All of this paper was locked up by the decree of a misguided governor whose great-grandfather had held his first book signing in the basement. Notable Narratives had been designated as a historic site, a national treasure of sorts, which meant it could exist but not operate. Mr. North tried to understand, but when he looked around the store, all he could see was the misuse of a valuable resource. Before the implementation of Paperless Doctrine No. 2152, which outlawed the sale of printed material, he had offered to buy the store from its owner, like his special interest group had done with hundreds of other bookstores. However, the old man in the *Star Tribune* visor, circa 2030, had refused.

Mr. North moved toward the back aisles, through History and Social Sciences. He turned at Photography and took the claustrophobic stairs leading down to the basement. The stairs groaned with each step. The ceiling was much lower in the basement. Mr. North had to watch for the eye-level lights as he passed Children's Picture Books and Young Adult Novels. He unfolded his hands from his coat sleeves, and he pushed his hood back. Settling into a wooden chair surrounded by boxes upon boxes of faded paperbacks, he picked up one of the books and opened it to the copyright page, 2010.

Mr. North remembered not wanting this assignment. He remembered waiting outside a large oak door to talk it over with his boss, Danielle Serif. James, the owner of the bookstore, was a friend, an acquaintance, really. Nevertheless, Mr. North's number had come up. The next assignment, like it or not, was his. He had argued with Ms. Serif, a direct descendent of Gilbert Serif, the famous architect who had designed their paperless society...

"What's the harm?" he had said.

"It's the last one."

Mr. North took the black briefcase off the table that divided them and placed it gently on the floor. "It will die in time."

Ms. Serif shook her head and removed her watch from her wrist. She looked at it before setting it down on the table. "Time. All things come back into fashion. Watches," she snorted, "and smoking tobacco, for example, banned in the early 21st century, only to return like a plague 100 years later." She frowned. "Do I need to find someone else?"

"No." He pulled up his hood, preparing to go out into the cold.

"Good. Remember, with this victory we will have finally fulfilled Gilbert's dream." She smiled. "Do I need to remind you that every book downloaded earns ad revenue? And that we have a 96% market share in those suggestive ads?"

Mr. North watched from inside his hood as she picked up a reader from her desk. She tapped it a few times before turning it around. It displayed a simple red line that started at the bottom left corner and arced toward the upper right hand corner.

"We cannot afford to let even one opportunity slip though our fingers." Ms. Serif stood up. "Now, do your job."

Gingerly, North wrapped his fingers around the handle of his briefcase before easing the door to her office closed.

Mr. North looked around the bookstore. It was empty of people. So much worry over such a useless and outdated medium. Why would anyone want to read this way? It was so slow. Plus, there were the new laws like PD 2152. Reading from bound paper books was a thing of the past.

Quietly, James walked out from the Mystery section carrying a stack of crime novels under his left arm. He inquired, "May I help you?" He pushed a pair of round glasses up his nose. "Oh, Mr. North, it's you. So sorry to interrupt." He started to back away, "I know how you like your privacy."

Mr. North smiled. "I have a lot of paperwork to get through tonight." He ran his hands through his short gray hair, feeling his implants vibrate behind his ears. "Could you bring me something to eat?"

"Sure thing, Mr. North." James set his books down and headed for the stairs.

"Wait."

"Yes?"

"I need a clean table and seclusion." Mr. North held up the briefcase, as if to set it down on a table that wasn't there.

"Sure, Mr. North."

"I may be a while. Do you mind closing? I'd like the store to myself again today. I'm on deadline."

James paused in the doorway, hiding his hands in his apron. "Researching another story? How long do you need?"

Viciously Mr. North thought, He's a nice fellow, but the crystals have made him daffy. Who researches anything off-line anymore? He could see that James's hands were shaking under the dirty fabric. "I don't know." He let his own hands drop to his sides. "The rest of the day? A few hours?"

James cleared off a nearby table and set it in front of Mr. North, who opened his briefcase and then quickly closed it. James was hovering, and Mr. North didn't want him to see what was inside.

"What is it, James?"

"I don't normally ask this of you, Mr. North. Can you pay up front?"

Without looking up, Mr. North replied, "I'm good for it."

"I know, sir. It's…I'm a little…business is…you know, the PD." James repositioned his visor over his bald spot.

"I'm good for it."

"Just a little down, Mr. North. I don't need it all, just a little to get free."

"Here." He held out a vial of light pink crystals. "It's all I've got. The rest will have to come later."

"Thanks, Mr. North." James took the vial and opened it. The pink crystals sparkled. "I'll be back in a second with something to keep starvation off."

"James," Mr. North called as the old man hurried out of the room. "Don't take all of those at once this time. Only one at a time."

The last of the stairs creaked like an old chair. Mr. North stood in front of the table. Places like this should be a thing of the past, he consoled himself. They do no one any good. He pulled out his halo headset and connected it to his thumbnail-sized implants located just behind his ears. Once attached, the electronically charged gas in his halo ignited. It flickered like a disco ball reflecting a rainbow before settling on neon-blue as it connected to the Global Village data bank. The light from Mr. North's halo made his skin look jaundiced and the whites of his eyes appear an eerie pale blue, as if he'd stepped out of Frank Herbert's novel *Dune*.

Mr. North picked up the book he had been looking at, *Moby Dick*. He thought about the title, sending signals out into the Global Village network via his flickering halo. As the book opened in his mind, he instantly knew every word by heart, along with every piece of commentary written about the book over the past five hundred years. Some of the essays were good, others weren't, but Mr. North now possessed the accumulated human knowledge on the subject. He was amazed that he liked the book and reasoned that he felt both compassion and anger for Captain Ahab. Mr. North understood blind obsession. To think that humans used to hunt whales as a means for economic gain; it was no wonder they were extinct.

He also had a strong craving for a fish sandwich from McDonald's. He knew that 5 oz. canned tuna was on sale for $23.75 at the local market around the corner, and that he could take a North Pacific cruise aboard a vessel called the *Pequod*, all thanks to the profitable ads that accompanied the book. North thought about Ms. Serif as he discarded the ads, but his stomach grumbled and he still longed for the fish sandwich.

The hinges on Mr. North's briefcase were stuck, forcing him to pry it open carefully. A few wires and a brick of gray clay fell out on the table. He placed the clay back into his briefcase gently and untangled the wires. There were easier, more efficient ways to demolish a building, but they were also easier to trace. Some things, if done well, simply require an antiquarian touch.

"Looks like something technical." James held a tray in one hand. A simple peanut butter and blueberry sandwich, cut in half, rested on a chipped, yellow plate next to a red apple, a glass of water, and a cup of black coffee. "Can I help?"

"Not this time."

“Sure.” James looked slightly rejected. He pinched his eyebrows, and a deep furrow snaked across this forehead. “I closed up like you asked. Not that it really matters. You’re the first person through the door in weeks.” James set the tray down on the table where Mr. North was working and turned back to the stairs. “Anything else?”

Mr. North shielded the contents of the briefcase from James. “If you had to make a choice, could you live without the store, or would you go down with the ship?”

“I think that silly halo-thing of yours is transmitting a little too quickly.” James smiled, as he pulled out the vial of pink crystals and shook them. “I’ll be upstairs if you need me.”

Mr. North walked out from around the table. “Seriously, could you live without the store?”

James paused at the base of the stairs. A poster of Marcus Pfister’s *Rainbow Fish Counting* hung on the wall above a dusty green beanbag chair. James rubbed his face with his left hand. “I guess I’m more like Ahab than I’d like to admit.” Without waiting for a reply, he made his way up the steps.

Mr. North shook his head and went back around the table. He reopened the briefcase and pulled out the tiny red wires. His halo flickered as he accessed a restricted information port on the demolition of small building.

2.

Upstairs, in his private apartment, James sat behind a large, purple counter, grinning stupidly from ear to ear. Too high from taking Mr. North’s vial of pink crystals to sit up straight, he leaned his head on one hand and his elbow on the smooth surface. No one ever came in any more, except for Mr. North. With the creation of the Paperless Doctrine of 2152, owning paper had become a misdemeanor, as uncouth as driving a car with a combustion engine had been in the late 21st century. He was grateful that his books hadn’t been recycled into compost to fertilize the fields of the Global Village like the rest of the printed material had been years ago. But deep down, he was angry. If someone wanted to buy a book or a poster, even though it was illegal, he’d sell it. The risk of being caught was minimal; however, collectors of paper products were seen as dirty miscreants caring only for themselves.

James, through his hazy thoughts, reminisced about the day he had first seen the announcement about the PD, which had been printed in the final issue of the *New York Times.* The yellowed, fifty-year-old article was framed and hanging on the far wall, with his collection of propaganda posters, including one of his favorites that read, "Viva El Mundo de Latinos!" from the Latin Labor Uprising of 2092.

Interest in print books, printed anything for that matter, died immediately after the creation of the PD. The Governor's decision to declare the bookstore a state treasure had transformed his business into a museum. James had no overhead, but he barely made a living. Most people would not pay to browse or handle books, old newspapers, and political posters. If not for the regulars, like Mr. North, who would buy or barter for two or three books and leave a little extra on every visit, he would have starved. It was obvious to James that Mr. North still loved to read books, to hold them in his hands. He did, too. There was nothing like feeling the weight of *Tale of Two Cities* by Charles Dickens, as he read the actual words on the printed pages. After the introduction of implants, reading had become like everything else in their society, fast and weightless.

James had taken the crystals, so that he, too, could feel fast and weightless. He was soaring, and he was happy watching the hours pass. He should have locked the store hours ago, like he had promised. But James had forgotten, and now, he didn't care. He was amid purples and deep blues and stark whites. And oh, the smells—hot gingerbread and cocoa. James didn't have implants like the rest of them. He didn't care for wires or worry about connection speeds. All James cared about was flying and books. When he couldn't fly, he read the old-fashioned way, book in hand.

At first, there were a few people looking to make a quick credit by illegally selling their books and collectable posters to James, but he soon ran out of money. He depleted his saving for one last acquisition, a first edition set of Mark Twain's novels and memoirs. After purchasing the first editions, he had to turn people away.

It was hard, but James had come to understand his place in the world. He was dead to the current age. He chose to ignore it. He wanted a revolution like the one that Russia had experienced in the days of Lenin and Stalin. Except that James didn't care about the people or social justice. James wanted to witness the end of something that no one thought would end and the birth of something new and unexpected. He longed for something tangible to replace the Paperless Doctrine. He craved something more, something terrible and violent.

3.

About two in the morning, James slid off his stool. He stunk. His skin and clothes were sticky with sweat. His apartment contained a refrigerator, a hot plate, and a large dingy couch that smelled of eggs and cat piss. His clothes were a mass of earth tones, piled in the corner under the only window. The walls and ceiling were covered in dusty, gray, popcorn stucco, worn smooth in places. James had thought about a bed once. A few months ago, he'd passed the store Everyone Deserves a Chance on his way home from the Food Outlet Ration Center. In the front window on the second floor, a small, single bed was done up in green sheets, with a hand-sewn quilt folded and place on the end. The price in the window read, $120.00 USD. A good price, but it was more than he had. The light had changed, and the transport he was on moved on to the next stop. Good thing, too, because James had been too high on crystals to make his way up to the second level.

He staggered to his feet, knocking into a small bookcase of Stephen King first editions. *Carrie* and *Tommyknockers* went flying across the floor. James stepped on *Desperation* and fell forward, lying still for a few minutes.

When the shock of the fall wore off, he picked up the copy of *Desperation*. It had been his favorite of all King's novels. It was about a coal-mining town somewhere in the American West that was overrun and possessed by earth demons. The main character was a writer, a best-selling author like King. It made James smile to hold the book. Happy memories of his youth flooded through him. He opened the book to see what he was asking for it.

"Two credits!" He stood and rubbed his back. His speech slurring, "Publisher printed too damn many copies. Flooded the market, they did. Over-anticipated the demand." James wondered how many copies he had in the store, how many he'd been able to save.

James righted the bookcase and picked up the displaced and scattered novels. He held up a copy of *Times Change*, King's final novel, and most would say, his best. It had won both the National Book Award and the Pulitzer Prize in Fiction in 2025.

He'd read all King's novels except this one. James put it back. He just couldn't bring himself to read the last King novel. He'd read a couple of reviews, but couldn't bare to break the binding on the book. *Times Change* was about a little black girl in the year 2001, just after September 11th, who wrote and mailed letters to Martin Luther King, Jr. Somehow her letters traveled into the past and were delivered days before his assassination. She asked how she was supposed to forgive bad men who did really bad things. Her letters would eventually inspire Martin Luther King, Jr. to give his "I Have a Dream" speech.

Leaving *Times Change* on his desk, James put *Desperation* under his arm and headed to the stairs. He held onto the wooden railing as he eased his way down to the first floor, step by creaking step. He thought he remembered turning off the lights, but he saw that they were still on. Mr. North was attaching something to the base of the wall near the section of Western Mediterranean Cooking.

"You're still here?"

Mr. North looked up. "I'm almost through." He finished taping whatever it was to the wall.

"You helping me with improvements?" James swayed. He could feel that he was about to take off again. It was sad that the high only came in waves. James longed for the high to be constant.

"You took the whole bottle."

"I'm free."

"I can see that." Mr. North helped James into an old wooden school desk with a fixed desktop.

"James."

James nodded his foggy head. "Good, good. Just make sure that you lock up on your way out."

"James. You need to choose."

"I'm free."

"James, it's over."

"Yes."

"Goodbye, Ahab."

James looked up at Mr. North. Blue light arced in the air around the man's head. "Ishmael, is that you?" James chuckled. Then he noticed one of the books on the desk in front of him. "*Times Change*," he said. "Ishmael, have you read it?"

Mr. North didn't answer. The LCD-like clock in his mind displayed a series of numbers that were counting down.

"Maybe it's time." James opened King's final novel to the first page. The binding made that new book cracking sound that James hadn't heard in years. A stupid grin showed his blackening teeth.

Mr. North shook his head and put his hand deep in his pockets. As he exited through the front, the small bell above the door tinkled.

4.

Mr. North wished that the inevitable could have gone some other way. He pulled something out of his coat pocket. Thank you, James, for everything," he said, fingering the old paper. He thought back to the first time he had met the man with the quaint visor. James had been waving a flag that read, "Remember *Fahrenheit 451*" outside a PD recycling center. The corners of Mr. North's mouth raised and his eyes softened.

There was a flash of green light. Then, the two-story building that contained the last printed books for sale on Earth fell intc rubble. Turning away, Mr. North walked slowly down the street, avoiding the smoldering pages that rained from the sky. Then, he shook his head before tucking the yellowed copy of *Moby Dick* back into his pocket.

Origins
by
Liz R. F. Coley

Morning has just broken. Long shadows stretch across the sand. Slivers of pink light catch the crests of the morning breakers. Early sandpipers scurry in and out of spent wavelets along the shoreline, while gulls wheel above. Without warning or sound, a silver teardrop appears in the sky, hovering over the Pacific, reflecting the dawn.

The cameraman clears his throat and raises spread fingers. "Camera's rolling in five…four… three…two…."

One…zero…blast off. Carolina imagines the upcoming launch countdown, her chest tight in anticipation. She plasters on what she hopes is a photogenic smile and smoothes the white lab coat they told her to wear over her blue mission jumpsuit. But the lens isn't focused on her. The camera rests on President Langston, who is beginning his recorded address to the American people. At his gesture, the cameraman pans across the tarmac to the silver teardrop-shaped vessel. About the size of the presidential chopper tipped up on its nose, the alien craft hangs a foot above the ground in bold defiance of all that Earth's physicists understand about gravity. The cloudless California sky is reflected as a shifting, brilliant blue in the mirrored surface of the vessel.

The open hatch beckons, but Carolina restrains her feet from leaping aboard before the designated time. Under the midday sun, air rises in shimmering waves from the runway at Miramar and blurs her view. Must be the mirage, she thinks, not tears. She wants this, more than anything.

The president's Kentucky twang pours past her ears. "…Settin' forth today, boldly, our scientist astronauts, Boston Peters and Caroleena Bennett…"

She frowns as the president mispronounces her name again. She's politely corrected him in private, twice. *Carolina, like the state.*

"North or South?" he'd asked with studied charm.

Of course, she'd laughed. Then she proposed the greatest origin-of-life experiment the human race has ever imagined. No false modesty—it's *her* experiment.

Scientists? Yes—she's a microbiologist and her colleague Boston is a renowned paleobiochemist. But astronauts? Not exactly. A job title hasn't been invented for the kind of journey they are about to undertake together.

"...An opportunity of staggerin' proportions, a gift from an unknown benefactor, the chance for humankind to challenge the very fabric of space-time..."

Carolina wonders why the actual words she used to sell the president on this mission sound so trite coming from his mouth. A month earlier, in the Oval Office, she meant them with all her heart. Now, on a scorching pavement, the same words spoken to an imaginary audience sound melodramatic and overblown.

Finally, mercifully, the script ends. Carolina and Boston exchange grateful glances behind the president's back. The camera shifts to the two of them. Carolina embraces each member of the send-off group, her colleagues on the top secret Alien Craft Analysis Task Force. It's more wrenching than she expects to say farewell to the people she's known and worked with so intensely for the past six months. And she's still reeling from the final goodbye with her sister Jenna, who never accepted her decision to go. She isn't here. She won't watch. Even so, Carolina is determined to walk straight into the alien vessel with dry eyes and a full heart, leaving everything familiar behind her. Forever.

Sensing the unwavering gaze of the cameras on her back, Carolina strolls across the radiating tarmac with perfect posture. Boston walks at her side. He places a hand under her elbow, as she steps up into the open vessel. The doorway feels cool and frictionless to her damp hands, even after hours in the full sun. Boston hops up behind her, and spins to wave one last time.

"Camera hog," she teases.

She edges her way past their gear to the right-hand seat. The passenger compartment is stuffed. Their bedrolls are crammed under the control panel. Behind her seat looms a precarious tower of boxes containing a three-month supply of field rations and a lifetime count of multi-vitamins. The floor space is dominated by their respective lab equipment, a lab tent, fully-loaded handhelds, sample return containers made from imperishable diamond, and the solar-powered survival gadgets that will purify their water and extract supplementary oxygen.

Yes, it will be a claustrophobic ride, but only for a very, very brief time—a journey of two and a half billion years in the interval of a sly wink.

Carolina stretches her long legs under the alien control board and shifts in the seat that only approximately fits her human anatomy.

"Nervous?" Boston asks from the co-pilot position.

"No way." She gives him a reassuring smile that crinkles her eyes, probably accentuating the tiny squint lines. She doesn't think of them as signs of creeping age, more as merit badges for the hours she has spent peering into microscopes, for the years she has studied artificial cell membranes in her lab, trying to catch them in the act of behaving like real ones. "It's going to work perfectly. I just know it."

Boston pats the control board, careful not to jostle any of the four setting dials. The protruding controls are sensitive and small for human fingers. "Mars or bust, right?"

Carolina studies his profile, thinking back to the days she played "who would you most like to be marooned with?" with Jenna and her friends. Funny that it was always Jenna's friends. She never had time to make any of her own—she was too busy studying. She can't recall the names of the rock stars and athletes the older girls adored. She just remembers saying, "Louis Pasteur, or maybe James Watson." Some biologist hero. The other girls laughed at her weirdness, but even then she knew where her future pointed. She just didn't know it would end up so completely linked with Boston's.

She's never been this close to him in all the weeks of task force meetings. Now Carolina notices the rough strip of scar that runs under his chin. His crooked nose must have been broken more than once. All in all, she has to admit, he can't be called handsome. Rugged is a more honest description. He could possibly pass for Robert Redford's younger, homelier brother. But none of that matters. She doesn't want a movie star. He's a scientist of the top caliber, and they are going to be marooned together. Her childhood fantasy has turned out to be prophetic.

"They look a little nervous, though, don't they?" Boston points through the transparent viewscreen to the send-off committee.

Carolina agrees. There's a sense of waiting tension. "You think they're afraid the ship won't come back to them after all? I practically promised the president he would have it back before it even left."

"Can't do that." Boston laughs. "It would introduce an anomaly in causality. A time-travel paradox."

Carolina waves away his comment. "I don't know about all that sci-fi stuff. I just know Stan worked it all out to the president's satisfaction."

"Of course he did. They've got a lot to lose if this amazing piece of technology vanishes forever. Frankly, I'm in awe over the way you pushed the plan through."

Carolina meets his admiring gaze square on. "I had to. It's the culmination of my life's work."

Always fascinated by the origin of life, for her doctoral research Carolina had studied mitochondria, the tiny organelles that power the cells of Earth's respiring organisms. Scientists had already deduced their distant history as free-swimming, independent, single-celled entities. It was widely believed that in a pivotal development about 1.5 billion years ago, some mitochondria were engulfed by simple, predatory cells. Rather than being digested, the microscopic energy factories entered into a symbiotic relationship with their primitive captors. Though these mitochondria eventually lost the genes to live autonomously, they gained indefinite protection and survival within their hosts, setting the stage for evolution's next leap forward.

Over the course of six years, Carolina reverse-engineered the lost genes, reconstructed the missing DNA sequences, and inserted them into the mitochondrial genome. In recreating this extinct form of early life—free-living mitochondria—she had proved the endosymbiosis hypothesis beyond doubt. The publication of her dissertation gave her instant star status in the world of microbiology.

Now the cargo hold beneath the metal floor carries the greatest experiment she has ever designed. Belowdecks teems a mixture of billions of unicellular microbes—photosynthesizers, chemosynthesizers, thermophiles, cryophiles, aerobes, anaerobes—chosen representatives from all of Earth's Kingdoms: the protists, fungi, animals, plants, bacteria, archaebacteria, and megaviruses. Even Carolina's own free-living mitochondria swim in the nutrient-rich bath.

Seeding ancient Mars with life is going to be her most magnificent experiment.

Again, she offers silent thanks to the anonymous inventors of this craft. When it popped into existence in Earth's sky over the

Pacific Ocean six months ago, the United States wasted no time in snubbing the United Nations and declaring exclusive ownership of the vessel. The craft proved to be empty, except for the organic residue in its cargo hold. At the right university, in the right field of study, at the right time, Carolina was summoned to the ACA Task Force to analyze the remains. And what she found set the rest of this scheme in motion—desiccated cells, built on a genetic design close enough to Earth's to suggest a relationship, yet different enough to prove their alien origin.

Once the multidisciplinary Task Force put together all the clues—the organic debris, the large cargo hold, the incredible range of the vessel—they were inclined to believe her conclusion, that its purpose was panspermia, the spreading of life to other planets. At the precise moment of this seductive realization, Carolina conceived her plan. Then she sold her vision for this *Seedship*, as she called it, to the president on the eve of his re-election campaign.

The timing was perfect.

"So what did you think of the president's canned speech?" she asks.

Boston laughs. "What a windbag! I still don't know how you got him to see this ship as more than a potential war plane. He told me he's going to hold all the footage of his speech and our departure until just before the election, then announce his plans for the first manned Mars mission. He's running as the 'new frontier' president."

"Playing off that ol' Kentucky voice, I bet." Carolina rolls her eyes. "First manned Mars mission? Shoot, we're getting there two and a half billion years before he does."

Boston winks. "Sure, but we'll be dust. Can't speak for ourselves. He imagines he'll be here to claim the glory." He nudges her elbow. "Good thing he doesn't really understand time travel."

"What do you mean?" she asks.

"Divergent paths," he says briefly.

She looks at him blankly.

He explains. "What if your seeding project works brilliantly? What if life takes hold on Mars and persists? Who's to say that having a green Mars shining in the sky won't completely change the history of Earth's space program? Think about it."

Carolina does, and suddenly it clicks. "You mean we wouldn't have been content to stop with the Apollo moonshots? We would have pushed ahead sooner?"

"Well, yes. Something like that, assuming there isn't a much earlier divergence."

Carolina feels a cold breeze cross her neck, which is impossible in the confined cabin. She shakes it off and peers through the window. "I wish they'd get on with it. What are they waiting for?"

Boston checks his watch. "Not quite time yet. The displacement coordinates are calculated for transferring exactly at noon. We've got a little while to wait. Look, Stan's doing the calculations again."

Carolina glances at the small, bald genius who worked out the navigation system for the alien vessel. When the military finally yielded the craft to the scientists for study, Stan was the first one allowed to touch the simple controls. It took him less than a week to decode their symbolic system and, in the boldest—that is, stupidest—spirit of science, test it on himself. Three dials represent the logarithmic distance displacement in three dimensions from the starting point. The scale apparently goes out to parsecs, a distance Stan hasn't dared verify personally, thank goodness.

The fourth dial is the magic one, the miraculous gift to Carolina and Boston and to mankind in general. It directs the vessel through time, starting at a mysterious O point. Could it be the beginning of time?

With tiny, careful adjustments, Stan has determined that the vessel can jump backwards in time, instantly from the point of view of the occupants. Traveling forward, however, the passenger experiences real time elapsing, which Stan learned the hard and hungry way. When he programmed the ship to travel two days ahead, he shifted into some sort of colorless, opaque limbo for forty-eight interminable hours. Then, without any warning, the viewscreen cleared to reveal the morning guard at Miramar picking himself up from the ground, knocked off his feet at the unexpected reappearance. A quick comparison showed Stan's chronometer exactly matched the guard's. That's when he grimly realized a return trip from the deep past would be impossible for a living crew. They wouldn't survive the passage of real time.

"Stan's giving us the okay sign," Boston says.

"I see that," Carolina answers. "So how many times did you check the coordinates?"

"Four," Boston confesses. "You?"

She laughs. "Got me. Three."

Next to Stan, another man is grinning wildly and waving at them. Carolina places a hand on Boston's arm. "Look at your brother Francis. He's as excited as we are." Then a thought hits her. "You didn't tell him, did you?"

Boston avoids her gaze.

She grips his arm. "You didn't tell him this is a one-way trip. Why not?"

"I just couldn't." He shrugs. "He'd blame himself."

"How do you figure?"

"He made me who I am." Boston's eyes are moist. "Taught me to read. Introduced me to Robinson's *Mars* trilogy. He shared his stacks of *Analog* and *Asimov's*." His lips twist. "He quizzed me mercilessly on *Star Trek* trivia. He made me love all the possibilities of science, and he made me insatiably curious about our universe."

"Wow. That's some tribute." Carolina tries not to compare him to Jenna, a sister who really never understood her.

Boston blinks hard and coughs around the catch in his throat. "Yeah. He's been some brother." He tightens his lips in what might pass for a smile and waves at Francis.

Carolina has to ask. "So why are you here with me and not out there with him? Why did you volunteer?"

"Volunteer? I think I ran over everyone else trying to get in line. It's *my* life's work, too."

Carolina hears the same conviction in his voice that she knows is in her own.

Like Carolina, Boston Peters is a funded member of NSCORT, NASA's Specialized Center of Research and Training. Before all this, they crossed paths occasionally at conferences, but his lab is a couple of miles away at the Scripps Institution of Oceanography, and his work a separate discipline, the chemistry of young Earth's oceans and atmosphere. His research has been central to figuring out the pathways of prebiotic chemistry, how all the organic molecules necessary for life could be produced in the primordial soup. This opportunity—literally the chance of a lifetime—to go back in time to conduct field studies, stop all the guesswork, and see what really happened must have drawn him irresistibly. It certainly had that effect on her.

They plan to send their lab notes and samples forward in time as their final academic legacy. A new twist, she thinks. Publish *and* perish.

Stan holds up two fingers and points at his watch.

Carolina catches her breath in a slight gasp. "Now?"

"Time to batten down the hatches." Boston reaches toward a depressed spot beside the open door.

"Wait," she chokes out.

"What?"

"Fred's running over here. Blast it. I hope nothing's wrong."

Fred Xu, the president's special advisor on planetary exploration is hustling across the tarmac. He reaches through the open door and grasps Boston's outstretched hand.

"Thank you," he says between breaths. "Godspeed and…just thank you."

Boston smiles, nods, takes Fred's hand in a firm grip. "Okay, Fred. Best give us a little clearance here." As Fred withdraws, he closes the door.

"What do you think that was all about?" Carolina asks.

"I think he just got it," Boston answers. "I don't think he understood until this moment just how monumental this journey is going to be."

"What a dingbat," Carolina offers unsympathetically. "He wrote all those words about healing our barren sister planet, about the living laboratory, about dispersing the seeds of life, without really comprehending anything. Gads, I'm glad we don't have to deal with politicians anymore."

"So does that mean you won't support me for president of the Precambrian then?" Boston asks. "Hey, look. That's it. Stan just gave us the go."

Tears spring unbidden into Carolina's eyes, and she clasps her hands tightly together against her chest, like a little girl praying. "You…you can drive." She can't trust her trembling fingers.

Boston touches the activation sensor. After a moment's delay, the view through the screen changes abruptly to a neutral gray, then just as suddenly to a rocky, furrowed landscape. The vessel hangs above red Mars at an altitude of five hundred feet. Carolina realizes she's holding her breath.

"Ding. Mars station," Boston intones. "Last stop before the Precambrian." Then he sinks back into his seat, dazed. "Oh, wow. Pinch me."

She hasn't felt a thing. Not even a jostle, and the first step is already accomplished. Carolina gives him a gentle punch in the arm. "Good job, co-pilot. You got the *where*. Now for the *when*. Let's see a beautiful, blue Mars."

Boston shakes his head from side to side, continuing to gaze out the viewscreen. "Hey, what's the rush? Give me a second to take this in. It's gorgeous." He sighs deeply. "You know, we should have been up here forty years ago. Amazing."

Carolina forces herself to admire a view familiar from NASA photographs. Rusty boulders litter the ground. In the distance, the immensity of Olympus Mons shadows the plains below. In person, though, the crispness of the air is almost tangible, the shades of red more vivid and subtle.

As he floats in his personal heaven, Boston seems content to watch all day. Carolina counts ten breaths with a growing sense of urgency. A glitter of white in the crevice folds of the mountain catches her eye, and her heart leaps with the thought, *there is ice here*. Her patience cracks.

"Okay, Boston, that's long enough. I don't want us to mess up the calculations. Besides, we're going to be right back here. Two and half billion years ago. In just a second."

"That sounds weird." He gestures to the controls. "Okay, ma'am. You want a turn?"

"Sure." Suddenly, unexpectedly, Carolina suffers a twinge of doubt. They can call it off now; they have the settings for a return to Earth, but there's no turning back once they slide through time.

What if the planetary geologists are wrong about Mars's warm, wet past? Or wrong about how long ago it was?

She pushes the negative thoughts away. Besides, both of them have been relentlessly drilled in the coordinate system so they can make minor adjustments for the unexpected. And this leg of the journey was right on target. So three cheers for Stan. Time to go.

Carolina checks her notes, resets the controls, takes a deep breath, and touches the activation sensor. Another smooth, imperceptible transition.

All that changes is the view, and it is stunning.

The vessel hangs above a calm sea, a huge, blue expanse in a basin, surrounded by red mountains. The intense colors in the thin air tug at Carolina's heart. A second Eden, indeed, she tells herself.

"Will you do the honors, Mars mother?" Boston teases.

Carolina eagerly reaches for the lever and releases her precious cargo into the womb of Mars.

In a way, it's cheating, dropping fully functioning cells into the ancient seas of this wet, warm Mars. On old Earth, the rich endowment of organic molecules had to figure out for themselves how to take the first leap forward to becoming the first true cells.

For the past five frustrating years, Carolina has studied the original missing link—the cell membrane—the root of such tantalizing mysteries. Sure, simple passive vesicles could form under the right conditions, and simple molecules had been shown to self-organize into complex proteins and even the building blocks of DNA and RNA. But how did these self-replicating chemicals wrap themselves up in a dynamic *living* membrane, pulling nutrients in and pushing waste out? How did a dumb vesicle become a membrane that actively participated in cell division and propagation? How did a strand of raw genetic material floating around put this clever wall between itself and the hostile environment to become the original cell, flourishing to reproduce this remarkable innovation again and again?

In the lab, her experimental membranes have remained stubbornly and stupidly inert. Maybe now, finally, she can find answers in Earth's deep past. Or maybe she will learn that an extraordinary catalyst was required to kick off life as we know it.

Is this what the aliens did before they sent the *Seedship* to a primordial, cooling Earth? Did they plant their primitive cells in Earth's tidepools and oceans at the dawn of ages and leave them for later study?

Carolina chuckles at her speculations. Aliens? That's Boston's department, not hers. "How I wish we could come back and see what happens," she says. "I left instructions for my grad students on the primary lab computer. I just hope they're smart enough to find them when my resignation is announced."

Boston raises an eyebrow. "If your students still exist, I'm sure they will."

"What do you mean, *if* they still exist?" Carolina asks with a laugh.

"We have no idea of the robustness of history," Boston says with a shrug. "Can the whole of history be crushed like a butterfly, as Bradbury suggested? Do alternate timelines split off into parallel universes, creating a multiverse, as Steele proposed? Is the past self-correcting, killing you before you can give your grandmother contraceptives?"

Carolina is confused. "But we're not trying to change Earth's past. Just Mars's. We're only doing field studies on good old Earth. I can't imagine how that would affect anything in Earth's future."

"Don't forget the observer phenomenon." Boston wags a finger in the air. Is he lecturing her? "You can't look at something without changing it. What if the algae you scoop up to put under your microscope is the great-to-the-sixtieth-power granddaddy of the California redwoods? What about all the algae cakes we're going to eat?"

Carolina turns over these perturbing ideas in her head. "I don't remember you saying anything about this during our mission planning meetings."

"I certainly tried, at least at the beginning. I don't remember anyone being receptive to hearing them," he shoots back. "The focus was on Mars, as you said, not Earth. Besides, I didn't want to risk the mission. Or my place in it."

"So what about our waste products? Our breath? Does that change anything?" Carolina's voice rises a notch with agitation.

Boston pats her arm. "Calm down. I'm not that concerned. We're so miniscule compared to an entire planetary ecosystem. I just wanted to make my point."

"Well anyway, I can't believe that all of evolution is so fragile," Carolina argues. "The same things had to have happened randomly over and over again for evolution to occur. You can't tell me that one single, particular bacterium is the parent of us all."

"You're correct. I can't tell you what neither of us knows. But when we send all of our research back to the future on the *Seedship*, someone will know. That's what we're here for, right? It's a scientist's paradise."

"There's really no turning back now," she says practically. "Onward. Earthward."

Her matter-of-fact tone masks the surge of excitement building within her. They are heading for a time when the oceans of Earth teem with unicellular life, maybe even organisms so simple that her mitochondria look like the hottest new thing in microbes. Now, she has a lifetime to collect samples, map thousands of genomes, and tease out the story of evolution from its early roots.

Fortunately, on their first try, the ship appears over land, a beach, rather than the nearby ocean. From only a hundred feet above Earth's surface, Carolina can't make out the shape of the landmass, can't orient to a world that predates the map of Pangaea by more than two billion years and predates the ancestral supercontinent Rodinia by more than a billion. The timescale is simply inconceivable.

Boston adjusts their altitude to a mere hover above the sand. After slipping on his lightweight oxygen mask, he uses a buckyfilament cable to slide down to the ground, then pulls the unresisting ship down to kiss the face of the ancient Earth. He holds out his arms to catch Carolina on her way out.

"Carry you over the threshold, ma'am?" he offers.

Carolina ignores the way her heart skips a beat at the slightly suggestive remark and frees herself from his arms to look around. They are about a quarter-mile from a shoreline—that worked out very well. The ground underfoot is sandy and rocky, but the rocks can be moved for a softer sleeping area. Except for the sound of crashing waves, the silence is eerie. Carolina realizes that her former life had a sound track of vehicles, insects, birds, voices.

She lifts her mask experimentally and takes a deep breath. The air smells different from what she imagined—dry and crisp, almost like mountain air, except without the trees. Thin, but at least she can breathe, and *that's* unexpected. She calls to Boston, "Hey, this air is full of oxygen."

Everything around her is painted in shades of brown and gray. No green, of course. Not on the land. The setting sun casts a reddish glow onto the pale sand.

Carolina calls out, "Race you to the water!" Her long legs speed across the ground, and she hears Boston chasing her down. He dashes ahead of her on wiry runner's legs, plunging into the warm, salty sea. When she catches up, breathless, he splashes her until she is soaked. In the thin air, their lungs heave with the effort of play, so they slow down for a time, relaxing into the swells' soft caress, floating out beyond the breakers.

When the sun touches the horizon, they walk back to the ship to set up camp. Discreetly turning their backs to each other, they slip out of wet clothes and into dry. Carolina only peeks once. Boston, twice.

The lab tent is easy to assemble, and they set up the equipment inside, with solar collectors on the roof. Carolina is tempted to do a quick water test before dark, but for now she hates to spoil the mood. There's more than enough time ahead for work.

She leaves the lab and locates a relatively rock-free spot for the bedrolls. Neither of them is sleepy—it's still mid-afternoon to their bodies—but they sit near each other and watch the waves roll in the dusk.

"This is great," Boston says. "No bugs."

"Yeah. And it's so quiet." Around them, nothing stirs, nothing chirps, nothing buzzes. Maybe a little too quiet. "So, you want to watch a movie?" Carolina sets her handheld to the entertainment setting and calls up a menu.

Boston nods and moves closer to her. "Wish I'd packed microwave popcorn. What's on?"

"Everything. These things are loaded. How about *The Land Before Time*? Ha, just kidding. Here, you choose."

As the show plays out on the tiny ten-inch screen, their heads and bodies move closer together, their breath mingling. When it ends, Carolina realizes she is tucked comfortably against Boston's chest. He smiles down at her and says, "Five hours till dawn. I'm not at all sleepy. What do you want to do?"

What the heck, Carolina thinks. It's like a movie, a slice of someone else's story, but here she is, against all expectations, cast as the leading lady. The romantic stage has been set by silence and stars. Even without a script, the next move is obvious. She tips her head back to meet his lips.

"Okay," he murmurs. "That sounds good."

At sunrise, they wake, untwine, and walk back down to the water for a quick dip, not bothering with clothes. It feels like late afternoon, and Carolina's stomach is beginning to growl. Getting used to these fourteen-hour days is going to be a challenge. They sift through the rations carton for lunch bars and eat their picnic down by the shore.

"We've got to get some water going," Carolina suggests. So they carry a couple of gallons in plastic sacks to the solar still.

No one has brought up science yet. For the first time in years, Carolina feels completely relaxed, content. As they head off for a long walk down the beach, hand in hand, Carolina surveys for shells along the shore until she reminds herself not to be ridiculous. Shells are far, far in the future. She settles for collecting wave-polished rocks instead. The quiet sinks into her bones, calming now, rather than unsettling.

The landscape consists of rock, sand, and more rock. Eventually, they come to a tide pool. Since starfish and crabs haven't invented themselves yet, they expect to see only algae. But the small pools are crystal clear.

They shrug at each other, and carry on with their walk. The conversation ranges across many subjects, and Carolina is tremendously glad that if she had to be marooned, it turned out to be with someone as compatible as Boston. Miles later, they notice the sun sinking again and turn back for home base. When the tent comes into sight, Carolina grabs Boston's hand, drags him to their tumbled bedrolls, and wrestles him to the ground.

"God, I love the Precambrian." Boston sighs.

An enormous moon beams down on them.

Reality hits at the next sunrise. The scientists within them can no longer wait. After another rations picnic, they head down to the beach to collect samples for analysis, some from shallow water, some from deep, some from the tide pools. Boston conducts his molecular analysis, while Carolina makes slide after slide for microscopic viewing. A slow feeling of dread grows as each slide turns up empty. Boston is whistling tunelessly over his experiments. He seems so cheerful, Carolina hates to disturb him with her worries.

"Um, Boston, what are you finding," she asks.

"I've got decent concentrations here of amino acids from the tide pool water. I haven't gotten to the open ocean yet. Why?"

"Well, I'm not coming up with anything."

"What do you mean?" he asks.

"There's nothing alive in my samples."

"Oh. I'm sorry. How about if we go collect more samples after lunch?"

"Yeah, okay." Disheartened, she dries off the slides. No need to sterilize them.

To Carolina's great dismay, all her samples from along the beach turn up sterile. She eats her dinner ration very slowly as she prepares to rain on Boston's parade. She's surprised he hasn't figured it out yet.

"We're going to have to move camp. Find a new body of water to test," she says.

Disappointment shades his eyes. "So soon?"

"Oh yes," she says, licking every crumb from her fingers. "We'd better find something alive soon or we'll have nothing left to eat."

"Ah, yes. I see," he responds gravely.

They cut their rations to five hundred calories per fourteen-hour day as they continue their search. Both athletic and lean to begin with, they have no reserves to speak of. As the days pass, each sees their increasingly hollow eyes and gaunt figures reflected in the other. Carolina tests salt and fresh water sources across the Earth for weeks, until the evidence can't be disputed any longer.

"I don't understand it!" Carolina complains. "This isn't the way it's supposed to be. It doesn't match the fossil record. Why isn't anything alive?"

"Oxygen poisoning?" Boston suggests. "Most researchers in my field believe Earth needed a reducing environment to get the right reactions started. For some reason, this atmosphere has much more oxygen than it's supposed to. I think that it's suppressing the chemistry for life. The primordial soup is much too thin." He spreads his hands in a gesture of helplessness. "This isn't the early Earth of our models."

"Are you suggesting we aren't on Earth? Why didn't you stop and ask for directions?" It's supposed to be a joke, but her voice comes out far more anxious and strident than she expected.

"No, I'm serious. The chemistry is all wrong here. And apparently so is the biology." Boston dredges up a theory from his wide-ranging imagination. His voice switches to lecture mode. "Perhaps when we jumped so far back in time, we derailed from our own timeline. In that case I would hypothesize that we're in a divergent reality, one where we have the raw ingredients for life, but apparently not the starter kit. Or maybe life isn't self-organizing, not at the start. In the reality that produced us, maybe Earth was seeded with life a few hundred-million years into its existence. The Greenland fossils support a start long before now."

"Divergent reality?" Carolina purses her lips and creases her brow skeptically.

Boston attempts another explanation. "Or maybe we screwed up a causal time-loop and delivered our cargo to the wrong planet. Maybe we are on our own Earth but it was supposed to be seeded with oxygen-loving microbes one point five billion years after it was formed. By us."

Carolina has never read science fiction, and she doesn't follow the time travel paradoxes and these weird multiverse scenarios that spring easily into Boston's mind. Causal loops? What is he talking about? She feels scared, frustrated, confused, and hungry.

"But what do we do now?" she asks him.

In a slow, soft voice, Boston confirms her worst fears. "I see two choices. We can explore the universe in that ship for about four more months on starvation rations, hoping to find a planet with edible life on it or try to enjoy the rest of our short lives here in this almost-paradise."

"And quietly starve, you mean."

"Yeah, quietly."

"Boston, did we destroy the world? Did our coming back here wipe out everything?"

He is silent for a full minute before he answers. "I'm not sure. I'd rather think we skipped out of our groove and that our old world carried on its merry way. But I don't know."

They return in somber spirits to their base camp.

Carolina catches Boston purposefully searching their medkit a few hours later. She asks him, "What are you looking for?"

He meets her gaze with heavy eyes. "I was wondering if we could concoct something out of these drugs to help us out." Defeat weighs down his bowed shoulders. "I just…don't want you to suffer."

She takes his meaning immediately and offers him a patient smile. She gestures to the barren land, the empty sea. The low, red sun dazzles her eyes. Orange clouds streak the indigo sky, the most beautiful she's ever seen. "Life was the most precious gift of all," she whispers. "I won't refuse it."

"Right. I understand." Boston puts away the small, deadly pile of opiates without another word. He holds her tight and warm in his weakened arms and watches the approach of night.

"Do I have great cheekbones?" Carolina asks several days after the food runs out.

"You've always had great cheekbones," Boston replies. They spend most of the day lying on their bedrolls, talking quietly, twining their toes together. Conserving their strength. While they still had energy, they moved camp closer to the high-tide line so they could hear the soothing crash of waves and wander down to the water. Now it's all they can do to fetch sea water to the still to keep their supply going.

"Carolina, I'm really sorry about this."

"What? Like this is your fault?"

"No, that's not what I mean," he says. "I mean I'm sorry that I'm leaving you with all this mess."

"Stop talking like that. As soon as we feel a little stronger, we can tackle it together."

Actually, there isn't much mess. All their samples are loaded into the cargo hold. Their field notes and diaries are entered into one of the handhelds and placed in the craft. The lab has been dismantled and stowed. There's nothing more to study.

"I've always wanted to be buried at sea," Boston comments.

"No one's ready to be buried!" Carolina shushes him.

But in the darkest part of the night, under a new moon, Boston quietly passes away.

In the morning, Carolina is too spent to weep. Inwardly, she curses him for being male, for being more fragile than herself, for leaving her with all this mess. She gathers what remains of her resolve. Placing a tender kiss on his brow, she rolls his body with all her might into the waves until they bear him away.

Then she drags herself to the *Seedship* and pulls herself up through the opening. She sets the controls to take it forward two-and-a-half billion years, to what was supposed to have been their future. She stands ready at the opening, pushes the activation button, and hurls herself out onto the sand. The *Seedship* vanishes into an unknown unfolding.

Carolina crawls to the very edge of the water at low tide. She curls up on the warm sand and falls into the deepest sleep.

The ocean returns to claim her as the sun sets in a brilliant blaze.

Two bodies roll in the waves. Inside them billions of cells, billions of microbes dissolve the flesh that houses them and find a new home in an ancient sea.

Morning has just broken. Long shadows stretch across the sand. Slivers of pink light catch the crests of the morning breakers. Without warning or sound, a silver teardrop appears in the sky, hovering over an ocean teeming with simple life, reflecting the dawn. It waits for a thousand millennia. And then a strange craft descends from the fourth planet—the first expedition to its blue-green sister world. The creatures aboard collect the odd artifact for further study, unknowing that it will unravel the mystery of their origin.

Ozymandias
by
Percy Shelley

I met a traveler from an antique land
Who said: Two vast and trunkless legs of stone
Stand in the desert. Near them, on the sand,
Half sunk, a shattered visage lies, whose frown
And wrinkled lip, and sneer of cold command
Tell that its sculptor well those passions read
Which yet survive, stamped on these lifeless things,
The hand that mocked them and the heart that fed.

And on the pedestal these words appear:
"My name is Ozymandias, king of kings:
Look on my works, ye Mighty, and despair!"
Nothing beside remains. Round the decay
Of that colossal wreck, boundless and bare
The lone and level sands stretch far away.

Omega Museum
by
Jaleta Clegg

I.

The tour guide paused at the door of the final exhibit, one hand resting on the handle. A hush fell over the group trailing her. "Sisters, counselors are available upon exiting should you find this exhibit too distressing." Her smile turned to the younger members of her audience, a school group on their required visit. "All of you have your signed release forms? Good. Come this way, please." She pulled on the handle. The group sighed in unison as the dim interior was revealed.

Shieyl followed the others inside, hiding her rising excitement under a pall of awe and shock. This final room of the Omega Museum, showcasing extinct species, paid homage to the missing half of their own race—man.

The tour guide bowed her head, posing near the first softly lit case. "The last male ruler of any planet in the Hegemony."

Shieyl shuffled forward with the others, staring at the plastaflesh image posing under glass. A hawk-like nose and dark stubble marked the face. The schoolgirls gasped in shocked revulsion. One whispered to her friend, pointing to the strangely flat chest. Shieyl let her gaze drop lower. The clothing on the figure teased her imagination. What really lay beneath on a man?

The tour guide's voice ushered them further into the exhibit. "As you should have learned in school, radiation and the effects of targeted warfare devastated the male half of our population. Efforts to counteract the damage through cloning also proved futile. Only the female clones survived."

The last male fetus bobbed gently in a jar of preservative fluid. The schoolgirls pressed their noses to the display. One girl turned, hands covering her mouth, her face a delicate green. Her teacher hustled her to a nearby exit.

Shieyl lingered, studying the pitiful thing. Strange emotions stirred in her breast. He was tiny, and not so different from a female fetus. What would it be like, to carry a male child? Or to carry any child at all? She pressed her hands to her flat belly.

The group filtered through the dim room, hushed as if in a cathedral, as they examined the tribute to the last males of their species. Women and girl children stared at the oddities. Shieyl drifted behind, waiting for the guide to reach the far end, to pause at the most revered shrine known to women.

The guide waited as the group slowly assembled by the final exhibit. Shieyl dampened her impatience. The woman smiled in a gesture calculated to show the proper amount of respect and authority. "Behind this door, lies the greatest treasure in the Hegemony. The last sperm, preserved forever in cryogenic deep freeze."

The door opened, releasing a wash of frigid air. Bright light bathed a tank of clear acrylic that was centered in the steel-lined chamber. The group filed inside, circling the exhibit. Shieyl clutched her hands, fingernails digging into her palms. She longed to conceive a child the natural way. She wanted to give birth to a male. Her dream was only possible with the sperm preserved in the vault.

"No images are allowed," the guide chided one schoolgirl gently.

Shieyl glanced around the chamber, confirming the position of security devices. Nothing had changed from her previous visits. The theft would not be easy, but it was possible. She leaned close to the tank, her breath frosting the surface. The tiny container embedded deep inside held her hope for immortality as the first woman to bring men back to existence. The cloning establishment had managed with lower vertebrates, even returning some species to the wild to procreate at will. But higher vertebrates, especially humans, had proven too difficult. Despite their best efforts, only a portion of the females survived.

Shieyl planned to change that, with the assistance of the last vial of male sperm in existence. She breathed her promise to her unconceived child before following the shuffling crowd through the exit.

II.

In a cubby above the restroom stalls, Shieyl crouched, waiting for the lights to dim to a twilight level. An architectural anomaly, the space had originally held an air processor that had been long since removed and replaced with a smaller, more efficient model. No security cameras covered the spot.

Shieyl tugged on the silvery gloves and facemask that matched the bodysuit hidden under her clothing. She contorted in the tiny space, stripping off her pants and sweater, tucking them into the far corner.

The guards should have finished their rounds. She lingered on the lip, listening to the hush of the empty museum. Breathing a prayer to the Mother Goddess, she slipped from her hiding spot. The camera at the door of the restroom swiveled. She flattened herself to the wall, trusting the suit's ability to render her invisible to security scans. The camera finished its pass and fell silent, its lens refocused on the stalls.

Shieyl crept along the wall, in slow and steady movements that allowed the suit to hide her form from the monitors. Ten minutes until the next camera sweep. Her fingers curled around the door handle to the museum's main exhibit hall. She eased it open just far enough to slip her slender body through.

Eerie twilight reigned in the displays. Shadowy shapes of extinct animals and plants loomed, curious and menacing. Shieyl drifted through the exhibit, like a ghost herself, as she hid in the shadows out of the direct path of the sensors.

Silence held as she approached the final door. The Last Men waited inside, and the promise of a future free of cloned reproduction. Her heart raced. A triumphant smile flashed across her face, unseen under the mask. She placed both hands on the door, the circuitry in her gloves unlocking the bolted mechanism.

"Father God, above all, let this work." She breathed her prayer, a tiny whisper of sound. The old religion would return when she presented the worlds of the Hegemony with the heir, a boy child, sturdy and strong and whole. She felt conviction in her soul as she eased the doors apart. With the last sperm, preserved for generations, she would resurrect the male half of her race.

She glided through the security net, past the plastaflesh figures so alien in their maleness. The final goal, her holy grail of desire, glowed gently blue, beckoning her. Shieyl entered the sacred chamber, pausing where the billows of chilled air condensed into fog around the base of the display.

"Mother Goddess, Father God—"

The lights flicked on in a harsh white accusation of violation. Shieyl dove for the vial resting in the heart of the display. But a stasis field snapped into place, freezing her in mid-reach.

Two security guards stepped from the far alcoves surrounding the display. The heavy-set brunette shook her head. "Poor deluded woman."

The second one, a muscular blonde, slapped Shieyl's shoulder sending her spinning inside the field. "Museum of the Last. Ever wonder why there's no display for the Last Thief? Third one this month."

"Let's get her processed." The brunette attached a controller to Shieyl's back before tugging her away from the display.

Shieyl struggled against the mechanism that controlled her muscles, but to no avail. She moaned as the doors to the exhibit slid closed, cutting off her view of the future.

"This might sting," the brunette said.

Shieyl's arm burned just before the world went blank.

III.

Shieyl blinked through crusted eyes. She took in the industrial lights, the cement walls, and the sharp smell of antiseptics that surrounded her. Shifting, she found her hands secured to the railings of a bed. Her belly ached with a deep fullness that was not quite pain. She lifted her head, straining to see.

She lay in a hospital cot with a thin gown rucked up around her thighs, her arms and legs exposed. Restraints circled both wrists, chaining her in place. Her bare feet, pale and sickly under the lights, framed a locked cell door in the far wall.

She dropped her head to the hard mattress, after frantically searching for an escape. Her legs twitched, still heavy from the sedation drugs.

The locks clanked and whirred. The door swung open, admitting a woman in a white coat. She paused by the bed as she scrawled in a notepad, then snapped her notepad closed, and aimed a perfunctory smile at Shieyl.

"Your vitals are well within norms. We'll take you to your cell as soon as you can walk."

Shieyl licked dry lips. "What about a trial? What about my rights?"

The woman dropped the notepad across Shieyl's thighs. "You attempted to steal the greatest treasure in the Hegemony. It makes no difference that the vial is a fake. You have given up your rights. You, and the others who attempt to steal the last sperm, simply vanish."

"A fake?"

The smile crept back, cold and harsh in the unforgiving light. "There is no sperm. There never was."

"Where am I? What are you going to do to me?" Panic clutched Shieyl's belly.

"It's already done. Welcome to the experimental breeding program, number one-one-seven-five-three." The woman tapped the notepad. "The procedure appears to be a success. At least in the initial stages."

Shieyl swallowed bile. "You implanted me?"

"Five embryos. With drug treatments, at least one should take." The woman patted Shieyl's naked leg. "We may not have sperm, but we do have three complete male genome patterns recorded. With the new advances in cloning techniques, we've managed to create a few viable male embryos."

Panic transformed to triumph. "And how many births?"

"None yet." The woman unclipped the restraints. "It's our last chance. Without men, we are doomed to extinction. The failure rate for clones has been rising steadily over the last hundred years. Each batch introduces more genetic defects into the population. Only one in three survives the pregnancy."

Shieyl sat up, her hands cupped protectively over her belly. A beatific smile wreathed her face. She glowed like a Madonna in her thin hospital gown. She let the doctor's warnings rush past her like empty wind. She would birth a son; she felt it in her soul. Shieyl closed her eyes, dreaming of her future glory as the first Mother of a Son, the resurrection of their race as the first Mother of a Son, the resurrection of their race.

Turning In
By Caitlin Kenzie Scott

They say the earth
is a wounded organ,
or was it infected? with sickness
mutated and recurring
and always the body
of a woman

She is swollen, capped off
or raked open,
they say
"he is not herself"
she is rotting

If not a woman then, an opening
mark, a passage that repeats
"these things are closing in"
folding up upon themselves
as one walks back on the fanning graves
of his own feet in a black loam

The earth is not defraying
like a shoelace,
or its plastic grommet unpeeling
from a sturdy knot
to an unbound bloom
like age to nerve endings
wearing slimmer,
the flossy telomeres unbind,
from spools of tender marrow

The air is only readying
anew to know different
feet on its broad face,
breath in its night
like bright light bulbs
of mood and thought,
a glow of dials in the atmosphere

The tones of day are multicolored
hovering strata,
the fattening of matter
from the bellows of our lungs, a tinted air
will gut the blue
red now, we tune the lightening tight

The earth is sucking back to its center
as directions of the compass
press backwards to their pin;
plasma magnetized and dense

In due course we too,
will be sucked back
with the clap of an atom's sneeze,
to a small electric point,
to become nuclear leaven
for a fresh crust
of a source-less dawn.

Fire and Ice
By Robert Frost

Some say the world will end in fire,
Some say in ice.
From what I've tasted of desire
I hold with those who favor fire.
But if it had to perish twice,
I think I know enough of hate
To say that for destruction ice
Is also great
And would suffice.

Under Erasure
by
Murray Leder

I grew up loving the stories of unsolved disappearances: Amelia Earhart, Ambrose Bierce, the Roanoke colony, the Anasazi Indians. I read everything I could about famous people who vanished in my lifetime, like D.B. Hooper and Jimmy Hoffa, both of whom were mysteriously missing and probably dead. But I wondered if they really were dead or whether they were occupying another place in the imagination, a place suspended between present and absent, alive and dead.

My favorite story was about the *Mary Celeste*, a ship found adrift in the Atlantic Ocean in 1872. The vessel was intact, but not a soul was aboard. Some accounts claimed there were steaming cups of tea and full plates of breakfast left on the dining table, untouched. These were pure embellishment. But they made for a good story. I first read about the ship in a book of great mysteries my uncle had given me as a birthday present. I remember the name of the ship's captain, Benjamin Briggs. Today, when I close my eyes, I can still feel the book in my hands.

What must it have been like to walk that ghost ship, those decks of the *Mary Celeste* that resounded with emptiness? Did the crew who boarded her know that they were entering an enigma that would never be solved?

Now, I know just how they felt.

It is March 31, 2010 and I'm sitting at the back table at "Heroes and Villains," a comic book store on James Street. I'm writing on a piece of lined paper. Underneath it is a copy of *Crisis on Infinite Earths.* My every word scratches a trace onto its cover. I wonder if what I'm writing will ever be read, and by whom. I wonder if I will last long enough to finish writing. But most of all, I wonder why I'm writing this piece, at all. For my own sake, I suppose. Like a diary. The diary of Carl Chalk, B.A., M.A., Ph.D. Associate Professor, Philosophy Department, Challis University, a member in good standing of the Canadian Philosophical Organization and other sundry organizations.

And the Last Man Alive.

At least as far as I know. Some might call me the most the important person in all of human history. But I know better; I am nothing more than a walk-on spear-carrier who happens to be present at the final curtain.

It happened a week ago, during a third-year undergrad class called "Twentieth Century Critical Thought." We were covering the concept of *sous rature,* "Under Erasure," as it applied to the writings of Jacques Derrida. The concept is the typographic expression of deconstruction—meaning a term from western metaphysics that is written out and struck through. "Under Erasure" applies when we question the term, but still need it. The word remains legible and yet, troubling the binary between presence and absence.

The fluorescent lights blared down on us. I heard stifled yawns. It was an advanced concept but if they grasped it they would begin to understand deconstruction.

I faced the chalkboard and scratched the word MEANING on its slate surface. Then I struck it through, placing it under erasure.

MEANING.

When I turned back, they were gone. *Gone.* There is a terrible finality to that word. A room of thirty students and then, nothing. Empty desks.

I had almost no reaction at first. It did not register as reality but as some strange dream. I took a sip of coffee and stared at the vacant room. Drinks, even half-eaten sandwiches sat on their desks, along with notes that trailed off in mid-sentence.

I went to the window and looked down at the quad. No one was there, either, just the wind kicking papers around the concrete. No birds sang. There was not a noise to be heard, not even the sound of traffic in the distance.

I walked into the hallway in a daze. My heart started to beat faster and I felt real anxiety. This was no dream. I ran my hand over the wall to feel its hardness. I even bit my cheek until it bled.

There was no denying it. I was awake. I was alive. I *existed.* I knocked on every door I could find, but I could not see or hear another living soul. I went to my office, picked up the phone and dialed information. I dialed emergency. And then I dialed random numbers just to see if anyone picked up. No one did. I tried everyone I cared about and got no answers.

Though I had much cause to doubt it, I knew I was sane. I was lucid. The world was real and almost unchanged, except for what had happened. My senses processed the world around me as always. As I walked out of the building, I smelled something familiar. Smoke. I followed the scent to one of the residence cafeterias where tables were littered with trays and half-eaten meals. Burgers were hardening into pieces of charcoal on the still-blazing fryers and acrid smoke filled the air. I switched off every machine I could find. There was a television in the corner of the cafeteria that showed nothing but leaping static. I could not stand to look at it and switched it off, too.

I walked outside and sat on top of a grassy hill. I stared up at the indifferent sun crawling across a blue sky. Part of me wanted to yell my lungs out, to call to whoever could hear me. But somehow I could not bring myself to disturb the silence that hung over everything like a drape.

I couldn't work up fear or despair. As far I could tell, no one had *died*, exactly. It felt like they had never been born, and I was not in the habit of mourning those who had never existed.

Yet I remembered them. As the hours turned into days, face after face flashed through my mind, faces that I had no name for: the superintendent at my building, the women behind the desk at the nearby laundromat, a parking attendant at my gym. And then people close to me: colleagues, students, friends, acquaintances, old lovers. But I steeled myself and pushed it all from my mind. I tried hard to not to think of anyone or anything I would miss. This wasn't the time for that, not if I wanted to keep going.

The sun hung low over the mountains by the time I left campus. Slowly I walked toward downtown. Driving wouldn't have worked too well. Cars sat inert in the middle of roads. Traffic lights changed, uselessly. The silence was the worst part. The city was like a hushed cathedral, a sense of silent fate hanging over everything. I saw no birds, no dogs or cats or squirrels, though the trees swayed in a warm spring breeze. At one point I found myself thinking that even an ant crawling across the sidewalk would seem like a gift from the God I did not believe in. But I did not find a living thing, not even an insect.

I walked into supermarkets for free food; the doors still parted for me. I thought about how I could preserve some of the food before it went bad. I would need a generator, and then I would have to figure out how to work it in anticipation of the day when the power grid inevitably failed. But I was too old to retrain as a survivalist. I had been an academic all my life, and I knew I would never be anything else.

"What's the point in surviving?" I asked myself. They were the first words I had spoken aloud since it had happened.

It would not have taken too long to walk to my apartment but I had no desire to do so. I did not want to see pictures of loved ones staring at me from the walls. I did not want to be nostalgic. I did not want to be confronted by my losses.

I needed to go back to where I belonged, to where I could feel useful. I grabbed some bedding from a department store and headed back to the university where I had worked for three decades.

In the courtyard before the library, a statue of the university's first president, David Tartelton, stood in a formal gown with a flat cap and a book under his arm. It had always struck me as a particularly ugly statue, with a fatuous smile on the bloated administrator's lips. "KNOWLEDGE IS FOREVER" was scrawled on its base. But now I knew, more keenly than ever, that knowledge isn't forever; it is temporary, contingent. Every book in the library will eventually become nothing but dust.

But do you know what is eternal? Or nearly eternal? Copper statues. I once read that when everything else has decayed, copper statues and nuclear waste will be the last traces of human habitation on Earth.

No more *Mona Lisa*, Beethoven symphonies, Ibsen plays, Woody Allen movies. But Tartelton will still be here. I unzipped my pants and pissed on the statue.

I laid out my bedding in the Philosophy section. No doubt if a science professor was in my place, he would be using his lab equipment to take readings from the air or constructing devices to look for survivors in faraway places. A younger, more adventurous man would find a fast car and hit the highway in an effort to see what was left of this mangled shadow of civilization. But me? I surrounded myself with books. I passed the days reading my way through Derrida, Eco, Ricoeur, Nietzsche, Heidegger. I tried to make Apocalyptic Literature and Thought my new area. I designed course lists on the subject. I hunted for answers in the texts. Maybe it was foolish to even ask why this had happened. What answer would be good enough?

On Mondays, I hiked to the nearest department store and came back with a shopping cart full of new clothes, canned goods and toiletries, as well as batteries for the flashlight I used to read at night. I parked the cart in the lobby of the library and carried the goods up the stairs to my nest on the fourth floor—I dared not take the elevator. Save for those trips off campus, the farthest from the library I ever went was the gym, where I took my showers.

The library was my base and the center of my existence. Even as I tried hard not to personalize my space, it slowly became my home. I became fastidious about where I placed my coffee thermos, where I laid my copy of *Difference and Repetition*, and where my notes were stored. I read twelve to fourteen hours a day. I moved on to poetry. Eliot and Yeats felt right. Lines that I knew from childhood took on a new resonance. "Turning and turning in the widening gyre. The falcon cannot hear the falconer; Things fall apart; the centre cannot hold."

I made myself read the book of Revelations in every edition of the Bible I could find, and then every commentary in the theology section. The descriptions of the Four Horsemen, the Seven Seals, the Dragon and New Jerusalem used to inspire me. But they had it all wrong; a mere glance out the window across the empty courtyard told a different story of what the real apocalypse looked like.

The truth is, I was living in regressive paradise; in a strange way, I was having the time of my life. There were no lectures to prepare, no papers to mark, no administrative headaches to untangle. I had no responsibilities in the world and had nothing to do but read.

But a devil whispered in my ear, a poststructuralist devil. The fear about the end of the world is the fear of the destruction of the archive—meaning of civilization's most significant works. I clung to the books because they counted for something beyond human life. But the destruction of the archive meant not only the end of humanity but also its *erasure*. All the books in the world could not keep us immortal. Neither could our cathedrals, nor our skyscrapers, podcasts or landfills. Decay and entropy would win out against the archive sooner or later. I just never thought I'd live to see the day.

One night, I went to the top floor of the library and stared out on the city. It looked like Las Vegas. So many lights were burning against the blackness. But light did not mean life; far from it. It just proved there was no one out there to switch them off. Soon enough, the grid would crash and a curtain of blackness would fall forever.

A face flashed into my mind as I stared out onto the bright-burning city—so random—a plump-faced girl with pigtails. I think she might have been a student I had many years ago. Then another. And more faces. Gas station attendants, clerks, contestants on TV game shows from decades ago. My memory swept over me. Loved ones and enemies alike. The nobodies and the people who meant the world to me. Everything I had tried to dam up came out in a torrent. A thousand faces flashed in my face in succession. They could not be denied.

I fell to my knees and cried. I couldn't remember the last time I had cried but I wept like an infant.

MEANING.

And I thought, *now, I am the archive.* So, like Prospero, I drowned my books. There would no peace for me in the library.

Without a plan, I set out into the silent, empty city. The sun was streaming between the towering skyscrapers. The landscape was picturesque, postcard pristine, but with a hollowness beneath the veneer. I fancied I could detect a certain almost imperceptible decay creeping across the face of the cityscape—the process of entropy that would ultimately reduce it all to ashes and ruins and dust had begun. But then I heard something, a sound I had almost forgotten. Music. I would never have noticed it at this distance if everything else had not been so quiet. I was excited, yes, legitimately excited for the first time in the weeks since the vanishing occurred. My heart was in my mouth as I ran through the streets trying to find the source. I was so ready for disappointment.

It was an old blues record, playing at a piercing volume over a sound system. It crackled and hissed over the streets. I could barely make out the words; the gruff, resonant voice sounded like it was coming from another planet. Instead, it was coming from Heroes and Villains, a comic book store. The door was propped open and I walked through.

I almost slipped on a comic book. Dozens of them covered the floor in neat piles. More were pinned to the walls, already open to particular pages. As the music played, I walked gingerly through the brightly lit store to avoid stepping on the covers, past the racks and shelves. I saw a movement at a table at the back. There was a faint smell of pizza in the air.

He saw me before I saw him.

In a motion he was on his feet and running towards me with a muffled cry of excitement. In a flash he was at me and I flinched, but he merely put his arms around me.

"Dear God, dear God!" he yelled. "I'd lost hope! And to think, Charley Patton brought you here to me." There were tears in his eyes.

I guessed he was in his late twenties, looking scruffy with a week's beard. He smelled like he might not have bathed in a week either. A red Superman logo was on his black shirt, which hung loose on a plump frame. He smiled widely, as if his entire world had just turned around. I tried to match it, but I wondered if my smile looked forced.

"Charley Patton," I said. My voice rasped. Like some cloistered monk, I hadn't spoken in weeks. "Is that who we're listening to?"

"I'll turn it down, I'll turn it down." He dashed to the turntable and switched it off. "Thought he seemed like a right soundtrack for this thing we're in. He had a song called 'High Water Everywhere' about the great flood in 1927. Seemed right." He turned back to face me, wiping the tears from his ears. "I'm sorry. It's just that I was seriously starting to doubt if I'd ever see another human face again. At this point I'd settle for Jeffrey Dahmer. I should introduce myself. I'm Alvin."

"Alvin, good to meet you," I said. "I'm Carl Chalk. I teach philosophy at the university. Or I guess I mean taught."

"Tenses are hard, aren't they?" he said. "So you're Professor Chalk, then. Pleased to meet you, another live person."

"You haven't seen anyone else?" I asked.

"No," Alvin said. "Nobody. And not for a lack of looking. I spent days wandering all around the city. Never saw a soul. Not a cat or dog or a pigeon. Wait, did you actually see it happen? I was sleeping off a hangover."

"I was looking away," I told him. "I was lecturing. I don't think I saw them disappear—I think I was looking away. But they were gone. Just gone."

"Not a noise?" he asked. "Nothing?"

"Nothing." I saw something die in Alvin's flabby face. He turned from me and paced the floor.

"So it's just the two of us, maybe in this whole city, or the world. Why?"

"I don't know," I said.

"Did aliens scoop up everybody to their mothership but miss us somehow?"

"I don't know."

"Maybe this is purgatory. Maybe the world's still as it was, but we've died and slipped into a parallel world for lost souls, or fallen out of time somehow."

"I don't know."

"I KNOW YOU DON'T KNOW!" he shouted, banging his fist against a bookcase, and setting it trembling. "There has to be an explanation."

"Does there?" I asked.

He looked at me without comprehension. "What do you mean? Of course there does. Things just don't happen for no reason."

I thought of the name on the store, "Heroes and Villains." Black and white, right and wrong. True and untrue.

"Sure they do," I said, slipping into lecture mode. "Every day of your life things happen for no reason. Any reason you come up with is your invention—your answer, not the truth."

He looked confused, maybe even appalled. "So that's enough for you? Not to even bother asking what this all means?"

"I've given it a lot of thought," I said with a sigh. "That's all we can do. But we should be prepared for the likelihood that we won't get an answer." After a pause I added, "Look, there's one detail that seems wrong to me in all of this."

"What is that?" asked Alvin.

"Writing. When my students disappeared, everything on them did too. It's not like there were piles of clothes left. But when I looked, the notes in front of them—those remained. Some ended mid-sentence, some even mid-pen stroke. The people disappeared but their writing remained."

Alvin lit up. "Yes! Yes! Writing survives. That's something. That's big."

"Western culture often thinks of writing as the thing that outlasts us. Our bones and our words."

"Pictures too." Alvin pointed to the nearest comic book, pinned on the wall, indicating the brightly colored images in it. My eyes narrowed on one that showed the process of depiction—a man crouched in a cave, his shadow cast against the wall by a flaming torch on the floor. He was etching something on the rock.

I suddenly realized the comic books were pinned to the walls and spread around the floor for a purpose. He was working on something, trying to crack a code.

Alvin was just like me. He was burying himself in the archive.

"You want some pizza?" he asked suddenly. "I've also got Coke."

He had worked at a pizza place nearby and continued to feed himself from it. I had to admit, junk food would really hit the spot. We sat at the back table and shared details about our lives, before and after the event. I wish I could remember more of what he said about his sister and his parents. How he had desperately gone looking for them but came up blank. He got teary more than once. All of this had hit him harder than me, I think. He had lost more than me.

"Are we really talking about the end here?" Alvin asked. "The end of the world? The end of everything?"

I sighed. "The Earth's still here. The stars are still up there. Geologically speaking, humankind was just a blip anyway. So no, I guess it isn't the end of everything."

"Just *our* everything."

"The end of history," I said, thinking of Alexandre Kojève and Francis Fukuyama. "My students often have trouble with this concept. It just means the end of a way of thinking about the course of time."

"So it's the end of history, then," said Alvin.

"It's a cruel trick," I said. "Instead of an apocalypse where our works die and we survive, it's the reverse. Humankind vanishes and all of our art and buildings and statues survive. But of what possible use is that now?"

He cleaned his fingers of pizza grease and reached for a comic book. "You probably think I'm a real nerd to spend all my time here. Did you ever read comics?"

"As a matter of fact, I did." I hadn't thought about it in years. "I read the Classic Comic books, things like *Moby-Dick* and *The Iliad,* when I was a boy. And I read the superhero stuff too. I used to like Captain Marvel."

"Shazam!" Alvin said.

I smiled. "Captain Marvel was great because he was a kid imagining that he was a big strong man. It was easy to pretend to be him."

"He started out with Fawcett Comics and was acquired by Charlton Comics, but the rights were eventually bought out by

D.C. Captain Marvel's still in the D.C. Universe now. Or..." He looked down at his hands. "Damn those tenses."

"If writing and pictures survive," I said, gesturing to the shelves of comic books, "then Captain Marvel is still around."

"Yeah." Alvin seemed happy with that thought. He leaned closer to me. "It just makes sense to me. This is where I learned about the idea of the apocalypse—the idea that the world *can* end. The universe is always teetering on the brink of extinction, and the heroes have all they can do to save it... Until the next time." He laughed painfully. "That's how it was supposed to be, you know?"

"Did you ever read T.S. Eliot, Alvin? 'This is the way the world ends. Not with a bang but a whimper.'"

"Right about now," said Alvin, "I'd settle for the whimper."

I bit into the lukewarm slice of pizza and drank from my bottle of Sprite.

"You say you were looking away when it happened, right?" asked Alvin. "I think I would have liked to have seen it happen. Seen their faces." He took a sip of his drink and then his tone grew darker. "I always knew it would happen like this." he said, his voice distant. "Even back then, as a kid reading comics, I *knew*. I knew I would live to see the end and that it would be something like this. No worlds exploding, no meteorites hitting Earth. It would happen quietly, suddenly. People wouldn't be huddling in shelters. They wouldn't even know and they'd be gone. Maybe we were always in the wrong world—we should be in the one with superheroes. Professor, you'd think I was mad if I said what I really thought was going on."

"Try me," I said.

Alvin reached over, grabbed a book off the shelf and put it in my hand. It was *Crisis on Infinite Earths.* Dozens or hundreds of costumed characters floated around the cover, and when I flipped through the pages, I was astonished to find endless characters stuffed into every panel, including a one page that had easily a hundred figures crammed in. I recognized Superman and only a few others.

"It's like one of those Russian novels from the 19th century," said Alvin. "Nearly every character in the D.C. universe appears somewhere. I was about twelve when it came out, and it seemed like the biggest thing that ever happened. They needed to do it because the D.C. universe was getting too complex. There were dozens of parallel universes and parallel timelines. Continuity grew impossible. It was hard for new readers to come in. The editors decided to do something about it. In a year of crossovers that told the biggest comic book story ever, characters died left and right, even big ones like Supergirl and the Flash." He flipped through the book till he found a page near the end, and pointed to what looked like a piece of glass shattering in space. "This is the end of the universe at the beginning of the universe. See what it says?" He tapped the dialogue box with his finger. TO BE CONTINUED? "I took it seriously at the time." He grinned. "So basically, the entire *multiverse* was destroyed. The many worlds became one, an amalgam of the old and new. This allowed writers to rewrite the world however they wanted. They could go with the continuity when they felt like it, or ignore it. Countless universes ended. Presumably billions of people died. But then again, they didn't exactly die. They were erased from continuity. They were written out."

His words set a tingle at the back of my neck. "So, that's what you think has happened?" I said. "That we're—"

"Between continuities. Like the Limbo that Animal Man visits during Grant Morrison's run; a place for the de-canonized. It's what we call a retcon for *retroactive continuity*—when writers find ways to toss away old continuity in favor of a new one, which can be revised however they decide. They're changing continuity out there—our continuity, and we've been left behind somehow."

"Who?" I asked. "Who are 'they'?"

Alvin shrugged. "Our writers? Maybe they want to change around mankind, hopefully for the better. Maybe there're parts for you and me, just with a changed back-story or something like that. Or maybe mankind is being written out altogether, and being replaced by something else, something that we kept from evolving. You've got to shake up the continuity every once in a while." Alvin shrugged. "Look, Carl, I realize this sounds very silly. Maybe you're right—maybe there is no answer. But for me, for now, this is my answer."

Part of me wanted to tell him about Heidegger and Derrida, to talk through what kind of shared logic we could find between comic book logic and continental philosophy. I wondered if being "Under Erasure" was the same as being out of continuity. Derrida, a blue-blooded snob underneath it all, would hardly think so. But all I said was, "Alvin, you've given me something profound to think about." I picked up *Crisis on Infinite Earths.* "And some new reading material."

Alvin smiled sadly.

"Alvin," I asked, "have you ever heard of the *Mary Celeste*?"

But Alvin never answered my question. Something fluttered through him, something palpable. I could see it on his face. With sudden urgency, he reached out and grabbed both of my forearms. "Look me in the eye, Professor," he said. "And remember."

I stared at Alvin's face, his eyes popping with intensity. Neither of us said another word. He clasped me as if in a death grip, but I did not blink. And before I realized it, I was looking at the wall behind him. What did I see as I watched Alvin erased from existence? Not some vanishing woman in a magician's act, not some trick. There was nothing cheap about it. It was profound. It was a rejoining with nothingness, a surrender to entropy. I tell myself that I saw peace on his face in those last moments. The peace of oblivion. And I can still feel the pressure of his hands on my arms.

He was real. He was here. And now he's gone. And I think, *He should have written down his ideas.* I need to do it for him. Enough reading; it is time to write.

But first I read *Crisis on Infinite Earths* from cover to cover. I do not try to follow the plot or keep track of the thousands of characters. I simply experience the art and the color and the clumsy grace of the dialogue. The sweep and volume of the story would shame Milton.

In a lonely dialogue box in the bottom, right corner of the last page, after all the destruction and remaking of universes, there's a simple declaration. "NOT THE END. THE BEGINNING OF THE FUTURE."

Maybe Alvin is in that new future now, and maybe I will join him. Or maybe not. Maybe I will never vanish, but will stay in this world as its orphan. I eat another slice of pizza and think about the crew of the *Mary Celeste.* I am going to tell Carl that if we knew what had happened to that vanished crew, I bet the answer would be damned disappointing.

Thus ends the last narrative of Carl Chalk. I am done with writing, and dubious about what putting this down has accomplished.

~~The End~~

The Star
by
H. G. Wells

It was on the first day of the New Year that the announcement was made, almost simultaneously from three observatories, that the motion of the planet Neptune, the outermost of all the planets that wheel about the Sun, had become very erratic. Ogilvy had already called attention to a suspected retardation in its velocity in December. Such a piece of news was scarcely calculated to interest a world outside the astronomical profession, where the majority of inhabitants was unaware of the existence of the planet Neptune and where the subsequent discovery of a faint, remote speck of light in the region of this perturbed planet would cause little excitement. Scientific people, however, found the intelligence remarkable enough, even before it became known that the new body was rapidly growing larger and brighter. Its motion was quite different from the orderly progress of the planets, and the deflection of Neptune and its satellite was becoming now an unprecedented phenomenon.

Few people without scientific training can realize the huge isolation of the solar system. The Sun, with its specks of planets, its dust of planetoids, and its impalpable comets, swims in a vacant immensity that almost defeats the imagination. Beyond the orbit of Neptune, there is space, vacant so far as human observation has penetrated, without warmth or light or sound for twenty million times a million miles. That is the smallest estimate of the distance to be traversed before the very nearest of the stars is attained. And, saving a few comets more unsubstantial than the thinnest flame, to human knowledge, no matter had ever crossed this gulf of space until early in the twentieth century, when this strange wanderer appeared. It was a vast mass of matter that rushed with no warning out of the black mystery of the sky into the radiance of the sun. By the second day, it was clearly visible to any decent instrument as a speck with a barely sensible diameter in the Leo constellation near Regulus. In a little while, an opera glass could attain it.

On the third day of the new year, the newspaper readers of two hemispheres were made aware for the first time of the real importance of this unusual apparition in the heavens. "A

Planetary Collision," one London paper headed the news and proclaimed Duchaine's opinion that this strange new planet would probably collide with Neptune. Leading writers expanded the topic further, so that in most of the capitals of the world on January 3, there was an expectation, however vague, of some imminent phenomenon in the sky. As the night followed the sunset round the globe, thousands of men turned their eyes skyward to see...the old familiar stars just as they had always been.

Until it was dawn in London and Pollux setting and the stars overhead grown pale. It was a sickly, filtering accumulation of daylight in the wintertime, and the light of gas lamps and candles shone yellow in the windows to show where people were astir. But the yawning policeman saw it; the busy crowds in the markets stopped agape, workmen, milkmen, the drivers of news-carts, homeless wanderers, sentinels on their beats all stopped agape; and in the country, laborers trudging afield, poachers slinking home were paused on their ways. All over the dusky country it could be seen, as well as out at sea by the seamen watching for the day. A great white star had come suddenly into the eastern sky!

It was brighter than any star in our skies, more luminescent than the evening star at its brightest. It glowed white and large; no mere twinkling spot of light, but a small, round, clear shining disk that had appeared an hour after first daylight. And where science has not reached, men stared and feared, telling one another of the wars and pestilences that are foreshadowed by these fiery signs in the Heavens. Sturdy Boers, dusky Hottentots, Gold Coast Africans, Frenchmen, Spaniards, and Portuguese peoples all stood in the warmth of the sunrise to watch the setting of this strange new star.

In a hundred observatories, there had been suppressed excitement, rising almost to shouting pitch, as the two remote bodies had rushed together, and a hurrying, to and fro, to gather photographic apparatuses and spectroscopes to record this novel, astonishing sight: the destruction of a world. For it was a world, a sister planet of our earth, far greater than our earth indeed, that had so suddenly flashed into flaming death. Neptune had been struck, fairly and squarely, by the strange planet from outer space, and the heat of the concussion had incontinently turned two solid globes into one vast mass of incandescence. Around the world that day, two hours after dawn, the pallid star was a fleeting image, fading only as it sank westward and the Sun mounted above it. Men everywhere marveled at it, but of all those who saw it, none could have admired it more than those sailors, habitual watchers of the stars, who far away at sea had heard nothing of its advent and saw it now rise like a pigmy moon, climb zenith-ward, hang overhead, and sink westward with the passing of the night.

And when it rose over Europe, crowds of watchers were everywhere on hilly slopes, on rooftops, in open spaces, staring eastward for the rising of the great new star. It rose with a white glow in front of it, like the glare of a white fire, and those who had seen it come into existence the night before cried out at the sight of it. "It is larger," they cried. "It is brighter!" And, indeed, the moon a quarter full and sinking in the west was, in its apparent size, beyond comparison, but scarcely in all its breadth had it as much brightness now as the little circle of the strange new star.

"It is brighter!" cried the people clustering in the streets. But in the dim observatories, the watchers held their breath and peered at one another. "*It is nearer,*" they said. "*Nearer!*"

And voice after voice repeated, "It is nearer," and the clicking telegraph took that up, and it trembled along telephone wires, and in a thousand cities, grimy compositors fingered the type. "It is nearer." Men writing in offices, struck with a strange realization, flung down their pens; men talking in a thousand places suddenly came upon a grotesque possibility in those words. "It is nearer." It hurried along wakening streets, it was shouted down the frost-stilled ways of quiet villages. Men who had read these things from the throbbing tape stood in yellow-lit doorways shouting the news to the passersby. "It is nearer." Pretty women, flushed and glittering, heard the news told jestingly between dances and feigned an intelligent interest they did not feel. "Nearer! Indeed. How curious! How very, very clever people must be to find out things like that!"

Lonely tramps wandering through the wintry night murmured those words to comfort themselves, looking skyward. "It has need to be nearer, for the night's as cold as charity. Don't seem to be much warmth from it if it *is* nearer, all the same."

"What is a new star to me?" cried a weeping woman kneeling beside her dead.

A schoolboy, rising early for his examination work, puzzled it out by himself, with the great white star shining broad and bright through the frost-flowers of his window. "Centrifugal, centripetal," he said, with his chin on his fist. "Stop a planet in its flight, rob it of its centrifugal force, what then? Centripetal has it, and down it falls into the sun! And this--!

"Do *we* come in that way? I wonder--"

The light of that day went the way of its brethren, and with the watchers of the frosty darkness, the strange star rose again. It was now so bright that the waxing moon seemed but a pale yellow ghost of itself, hanging in the sunset. In a South African City, a great man had married, and the streets were alight to welcome his return with his bride. "Even the skies have illuminated," said the flatterer. Under Capricorn, two lovers daring the wild beasts and evil spirits for love of one another crouched together in a break in the cane where fireflies hovered. "That is our star," they whispered, feeling strangely comforted by the sweet brilliance of its light.

A master mathematician sat in his private room and pushed papers away from him. His calculations were already finished. In a small white vial, there still remained a little of the drug that had kept him awake and active for four long nights. Each day, serene, explicit, patient as ever, he had given his lecture to his students and then had come back at once to this momentous calculation. His face was grave, a little drawn and hectic from his drugged activity. For some time, he seemed lost in thought. Then he went to the window, and he pulled the blind up with a click. Halfway up in the sky, over the clustering roofs, chimneys, and steeples of the city hung the star.

He looked at it as one might look into the eyes of a brave enemy. "You may kill me," he said after a silence. "But I can hold you, and all the universe for that matter, in the grip of this little brain. I would not change. Even now."

He looked at the little vial. "There will be no need of sleep again," he said. The next day at noon, punctual to the minute, he entered his lecture hall, put his hat on the end of the table as was his habit, and carefully selected a large piece of chalk. It was a joke among his students that he could not lecture without that piece of chalk to fumble in his fingers, and once he had been stricken to impotence when they hid his supply. He came and looked under his gray eyebrows at the rising tiers of young faces and spoke with his accustomed, studied commonness of phrasing. "Circumstances have arisen, circumstances beyond my control," he said and paused, "which will debar me from completing the course I had designed. It would seem, gentlemen, if I may put the thing clearly and briefly, that man has lived in vain."

The students glanced at one another. Had they heard correctly? Was he mad? There were raised eyebrows and grinning lips, but one or two faces remained intently focused on his calm, gray-fringed face. "It will be interesting," he was saying, "to devote this morning to an exposition, so far as I can make it clear to you, of the calculations that have led me to this conclusion. Let us assume..."

He turned toward the blackboard, meditating a diagram in the way that was usual to him. "What was that about 'lived in vain?'" whispered one student to another. "Listen," said the other, nodding towards the lecturer.

Presently, they began to understand.

That night, the star rose later, for its proper eastward motion had carried it some way across Leo toward Virgo, and its brightness was so great that the sky became a luminous blue as the star rose. Every star was hidden in its turn, save only Jupiter near the zenith, Capella, Aldebaran, Sirius, and the pointers of the Bear. It was very white and beautiful. In many parts of the world that night, a pallid halo encircled it. It was perceptibly larger; in the clear, refractive sky of the tropics, it seemed as if it were nearly a quarter the size of the moon. The frost was still on the ground in England, but the world was as brightly lit as if it were midsummer moonlight. One could see to read ordinary print by that cold, clear light, and in the cities, the lamps burnt yellow and wan.

The world was awake that night, and throughout Christendom, a somber murmur hung in the keen air over the countryside like the belling of bees in the heather, and this tumult grew to a clangor in the cities. It was the tolling of the bells in a million belfry towers and steeples, summoning the people to sleep no more, to sin no more, but to gather in their churches and pray. And overhead, growing larger and brighter as the earth rolled on its way and the night passed, the dazzling star rose.

The streets and houses were alight in all the cities, the shipyards glared, and whatever roads led to high country were lit and crowded all night long. On all the seas, ships with throbbing engines, bellying sails, crowded with men and living creatures, were out at sea, looking to the north. For already, the warning of the master mathematician had been telegraphed all over the world and translated into a hundred tongues. The new planet and Neptune, locked in a fiery embrace, were whirling headlong, ever faster toward the Sun. Already, this blazing mass flew a hundred miles during each second, increasing its terrific velocity along the way. As it flew now, indeed, it must pass a hundred-million miles wide of the earth and scarcely affect it. Near its destined path, though, as yet only slightly perturbed, spun the mighty planet Jupiter with its moons sweeping splendidly around the Sun. Every moment, the attraction between the fiery star and the greatest of the planets grew stronger. And the result of that attraction? Inevitably Jupiter would be deflected from its orbit into an elliptical path, and the burning star, swung by its attraction wide of its sunward rush, would take a curved path, perhaps colliding with and certainly passing very close to our earth.

"Earthquakes, volcanic outbreaks, cyclones, sea waves, floods, and a steady rise in temperature to unknown limits," prophesied the master mathematician.

And overhead, to carry out his words, lonely and cold and livid, blazed the star of the coming doom.

That night, to many who stared at it until their eyes ached, it seemed that it was visibly approaching. The weather changed, too, and the frost that had gripped all of Central Europe, France, and England softened into a premature thaw.

However, you must not imagine that because I have spoken of people praying through the night, going aboard ships, and fleeing toward mountainous country that the whole world was already in a terror because of this star. As a matter of fact, use and wont still ruled the world, and save for the talk of idle moments and the splendor of the night, nine human beings out of ten were still busy at their common occupations. In all the cities, all but a few shops the shops opened and closed at their proper hours; the doctor and the undertaker plied their trades, the workers gathered in the factories, soldiers drilled, scholars studied, lovers sought one another, thieves lurked and fled, politicians planned their schemes. The presses of the newspapers roared through the night, and many a priest would not open his holy building to further what he considered to be a foolish panic. The newspapers insisted on the lesson of the year

1000, when people had also anticipated the end. The star was no real star, only gas, a comet. Were it a star, it could not possibly strike the earth; there was no precedent for such a thing. Common sense was sturdy everywhere, scornful or jesting even, and a little inclined to persecute the obdurate fearful. That night, at seven-fifteen by Greenwich time, the star would be at its nearest to Jupiter. Then the world would see the turn things would take. Many treated the master mathematician's grim warnings as elaborate self-advertisement. At last, common sense, a little heated by argument, signified its unalterable convictions by going to bed. So, too, barbarism and savagery, already tired of the novelty, went about their nightly business, and save for a howling dog here and there, the world of beasts left the star unheeded.

When at last the watchers in the European states saw the star rise, an hour later than the day before, it no larger than it had been the night before. There were plenty awake to laugh at the master mathematician and to bear testimony that the danger had passed.

Shortly thereafter, the laughter ceased. The star grew; it grew with a terrible steadiness hour after hour, a little larger each hour, a little closer to the midnight zenith, and brighter and brighter until it had turned night into a second day. Had it come straight to the earth instead of moving in a curved path, had it lost no velocity to Jupiter, it might have leapt the intervening gulf in a day, but it instead took five days total tc come past our planet. The next night, it had grown to one-third the size of the Moon before English eyes set upon it and the thaw was assured. It rose over America, now nearly the size of the Moon, blinding to look at, and *hot*. A breath of hot wind now blew with its rising and gathering of strength, and in Virginia, Brazil, and down the St. Lawrence valley, it shone intermittently through a driving wall of thunder-clouds, flickering violet lightning, and hail. In Manitoba, there was a thaw with devastating floods. Upon all the mountains of the earth, the snow and ice began to melt, and all the rivers coming out of high country flowed thick and turbid, carrying swirling trees and the bodies of beasts and men. The waters rose steadily in the ghostly brilliance emanating from the star.

Along the coasts of Argentina and the South Atlantic, the tides were higher than they had ever been in mankind's memory, and the storms drove the waters scores of miles inland, drowning entire cities. So great grew the heat that during the night, the rising of the Sun was like the coming of a lone shadow. Earthquakes began and grew from the Arctic Circle to Cape Horn until hillsides were sliding, fissures were opening, and houses and walls were crumbling to destruction. The whole side of Cotopaxi slipped out in one vast convulsion, and a tumult of lava poured out so high, broad, swift, and fluid that in one day, it reached the sea.

The star, with the wan Moon in its wake, marched across the Pacific, trailed the thunderstorms and the growing tidal wave that toiled behind it, frothing and eager, like the hem of a robe. The largest wave came at last, in a blinding light and with the breath of a furnace, swift and terrible, a wall of water fifty feet high, roaring hungrily against the long coasts of Asia and sweeping inland across the plains of China. For a time, the star, hotter, larger, and brighter than the Sun, illuminated with pitiless brilliance the wide and populous country: towns and villages with their pagodas, trees, roads, cultivated fields, and millions of sleepless people staring in helpless terror at the incandescent sky. Then, low and growing, came the murmur of the flood. That was how it was for millions of men that night: flight not an option with limbs heavy with heat and breath fierce and scant and the flood like a wall, swift and white behind them. Then, inevitably, death.

China was glowing white, but over Japan, Java, and all the islands of Eastern Asia, the great star was a ball of dull red fire due to the steam, smoke, and ash from volcanoes that were spouting to salute its coming. Above the floods were lava, hot gases, and ash, and below them, the whole earth swayed and rumbled with earthquake shocks. The immemorial snows of Tibet and the Himalayas were melting and rushing downward by way of ten million deepening, converging channels toward the plains of Burma and Hindustan. The tangled summits of the Indian jungles were aflame in a thousand places, and below the hurrying waters were dark objects that still struggled feebly and reflected the blood-red tongues of fire. In a rudderless confusion, a multitude of men and women fled down the broad river-ways to the one last hope of mankind: the open sea.

The star grew larger, hotter, and brighter with a terrible swiftness now. The tropical ocean had lost its phosphorescence, and whirling steam rose in ghostly wreaths from the black waves that plunged incessantly, speckled with storm-tossed ships.

Then, something wondrous happened. It seemed to those in Europe who watched for the rising of the star that the world must have ceased its rotation. In a thousand open spaces, people who had fled from the floods, falling houses, and sliding hill slopes watched for that rising in vain. Through hour after hour of terrible suspense, the star did not rise. Once again men set their eyes upon the old constellations they had thought were lost to them forever. In England, it was hot and clear overhead, though the ground quivered perpetually, and in the tropics, Sirius, Capella, and Aldebaran shown through a veil of steam. When at last the great star rose ten hours late, the Sun rose close behind it, and in the center of its white heart was a disk of black.

Over Asia, the star had begun to fall behind the movement of the sky, and then, suddenly, as it hung over India, its light had been veiled. All the plains of India, from the mouths of the Indus to the Ganges, were shallow wastelands of shining water, out of which rose temples and palaces, mounds and hills, all black with people. Every minaret was a clustering mass of people who fell one by one into the turbid waters as heat and terror overcame them. The whole land seemed to be silently wailing of the disaster, until a shadow suddenly swept across that furnace of despair, carrying a breath of cold wind and a gathering of clouds out of the cooling air. Men looking up at the star, nearly blinded by it, saw that a black disk was creeping across the light. It was the Moon coming between the star and the earth. Even as men cried out to God at this respite, the Sun sprang out of the East with a strange and inexplicable swiftness. The star, Sun, and Moon rushed toward each other from across the heavens.

To the European watchers, the star and Sun rose alongside each other, driving headlong for a time and then slowing down until, at last, the star and Sun came to rest, merging into one glare of flame at the zenith of the sky. The moon no longer eclipsed the star, but it was lost in the brilliance of the sky. Those who were still alive regarded it for the most part with the dull stupidity that hunger, fatigue, heat, and despair engender, though there were still men who could perceive the meaning of these signs. The star and Earth had been at their nearest, had swung about one another, and the star had passed. Already, it was receding, swifter and swifter, into the last stage of its headlong journey downward into the Sun.

The clouds gathered, blotting out the vision of the sky, and thunder and lightning wove a garment round the world. All over the earth was a downpour of rain as men had never witnessed, and where the volcanoes flared red against the cloud canopy, there descended torrents of mud. Water was pouring off the land, leaving mud-silted ruins, and the earth was littered like a storm-worn beach with the dead bodies of the men and brutes. For days, the water streamed off the land, sweeping away soil, trees, and houses, piling up into huge dykes, and scooping out titanic gullies all over the countryside. Those were the days of darkness that had followed the star and its accompanying heat, and the earthquakes continued throughout.

The star had passed, though, and men, hunger-driven and slowly gathering courage, might creep back to their ruined cities, buried granaries, and sodden fields. Few ships had escaped the storms of that time, but some cautiously came stunned and shattered through the new marks of once familiar ports. As the storms subsided, men perceived that the days were hotter than those of previous years, the Sun larger, and the Moon, shrunk to a third of its former size, now took fourscore days between the commencement of consecutive new phases.

This story does not tell of the new brotherhood that grew among men; of the saving of laws, books, and machines; of the strange change that had come over Iceland, Greenland, and the shores of Baffin's Bay, so that the sailors coming there presently found them green and gracious and could hardly believe their eyes. The movement of mankind now that the earth was hotter, northward, and southward towards the poles of the earth are not to be told in this recapture; it solely concerns itself with the coming and passing of the star.

The Martian astronomers, for there are astronomers on Mars, although they are very different beings from men, were profoundly interested by these happenings. They saw them from their own standpoint, of course. "Considering the mass and temperature of the missile that was flung through our solar system into the Sun," one wrote, "it is astonishing what little damage the earth, which the missile missed so narrowly, has sustained. All the familiar continental markings and the masses of the seas remain intact, and indeed, the only difference seems to be a shrinkage of the white discoloration, frozen water, around each pole." This only goes to demonstrate how small the vastest of human catastrophes may seem at a distance of a few million miles away.

Depletion
By Mark Brandon Allen

Luminescent Nova,
Anamorphosis anomaly
In ethereal skies
With different cosmological constants
Grows in mass and distension
Moving through a rift in time
Stretching
Chromospheres source depleted
Relapses into final configuration
A fatal turbulent collapse
Event horizon
Black hole,
Climax.

Old Gods at the Armageddon
by
Jeffery Ryan Long

The planets had ceased their rotation around the Sun, and all their moons were frozen in cold, universal blackness. Zeus, king of all gods, had stopped time. Watching the stars burn light years away from him, Hermes, the patron god of travelers, attempted to gauge how long he'd been away from Earth.

When Hermes had first arrived on his home planet Mercury, he lay out on the barren, rocky plain, and his god-skin bronzed. Although time had stopped, the Sun and stars still flamed. As he tanned, Hermes looked into the center of the Solar System and watched the Sun until he tired of watching the pulsating fire-bursts.

Shading his eyes, the god turned to Earth, two worlds away. Frozen in mid-revolution, it appeared as a glowing, three-dimensional photograph. Zeus had paused humankind in the middle of blowing itself up. Hermes studied the patches of darkness spread throughout the Earth's small globe. These blots were wide-arching caps of mushroom clouds, the smoky residue of nuclear explosions.

There was no time, and yet there was an eternity for the Immortals. Although seconds did not move on any clock in the galaxy, and no tide gained ground upon any sandy beach, Hermes felt himself change in the way only gods can change: he grew eternally different. Not better, not older, just different.

Eventually, the invisible finger of Zeus beckoned back to counsel on Mount Olympus. But first, Hermes wanted to see what these nuclear bombs had really done. Beyond luxury cars and MP3 music players, Hermes had never been interested in the technological advances of humans. The patron god of travelers avoided the burden of excessive baggage. When he received the silent call from his father, Hermes reversed his Cadillac out of its diamond garage, gassed it with liquid planetary essence, and began his trip home.

Hermes let up on the gas pedal of his silver convertible as he drifted into the Earth's atmosphere. The heat from atmospheric friction caused his back to sweat against the upholstery. He closed the convertible's windows, pulled up the top, and turned on the air-conditioning. Descending first through the layer of ozone, then in a steady plunge through the center of a mushroom cloud, Hermes inhaled the stillborn, radioactive dust and debris that entered his craft through the cooling vents. He chose to see each particle of the nuclear reaction broken down into its molecular components, the halted motions of neutrons and electrons. He was impressed by the molecular complexity of these atomic weapons. Hermes traveled down the vertical length of the cloud and parked just outside its explosion base.

The god opened the adamantine doors of his Cadillac and walked around the explosion's circumference. Surveying the destruction, he closed his eyes to the people held captive by the bomb's spectacular effect, though he knew they were there. He did not see the buildings or the ravaged foliage and fauna; he focused only on the ground, the brown, bald surface surrounding the great, gray-green trunk of the mushroom cloud.

This particular cloud had been released in Canada, but dozens of others stood suspended on landmasses all over Earth, with different shades, shapes, chemical reactions, and molecular combinations, each the result of a simultaneous worldwide detonation. When Hermes's mind wandered, the real world he had chosen not to see appeared to him, especially the dead. He witnessed their surprise as the flesh tore away from their bodies, each individual expression imprinted onto the still air. In grotesque accompaniment, Hermes heard the echo of screams and sirens, the sound of a magnificently complete breaking apart. And over the multitude of noise, the lingering single note of a sonic boom not yet complete. In that instant, Hermes felt the world's horror melt into him.

With great effort, Hermes pulled himself away from the vision. The god remembered Prometheus, and how proud he'd been when he'd first shown Zeus the entertainment value of humans and their insignificant desires. He then recalled how upset Zeus had been when Prometheus delivered fire, the beautiful flames of destruction, to his tiny race of bipeds. And what did Prometheus think about his humans now? There was no glory or triumph in this bomb, not even the comforting mania of bloodlust. Only horror. Hermes felt this horror all the more acutely because he was a god.

After Hermes had seen *what* had happened, he wondered *why* it had happened. Prometheus would know. Hermes flew to the Titan, still captive in Caucasus.

After eons, Prometheus remained a prisoner to the world, his arms and legs held by stainless manacles attached with chains to the mountainside. Shocked, Hermes could see through the Titan to the rocks underneath his great, splayed body. Prometheus had gone nearly transparent. His being, his flesh, bones, and Titanic interior organs, had only the substance of fog; except for his blood-red liver, shiny and pulsing, solid in his abdomen, exposed by an irreparable incision. And perched upon Prometheus's hipbone was the vulture with which Zeus had cursed the Titan, its black talons clutching his almost invisible skin. The vulture's pink, flabby head was completely immersed in Prometheus's middle, its curved beak frozen in mid-chew. Hermes hadn't quite gotten over how creative Zeus had been in his revenge.

"I suppose you've seen," Hermes said, looking at the chained Titan, speaking upward from his knee. Compared to Prometheus, Hermes was the size of an infant; such is the distinction between gods and Titans.

As Hermes spoke, a large being, composed of the same granite that formed the mountain, stepped awkwardly away from a cliff and placed a fist upon the god's shoulder. As the being wasn't necessarily alive, Hermes assumed that it could not be affected by Zeus's suspension of time. The giant spoke from his blank, rock head.

"It's not my fault," the granite being said.

"Don't mind 743936," Prometheus called wearily from behind the rock figure. "He's imperfect, like the rest of them. He operates from my brain waves."

Hermes shook off the giant's grip. Just as Prometheus had invented humanity from the essence of dust, he had apparently attempted to make a friend from the environs of his prison. The granite being, telepathically ordered by Prometheus not to be a pest, collapsed onto the ground in a sitting position, its knees drawn up to his chest.

"His bite is more like a pinching now," Prometheus said, watching Hermes, whose gaze had been pulled back to the vulture. "You should see when he's really going at it."

Hermes turned to the chained Titan's face. He was surprised he'd been staring—unless they are considering sexual conquest, gods never stare at anything for long. Despite the years on the mountain, Prometheus' countenance had grown neither weather-beaten nor unkempt. In fact, the Titan still had the glow of a youthful Immortal, but now that glow emanated from his near-transparency.

"It gets lonely here," 743936 said in echo to Prometheus's unspoken thoughts. The chin of the giant's head-without-a-face rested on hands-without-fingers. 743936 waited on the side of the mountain. Hermes wondered at the giant's ability to appear despondent when he lacked the physical characteristics necessary to display feeling.

"I made 743936 from what I had—this mountain," Prometheus said. There were deep grooves in the rock under the Titan's left hand, upon which the thumb and forefinger were enlarged. Hermes presumed the granite giant had been created from that left hand.

"He's the result of 743,936 attempts to create life," Prometheus said before turning his head to study the rocks under his unbreakable nails. "But he's systematically flawed, like all the rest. Everything he says is a result of what I've thought. We've never even had a real conversation because he can't disagree."

"I'm not as effective as I should be," 743936 said. Even without eyes, the stone giant appeared to be looking out to the world, dreamily, contemplating his melancholy.

"Oh, he's all right," Prometheus said. "I've also programmed him to function as a clock radio, so he can wake me up when I nod off." Immediately, 743936 erupted into a cacophony of noise and static, as if caught between stations. Just as suddenly, he went silent—the result of a telepathic snooze button being pressed.

Hermes cleared his throat. "Your humans are destroying one another," he said, remembering the purpose of his visit.

"I know. I still see everything, so I don't forget. But I'm sure the mortals won't die off completely, even after this."

"But why? Why try to blow themselves up? You know them better than anyone."

Prometheus laughed at Hermes, loud and long, his intestines shaking in his exposed midsection. Blood spilled over the side of the wound, melting into the rocks below. "Ah, it hurts," he said. His head hung over his chest, as he caught his breath. "*Why* is an irrelevant question when trying to understand the motivations of mortals."

"What will happen to us?" Hermes asked, "What will happen if they do die?" Like the rest of the gods, Hermes instinctively knew how hard it was to exist when no one believed in you anymore.

"They won't," Prometheus said. "And besides, it won't affect me. I can't change. When Zeus brings time back, I'll be right here, as always." Prometheus's arms grew tight against the unbreakable chains, and for the first time, Hermes witnessed the power of the ancient Titan as the mountain split in fissures behind the prisoner's broad back. Then, Prometheus fell against the mountainside again, deflated. "But things are going to be uncomfortable for a while. Humans aren't the only ones who make poor decisions."

Hermes kicked a boulder that had rolled onto one of his shoes, knocked loose by 743936 as he settled deeper into the mountain. For a second, the god wondered what it was like to be Prometheus, to have created something so arbitrary, and yet so nihilistic. "Zeus called a counsel to discuss what happens next."

"Then you better go. You gods have a big mess to clean up." Prometheus sighed, his head drooping.

As Hermes stepped into his Cadillac, 743936 grabbed him around the arm. "Do something for me," the rock said. "Tell Zeus that I'm sorry."

The messenger god's hand shook as he positioned the rearview mirror downward to study his face. It looked the same as it had always looked. *I've been a god for too long. I interpret everything as monumental.*

The brilliant and smooth terrain of Mount Olympus glowed phosphorescently upon Hermes's windshield, and he killed the engine of the Cadillac alongside the mythical animals his fellow gods preferred to use for travel. As mythical animals, they had not been handicapped by Zeus's control over time. A chimera was tethered to the post of a star-burning lamp, Pegasus dug its face deep into the feedbag attached to its head, and other creatures that were only seen by Immortals, indescribable in human terms, weaved in the air, their scaled muscles decorating the wind with sibilant motion. Hermes waved to his incestuous relatives before speeding past them to his father.

Hermes caught Zeus as he stomped through the golden corridors lit by refractions of intensified sunshine that glowed against the prismatic metal mirrors cunningly crafted in the workshop of Hephaestus. The King of the Gods, his white toga rustling around his barrel chest, hurried toward the meeting room in the eastern wing of the halls of Olympus. Or rather, the golden corridors submitted to Zeus's stomping, so that his highness was able to hasten to his destination unimpeded.

"Dad, wait a second," Hermes said. "I have a message from Prometheus."

"Prometheus?" Zeus said, his two magnificent eyebrows furrowing into one.

"He told me to tell you he's sorry."

Zeus stood in place silently, looking through his son. In synchronicity to the King of the God's wordless contemplation, the stones and trees of Olympus, as well as the cattle and serpents, bowed their heads in universal quiet.

Finally, Zeus roused himself. "It doesn't matter," he said. "This goes beyond Prometheus."

"What do you mean?" Hermes said.

"That's why we're all here," Zeus said, as Hermes followed his father into the conference room.

All the gods, excluding Ares, were already present around the marble table. Zeus, in an elegant PowerPoint presentation with diagrams, explained that Ares was on Earth, tending to the atomic blasts, recording statistics concerning potential casualties and collateral damage. This new kind of warfare had excited the God of War as no other had before. Ares wanted to evaluate every possible outcome. Zeus let the presentation linger on the concluding slide that read *WHAT NEXT???* "That's why we're all here," the King of the Gods repeated.

Zeus's brother, Hades, who to his displeasure, was referred to as the Lord of the Dead by mortals, spoke next. In a lilting, musical voice that sounded eerie and peculiarly vibrating, he asked, "What next? A good question. What is most necessary," Hades continued, the black spaces of his eyes narrowing, "is more land for the Underworld. It is already overcrowded. Once these bombs finish detonating, there will be no room to accommodate the billions of people who will die."

Every god present knew Hades's concern well. For every counsel on Olympus since 2500 AF (After Fire) Hades had requested, and then demanded, more room for his kingdom. When Hermes had last escorted a trainload of the newly deceased down to the Charon's crowded ferryboat on the River Styx, Hades was overseeing the construction of high-rise apartment buildings. Hermes thought it *had* become cramped down there. Before, meaning near the dawn of recorded time, there had been palaces in the Underworld, great estates housing the families of innumerable spirits, all confined to their particular fate as decided by the god who ruled them. If punishment dictated that a large lawn be acquired for a dead spirit so that it could cut every blade of grass save one before the lawn would immediately regrow, then a tract of land was procured.

Now, there were structures piled on top of one another, the result of overlapping punishments so that the dead had company in their unlimited suffering. Hades hated the fact that misery loved company. In order to solve the population problem, Hades first had personally eliminated any further assigned eternal punishments and then categorized the existing sufferers into group classifications: eternal work, eternal pain, eternal fear, eternal temptation without satisfaction, etc. But it hadn't helped. Hades had become squalid and overrun.

Despite the overcrowding, Zeus had ordered his brother to put a hold on the high-rises, which nearly reached to the surface of the Overworld and threatened to break through the crust of land that separated the dead from the living. But he had always promised he would find space for the crowded, depressing kingdom.

"What about sending dead souls to another planet?" Hera said, moving the single peacock feather in her hair from one ear to the other.

Hades scoffed at his sister-in-law, his dark moustache trembling over his open mouth.

"What?" Hera said, changing the position of the feather once again. "Hermes has his fancy Cadillac. Let him lead the poor souls to Pluto. You could put them to work mining for precious metals."

"Oh, come off it, Hera," Hades said. "We all know that Pluto isn't much more than an oversized moon. Besides, I can't split my time between two worlds. If the dead people of Earth don't stay on Earth, they'll have no resonance with the living. The living will forget what it means to be dead."

"But what if there are no more mortals?" Hermes asked. "What if our time is up?"

"Stop," Poseidon said, and all of the assembled gods felt a salty spray against their unblemished skin. The God of the Oceans raised a wet hand that fell limply onto the marble tabletop with a splash. Cuttlefish swam through the seaweed of his beard, all of them simultaneously assuming a dull purple hue. “I hereby give over all of the seas to the Lord of the Dead.”

A collective murmur rose from the table. To human ears, the murmur would’ve sounded like the downward rush of a waterfall or the ambient interlude of a classical score between themes.

“You can't be serious,” Artemis said, her broken arrows on display in front of her place at the table. She remembered skinny-dipping with her nymphs in many a secret stream. She remembered floating in rivers, on her back and under the stars, as she waited for the elk to drink.

“I think he might be serious,” Aphrodite said. The goddess of beauty had aged, but she still wore her toga with the straight-backed grace of a handsome woman.

“I relinquish my kingdom,” Poseidon said. “The sea is dead anyway. Radioactive fall-out from these bombs will destroy all underwater life in the Earth’s streams, ponds, rivers, and oceans. All of them floating graves. I won’t have any power. Let Hades have the sea. Better it go to him all at once, rather than by a slow poisoning.”

“Is that really a good idea?” Hermes imagined himself, outfitted in a wet suit, winged shoes soaked and heavy with salt, leading the overcrowded souls by submarine to the Oceanic Underworld. “I mean, doesn’t water cover seven-tenths of the planet?”

Poseidon brushed Hermes's concerns aside—or, rather, washed his concerns away like a wave washes away a letter in the sand—and continued. “I’ll go to the frozen continent at the bottom of the world.” Poseidon shrugged and then frowned. “I’ll amuse myself with earthquakes.”

“The dead claim the sea, “the King of Gods said, nodding to his brother. “The world goes on. This arrangement will have to be formalized.”

Hades leaned over the table “What are your terms, Poseidon?”

“There are no terms. I’ll simply give you the deed.”

Hermes panicked, anxiety drumming over his heart as quickly as the flapping wings of his flying shoes. “You should think about this.”

“I have thought about it.” Poseidon folded his arms and sighed. “I don’t want anything to do with people anymore.” A piece of parchment materialized in his open hand, and the former God of the Sea signed his name on the dotted line with squid ink. He pushed the paper over the table to Hades.

Hermes intercepted the deed before the Lord of the Dead could take it.

"What are you doing?" Hades tore the page away from Hermes.

"This can't be happening," Hermes said.

"It's a bummer, but it's a done deal," Apollo said, pushing his bangs out of his eyes. His gelled hair, normally an impressive pompadour, had wilted and sagged over his ears and forehead.

Zeus agreed. "There will be a new order. The seas will be dead, but the mortals will survive. We all go on."

"What, no one wants to refute this?" Hermes looked around at his siblings. "This isn't just about water. We're reshaping the entire planet!"

"Who are you to overrule an agreement of the gods?" broad-shouldered Athena said, scandalized.

Artemis bowed her head and sniffed softly.

Hermes's face flushed as the other gods stared at him. "You're going to let him get away with this?"

Zeus waved his hand, and the gods felt a ripple through their bones. "The pact has been made. You have my approval, Hades."

Hades didn't laugh; he lacked the capacity to laugh. He didn't gloat either. None of the gods would be impressed. He simply left the table, the deed to the sea rolled up in his fist.

"The god of wealth gets his due." Hera reached for a cigarette.

Poseidon, refraining from goodbyes, saddled the Loch Ness Monster and "hee-yahed" him away. From their marble table on Mount Olympus, which Zeus had transformed into a digital viewing screen, the gods watched as Poseidon flew over the Aegean Sea and above the Indian Ocean. After he plunged through the water's glassy surface to its depths, he removed the bridle and saddle from Nessie and petted its tail before releasing it. The beast swam away, the only moving creature in the dark ocean.

The gods continued to watch as Poseidon took a last look at his corral of frozen sea horses, then he placed both of his hands on the surface of the ocean floor. The viewing screen shook as Poseidon rumbled the seabed with the power of his earthquakes. A large mountain at the bottom of the sea began to wobble, and crumbling chunks fell away. Through these falling mounds of sea dirt and rock, an eye became visible under the mountain, then a head, then great webbed fins, and finally the slick body and forked tail of Poseidon's favorite pet, Leviathan. Poseidon swam over to the great beast and pulled it out of suspended time.

Leviathan's yellow, glowing eye came to life, and its beams illuminated the frozen surroundings. Poseidon reached into the sea beast's gills and extracted them, installing a set of air-breathing lungs in the process. He dragged Leviathan to the surface by its whiskers before it drowned, and set his enormous pet onto the coast of Antarctica. Suddenly, a thick, brown fur bloomed over its slick, slimy fish body. Leviathan followed his master from the beach, sliding across the icy land on its belly. Once Poseidon found a suitable setting of white desolation, he crawled onto Leviathan's back and sat down.

"It's just you and me, kiddo."

The sea beast, now a mutated land creature, moaned from underneath him.

The gods at the conference began to argue, for gods have the ability to misunderstand one another about everything; the more trivial the matter, the greater the misunderstanding. Eventually, Zeus, weary of Hera's complaining, Apollo's distraction with a melody he heard in his head, Aphrodite's worsening complexion, Artemis's sulking, and Hermes's preoccupation with evading anything important, began to bellow commands and didn't stop until everyone around the table had properly shut up.

"Just tell me what you want me to do," Hermes said, tired of being there, tired of being anywhere.

Zeus told all the gods he'd restart time as soon as they understood their roles in the new world.

When the meeting concluded, Hermes wandered into the great living rooms of Olympus, among the chairs of infinitely-cushioned comfort and the divans of sensuousness to the *n*th degree. Tapestries, each depicting a scene from the history of the gods, hung from the walls brilliantly in metallic, unearthly fabrics. There was Zeus with the renegade Titans, sealing up his father, Cronus, at the bottom of the universe. In another tapestry, Athena emerged through a wet split in the skull of Zeus, her helmet, armor, and shield covered in reddish birth fluid.

The other gods were in their bedrooms, preparing themselves for the messy restart. Hermes frowned as he watched Apollo tear the Jimi Hendrix poster from his wall; it had been there so long that it was practically an artifact. Across the hall, Athena rolled up her deer-hide rug, a present from Hermes after her first kill.

"Nobody will care after this," Apollo said, putting a rubber band around the poster. "They might remember music after a while, but not for a *long* while. Who's going to care about the greatest guitar player that ever lived when everyone will be fighting for survival?"

Apollo picked up a turtle shell lute and held it out to Hermes. "Remember this? Man, I used to think that this was *it*." He plucked the strings of the instrument and an obsolete Doric melody rose to the top of the room. "They don't make them like this any more. Now it's all digital. You want it?"

"No," Hermes said. "You keep it."

"I don't know what I'm going to do with it," Apollo said. He set the lute in a corner of the room. "You know," he said, turning to his younger brother, "I'm kind of looking forward to this Armageddon. Who knows what human beings might be capable of next? I mean, culturally, things weren't really, you know, progressing. Not for a long time. Take music, for instance. I tend to think, and maybe I'm a purist here, that human music peaked at modal jazz."

"I liked the way things were," Hermes said.

Apollo looked at him. "Ah, you're just upset that you'll be going underwater all the time. But it's still the land of the dead, right? Same thing. If you don't want to do it, the whole messenger thing, then just don't do it. You've always had a knack for figuring ways to get out of things."

Athena passed Hermes as he stepped back into the hall. His sister had shaved her head, and instead of her customary armor, she now wore the saffron robes of a Tibetan Buddhist.

"What gives?" Hermes said.

"What do you mean?"

"The new look."

Athena smiled. "I only have to search for wisdom now. Humans don't need me as their battle goddess anymore. After Armageddon, their wars will be brutal and savage, the violence of animals. That's more Ares' dominion. Governments will cease to exist; all order will be gone. But eventually, individuals will once again strive for wisdom. I have to give what I can to that cause. Even if I have nothing to offer to their warfare or to their democracies."

"All order gone?" Hermes said. If there were no rules, then there was no way around the rules. There was no way to cheat, no way to be himself.

"Complete chaos," Athena said. She smiled again and walked past him to her own quarters.

Hermes walked up the curved platinum staircase to Zeus's penthouse on the second floor. Captured lightning glowed in bulbs that hung from the high ceiling. Every species of bird, mythical and real, sang from a long shelf that ran across the four walls. While clouds moved across the blue-painted ceiling, changing forms from animal-shapes to indistinct, lumpy masses, Zeus sat in a reclining leather chair in front of a multitude of television monitors, all showing scenes from newscasts all over the world. The images on the screen were paused.

Zeus didn't hear his son come in from behind him. He simply stared at the screens and bit at a fingernail.

"Dad," Hermes said.

"Oh, it's you," Zeus said, pulling the finger from his mouth. He turned back to the screens. "Even I can't tell how all this will turn out."

"So what do I do?"

"You're the messenger, relaying correspondence from Olympus to Earth. You do what you always do. You lead the dead souls to Hades."

"I don't want to do that anymore," Hermes said. "You know, I never liked water all that much when it was alive. Now that it's dead—"

"That's irrelevant. It doesn't matter what you like, it's what you are able to do. You'll lead dead souls to the bottom of the sea."

"Maybe we can talk Poseidon into taking back the ocean. To give it up like that…maybe he's just getting old."

"Gods don't get old, Hermes, they just get bored."

"But maybe we could talk to Hades…"

"And maybe I could reverse time so these nuclear explosions don't happen. Maybe I could subjugate reality to my own whims. It doesn't work like that." Zeus held up a large remote control to the television monitors. He pushed play, and all of the paused images on the screens went live.

At once, all over the world, the nuclear bombs continued their cycle of destruction.

And at once, all the slow and stuck drains in the world were unclogged. Every human hair that had been stuck together with blood, skin, and semen was flushed from the pipes of every household into the sea, collecting upon the dead waves into a mass, growing larger and larger, as big as the seas themselves, a great floating wig that covered the surface of all five oceans. The few survivors of the nuclear blasts looked out to the coasts and saw only a great moving body of dark wet hair. Mountains of it washed onto the shore.

As it soaked completely through, the hair became heavy and sank toward the bottom of the sea, catching crabs, dolphins, and tuna in its tangled net, all the sea life that had begun to float up after death. Soon the hair was a blanket at the rocky bottom, every marine animal stuck in its coils, rotting with it.

Hades built an opulent bone palace upon this foundation of lost hair deep below the waves. What had been living in the waters was now buried in hair, strangled, poisoned, or simply murdered by Hades' presence. He strolled several times through the oceans to admire the emptiness before the first dead souls arrived, already feeling the bursts of a reawakened creativity. Just punishments in death could once again be instituted for unjust actions in life. The possibilities were endless. *Perhaps it is the change of scenery*, he thought. He felt the richest of all the gods.

The passage to the new Land of the Dead lay under the crest of a certain wave off the coast of Australia, a wave Zeus had instructed Hermes how to recognize. "The wave comes in like this, and as soon as it breaks, you have to dive through and take all of them with you," Zeus had said. "Then you keep going lower until you see the palace. Hades will take it from there. But if you miss the wave, then you've got to wait for the next one, and by that time the dead souls will start piling up. So make sure you get through correctly when the wave breaks."

Hermes stood on the beach at the darkest hour before dawn and watched the dead souls shivering in their swimming trunks. Some of the spirits began to wander away and Hermes left the sand to herd them into a large clump. "Get in line," he repeated. "All I see is a blob." He looked out towards the ocean and saw the wave moving in from the distance. "There it is," he announced to the gathered dead, and they all shot into the wave in rocket positions and dissolved into the salt water.

This isn't so bad, Hermes thought. He could see the palace up ahead, bursts of lava shooting out from chimneys and clouding the water. *It's rather empty and peaceful down here.* He motioned downward to the souls that had lost their individual wills, and they drifted past him listlessly, toward their destinies, to the whims of their Lord.

Hermes was about to swim back to the surface, but instead let his body sink to the depths, all the way to the sea floor. *Strange that it would feel so comfortable,* he thought. *It looks like hair.* He let the hair wrap around his arms and his legs, not wanting to pull himself free. The hair waved all around him, pulsating. *How nice it would be to only feel the ebb and flow of the current on the bottom, to simply be and not think.* He fell farther through the hair and saw the dead things that had been caught: the porpoises, the fishermen, the whales, the sharks. Soon he was underneath the blanket of hair, breathing it in through his nostrils along with the water.

There was no place on Earth for him anymore. If only he could learn how to die.

Helen of Troy
by Sara Teasdale

Wild flight on flight against the fading dawn
The flames' red wings soar upward duskily.
This is the funeral pyre and Troy is dead
That sparkled so the day I saw it first,
And darkened slowly after. I am she
Who loves all beauty, yet I wither it?

Why have the high gods made me wreak their wrath,
Forever since my maidenhood to sow
Sorrow and blood about me? Lo, they keep
Their bitter care above me even now.
It was the gods who led me to this lair,
That tho' the burning winds should make me weak,
They should not snatch the life from out my lips.
Olympus let the other women die;
They shall be quiet when the day is done
And have no care to-morrow. Yet for me
There is no rest. The gods are not so kind
To her made half immortal like themselves.

It is to you I owe the cruel gift,
Leda, my mother, and the Swan, my sire,
To you the beauty and to you the bale;
For never woman born of man and maid
Had wrought such havoc on the earth as I,
Or troubled heaven with a sea of flame
That climbed to touch the silent whirling stars
And blotted out their brightness ere the dawn.

Have I not made the world to weep enough?
Give death to me. Yet life is more than death;
How could I leave the sound of singing winds,
The strong sweet scent that breathes from off the sea,
Or shut my eyes forever to the spring?
I will not give the grave my hands to hold,
My shining hair to light oblivion.
Have those who wander through the ways of death,
The still wan fields Elysian, any love

To lift their breasts with longing, any lips
To thirst against the quiver of a kiss?
Lo, I shall live to conquer Greece again,
To make the people love, who hate me now.
My dreams are over, I have ceased to cry
Against the fate that made men love my mouth
And left their spirits all too deaf to hear

The little songs that echoed through my soul.
I have no anger now. The dreams are done;
Yet since the Greeks and Trojans would not see
Aught but my body's fairness, till the end,
In all the islands set in all the seas,
And all the lands that lie beneath the sun,
Till light turn darkness, and till time shall sleep,
Men's lives shall waste with longing after me,
For I shall be the sum of their desire,
The whole of beauty, never seen again.

And they shall stretch their arms and starting, wake
With "Helen!" on their lips, and in their eyes
The vision of me. Always I shall be
Limned on the darkness like a shaft of light
That glimmers and is gone. They shall behold
Each one his dream that fashions me anew;
With hair like lakes that glint beneath the stars
Dark as sweet midnight, or with hair aglow
Like burnished gold that still retains the fire.

Yea, I shall haunt until the dusk of time
The heavy eyelids filled with fleeting dreams.
I wait for one who comes with sword to slay,
The king I wronged who searches for me now;
And yet he shall not slay me. I shall stand
With lifted head and look within his eyes,
Baring my breast to him and to the sun.

He shall not have the power to stain with blood
That whiteness, for the thirsty sword shall fall
And he shall cry and catch me in his arms,
Bearing me back to Sparta on his breast.
Lo, I shall live to conquer Greece again!

The Suicide of the World
by
André Saglio, Tr. Michael Shreve

"No more than a thousand years!"

The Earth was slowly following a long ellipse around the red sun. The planet had flattened to the point of becoming a monstrous lens of snow, and its equator had cracked into a circling chasm, a dark and smoky mouth that gaped at the last rays of heat and light.

In the warmth of this valley, life took refuge. Of living beings, there remained only some stunted plants, a few hairy beasts and some humans. But there were many more humans than beasts or plants because they had learned how to defend themselves against the mortal invasion of cold. The humans had dug deep galleries in the rock close to the still-bubbling core of the Earth, and by their industry, they had fabricated machines that allowed them to survive the frigid light of day in its revolving course.

In fact, these last men had great knowledge. They had amassed all the discoveries of the countless preceding generations and had reduced physical effort to a minimum. They didn't have to hunt for food because for a long time they managed to take the basic necessities of existence from the air and earth and materialize them. All illnesses had been eradicated, and everyone passed away peacefully at a very advanced age, when their organs had worn out.

Human intelligence had found its immutable limits only in searching for the cause and purpose of life. Here it remained where it had always been when trying to discern the foundation of absolute truth in the seductive affirmations of religion. Everything was reduced to the recognition of universal movement and first impulse. But the representation of this impulse, its origin and its end, escaped the efforts of the human brain, which darkened as soon as it broached the problem.

So, despite not caring about material needs and despite being free of bodily suffering, the men of this dying Earth were not happy; they had more time to think than the men of old who had been distracted by the struggles of daily life, and all their thoughts ended up in one eternal interrogation that remained unanswered. From the time that children were old enough to reflect on things, a deep crease formed on their forehead and never left them. The words "laughter," "joy," and "hope" fell out of use, as if belonging to an ancient, naïve epoch. Many people never left the Valley because their sadness turned to bitterness at the sight of the bowing sun in the rosy haze of sky and the dusting of stars that no longer faded. They preferred to shut themselves up in the subterranean rooms in which the debris of ancient civilizations had accumulated, and they tried to live by imagining the past with the stubbornness of an old man remembering his youth.

Yet they never got used to seeing the archaic invocations to a just, good, and wise god in the yellowing books or on the sculpted fragments of temples. When they, or one of their brothers of the human tribe, had to allude to the inexplicable principle of Force, they used a word that contained the threefold meaning of "Breath," "Blindness," and "Folly." But everyone avoided this dismal expression, which stirred up hatred by evoking thousands of centuries of suffering and fatal collapse.

In a world without material needs, there were no rich or poor. Everyone had the same right to use the necessities—the machines that fought off fatigue and the food gathered in public places like libraries and museums. By tradition, those who had the most experience supervised all the institutions that maintained life, and handed out to the young men the little work that was useful to the community.

Among the elderly, there was one who delved deeper than the others in all the knowledge of the past. His name was Orgouzalam. His smooth face was like wax; on his forehead, the wrinkle of melancholic reflection that marked all men was deep like a wound, and his water-colored eyes reflected nothing of temporary things. He lived with his large family in an underground apartment that looked out upon a point in the Valley through a large opening enclosed by crystal. Like many of the old people, he hadn't gone outside to follow the vivifying light of the sun for a long time; he remained in contemplative silence buried in furs, constantly looking towards the infinite sky—first black, and then rose-red in the course of a day. Sometimes, however, his relatives saw his lips move, as if he were speaking to himself, and his finger traced invisible numbers on his knee.

One morning, as the massive iron star rose, Orgouzalam saw a long, bloody sparkle on the crest of the steep wall that enclosed the Valley—a miraculous fringe of rubies that followed the contours of the rock as far as the eye could see. It was the ice, which in its implacable march of destruction had finally reached the last refuge of humanity. A cry escaped his mouth because his calculations measured exactly the very short time that would pass between the coming of this sign and the complete extinction of life.

"No more than a thousand years!"

The sound of his voice ran through the galleries and echoed off the walls, so tragically, that whoever heard it raced out. But they read nothing in the old face, already stilled, and did not notice the flame behind the colorless eyes.

The murmur of the crowd that filled the room seemed to be the only thing that woke the old man from his reverie. He contemplated the men, women, and young children for a long time; he sighed deeply, and then ordered everyone to find ten elders, renowned in wisdom, and also ten young men who had recently started families.

Around noon, all twenty came, one after another, bowing silently before the master as they sat in a semi-circle. They looked like twenty brothers, for the uselessness of anticipation had frozen their faces into identical lassitude; or rather, into twenty portraits of the same man chiseled in stone at different periods of his life.

After the doors had closed, Orgouzalam spoke. In few but magnificent words, he recalled the formation of the world; it had started as gas set afire in the incomprehensible *Nothingness.* He told of the slow solidification of the globe, the appearance of life, and the birth of intelligence in an animal's nerve that accidentally bloomed in the brain; but he skimmed over the bitter struggle of human generations to survive, then expanded it, bit by bit, to the domain of thought. He spoke of the victories that had swelled men's pride and made them insane with the illusion of being the direct instruments of justice and kindness, but that despite their progress, the Earth began to die.

The voice continued, burning with hatred, "Men, in you I am speaking to all of humanity! The ice has reached us. Today, it is touching our cavern; tomorrow it will enter it, and in exactly six centuries, the last twitch of life will fade away under its glassy shroud. Men, will we allow the works of man to disappear like this without revolting against the blind force that gave rise to us? Will we allow the world to fall back into nothingness by a briefer but more dreadful torment than was the birth of intelligence? Will we not even have a curse worthy of the genius created by our race against this demented game that produced the Earth and its people, and that kills them at the very moment when they have reached perfection?

We are united as brothers. We have dispensed with physical suffering, our descendants can live a soft life, thanks to our labors, without even worrying about death, because they can see themselves live again in the children destined to enjoy the good and beautiful things that they know. It's at this culminating point that we must accept the fact that human intelligence fails in the face of bodily pain, and so, in a thousand years, there will be nothing left in the last man's brain except the light of wild, animal instinct, howling before death and after finally being beaten down, the light will moan on the debris of civilization in darkness and ice!

No, no! We shall revolt, men of the Earth! Let's cheat the eyeless, earless, monstrous thing, and because we are powerless against annihilation, let us, at least, rob it of ten centuries of suffering! Let humanity perish just like that, in an apotheosis, and let this old Earth, which had the glory of seeing the soul of man take shape, collapse with us instead of continuing to turn for thousands of years in the infinite void of space, a desolate and dead planet, the wreckage of this world!"

He continued shouting frighteningly for a long time, until the red sun had set behind the edge of the mountain. Twenty men stood up, won over by his grandiose emotion; they cried out anathemas with him and groaned, their arms stretched toward the immensity overhead like a chorus responding to a dirge. "Cheat the Breath! Change the Law! Let man have his revenge at last! Tell us, Master, what should we do? Speak your thoughts, Master!"

The old man gestured for them to huddle together around him and lowered his voice to a barely audible whisper, as if he feared he could be heard by an invisible, prowling power. He explained his formidable plan—to dig into the ground of the Valley at points equally far apart, to penetrate to the fire, and to make burning springs gush out, emitting light and heat, long forgotten in the world, until the nourishing flanks had emptied.

But before the fatal depletion, at a moment that he, Orgouzalam, alone would determine, the Earth would disappear, just like that. It was useless to explain his method; the annihilation, he swore, would be as quick as the blink of an eye, and so final that the dust on the road would seem thick compared to the vapor that would remain where the Earth had once stood.

The bedlam of activity that followed shook up humanity, which had been frozen for centuries in the dreary expectation of the inevitable end. In all the subterranean galleries, the beings bustled about, swarming so densely that you'd think the species had suddenly increased tenfold. A huge murmur of voices rumbled through the labyrinth of vaults flooded with electric lights and mingled with the din of rolling, striking machines. The open doors of the tunnels in the sides of the Valley were continually streaming with files of workers. All day long, the invalids, the women, the children, the elderly clung in layers to the sloping rocks, like shifting patches of lichen, in order to see the liberating work progress.

Six colossal drills rose up toward the sky, piercing the ruby-red fog with their steely needles. They started to come alive in panting rhythm, smashing the clay, pulverizing the granite and around their bases, dumping cascades of debris that piled up like craters. Finally, one morning, almost all at the same time, they reached the liquid globe of fire that formed the core of the planet, and lava rushed into the wells with the clamor of a herd of beasts, blasting the carcasses of the machines into the far-off ice, spurting up into the air, so white, so dazzling that the sun was eclipsed and the sky itself seemed to lose all color. The jets rose above the mountains, mushroomed, and fell back down in large drops that splattered on the ground with a dull sound that blossomed into sparks. Six boiling lakes were formed in a few hours; they extended to the heart of the Valley and flowed toward one another in swelling rivers that joined together.

That evening, for the first time since the origin of the world, there was no night for humanity. The light and heat near the fountains of fire were scorching, but at a short distance, everyone could enjoy the warmth of a tropical noon such as had existed in the middle age of Earth, or from a farther point, the soft gentleness of Mediterranean rivers, or farther still, the subtle sensation of spring twilight in the forgotten country where the Seine had flowed, cumbered with flowery islands.

These were the charming, poetic regions that many preferred. Young couples wandered about in joy, happy for the silence of their steps on the carpet of grass that magically began to turn green; a thousand singing brooks flowed down the rock walls from where the ice had retreated. Sap flowed back into the old, black trunks of the stunted trees and adorned them with buds like pink and purple gems; tiny animals, numbed in their crevasses, made their appearance.

Nothing was more wonderful than this immense, endless day after everything had been exquisitely, violently reborn. When the couples were weary, they stretched out wherever they had aimlessly wandered, in the perfume of young plants, and slept, holding hands. Near them, without fear, birds nuzzled their tiny heads in their ruffled feathers, and insects stood motionless in the soft pollen on the calyx of flowers.

No one dreamed that this golden minute of eternity would end except old Orgouzalam. While the machines had been digging up the worn out corpse of the Earth, he had shut himself up with the books of past ages that guarded the secret of chemical inventions, so destructive that, in common accord, men had once renounced war to save the race. But the formulae of this devastating matter, as complicated as they were, were still quite infantile for a brain that had collected the knowledge of the whole of humanity.

By the time the radiant plume of the wells nearest his dwelling appeared, Orgouzalam had learned of a combustible combination, an explosive reaction so terrifying that it exceeded man's dreams. He heard the cries of joy of the beings scattered in the Valley while he gathered a powder that had been crystallized in the walls of an animal's horn—a powder so light and of such a precious quality that it looked like the skin shed from the wings of a butterfly. He had enough to fill up a little box; it was more than enough. He sealed the cover and brought it to the heart of the deepest gallery deserted by men. A wire ran from it to his room, and the wire was connected to a small, shiny machine that looked like a golden ball forgotten after a game in the corner of the room.

When all was ready, the old man went back to his usual place in front of the round window. He broke off the crystal. The aroma of flowers, mingled with the tinkling of laughter in the warm air, enveloped him with caresses. But his soul remained as rigid as his face. He traveled through the immensity in his mind and became like the universe of stars wending endlessly in circles and succeeding one another according to the inexplicable impulse of the blind Breath. His mind imagined, without limits, the sources of life lit up, shining for a moment, and then extinguished in an agony like that of the Earth. Hatred filled him, enormous hatred. He wanted the Principle, the motor of the atrocious game of things, to paint itself in his imagination in a tangible form so that he could experience the naïve beliefs of former times. He imagined the furious spasm of Its face, when humanity, violating Its hapless law, would escape in one fell swoop from the encroaching grip of Its icy claws. But he came to find even this revenge was too menial—to kill the Earth before its time—he found he wanted to annihilate everything that moved in eternity.

It had been eighty-two days since life had been reawakened in the terrestrial Valley. Orgouzalam, after dozing for several hours, woke up to a fresh and pleasant twitter. He looked in front of him and noticed, on the perfumed foam of violets, a naked child, the last of his great-grandchildren, who was groping and waving his pink limbs, just happy to be alive. And while the old man was watching him, he had the sudden impression of a thin veil unexpectedly falling upon the world. He raised his eyes and saw that the torch of fire at the end of the verdant gorge had stopped reaching the level of the high walls. The bowels of the earth were wearing out; the lava was beginning to lower. No one but he, no doubt, had noticed this yet; he had to act before dread entered the hearts of men.

Orgouzalam stood up, but right away a thought crossed his mind that lit up his face with a superhuman and triumphant glow. He took the little, smiling child, the being, and raised him toward the sky in his outstretched arms as if to make the Unknown see more clearly the enormous mockery of his forceless gesture. Then he put him on the floor of his room, very gently, and watched.

On his tiny hands and knees, the little one wandered, stood, stumbled. The golden ball attracted his attention; he approached it shouting and laughing. He stretched out his trembling fingers, lost his balance and with all his feeble weight fell upon the toy.

A sparkling dust bloomed in the immensity for a moment and then went out. And the bloody eye of the sun searched in vain for the world.

Nuclear Winter
by Nicolas Samaras

This far I know: we will all singularly choose where to lie down, stoke the night, read Darwin, Writings of the Desert Fathers. Those with tattered dissertations may migrate to New York City or Princeton, arguing our occlusion. They will peer as through tinted glasses, unpack hasty papers, briefs, workable stopwatches, ampoules of cologne. Soon, I will move to the furthest part of myself. I will shore up the framehouse in the foothills of Wyoming, wedged between a rusted mesa and a railway trailing its February breath. I have weighed my days against the distance on the horizon I think my sight may carry me. I plan this, the temperature of our lives forcing the choice. I will lie down in my father's bed, open windows and let glassy winds bleach me like the femurs and spoked teeth of sagebrush. Far-off, the sounds of frenzy in the dark hills. Echoes of dull explosions. Pocks of fires against the nights and the smudge of smoke. Cries of hunger ebbing. The long, brittle ache in my bones. Outside, I'll feel the earth cool, blur and deepen, watch muledeer and hinterland wolves approach warily for warmth. Together, we'll huddle in the garden, face to fur, embracing what is human, what is animal, look up to the light unraveling, the sky's cataract.

Gip
by
Mark Taylor

The footage of two nuclear explosions played on the screen again—one following the other by only a few moments—two great, white, billowing clouds appearing from nowhere. As the reel continued, the beautiful seas of the Earth, the dark mountains and land, and lush green vegetation all disappeared beneath a gray smudge.

Gip watched it for the hundredth time aboard the satellite weather station *Forth.* He drummed his three rubber-alloy fingers on the desk impatiently, waiting. When was the International Culture Board going to come back online? He had lost contact with Central Transmissions shortly before the first explosion. When he left Earth, the politicians were arguing over landmasses, population dispersal, and money. Gip's historical records showed that arguments over these things usually ended in war. Still, he had waited.

Twisting his wrist, he looked at his watch. It had been four… no, five hundred years. Gip was supposed to have been retired at his ninetieth year of commission. It had been hard-wired into him by I.C.B. during his early days when the techs fired the circuits that brought him consciousness. Once he was out of warranty, Gip's functioning and programming had started to fail, but he still did his duties: report on the weather; be prepared to alert Central of impending problems, like asteroids; and monitor the vast constellations, looking for changes, disruptions. Day after day, Gip never received a complaint. But now, no one contacted him. No one told him, "Good job."

"Off," he ordered the monitor. Today's report had already been sent and the menial machines had already started computing, collating and cataloguing streams of data for tomorrow.

Let us in.

And there it was again. Gip was sure that the voices he had been hearing were echoes from his central cortex brain—memories or thoughts jumping between electrons that were slowly breaking down. "Shut up." His voice echoed in the empty Research Laboratory. If his creators at I.C.B. had been watching, they might have assumed he had gone slightly strange, a machine standing alone in a room, looking around for the source of voices that weren't there.

It's cold out here.

"I have no interest. I have work to do." Gip strode purposefully through two automatic doors, across Gantry B and onto the Observation Landing to check the monitoring of the star patterns flowing across Sector Four. That'd show them. Of course, the Obs Landing had as little for Gip to do in it as the lab. Everything on the satellite was largely automated and Gip was left to fill his days by gazing at the stars.

He picked up a chair next to the table and brought it to the Starboard window.

"Better." While Gip's face didn't show a smile, he felt bright inside. Perhaps this is what the humans felt like when they smiled. His face wasn't designed to draw a smile; it wasn't necessary. And it wasn't efficient, but after all this time he found that just the smallest of things could satisfy his circuits. It made him wonder if this is what the word *pleasure* meant. At first, he had associated it with oversized cumulus clouds, the perfection of the clouds forming without mathematical overlays or carefully drawn schematics; and now, it was seating. Actually, it had been a while since he had seen a cumulus cloud. It had been a while since he had seen any cloud. As he sat there, looking at the stark lines of the hard, white walls of the lab, he could have been mistaken for a casual tourist admiring the scenery. He had, of course, seen the lines from this angle many times before, but it gave him a purpose, if only briefly.

We're waiting for you.

Gip simulated a sigh. He didn't breathe—couldn't—but he was programmed to impersonate some physical human traits. It seemed to make the few *actual* people he had met feel better about themselves, to have the automatons they created mimic them so.

"What?" He stood. "What now?"

Let us in, we'll be friends.

"I cannot. I have work to do."

Not now. You're not doing anything now. Are you?

"Why? Why do you want to come in?" Gip walked back across the Gantry to the lab and started punching at the controls of the menial machine, trying to look busy, unsure whom he was trying to impress. "Reasons. I need reasons to do things."

We can keep you company.

"I don't need company. I.C.B. will come back online soon." He gestured at the port over-looking the planet.

You don't really believe that, do you? They're not coming back. Ever.

Gip hung his head slightly. He did not want to believe them, but somewhere inside his circuits he knew it was probably true. It had been so long.

"They will," he tried to convince himself, more than them. "They will be back... you will see." He imagined the voices outside, shaking their heads in pity. From beside one of the monitoring consoles, he pulled out the extension leading to the solar panel regeneration unit and plugged himself in to recharge. "Why can I not see you if you are out there?"

We're on the other side.

"The other side of what?" Gip asked, expecting an answer that might challenge his limited perspective of the universe.

The other side of the satellite.

"Oh." He looked across the room to the door of the Gantry. "Outside the airlock? They told me not to touch the airlock."

They're not coming back. It doesn't matter anymore.

"No. I do not think that would be right." Gip spoke with an air of authority; he'd been practicing it in his head for just such an occasion, when the voices started getting pushy again. He waited, cocking his head to the side. They didn't speak again. Good. Now, maybe he could get on. Returning to the Observation Landing, Gip moved the chair back to its original location and sat again.

After a day had passed, Gip uploaded the files that the menial machines had processed, going about his daily tasks with his usual vigor, as if it was the first time he had truly mastered them. As the files transmitted, a thought passed through his mind—where did the files go when they left the satellite?

Nowhere.

"Not again. Can you not just leave me alone?"

You're pointless. You have no meaning in the universe. You sit here, day after day, transmitting pointless details about the weather of a dead planet to its dead inhabitants. Pointless.

"So why do you want to come in, then?" Gip felt as though he had a winning argument for a second; it didn't last.

You're right. We don't want to come in now. You're too pathetic to be our friend.

Gip deflated. "Fine. Then maybe you should leave me alone. Hm?"

There was no reply. Maybe they'd finally left?

"Hello?" he asked, expecting a cutting retort or some such thing. After a suitable pause, Gip had no choice but to assume that they had actually left. He made a mumbling noise, somewhat unsure of how to take it. He had, after all, wanted them to leave, but did not actually expect them to go.

After the transmission had been completed, Gip checked on the Observation Landing, running through some routine procedures. He moved the chair from one side of the landing to the other, then back, sat in it a few times, and monitored the menial machine's progress. He came to a conclusion: the voices were right… probably.

"Hello?" He waited. "Voices? Are you there? I am…" He thought, sorry.

How sorry?

"You are still there. Good. I did not mean to offend you. Please do not leave me alone."

Then we're also sorry.

A warm brilliance grew within him while Gip started to plan where to move the chair.

"What do you think?"

It's pointless. Let us in.

"But the airlock. I am not permitted."

Then we'll leave.

"Wait." Gip pondered. "Thinking." What if he did let them in? What would the consequences be? What harm would it do? The question in his mind was whether there was anyone out there or not. "Voices. How? How do I open the airlock?"

Press the four buttons on the first door. This will open the inner door. The outer door needs to be opened past the inner door.

Gip walked onto the Gantry and looked down the long metal bridge to the airlock door.

"Lights on." The tube lighting overhead flickered and illuminated the path. With great care, Gip made his way down the bridge, a trench of metal beneath him, each step echoing in the chasm below. He had spent so long avoiding it, ignoring it, that it felt truly alien to him to be here, facing the large, solid door. He hesitated briefly; a final lingering doubt flitted through his circuits before he keyed the four buttons. As the door started to rise, air hissed out around it, the seal broken after hundreds of years.

"AIRLOCK OPEN." A booming voice carried around the satellite, the likes of which Gip had never heard before.

"Who is there?" he asked, looking around for the source, "What did I do?"

It's just a voice, Gip. It means nothing.

"Voices. Did I do something wrong? Have I broken something? Should I stop?"

You've done nothing. Enter the airlock. Press the four buttons by the outer door.

Gip stepped over the lip of the doorway into the white, walled airlock and crossed to the outer door. He had not been in here since the day he arrived. Putting his face against the glass, he peered out into the black universe.

"Where are you?"

Open the door, Gip. It will reveal all.

Gip looked at the keypad, then back out the window, trying to see the source of the voices.

Do it now.

"Do not bully me." Gip pulled away from the door. "Or I will not let you in."

Then we will leave.

"No. Wait." Gip stepped forward and keyed the four buttons to the outer airlock door, the air around the seal hissing louder than before.

"AIRLOCK OPEN," Gip heard again, but this time the voice of the ship's safety computer was masked by the escaping atmosphere. As the air inside the station was pushed out into space, Gip was carried along with it, the rush too forceful and Gip too slow, his flailing hands failing to secure a grip on any part of the satellite. As he floated away towards deep space, he called out for the voices. But out there, he couldn't even hear his own.

There Will Come Soft Rains
by
Ray Bradbury

August 2026

In the living room the voice-clock sang, *Tick-tock, seven o'clock, time to get up, time to get up, seven o'clock!* as if it were afraid that nobody would. The morning house lay empty. The clock ticked on, repeating and repeating its sounds into the emptiness. *Seven-nine, breakfast time, seven-nine!*

In the kitchen the breakfast stove gave a hissing sigh and ejected from its warm interior eight pieces of perfectly browned toast, eight eggs sunnyside up, sixteen slices of bacon, two coffees, and two cool glasses of milk.

"Today is August 4, 2026," said a second voice from the kitchen ceiling, "in the city of Allendale, California." It repeated the date three times for memory's sake. "Today is Mr. Featherstone's birthday. Today is the anniversary of Tilita's marriage. Insurance is payable, as are the water, gas, and light bills."

Somewhere in the walls, relays clicked, memory tapes glided under electric eyes.

Eight-one, tick-tock, eight-one o'clock, off to school, off to work, run, run, eight-one! But no doors slammed, no carpets took the soft tread of rubber heels. It was raining outside. The weather box on the front door sang quietly: "Rain, rain, go away; rubbers, raincoats for today…"

And the rain tapped on the empty house, echoing.

Outside, the garage chimed and lifted its door to reveal the waiting car. After a long wait the door swung down again.

At eight-thirty the eggs were shriveled and the toast was like stone. An aluminum wedge scraped them into the sink, where hot water whirled them down a metal throat, which digested and flushed them away to the distant sea. The dirty dishes were dropped into a hot washer and emerged twinkling dry.

Nine-fifteen, sang the clock, *time to clean.*

Out of warrens in the wall, tiny robot mice darted. The rooms were a crawl with the small cleaning animals, all rubber and metal. They thudded against chairs, whirling their mustached runners, kneading the rug nap, sucking gently at hidden dust.

Then, like mysterious invaders, they popped into their burrows. Their pink electric eyes faded. The house was clean.

Ten o'clock. The sun came out from behind the rain. The house stood alone in a city of rubble and ashes. This was the one house left standing. At night the ruined city gave off a radioactive glow, which could be seen for miles.

Ten-fifteen. The garden sprinklers whirled up in golden founts, filling the soft morning air with scatterings of brightness. The water pelted windowpanes, running down the charred west side where the house had been burned evenly free of its white paint. The entire west face of the house was black, save for five places. Here the silhouette in paint of a man mowing a lawn.

Here, as in a photograph, a woman bent to pick flowers. Still farther over, their images burned on wood in one titanic instant, a small boy, hands flung into the air; higher up, the image of a thrown ball, and opposite him a girl, hands raised to catch a ball which never came down.

The five spots of paint—the man, the woman, the children, the ball—remained. The rest was a thin charcoaled layer.

The gentle sprinkler rain filled the garden with falling light.

Until this day, how well the house had kept its peace. How carefully it had inquired, "Who goes there? What's the password?" and, getting no answer from lonely foxes and whining cats, it had shut up its windows and drawn shades in an old maidenly preoccupation with self-protection, which bordered on a mechanical paranoia.

It quivered at each sound, the house did. If a sparrow brushed a window, the shade snapped up. The bird, startled, flew off! No, not even a bird must touch the house!

The house was an altar with ten thousand attendants, big, small, servicing, attending, in choirs. But the gods had gone away, and the ritual of the religion continued senselessly, uselessly.

Twelve noon.

A dog whined, shivering, on the front porch.

The front door recognized the dog voice and opened. The dog, once huge and fleshy, but now gone to bone and covered with sores, moved in and through the house, tracking mud. Behind it whirred angry mice, angry at having to pick up mud, angry at inconvenience.

For not a leaf fragment blew under the door but what the wall panels flipped open and the copper scrap rats flashed swiftly out. The offending dust, hair, or paper, seized in miniature steel jaws, was raced back to the burrows. There, down tubes, which fed into the cellar, it was dropped into the sighing vent of an incinerator, which sat like evil Baal in a dark corner.

The dog ran upstairs, hysterically yelping to each door, at last realizing, as the house realized, that only silence was here.

It sniffed the air and scratched the kitchen door. Behind the door, the stove was making pancakes, which filled the house with a rich baked odor and the scent of maple syrup.

The dog frothed at the mouth, lying at the door, sniffing, its eyes turned to fire. It ran wildly in circles, biting at its tail, spun in a frenzy, and died. It lay in the parlor for an hour.

Two o'clock, sang a voice.

Delicately sensing decay at last, the regiments of mice hummed out as softly as blown gray leaves in an electrical wind.

Two-fifteen.

The dog was gone.

In the cellar, the incinerator glowed suddenly and a whirl of sparks leaped up the chimney.

Two thirty-five.

Bridge tables sprouted from patio walls. Playing cards fluttered onto pads in a shower of pips. Martinis manifested on an oaken bench with egg-salad sandwiches. Music played.

But the tables were silent and the cards untouched.

At four o'clock the tables folded like great butterflies back through the paneled walls.

Four-thirty.

The nursery walls glowed.

Animals took shape: yellow giraffes, blue lions, pink antelopes, lilac panthers cavorting in crystal substance. The walls were glass. They looked out upon color and fantasy. Hidden films clocked through well-oiled sprockets, and the walls lived. The nursery floor was woven to resemble a crisp, cereal meadow. Over this ran aluminum roaches and iron crickets, and in the hot still air butterflies of delicate red tissue wavered among the sharp aroma of animal spoors! There was the sound like a great matted yellow hive of bees within a dark bellows, the lazy bumble of a purring lion. And there was the patter of okapi feet and the murmur of a fresh jungle rain, like other hoofs, falling upon the summer-starched grass. Now the walls dissolved into distances of parched weed, mile on mile, and warm endless sky. The animals drew away into thorn brakes and water holes.

It was the children's hour.

Five o'clock. The bath filled with clear hot water.

Six, seven, eight o'clock. The dinner dishes manipulated like magic tricks, and in the study a click. In the metal stand opposite the hearth where a fire now blazed up warmly, a cigar popped out, half an inch of soft gray ash on it, smoking, waiting.

Nine o'clock. The beds warmed their hidden circuits, for nights were cool here.

Nine-five. A voice spoke from the study ceiling:

"Mrs. McClellan, which poem would you like this evening?"

The house was silent.

The voice said at last, "Since you express no preference, I shall select a poem at random." Quiet music rose to back the voice. "Sara Teasdale. As I recall, your favorite...

"There will come soft rains and the smell of the ground,
And swallows circling with their shimmering sound;

And frogs in the pools singing at night,
And wild plum trees in tremulous white;

Robins will wear their feathery fire,
Whistling their whims on a low fence-wire;

And not one will know of the war, not one
Will care at last when it is done.

Not one would mind, neither bird nor tree,
if mankind perished utterly;

And Spring herself, when she woke at dawn
Would scarcely know that we were gone."

The fire burned on the stone hearth and the cigar fell away into a mound of quiet ash on its tray. The empty chairs faced each other between the silent walls, and the music played.

At ten o'clock the house began to die.

The wind blew. A failing tree bough crashed through the kitchen window. Cleaning solvent, bottled, shattered over the stove. The room was ablaze in an instant!

"Fire!" screamed a voice. The house lights flashed, water pumps shot water from the ceilings. But the solvent spread on the linoleum, licking, eating, under the kitchen door, while the voices took it up in chorus: "Fire, fire, fire!"

The house tried to save itself. Doors sprang tightly shut, but the windows were broken by the heat and the wind blew and sucked upon the fire.

The house gave ground as the fire in ten billion angry sparks moved with flaming ease from room to room and then up the stairs. While scurrying water rats squeaked from the walls, pistoled their water, and ran for more. And the wall sprays let down showers of mechanical rain.

But too late. Somewhere, sighing, a pump shrugged to a stop. The quenching rain ceased. The reserve water supply, which had filled baths and washed dishes for many quiet days was gone.

The fire crackled up the stairs. It fed upon Picassos and Matisses in the upper halls, like delicacies, baking off the oily flesh, tenderly crisping the canvases into black shavings.

Now the fire lay in beds, stood in windows, changed the colors of drapes!

And then, reinforcements.

From attic trapdoors, blind robot faces peered down with faucet mouths gushing green chemical.

The fire backed off, as even an elephant must at the sight of a dead snake. Now there were twenty snakes whipping over the floor, killing the fire with a clear cold venom of green froth.

But the fire was clever. It had sent flames outside the house, up through the attic to the pumps there. An explosion! The attic brain, which directed the pumps, was shattered into bronze shrapnel on the beams.

The fire rushed back into every closet and felt of the clothes hung there.

The house shuddered, oak bone on bone, its bared skeleton cringing from the heat, its wire, its nerves revealed as if a surgeon had torn the skin off to let the red veins and capillaries quiver in the scalded air. Help, help! Fire! Run, run! Heat snapped mirrors like the brittle winter ice. And the voices wailed Fire, fire, run, run, like a tragic nursery rhyme, a dozen voices, high, low, like children dying in a forest, alone, alone. And the voices faded as the wires popped their sheathings like hot chestnuts. One, two, three, four, five voices died.

In the nursery the jungle burned. Blue lions roared, purple giraffes bounded off. The panthers ran in circles, changing color, and ten million animals, running before the fire, vanished off toward a distant steaming river...

Ten more voices died. In the last instant under the fire avalanche, other choruses, oblivious, could be heard announcing the time, playing music, cutting the lawn by remote-control mower, or setting an umbrella frantically out, and in slamming and opening the front door, a thousand things happening, like a clock shop when each clock strikes the hour insanely before or after the other, a scene of maniac confusion, yet unity; singing, screaming, a few last cleaning mice darting bravely out to carry the horrid ashes away! And one voice, with sublime disregard for the situation, read poetry aloud in the fiery study, until all the film spools burned, until all the wires withered and the circuits cracked.

The fire burst the house and let it slam flat down, puffing out skirts of spark and smoke.

In the kitchen, an instant before the rain of fire and timber, the stove could be seen making breakfasts at a psychopathic rate, ten dozen eggs, six loaves of toast, twenty dozen bacon strips, which, eaten by fire, started the stove working again, hysterically hissing!

The crash. The attic smashing into kitchen and parlor. The parlor into cellar, cellar into sub-cellar. Deep freeze, armchair, film tapes, circuits, beds, all like skeletons thrown in a cluttered mound deep under.

Smoke and silence. A great quantity of smoke.

Dawn showed faintly in the east. Among the ruins, one wall stood alone. Within the wall, a last voice said, over and over again and again, even as the sun rose to shine upon the heaped rubble and steam:

"Today is August 5, 2026, today is August 5, 2026, today is..."

The Last Man on Earth
by
Big Jim Williams

A man staggers out of the New York subway. He wears an old, tattered, dirty overcoat and an equally filthy hat, torn pants, and worn boots. He's been underground sleeping off a big drink for several days.

His friends call him Mac.

Mac ignores the yellow police crime-scene tape as he slowly climbs up the steep stairway from the end-of-the-line tunnel. He surfaces into an afternoon of smoky daylight. He coughs and rubs his red, watery eyes. He squints and tries to clean his glasses with his shirttail, then returns the thick lenses to his face. "Oh, my God," he says.

There is total destruction in every direction. Buildings are toppled, storefronts are smashed and burning, cars are overturned, fires and thick smoke are everywhere. The air tastes like burning trash.

Mac stares and then stumbles forward, trying to focus his eyes and alcohol-soaked brain on the devastation. His boots crunch on broken glass as he wanders the deserted streets and searches inside burning cars and abandoned buildings.

There isn't a sign of life. Bodies are scattered in the debris, but he won't go near them; they are reminders of his combat days in Vietnam. He scans the sky for birds and aircraft.

"Nothing," he says. His shoulders sag. He feels numb. There's an incessant pounding inside his head. "Hello! Hello! Is anybody there?"

The only sounds are his voice mixed with the churning wind and acrid smoke.

"Nothing's alive. Not even dogs or cats. Everyone must be dead!"

He slumps onto a curb, surrounded by broken glass, piles of bricks, and charred timbers. He has never felt so alone. He longs for his drinking buddies.

To his family, he's long dead—a worthless drunk and drifter, a moocher and bum forever lost in a city of millions.

"It must have been *the bomb*," he says. "Some damned madman finally pushed the button, blew up the whole planet and everyone on it. I said they'd do it someday, but nobody would listen."

Tears cut parallel lines on his dirty face and find sanctuary in his gray beard.

"I must be the last man on Earth."

Mac's hands shake as he rummages through his coat and produces a small bottle from a torn inside pocket. He unscrews the cap, presses the glass to his mouth, and realizes it's empty. He curses and hurls the half-pint against the side of a smoldering brick building.

Mac sees a half-smoked cigarette in the gutter. He retrieves the dead stub and with shaking hands, lights it on his third attempt and inhales.

"That's better," he says.

He staggers up the street and finds a liquor store, but it's empty. He moves on to a grocery store. Empty, too. "Damned looters," he growls.

"I was passed out for days, back inside the subway line that saved my life," he says. "Didn't hear no bombs. Too drunk to hear anything. Everything's gone. Everyone's dead. There's no food, no shelter. Everything's burning."

He rests against a lamppost and then slowly moves down the street, stepping over bent girders, around smoldering trash and overturned cars. The afternoon shadows have lengthened; it's near twilight, the end of the day. The western skyline is slowly turning a bright red. He cries out.

"Is anyone there?"

His response is only echoes. But then...

Suddenly, he's surrounded with the brightest lights he's ever seen, lights that cut into his rum-soaked brain and penetrate his soul.

"What the...?"

Amplified cuss words fill the air. "Hey, you," screams a voice. "Where in the hell did you come from?"

"What? Who's there?" says Mac.

"How in the hell did you get in here? Everything was cordoned off."

Mac shields his eyes from the brain-burning lights. "Where are you?" he asks. "I can't see anything."

"Hey, numb nuts," continues the disembodied voice. "I'm up here."

A long crane is poised high above the derelict's head. A man with a handheld megaphone is seated on the end of the crane, next to a large movie camera.

"Hey, dumbo," says the man. "We're shooting a disaster movie. We've been waiting all day for this sunset. Now, get the hell off our set before we call the cops!"

Eclipse
by
Alicia Curtis

The moon came down and licked the horizon
ever so delicately
one last giant's eye peeking
through the rim of the dome.

Tomorrow: permanent occlusion
so that men may dance without motion
and women without sense, our limbs
entwined with lead.

The sun, that old dotard grown sour
years hence, is to blame for this.
Men lay fat under lamplight
and begged to be other than warriors

but with the moon's rising
we mothers clung to monstrous oaths
and unceasing fires—

Dome, take my eyes instead
tender a sword to pry them out
that I may feel in the hairs of my arm
my neck's nape

a howl beyond the diamond case
beating to get at her lunar heart.

The Last Day of Sanity
by
Darryll B. Snyder

Midnight.

Awake. I can't believe I'm wide-awake watching the clock. It's six hours until the alarm goes off, and the digital sentinel stares at me with an unblinking, red LED eye. I try rolling over on my left side. No help. I roll onto my right, knowing I'm not going to sleep, but that it's worth making the effort. 12:27 a.m. and the Eye is still there, ever present and never blinking. Closing my own eyes, I count sheep and let my mind drift, hoping sleep will take me.

Suddenly, a sound forces my lids open. I glance at the clock expecting to see the passing of hours, but the unrelenting purveyor of time informs me that it is only 1:10 a.m. Dejected, defeated, and dismayed, I reach for the TV remote and press the power key. The room is flooded with light and sound. A bubble-headed, bleach blonde is informing me that "in just two weeks I could make millions of dollars in real estate if I just act now and call with my credit card number ready." I flick the channel to find my choices are old seventies movies, 24-hour news channels, and infomercials. I lie there watching without seeing, and allow myself to become lobotomized.

I hear the sound again. It's from outside.

I snap out of the brain-salad-surgery before its completion, and peer through the blinds on the windows. Nothing. Must have been my imagination, I suppose.

"Did you hear anything?" I ask the clock.

Its only response is to change its minute hand. The clock now displays 2:14 a.m.

No use. Rising out of bed, I throw the covers to the side and walk toward the kitchen, leaving the drone and blue-hued light of the "Brain-Box" behind. The linoleum floor is cold in the early morning. It's September and still officially summer. I can't believe I'm suddenly thinking about putting socks on! For a split second I consider a glass of milk. Then, returning to bed, I lay back down. No use in that. I hear the sound again and realize sleep is a lost cause. Back in the kitchen, I turn on the coffee pot and walk to the window to have a look. Nothing. Maybe it's the refrigerator condenser or perhaps the icemaker.

"Why are sounds at night so loud?" I ask the coffee pot.

The coffee pot is even less inclined for conversation than the infernal clock. I leave the percolator behind and search out my recliner.

I find my chair and ease myself into its comforting arms. I feel myself sinking into my steady companion.

Hello old friend, I think to myself, wishing it was a Sunday afternoon. The sounds of football echo in my mind, and out of reflex I grab the remote for the TV in the living room. My eyes open and I stare at the screen; my thumb pauses over the power button.

"Do I really want to turn this on?" I ask myself, and to my surprise the coffee pot answers, this time with a healthy gurgle of steam and brewing coffee.

I remind myself that I had just narrowly escaped the bedroom brain trauma. Did I really want to invite that bubble-headed, bleach blonde into another room in my home? I decided to leave her alone, trapped with the clock in the bedroom.

I look at the window wishing I had pulled open the blinds before I sat down. The sounds of the coffee pot going through the final stages of what sounded like a tortuous effort of brewing, stirred me into action.

I hop over the chilly linoleum again. The floor isn't that cold, I tell myself, but I don't want to admit that my socks are in the bedroom with the blonde and the clock, which, I'm sure, must be displaying something close to 6 a.m. by now.

As I reach for my coffee cup, I see the microwave, flashing its own version of time in green. So the clock and microwave are in this together. The microwave tells me it's 2:41 a.m. and I think about sneaking into the bedroom to check the alarm clock, except that I can still hear the blonde almost begging for my credit card number.

Coffee in hand, I leave the sounds of her voice behind, and this time I detour to the living room window before I claim the man-throne. With the blinds safely pulled up, I rely on my old friend's comforts once again and prepare for the sunrise.

I should see the first rays of light in a couple of hours, I guess. My first day at work isn't going to be fun. I hadn't planned on getting so very little sleep. I remind myself that working in downtown Manhattan is an opportunity not to be passed up and that the price of rent for this condo is outrageous, but worth it. I keep replaying the line the realtor told me after I had signed the lease—"location, location, location," somehow knowing that she would eventually wear me down. I finish my cup and contemplate what the day will bring.

Suddenly, I hear the noise again. Standing up, I watch as my cup, which had been quietly minding its own business on my lap, flies across the room. Sunlight peers through the open blinds. I recognize the sound. It's my own alarm clock—*or is it*—informing the world that it is now 6 a.m. and time for all taxpayers to begin their daily regimen. I had finally drifted off to sleep. Grasping my back and wincing at my sore shoulders, I curse the chair, and walk toward the kitchen.

I consider going back for my cup, but decide against it. Let my cup stay there for the rest of the day. "It'll teach you to let me fall asleep in that recliner again."

In the kitchen, I reach for the coffee pot, realizing I need my cup more than it needs me. I walk into the living room and back, this time grasping my new best friend. After all who needs a recliner like that anyway?

Swallowing a mouthful of what has become something more akin to engine oil than Folgers, I walk toward the bedroom to silence that digital devil. Upon entering the bedroom, I noticed the Blonde has been replaced by a rather well-fed chef in bare feet, who is explaining how to put chocolate frosting on an exotic desert.

"Too early in the morning for this," I proclaim and silence the "Brain Box."

Turning to the clock, I tell it to shut up, which of course does no good at all, until I turn it to the off position. Now in silent mode, it informs me that it's 6:08 a.m. and playtime is over. Still sore from my tussle with the chair, I hurriedly make the bed and head for the bathroom.

"No clocks, coffee pots, microwaves or evil recliners in here," I say to the mirror. I forgot about the cold toilet seat though.

I finish my morning ablution and get dressed. "I'm not even afraid to get my socks," I say out loud. "Maybe this won't be such a bad day after all."

I pour another cup of 10W-30 into a Styrofoam cup. *Let someone else save the planet today.*

I'm on time and out the door. After gliding down in the elevator, I open the door of my building, and step out into the most beautiful September morning I have ever seen. Everywhere I look, orange skies match the color of the changing leaves.

"Gorgeous, simply gorgeous." Even my back doesn't mind the effort of walking.

By the time I get to work, I've managed to forget about the LED Eye and the bubble-headed, bleach blonde.

It's my first day on the job, and even though I'm tired, work goes well. I can tell by 8:30 a.m. that I'm not only impressing my new boss, but my co-workers, too.

I inform the woman in the next cubicle, Jill, that I could really use a cup of coffee and ask her if she'd like me to bring one back for her. I'm rewarded with a smile, along with a friendly "Why yes please!" and directions to the unofficial office coffee mess.

After pouring two cups, one with "two creams and not too much sugar, please," I look out the window. The view is simply awe-inspiring. From this height, I can see all of Manhattan. Given the beauty of the day, I am relieved to be my old self again. I notice the plane. It's odd to see such a large plane this close to downtown. Then again, I am *new* to the city, so I better not say anything. A joke at this early stage might elicit ridicule from my new friends. I might ruin the carefully cultivated good "first impression" I had achieved.

I finish making Jill's coffee—"Remember, not too much sugar now!"—but can't take my eyes off that plane. Is it getting closer? Or is it a trick of the light through the glass?

Naw, I say to myself. It's just a lack of good sleep, that's all. I return to Jill's smiling face.

"So," she asks. "How do you like working here in the North Tower?"

I never get the chance to answer her question, because at that moment, the clock in my bedroom turns to 8:46 a.m. and the world changes for us all.

Immutability
by Janelle Schwartz

Pebbles collide, lilies flower, worms surface—
Around the shores of deserted earth
No step of man marks the tetchy landscape;
Nature lives but to descend into arrest.

Pebbles grind to sand and lilies drop their crowns,
spent out of Time, wormy cultivation blindly carries on a
wasted revolution, leaving the animalcule to withdraw below
into fleeting layers of forsaken affluence.

While singular grains settle into an unchanging terrain,
And the last lily stoops to survey encroaching monotony,
Vermicular conditions—scant—betray a twofold longing:
To preserve *the causes of life we must first have recourse to*
death. But no longer can such tandem sustain
It is the same!—No waking from a terrible dream.
No more worm to work the loam
No engineer to cast up
The soiled monuments of passing witness

Naught may endure.

The Last Unicorn
by
H. J. Liguore

The village market bustles with the music and motion of shoppers and vendors selling their wares. The cobbled street is lined on both sides with carts and stands dedicated to food. Silver fish overfill a basket. Beside it, eels and shrimp are piled high. Another vendor offers cloth bags filled with warm eggs; hanging over the eggs are the plucked hens that laid them. My nose takes me toward the aroma of fresh baked breads. On a small brick oven, the Baxter pulls out a rack of buns. He knows my face, and beckons me with a floured finger, offering me his specialty of the day, a mouthwatering meat tart with mint jelly.

The Baxter, as well as the other vendors, knows I'm here shopping for the king's jubilee, an event that only occurs once every fifty years. A Red Letter Day, marked in pen in the kingdom's holy writ, the jubilee marks a period of seven days of rest to all, including slaves. Much importance is put on the opening feast, where other lords, high officials, clergy, and landowners are invited to attend.

The task of preparing the meal has fallen to me, Sir John Whitfield, former knight, turned chef. I was chosen on the grounds of merit alone, having accidentally, on one drunken occasion, broke into the castle kitchen, and prepared a savory bean stew with turnips, lentils, breadcrumbs, and spices. The king on the very same occasion, also drunk and hungry, followed the aroma, and rather than throw me in the dungeon, promoted me to head chef.

My new position, which I've been at for over a year, came with the sever complaint from the former chef, my rival, William Thornyside, who descends from a long line of kings' chefs. It's no secret this jubilee will be the first in over three centuries where a Thornyside isn't chef. To believe for a moment William isn't plotting and planning my ruin would be an understatement. His tactics over the last few weeks have increased from playful pranks, like the hole in the cauldron, or the subtle removal of all kitchen knives, to more provocative attempts, like the ripped up vegetable gardens, or the sudden appearance of weevils in the flour. At the time of my promotion, William had been allowed to stay on as a sous-chef.

He was officially let go three days ago. That's when the real trouble started.

The morning after William's forced resignation, I was to receive a delivery of autumn pheasants. With sunburst plumage, these special birds were raised especially for the king and more particularly, for the jubilee. Autumn pheasant is the king's favorite dish. I've spent the last six months training at the best restaurants in the kingdom, learning the secret art of roasting the bird in such a way that it is neither gamey nor tough. But all has been for naught, for the shipment never arrived. William has struck again, though I can't prove it was him.

The market is bustling with the gossip of my arrival. There isn't a soul in the entire square that doesn't know I'm here to find a replacement for the pheasant, or that my head will be on the block if I fail.

The sky overhead is cobalt blue and devoid of any storm clouds. Pots of colorful flowers decorate the balconies of the townhomes outlining the streets. I pass a cart filled with nuts, seeds, and bins of olives, and notice the vendors lining up to greet me. They know I'm at their mercy.

The first vendor, a short man with a colorful cap, approaches me with a rose-petal trencher. In actuality, it is no more than a square loaf of bread topped with gravy and potatoes. I ignore him and move to the next stand. A plump woman with rosy cheeks leads me to the back of her wagon, and unveils an edible pastry sculpture, shaped like a pheasant, called an *entremets.* It's a fancy creation, but hardly hearty enough for the main course. The woman says she can fill the pastry with deer testicles and hard-boiled sparrow eggs, two of the king's favorites, but I've gone on to the next vendor, hoping for something better.

A scruffy peddler approaches me holding in each fist the uppers of a chicken and the nethers of a pig. "We call it a cockentrice." He spit as he spoke. "You put it together like this." In one smooth motion, he joins the two creatures together. "There," he says, putting needle and thread to the monstrosity. "If that don't please you," he adds, pulling out a bowl and brush. "With a few strokes, I can make it a *golden* cockentrice." He dabs the chicken's head with a gold paste.

I turn him down flatly, and continue down the line, where I'm bombarded with bread and fowl, ale-cakes and herbal soups.

I'm dazzled with tantalizing stews and roasted barnacle goose, but nothing the vendors show me is elegant or elaborate enough for the king. I need something grander than autumn pheasant, but I can't find it. I'm nearly ready to give up, and decide to duck into an alleyway in order to go back to the castle a different way, when a noble man, dressed in a sleeveless surcoat, approaches me from the shadows.

"Come with me, if you want to save your hide."

I hesitate only slightly, but seeing the man's regal attire, and hearing his claim, I go with him.

The man leads me through the winding village streets, away from the crowds and vendors, over the cobbled bridge. "The name's Vincent," he says, shaking my hand. "I've been following your recent turn of events and I want to help."

"Why?" I ask.

"Because we have a mutual enemy, William Thornyside. He owes me money for a shipment of grouse. I promised myself I'd find a way to get even."

"Unless you can produce a wagonful of autumn pheasant," I say, gloomily. "I'm afraid I'll be fated to face the consequences."

"Nonsense." Vincent leads me down a muddy path toward a barn, secluded by great pines and oak trees. "If you fail, old William Thornyside will have beat you. Besides, I have just the thing for you."

Vincent opens the barn door far enough so I can slide inside. He lights a lantern. The glow falls upon the most magnificent creatures I ever laid eyes on.

"They're unicorns," I say, with disbelief. "Where did you find them?"

"Never mind where I found them." Vincent strokes the coat of an elegant brown unicorn. There are close to twelve in total. Some are pale yellow, some white, each with golden manes, and a single spiral horn. "Roast unicorn is renown for its tender meat and exquisite taste. And it's a rare treat, one I doubt the king has ever had the occasion to eat."

"It's perfect for the jubilee. The king will be awed," I say, dreamily. I'm taken up with images of the king and his guests praising me for my ingenuity, my resourcefulness—my brilliance. "How much?"

"They'll cost you a pretty sum." Vincent gives me a figure.

"Done." I shake on it. "When can you deliver?"

"Tomorrow morning I'll send them to the butcher," says Vincent. "I'll have the meat and horns delivered the following day, just in time for the celebration."

"That doesn't give me a lot of time to tenderize," I begin, "but it'll have to do." I follow Vincent out of the barn.

"I'll have a carriage take you back to the castle." Vincent calls for a driver. "Best to keep this secret," he adds.

We shake hands again and I board the carriage. The drive is peaceful, as I avoid the hustle from the village square. I waste no time in conjuring up a recipe. It doesn't matter that I have never cooked unicorn before, or that I don't have enough time to consult any of the specialty chefs throughout the kingdom. I'll need to muster all my ingenuity to make the dish superb. Anything less will be the death of me.

On the morrow, I left nothing to chance. I snuck away from the castle, down into the village center, to the butcher, and found him working diligently on the dozen unicorns. I play the fool and ask him what he's butchering.

"Horses," the butcher says with a droll voice.

I smile, knowing for sure Vincent has protected our secret. On the way back to the castle, I stop by the tavern and purchase several cases of wine, which I spend the night mulling into Hippocras, a special cooking sauce I make by adding basil, ginger, rosemary, cloves, and cinnamon. It will be the perfect mixture to marinate the unicorn.

On the morning of the jubilee, I watch at the kitchen window as troupes of royalty from the surrounding kingdoms arrive in droves. Colorful banners fill up the sky the closer they get to the castle gates. The grounds swarm with people of different classes, dressed in diverse colored robes and dresses. I notice one rogue fellow, lingering near the kitchen gardens. When I call to him, the figure runs, and disappears through the gathering crowds. William Thornyside, I presume, here to put a kibosh on my royal meal. But he'll not get the best of me.

Behind me, in the kitchen, my staff is busy preparing the fifty or so side dishes, including, steamed cabbage with a mustard cream sauce; an apple and mincemeat pie made in honor of Saint Swithin, our patron saint; cheese and safflower dumplings; corn pudding, garnished with raspberries and cream; and my personal favorite, the dish that brought me to head chef, Whitfield's savory bean stew.

My young apprentice, Barnabus, a thin, sallow figure, who at fifteen hunches over like an old man, approaches me and tugs on my sleeve. "Sir Chef," began Barnabus. "Where is the main dish?"

The delivery of unicorn meat is late. I know it. Barnabus knows it. My staff knows it. As long as the king doesn't know it, I'm still safe. I am just about to think the worst—that William Thoryside has struck again—when one of the king's guards yells, "delivery!" I beckon Barnabus to follow, and together we bring the slabs of meat into the private end of the kitchen, which I've curtained off, to keep my specialty dish secret until it's unveiled to the king. I notice immediately the horns did not come with the delivery. I try not to fret, assuming Vincent will bring them.

My plan starts to come together as we cook the meat on an open fire, with herbs and the Hippocras sauce. Soon, voices just beyond the curtain start to inquire about the alluring smells. It is none other than the king, following his hungry stomach, beckoning to see and taste. I slide out underneath the partition, entrusting Barnabus with the brazing and glazing.

"My King." I bow formally, excusing my harried appearance. "The king's own meal is not finished."

"A small taste." The king holds up two fingers close together. "I can't wait."

Realizing I can't put off a hungry king, I see one of my bakers pulling a tray of hot buns from the oven. "Wait here, my Lordship." In a mad dash, I grab a hot roll, slather it with butter and parsley, a hint of mint, and pour on my Hippocras sauce. "Only a sample of the main dish," I say, handing it to the king, who scarfs it down in two bites. He licks his fingers—which I take as the highest compliment—and leaves, bidding me to be on time with the meal.

I return to my work with a sense of relief that the king's unexpected visit has gone well. Had he come any earlier, he would've seen the delay of the main dish as insubordination, and it could've been over for me. Now, the only hitch is that Vincent hasn't delivered the spiral unicorn horns. Without them, I only have horses, a slaves fare.

The jubilee trumpets have sounded, signaling the start of dinner, and I still don't have the horns. I procrastinate by sending out a side dish at a time. Barnabus continues to baste the cooked unicorn, and keeps it warm by the fire.

The jubilee song is nearly ended when Vincent arrives. He hoists a sack onto the table and opens it. The horns are dirty, but intact. Vincent makes excuses for his tardiness, explaining that the roads were jammed; he had to make the last leg of the trip on foot. I pay him his fair price, and tip him an extra sovereign for his efforts.

Barnabus and I take the horns to the nearest cauldron filled with boiling water. This simple process will clean and sterilize them. Barnubus asks why I've gone through the trouble of procuring goat horns. "They're not goat horns," I insist, pulling them from the scalding water, and decorating the meat platters.

"I know a goat horn when I see one." Barnabus is reluctant to take the dish to the main hall. "I'll not serve the king goat or horse."

"It's unicorn," I whisper.

"Unicorn," he whispers back. "There's not been a unicorn in these woods for a long, long, long, long, long, time."

"I had them imported." I push the covered platter into his chest. "Now take this out to the hall or both our heads will be on the block."

The jubilee song has long ended. All the secondary dishes have been taken out, and now, a long line of unicorn platters make their way into the refectory, where the king and his guests wait. I put on a clean coat, fix my hair with a little water and grease, put on a smile, and tag along behind the train of food.

Whispers follow me toward the king's table. The guests marvel at the spread. As customary, before the meal starts, I approach the king and queen. After my formal bow, I introduce many of the smaller dishes and lead up to the main dish.

"It is my honor, my Lordship and Lady, to present you with the dish of honor, only fitting royalty." I pull off the lid, motioning to my staff to do the same. "I present to you roast unicorn!" The jubilee trumpets squawk out a tune of celebration. "Oohs" and "aahs" travel through the hall. The king picks up a hunk of meat, oozing with sauce, and raises it to his lips. Thoughts of my reward circle my head: a tiny villa on a wooded hill, piles of gold to fill my coffer, a beautiful maiden, perhaps the king's own daughter, to share my hearth, and plenty of servants to cook for *me*.

But then a loud voice breaks through my dream and interrupts the service. A cloaked figure pushes through the crowd to get to the king. The guards are fast upon him. My smile fades, when I see the king hasn't tasted the meal.

"Who dares to interrupt the king's feast?" shouts the king.

"It is I, your humble servant." Beneath the cloak, the face of my enemy, William Thornyside, is revealed. "I have proof that your would-be-chef has served you a slave's meal. That meat you are about to eat." He points. "Is none other than common horse meat!"

A rush of discord descends upon the room.

"No," I interrupt, speaking loudly to be heard over the banter. "It's unicorn. I swear on my life."

"You have been fooled, amateur," says William. "The last unicorn went extinct when my father was a boy."

"No," I plead, "this isn't true. A man, Vincent, gave me his word it was unicorn. I saw them with my own eyes."

"The man who sold these to you is known throughout the kingdom as a swindler. His head is wanted for treason against the king." William folds his arms, arrogantly. "A *real* chef would've known the difference."

The king calls for a slave to be brought forward to try the food.

"All the slaves are free for the jubilee, my Lord," reminds the queen.

"Who will taste the food?" The king looks over the room for a volunteer. No one comes forward.

Before I can say another word, the king flicks his wrist, an order that sends the guards fast upon me. It's all over for me. The king pushes the dish of unicorn away, and orders my immediate execution. William kicks me as I'm dragged from the room. The last thing I hear is the king announcing William's reinstatement as head chef.

Outside the castle walls, a path is made through the crowds all the way to the scaffold. They are angry, feeling I have committed the gravest sin against the king.

"What do you expect from a former knight," one villager shouts.

"Only a fool would feed the king horse meat," shouts another.

Rotten food and mud is flung at me, as I'm taken to the front of the line, past the other prisoners. At the top of the stairs, the executioner is ready with his axe. I want to ask if he'll be sharpening it. If I know anything about cutlery, the duller the blade, the harder it is to cut through flesh.

My head is set on a stump stained with blood. Images of my entire career as a chef flash before me. I could've stayed a humble knight, but the grandeur of being the king's head-chef had dazzled me. Now, I would die without honor.

The jeering quiets down, as the executioner raises the axe. I swallow hard, and pray to Saint Swithin to guide me to the other side. Then a voice breaks through the quiet. "Wait," it calls. "Wait!"

Barnabus, straighter than I've ever seen him, climbs onto the scaffold. "Hold the execution!" Barnabus nears the executioner holding a small scroll. The executioner reads it thoroughly, and after several minutes, he sets me free. The crowd starts to jeer, unhappy with the turn of events.

Barnabus and I flee through the backwoods, toward the castle. On the way, Barnabus explains that when the king pushed his plate away, his fingers went into the Hippocras sauce. He licked the sauce from his fingers and found it to be delicious. Not wanting to be shamed for eating a slave's meal, the hungry king snuck to the kitchen and set to work on the meat, caring not whether it was unicorn or horse, and called for seconds.

At the castle, in private quarters, the king honors me with a handshake, and praises me for cooking one of the finest meals he's ever tasted. To save his reputation, the king explains, he would have to send me away. As a small reward, the king hand picks a small villa for me on the far edges of his kingdom. Barnabus is sent away with me, not his beautiful daughter. Instead, she is married to the son of William Thornyside, the man who would go down in history as the chef who saved the king's jubilee.

Legend has it that on the day of the jubilee, a knight-turned-chef, Sir John Whitfield, served the king horse and was put to death. I've also heard it was written in the Holy of all Holy Writs that way. Occasionally, when I venture toward the markets to pick out food for a meal, sometimes a vendor will approach me with a fine cut of horse meat, and in whispers tell me of a knight-turned-chef, who cooked unicorn for the king who spared his life. I smile, and buy the meat, knowing one day, maybe soon, the real story of my life will be heard.

The Last Hours
By D. H. Lawrence

The cool of an oak's unchequered shade
Falls on me as I lie in deep grass
Which rushes upward, blade beyond blade,
While higher the darting grass-flowers pass
Piercing the blue with their crocheted spires
And waving flags, and the ragged fires
Of the sorrel's cresset - a green, brave town
Vegetable, new in renown.

Over the tree's edge, as over a mountain
Surges the white of the moon,
A cloud comes up like the surge of a fountain,
Pressing round and low at first, but soon
Heaving and piling a round white dome.

How lovely it is to be at home
Like an insect in the grass
Letting life pass.
There's a scent of clover crept through my hair
From the full resource of some purple dome
Where that lumbering bee,
Who can hardly bear
His burden above me, never has climb.

But not even the scent of insouciant flowers
Makes pause the hours.
Down the valley roars a downward train.
I hear it through the grass
Dragging the links of my shortening chain
Southwards, alas!

Cassandra
by
C. J. Cherryh

Fires.

They grew unbearable here.

Alis felt for the door of the flat and knew that it would be solid. She could feel the cool metal of the knob amid the flames… saw the shadow-stairs through the roiling smoke outside clearly enough to feel her way down them, convincing her senses that they would bear her weight.

Crazy Alis. She made no haste. The fires burned steadily. She passed through them, descended the insubstantial steps to the solid ground—she could not abide the elevator, that closed space with the shadow-floor, that plummeted down and down; she made the ground floor, averted her eyes from the red, heatless flames.

A ghost said good morning to her… old man Willis, thin and transparent against the leaping flames. She blinked, bade it good morning in return—did not miss old Willis's shake of the head as she open the door and left. Noon traffic passed, heedless of the flames, the hulks that blazed in the street, the tumbling brick.

The apartment caved in—black bricks falling into the inferno, Hell amid the green, ghostly trees. Old Willis fled, burning, fell—turned to jerking, blackened flesh—died, daily. Alis no longer cried, hardly flinched. She ignored the horror spilling about her, forced her way through crumbling brick that held no substance, past busy ghosts that could not be troubled in their haste.

Kingley's Café stood, whole, more so than the rest. It was refuge for the afternoon, a feeling of safety. She pushed opened the door, heard the tinkle of a lost bell. Shadowy patrons looked, whispered.

Crazy Alis.

The whispers troubled her. She avoided their eyes and their presence, settled in a booth in the corner that bore only traces of the fire.

WAR, the headline in the vendor said in heavy type. She shivered, looked up into Sam Kingsley's wraithlike face.

"Coffee," she said. "Ham sandwich." It was constantly the same. She varied not even the order. Mad Alis. Her affliction supported her. A check came each month, since the hospital had turned her out. Weekly she returned to the clinic, to doctors who now faded like the others. The building burned about them. Smoke rolled down the blue, antiseptic halls. Last week a patient ran—burning—

A rattle of china. Sam set the coffee on the table, came back shortly and brought the sandwich. Alis bent her head and ate, transparent food on half-broken china, a cracked, fire-smudged cup with a transparent handle. She ate, hungry enough to overcome the horror that had become ordinary. A hundred times seen, the most terrible sights lost their power over her: she no longer cried at shadows. She talked to ghosts and touched them, ate the food that somehow stilled the ache in her belly, wore the same too-large black sweater and worn blue shirt and gray slacks because they were all she had that seemed solid. Nightly she washed them and dried them and put them on the next day, letting others hang in the closet. They were the only solid ones.

She did not tell the doctors these things. A lifetime in and out of hospitals had made her wary of confidences. She knew what to say. Her half-vision let her smile at ghost-faces, cannily manipulate their charts and cards, sitting in the ruins that had begun to smolder by late afternoon. A blackened corpse lay in the hall. She did not flinch when she smiled good-naturally at the doctor.

They gave her medicines. The medicines stopped the dreams, the siren screams, the running steps in the night past her apartment. They let her sleep in the ghostly bed, high above ruin, with the flames crackling and the voices screaming. She did not speak of these things. Years in hospitals had taught her. She complained only of nightmares, and restlessness, and they let her have more of the red pills.

WAR, the headline blazoned.

The cup rattled and trembled against the saucer as she picked it up. She swallowed the last bit of bread and washed it down with coffee, tried not to look beyond the broken front window, where twisted metal hulks smoked on the street. She stayed, as she did each day, and Sam grudgingly refilled her cup, which she would nurse as far as she could and then she would order another one. She lifted it, savoring the feeling of it, stopping the trembling of her hands.

The bell jingled faintly. A man closed the door, settled at the counter.

Whole, clear in her eyes. She stared at him, startled, heart pounding. He ordered coffee, moved to buy a paper from the vendor, settled again, and let the coffee grow cold while he read the news. She had a view only of his back while he read—scuffed brown leather coat, brown hair a little over his collar. At last he drank the cooled coffee all at one draught, shoved money onto the counter, and left the paper lying, headlines turned face down.

A young face, flesh and bone among the ghosts. He ignored them all and went for the door.

Alis thrust herself from her booth.

"Hey!" Sam called at her.

She rummaged in her purse as the bell jingled, flung a bill onto the counter, heedless that it was a five. Fear was coppery in her mouth; he was gone. She fled the café, edged round debris without thinking of it, saw his back disappearing among the ghosts.

She ran, shouldering them, braving the flames—cried out as debris showered painlessly on her, and kept running.

Ghosts turned and stared, shocked—*he* did likewise, and she ran to him, stunned to see the same shock on his face, regarding her.

"What is it?" he asked.

She blinked, dazed to realize he saw her no differently than the others. She could not answer. In irritation he started walking again, and she followed. Tears slid down her face, her breath hard in her throat. People stared. He noticed her presence and walked faster, through debris, through fires. A wall began to fall, and she cried out despite herself.

He jerked about. The dust and the soot rose up as a cloud behind him. His face was distraught and angry. He stared at her as the others did. Mothers drew children away from the scene. A band of youths stared, cold-eyed and laughing.

"Wait," she said. He opened his mouth as if he would curse her; she flinched, and the tears were cold in the heatless wind of the fires. His face twisted in an embarrassed pity. He thrust a hand into his pocket and began to pull out money, hastily, tried to give it to her. She shook her head furiously, trying to stop the tears—stared upward, flinching, as another building fell into flames.

"What's wrong?" he asked her. "What's wrong with you?"

"Please," she said. He looked about at the staring ghosts, then began to walk slowly. She walked with him, nerving herself not to cry out at the ruin, the pale moving figures that wandered through burned shells of buildings, the twisted corpses in the street, where traffic moved.

"What's your name?" he asked. She told him. He gazed at her from time to time as they walked, a frown creasing his brow. He had a face well-worn for a youth, a tiny scar beside the mouth. He looked older than she. She felt uncomfortable in the way his eyes traveled over her: she decided to accept it—to bear with anything that gave her this one solid presence. Against any inclination she reached her hand into the bend of his arm, tightened her fingers on the worn leather. He accepted it.

And after a time he slid his arm behind her and about her waist, and they walked like lovers.

WAR, the headline at the newsstand cried.

He started to turn into a street by Tenn's Hardware. She balked at what she saw there. He paused when he felt it, faced her with his back to the fires of that burning.

"Don't go," she said.

"Where do you want to go?"

She shrugged helplessly, indicated the main street, the other direction.

He talked to her then, as he might talk to a child, humoring her fear. It was pity. Some treated her that way. She recognized it, and took even that.

His name was Jim. He had come into the city yesterday, hitched rides. He was looking for work. He knew no one in the city. She listened to his rambling awkwardness, reading through it. When he was done, she stared at him still, and saw his face contract in dismay at her.

"I'm not crazy," she told him, which was a lie that everyone in Sudbury would have known, only *he* would not, knowing no one. His face was true and solid, and the tiny scar by the mouth made it hard when he was thinking; at another time she would have been terrified of him. Now she was terrified of losing him amid the ghosts.

"It's the war," he said.

She nodded, trying to look at him and not at the fires. His fingers touched her arm, gently. "It's the war," he said again. "It's all crazy. Everyone's crazy."

And then he put his hand on her shoulder and turned her back the other way, toward the park, where green leaves waved over black, skeletal limbs. They walked along the lake, and for the first time in a long time she drew breath and felt a whole, sane presence beside her.

They bought corn and sat on the grass by the lake and flung it to the spectral swans. Wraiths of passersby were few, only enough to keep a feeling of occupancy about the place---old people, mostly, tottering about the deliberate tranquility of their routine despite the headlines.

"Do you see them," she ventured to ask him finally, "all thin and gray?"

He did not understand, did not take her literally, only shrugged. Warily, she abandoned that questioning at once. She rose to her feet and stared at the horizon, where the smoke bannered on the wind.

"Buy you supper?" he asked.

She turned, prepared for this, and managed a shy, desperate smile. "Yes," she said, knowing what else he reckoned to buy with that—willing, and hating herself, and desperately afraid that he would walk away, tonight, tomorrow. She did not know men. She had no idea what she could say or do to prevent his leaving, only that he would when someday he recognized her madness.

Even her parents had not been able to bear with that—
visited her only at first in the hospitals, and then only on holidays, and then not at all. She did not know where they were.

There was a neighbor boy who drowned. She had said he would. She had cried for it. All the town said it was she who pushed him.

Crazy Alis.

Fantasizes, the doctors said. Not dangerous.

They let her out. There were special schools, state schools.

And from time to time—hospitals.

Tranquilizers.

She had left the red pills at home. The realization brought sweat to her palms. They gave sleep. They stopped the dreams. She clamped her lips against the panic and made up her mind that she would not need them—not while she was not alone. She slipped her hand into his arm and walked with him, secure and strange, up the steps from the park to the streets.

And stopped.

The fires were out.

Ghost-buildings rose above their jagged and windowless shells. Wraiths moved through masses of debris, almost obscured at times. He tugged her on, but her step faltered, made him look at her strangely and put his arm about her.

"You're shivering," he said. "Cold?"

She shook her head, tried to smile. The fires were out. She tried to take it for a good omen. The nightmare was over. She looked up into his solid, concerned face, and her smile almost became a wild laugh.

"I'm hungry," she said.

They lingered over a dinner in Graben's—he in his battered jacket, she in her sweater that hung at the tails and elbows: the spectral patrons were in far better clothes and stared at them, and they were set in a corner nearest the door, where they would be less visible. There was cracked crystal and broken china on insubstantial tables, and the stars winked coldly in gaping ruin above the wan glittering of the broken chandeliers.

Ruins, cold, peaceful ruin.

Alis looked about her calmly. One could live in ruins, only so the fires were gone.

And there was Jim, who smiled at her without any touch of pity, only a wild, fey desperation that she understood—who spent more than he could afford in Graben's, the inside of which she had never hoped to see—and told her—predictably—that she was beautiful. Others had said it. Vaguely she resented such triteness from him, from him whom she had decided to trust. She smiled sadly when he said it and gave it up for a frown; and, fearful of offending him with her melancholies, made it a smile again.

Crazy Alis. He would learn and leave tonight if she were not careful. She tried to put on gaiety, tried to laugh.

And then the music stopped in the restaurant, and the noise of the other diners went dead, and the speaker was giving an inane announcement.

Shelters... shelters... shelters.

Screams broke out. Chairs overturned.

Alis went limp in her chair, felt Jim's cold, solid hand tugging at hers, saw his frightened face mouthing her name as he took her up into his arms, pulled her with him, started running.

The cold air outside hit her, shocked her into sight of the ruins again, wraith figures pelting toward that chaos where the fires had been worst.

And she knew.

"No!" she cried, pulling at his arm. "No!" she insisted, and bodies half-seen buffeted them in a rush to destruction. He yielded to her sudden certainty, gripped her hand, and fled with her against the crowds as the sirens wailed madness through the night—fled with her as she ran her sighted way through the ruin.

And into Kingsley's, where café tables stood abandoned with food still on them, doors ajar, chairs overturned. Back they went into the kitchens and down and down into the cellar, the dark, the cold safety from the flames.

No others found them there. At last the earth shook, too deep for sound. The sirens ceased and did not come on again.

They lay in the dark and clutched each other and shivered, and above them for hours raged the sound of fire, smoke sometimes drifting in to sting their eyes and noses. There was the distant crash of brick, rumblings that shook the ground, that came near, but never touched their refuge.

And in the morning, with the scent of fire still in the air, they crept up into the murky daylight.

The ruins were still and hushed. The ghost-buildings were solid now, mere shells. The wraiths were gone. It was the fires themselves that were strange, some true, some not, playing above dark, cold brick, and most were fading.

Jim swore softly, over and over again, and wept.

When she looked at him she was dry-eyed, for she had done her crying already.

And she listened as he began to talk about food, about leaving the city, the two of them. "All right," she said.

Then clamped her lips, shut her eyes against what she saw in his face. When she opened them it was still true, the sudden transparency, the wash of blood. She trembled, and he shook at her, his ghost-face distraught.

"What's wrong?" he asked. "What's wrong?"

She could not tell him, would not. She remembered the boy who had drowned, remembered the other ghosts. Of a sudden she tore from his hands and ran, dodging the maze of debris that, this morning, was solid.

"Alis!" he cried and came after her.

"No!" she cried suddenly, turning, seeing the unstable wall, the cascading brick. She started back and stopped, unable to force herself. She held out her hands to warn him back, saw them solid.

The brick rumbled, fell. Dust came up, thick for a moment, obscuring everything.

She stood still, hands at her sides, then wiped her sooty face and turned and started walking, keeping to the center of the dead streets.

Overhead, clouds gathered, heavy with rain.

She wandered at peace now, seeing the rain spot the pavement, not yet feeling it.

In time the rain did fall, and the ruins became chill and cold. She visited the dead lake and the burned trees, the ruins of Graben's, out of which she gathered a string of crystal to wear.

She smiled when, a day later, a looter drove her from her food supply. He had a wraith's look, and she laughed from a place he did not dare to climb and told him so.

And recovered her cache later when it came true, and settled among the ruined shells that held no further threat, no other nightmares, with her crystal necklace and tomorrows that were the same as today.

One could live in ruins, only so the fires were gone.

And the ghosts were all in the past, invisible.

Cee Cee Was My Dog
by John Dudek

only since my
dear wife, Dawn
departed.
A miniature schnauzer,
twelve inches
at the shoulder
with a popgun bark
and fiber-optic
eyebrows.
Sure, we weren't
thick as thieves,
but we at least
had an understanding.
"Together till
the End" we—
I said. But again, we
were mutual
beneficiaries
with an understanding.
Cee Cee didn't
object any because
the kibble bin
stayed heavy,
the backdoor
always open.
In exchange, my
feet were warm
at night and that old
Turkish carpet left
unsoiled. True, blood-
buddy symbiotes
we were. So is it
any wonder,
considering our oath,
that I'm a little
stressed since
Cee Cee dug out
the fence
in back?

水
by
Jack Frey

The captain insisted there was nothing below decks. He said there was nothing worth inquiring about, only a sand ballast, so that the tanker didn't ride too high on re-entry. I was the *ship's third*—that's what the captain called me, hired on to help guide a decrepit oil tanker back to Earth. I was at the bottom of the pecking order. I didn't know much about ships, and the captain was quick to remind me of it. But I knew what sand ballast was—how a ship without a cargo still needed the weight in its hold to steer properly, even in outer space—and I couldn't help but wonder if something like that really needed to be kept under lock and key, and whether that key needed to hang around the old man's neck. I had only known Captain Xu for a few weeks, and I had no reason to distrust him, but I had no reason to trust him, either. The ship was at least a kilometer long, but the crew's quarters were small and cramped. As I lay curled in my bunk between watches, I found myself thinking about what the captain might be hiding in the hold below.

When I couldn't ignore my curiosity any longer, I waited until the captain wasn't around, and then slipped down the ladder to the cargo hatch to have a closer look. The doors were shut and fastened by a dull, brass padlock. Nothing unusual, until Captain Xu appeared at my side, dark eyes pinched behind thin lids.

"You've no business down here, Chunguang," he barked. "There's only sand ballast in there." The captain closed his fingers over the key hanging around his neck. "You hear me, boy? Nothing but sand."

I had no choice but to return to my quarters.

He was the kind of captain that there used to be more of, I suspect, before the Earth's seas had evaporated into the thinning atmosphere and revealed the yawning cavities beneath. He claimed to remember the days when water filled the vast expanses between the mountains. He used strange terms like *tides* and *undertow*, and swore that all sorts of improbable beasts had swarmed beneath the oceans. I knew of words like "waves" and "currents," but only in connection with the radio or electricity. As the captain stalked the deck, gnarled hands clasped behind his ragged wool sweater, blue cap perched on his head at a rakish angle, he seemed to me to be sniffing the air, as if searching for something. Maybe he was trying to find the smell of the sea, something that he had once described as a mixture of salt and wind, fish and rot—the smell of water, though I wondered how such a thing could have a smell.

I'd signed on at New Kashgar, a lonely rock at the ass-end of the solar system, where I'd spent six months out on the tar sands, driving a loader so large that I needed an elevator to reach the cockpit. I was sick of it: the paste-meals and the protective gear and the men that stank and talked about nothing but hookers. So I signed on with the captain to hitch a ride home. I had agreed to work my way to Zhengzhou-Shi, and then, finally, back to Earth. I don't even remember the name of the tanker, some number-letter combination, nothing special. There were only three of us: Captain Xu, me, and Sukhbaatar, a Mongolian who seemed particularly unsuited for the job of first mate. Sukhbaatar was jumpy and lazy and had zero mechanical aptitude. We were a skeleton crew guiding an empty tanker back to Earth. That the ship was empty seemed strange to me, considering the tendency for returning ships to be loaded to capacity with as much oil, tar, or hydrogen silt as was permitted by the port authorities. It was stranger still when I thought about how enormous the craft was, larger than some of the asteroids we'd passed beyond Zhengzhou-Shi. But the captain had his reasons, or so he had said to me again and again, that it only took three men to pilot a tanker, no matter how large.

All I really cared about was getting home. Space is no place for something as fragile as meat and bones and blood, if you ask me. Steel and silicon, maybe, but not human flesh. I wanted to be back in the crevices of Earth, down in the snaking folds of the crust, where the remnants of the atmosphere pooled like the ancient oceans that the captain had talked about.

I'd made ten times as much money working the tar sands in space as I would have made working for the same amount of time back on Earth. Even so, most of the guys out on the sands were broke because they spent all their money on cheap yeast liquor and whores. But I'd saved every yuan, enough to buy a flat in Mariana. I wanted to settle down, marry Zhao Yunyun, and start a family.

I wouldn't have to wait long. We were already near enough to Earth to hear that the tanker was turning on just three screws. A few hours earlier, the planet's gravitational pull had tripped the ship's sensors and forced us out of autopilot. I found Sukhbaatar in the wheelhouse, balanced on a threaded stool and licking the inside of a greasy wrapper. The air stunk of dead cigarettes and body odor. Sukhbaatar seemed nervous. His face was flushed, as if he'd been drinking.

He looked up when I entered and attempted a lame little wave. "Heya, Chunguang. Have you seen the captain anywhere?"

Captain Xu had a way of disappearing for hours at a time. That might sound easy on a ship so large, but the crew's quarters were actually fairly confined. The old man spent a few moments in the wheelhouse every now and then, inspecting the system. After that, he'd vanish. I hadn't seen him since breakfast.

But now, as we prepared to enter Earth's orbit, we needed him. The harbor above Mariana circled at an altitude of 185,000 meters, and it would take all three of us to dock safely. I could see from the dirty display above Sukhbaatar's head that we'd already been contacted by the port authorities.

"Do we have clearance to come in?" I asked.

Sukhbaatar nodded. "It's a busy day. Two freighters in front of us, another tanker right behind. Where's the captain?"

I ran my fingers through my lanky, black hair and said that I didn't know. I imagined the old man perched over the composting toilet, or holed up in an engineering shaft doing who knows what. Sukhbaatar had his feet on the floor now, and he was fiddling with the flat, gray knobs on the console. He throttled down to one screw.

"Six minutes till we engage," said the Mongolian. His forehead was beaded with sweat. "Did you check his cabin?"

"I haven't looked anywhere," I said. "I'll go see. But worst case, just contact the harbor and tell them we're skipping our turn. Take us back out, and we'll orbit a few times."

Sukhbaatar didn't seem to understand, and I wondered if I should make him go look for Captain Xu. I could stay and man the controls. But I also didn't believe that the Mongolian would find the old man, and it annoyed me to think about stepping out of queue and wasting a few more hours. I had Yunyun on my mind, and I was eager to hop on the first shuttle down to

Mariana. I could find the captain and be back in time to dock the tanker.

I left Sukhbaatar crumpling the wrapper in his anxious hands, and ran down the hallway. There were only a few places where the captain could be: the wheelhouse, obviously, the cabin, with its three small compartments and shared living area, the kitchen and the attached storage space, or the recreation room, with its two broken computers and a felt-less pool table. That didn't matter much, because one of the gravity spools that ran parallel with the ship's keel had malfunctioned a few days earlier. Since then, the pool balls had a tendency to roll unbidden into the corner pocket, which took a lot of the fun out of the game.

The cabin was empty. I listened, hoping to hear the sound of the old man's breathing. But all I heard was the steady thrum of the single screw and the occasional clunk of the faulty gravity spool trying to kick in. I tried the kitchen, but there was nothing but a few dirty bowls and the stink of old oil.

I looked at my watch. Four minutes 'til engagement. Just as I was about to run to the recreation room, it hit me. I laughed. The cargo hold. The captain was below deck. But why? What could be so important to the man that he had turned over the wheelhouse to someone like Sukhbaatar?

The hatch was at the bottom of an iron ladder. It was not the main entrance, which was located outside the ship itself. This entrance was just a rusty pair of doors that slid together on rollers. The padlock dangled, open. But when I tried the doors, they wouldn't budge.

A bit more than three minutes left. I banged on the door and shouted for the captain. I listened. Nothing. I kicked the doors without effect. Then, I looked into the minute gap between the two panels and thought I saw a latch. The door was barred from the inside. If I could just lift it somehow—

I was carrying my Mariana ID card. I didn't think it would be strong enough, but I was wrong. The latch lifted easily. I pushed the doors, and they slid apart. Two minutes and forty seconds left.

At first, everything inside was completely dark, and I saw nothing. The air was indescribable. It seemed to have a body, a smell unlike any I'd ever known, thick and round at the back of my throat. I thought of the captain's words—salt and wind and fish and rot. And I wondered.

I took a step inside, onto a narrow, steel catwalk that hung out over the black expanse. I squinted. Then I thought I saw a small point of light like a far-off star, moving slightly. My voice was dull in the darkness. The space was so large that I heard no echo. No echo and no answer. But the door was unlocked. The captain had to be in here.

There was no time. I stepped further out onto the catwalk, wishing for a light. There were no rails, and I felt as though I would stumble into the void and fall to my death in the belly of this ship. But the farther I moved away from the hatch, the brighter that pinpoint of light ahead of me became, until I thought I could make out the dull glow of the space around it.

I was confused. The light was not on the catwalk at all, but appeared to be balanced just off to the left, out over the black expanse. My eyes strained in the dark, and I thought I saw a broad curve against a shimmering mirror, a sheet of silver upon which something moved. It was a small wooden boat, like I had only seen in pictures.

And then I saw the captain was lying on his back in the bottom of the boat, his withered fingers wrapped around the base of the lamp. The white light poured over the underside of his face, seemingly pushing his eyes further into the hollows of his head. The man's cap was gone. I couldn't tell if he was breathing or not.

At first, I supposed that the boat was floating on oil. But the air was clear. I kneeled down to inspect the stuff. It was cool to the touch, and my finger came out clean. Could it actually be water? There had to be millions of cubic meters here—where had the captain gotten it all? Maybe the man planned to sell it back on Earth. I couldn't even begin to guess how much it was worth.

The tanker lurched as if the gravity spool had momentarily engaged. I saw the flat surface before me distort momentarily, and then the water appeared to rise from its dark bed and form a thousand tiny peaks. The boat shuddered and the catwalk shook. I dropped to my stomach, clutching at the steel.

It was too dark to see my watch, but I suspected that Sukhbaatar was trying to drag the ship further out of orbit. We were stepping out of queue. *Well,* I thought, *no question about it now.* There was no chance of docking without radioing for help first. From what I could tell, the captain was dead. His body was completely limp, his lips pressed lightly together, as though, at any moment, he might open his mouth and let out a low sigh.

Another jolt. I wondered whether it wouldn't be better for me to return to the wheelhouse. The captain didn't need me. I rose to my feet. But then the catwalk shook, and I heard a long series of thuds from somewhere far below. It was the faulty spool, pounding alongside the keel. In the darkness, it sounded like an enormous drum.

The water moved, inwards at first, or so it seemed, and then apart, towards the hull. I'd never seen anything like it. I'd never seen water outside of a drinking glass. The tanker quivered, and I fell. Water sloshed up between the thin, steel mesh beneath me, soaking me, stealing away my breath. The light inside the tiny boat lurched up and down, higher and higher, and then disappeared behind momentary walls of water.

One of these walls rose up beneath me, striking my face with such force that I gasped, losing my grip. How could something so soft, so completely conformable, become like iron? Another fist struck me, and I spilled off the catwalk into the water. I had never felt cold like that before as the water seeped deeper into my skin, into my open mouth, and down into my marrow. I tried to scream, but the air came out of my mouth in clumps that seemed to burst just inches from my face.

My hands clawed uselessly at the stuff. It moved between my fingers as easily as air, and I felt betrayed. Only moments before, it had been like iron. My feet flailed. I grabbed for a place to touch, to lock onto, anything. Then my head broke free, and for a moment, I saw through the lenses of water, the skeleton of the catwalk rising before me, and, beyond that, the tormented shell of the boat. A hand, my own, I think, grasped upwards, but I was already moving down again, into the dark.

Inside me, I felt a strange fire, lit by the water itself. I burned. My spine arched, my head tilted back until I thought my neck would snap. All around me, I heard the endless thud-thud that I no longer recognized as the spastic spool. But then my fingers were driven up against something hard and irregular. The boat. I gripped the wooden lip with both hands, coughing and heaving.

I pulled myself into the floating shell. I don't know where I found the strength. I felt as if I'd been beaten, as if I'd been dragged behind a moving vehicle. I could barely lift my arms. I shivered and vomited water. Captain Xu was there, motionless in the other end of the tiny craft, hands folded over the base of the lamp. His calm face seemed to smile at the lurching water and the death I'd narrowly avoided.

Inside the boat were two thin paddles. It now seemed obvious what they were for. I forced myself to drop the end of one into the water. I wanted to get back to the catwalk before the boat capsized and I found myself, once more, under the icy waves. But it was slow going, and several minutes elapsed before I reached the catwalk.

By the time I kneeled on the steel deck, the tanker was howling loudly. I wondered if Sukhbaatar had tried to override the safeties and throttled up all twelve screws. The hull twitched and throbbed. I had to get back up to the wheelhouse.

The tiny boat and its occupant had already moved into the distance, caught in an unseen eddy that pulled them deep into the cavernous hold. I crawled on my hands and knees towards the hatch, back towards the light, stopping each time another spasm shook the ship.

Outside again, the whiteness was unbearable, but the air was deliciously dry. I staggered toward the iron ladder and inched my way to the deck. My shoes squeaked as I stumbled to the wheelhouse, and I left a trail of tiny puddles.

Sukhbaatar was nowhere in sight. The stool was empty. The greasy wrapper was lying on the floor beside it. I looked at the display: 140,000 meters. We were falling. But all twelve screws were turning, driving the tanker forward. The port authorities had tried to contact the ship four times. Where the hell was the Mongolian?

The display flashed twice, and I saw the words "Lifeboat launch." The dirty bastard. He'd abandoned ship. Left me here to fend for myself. But maybe he wasn't so stupid after all, I thought. The ship was falling. There was nothing stopping it now. It would break apart or shatter into dust on one of the high, airless plateaus where people had once lived.

There were three lifeboats. The tanker was humming now, as if the walls might disintegrate at any moment, but I walked slowly back to the cabin, to my locker. I seized my money and stuffed it down the front of my pants. No way was I going to let six months on the tar sands be for nothing. If only I could bring a bit of that water with me, I'd be set for life.

I screwed the lifeboat hatch shut behind me and entered the sequence as it was posted on the wall. The engine came to life. I felt the craft slide free, out the chute, and into the emptiness beyond. From the portal, I saw the tanker, at first so large and so close that it appeared to be a flat gray wall. But then, the lifeboat moved farther away, and the colossal hull took shape. It seemed to turn in slow spirals. I watched the keel move upwards until it sat like a fin, a crest along the ship's spine. And then it was gone, rolled over into the darkness beyond.

Somewhere inside that ship was Captain Xu. I thought about the man. It seemed impossible that he could have existed at all, as though he had emerged from a stasis chamber after a thousand years. He was an unknowable mystery, like the fathomless oceans that still covered him. I felt as though I had breathed in and nearly suffocated on the forgotten majesty that still surged within his darkened depths that I would never really understand.

Far below, the familiar form of the highest mountains rose swiftly, incredibly high above the narrow valleys where air still lingered. The mountains, all white and honeycombed like the ancient molars of a mastodon were in sharp contrast to the curved emptiness of space. I shuddered and looked away.

The tanker still rolled, but its angle had changed. Its bow wobbled. I held my breath. And then it happened. The first cracks appeared near the screw case and traveled forward. One moment the ship seemed to contract, and the next it separated into a hundred tiny splinters. I watched as something like hair grew from the shards, moving outwards in an ever-expanding web, until the fringes were so delicate that it looked almost like cotton candy.

It was water, I realized; pressurized water that was expanding, freezing, and vaporizing. The lifeboat was plummeting now, down to the safety of Mariana, to Yunyun and the world I knew. But, as the shattered remnants of the tanker crawled across the sun, the light passed through the frozen filaments, and I saw in that matrix every conceivable color moving outwards in concentric rings. It was nothing now, just floss, sublimating, consumed by light. But I'd seen the depths, felt the waves, the currents, the majesty, and I think the captain would have wanted it that way.

My Blue Ribbon Pies
by
Jacquelyn Fedyk

My name is Abigail August Smith, and I wanted, more than anything, to be an expert baker. I wanted to be a connoisseur of crusts and a virtuoso of pastries. I loved to bake, and baking pies was my family's specialty. I truly considered baking an art form and, in my opinion, one of the most beloved ways to spend one's leisure time. I learned to bake from my mother, she learned from her mother, and so on, as far back as most women on my mother's side could remember. All of my female relatives were absolute masters in the kitchen, and I grew up basking in their glory. Our most coveted prize was the Wellington County Blue Ribbon for Best Pie. Over the years and generations, every woman on my mother's side had won this magnificent mark of achievement.

Everyone, that is, with the exception of me.

Every year for the past eight years, I had entered the Wellington County Fair Bake-Off, and every year I placed only within the bottom three. Not only did I want to win this prize more than anything in the whole world, but it was expected of me. I had been practicing at church bake sales and Sunday dinners. This year, I would not go down in shame! I would win the blue ribbon.

I must.

The day before the fair, I was in my kitchen going through the famous box of family recipes, looking for something to give me an edge, some inspiration. It was quiet. My housemaid, Sarah, had the day off, and the rest of the staff was busy with their duties. I paced the floor nervously. I sat down, alone and frustrated, trying to find something new and spectacular in my old, tattered box of the tried and true. Nothing. I could find nothing. I was running out of time. The fair was the next day.

An old apple tree stood outside our window. An apple pie was such a simple way to go, but what if I could do something new and wonderful with it? I became excited and inspired by the thought. I decided a walk might awaken my muse.

I was strolling along our estate, an act that had always brought me peace when I felt troubled. My eyes gazed blankly upon the scenery, lost in thought. I took pleasure in the rolling hills, the way they seemed to go on forever, beautifully blemished here and there with patches of clover and little white flowers. The ground was damp, but not muddy. The horses grazed leisurely alongside the sheep in the nearby meadow. It was such a lovely day; the summer sunshine warmed my shoulders. I was glad I had left my shawl at home, for the weather was much too warm for it now. There wasn't a cloud in the sky, but I did notice a dark shadow creeping over the hills. Suddenly, without much warning, the day turned black. It was a total eclipse of the sun! *Funny*, I thought. I had recently perused the Farmer's Almanac, and I could not remember reading anything that suggested an eclipse that day. However, as soon as a flutter of worry flickered in my stomach, the sun reappeared. Only a moment of confusing darkness had passed, but something was different. At first, I didn't know what had changed. I looked around, bewildered, assessing my surroundings, and then, right before me, I discovered a new fruit tree in our field.

I had never noticed this tree before. I had walked by this particular spot thousands of times, and I knew it well. It was beside a dip in the old farm fence near the border of our property. There had never been so much as a sapling there before, and now, here was a fully-grown fruit tree, several feet high, bearing strange fruit. The fruit of the new tree was similar to that of an apple, but larger and colored a dark purple like the color of an eggplant. It was like looking at a giant, black apple glimmering with purple hues in the beams of the afternoon sunlight. I studied this odd fruit carefully. Soon, I had absolutely no fear of plucking this giant, black apple from the tree. Immediately, I brought it to my lips to take a hearty bite. The thick nectar juices flowed from the corners of my mouth; it was extremely succulent and so delicious! Tasting this flavor was one of the most mouth-watering, delectable experiences of my life. Nothing had ever been so tantalizing as my yearning to take bite after exquisite bite. At the time, devouring this fruit was the single most fulfilling act I had ever engaged in.

The essence was hard to describe. It was both sweet and tart. Once the meat of this fruit was inside your mouth, the texture softened and spread over your pallet, coating your tongue with a warm, satisfying syrup. No other food could hold a candle to this experiment in taste. But the highlight from partaking from this fruit came after I had finished eating it; I was left with the most gratifyingly warm tinge in my mouth, a superb after-taste, and a craving for more.

I knew at once upon finishing this delicacy that I had to use it in this year's pie-baking contest entry. I thought about Great Grandmother Queenie. She was the pride of the family, a stern Christian woman standing six-feet tall with broad shoulders. She may have had the bold features of a man, and a slight beard, but nobody had ever lived up to her pie-baking accomplishments. She had the most wonderful recipe for Scottish Apple Pie. Everyone loved it, and it had been in the family for years, but she was the only one who was brass enough to bake it.

Lightening figuratively struck my brain, and I heard a strange voice inside me. *Mix the two fruits together*, it said in a slithering tone. Mix the black fruit with the apples? Yes, I dare say that they would complement each other harmoniously. I ran to the house bursting with enthusiasm. Quickly, I returned to the tree with baskets, filled them with the new fruit and apples and raced back to the kitchen to get started.

I used Grandmother Queenie's award-winning Scottish Apple Pie recipe as the base. When I was a girl, she'd won the blue ribbon with this pie in a crushing defeat of all other participants. Old Grandmother Queenie, she was a force to be reckoned with. I could almost hear words of encouragement from her as I held up the new fruit and apple together.

I do believe I was the first to discover this new fruit so I decided to name it. I called it queenfruit, in honor of my great grandmother. The two looked beautiful side by side, the queenfruit and the apple. However, seeing them together like this felt unnatural. When I sliced the fruit and placed it in a bowl for filling, the queenfruit and the apple fused together. They bonded into small bits of curious, hybrid dumplings, which were linked together by tiny purple veins. I paused and marveled. I took it as a good sign; finally, fate was lending me a hand. My cheeks flushed with the admiration of my ingenious new recipe. I worked the filling with new energy.

I was in absolute heaven as I rolled the dough and spread it across my pie dish. I mixed the hybrid dumplings with the appropriate spices and poured the filling into my piecrust, all the while fantasizing about my definite win. I saw myself center stage at the fair accepting the blue ribbon, then bowing to the judges and posing for the newspaper photographer. In my kitchen, I was performing a beautiful dance, a pinch of this and dash of that, twirling around like a dancer in a Degas painting.

I could feel the heat from the oven. It called to me that the pie was ready. I rolled out another layer of crust for the top and placed it over the filling, securing the edges with a fancy rope of dough. I cut vents into the upper crust in the shapes of small rounded hearts, forming a circle with their bottom points together. Appearance was as important to me as taste, and this was a beautiful pie. I stepped back and admired my masterpiece in its infant stage. Oh, wouldn't Great Grandmother Queenie be so proud if she could only see me now? I was certain this pie would win the blue ribbon.

I sat anxiously at the kitchen table the entire time the pie was in the oven. Every few minutes, I checked to make sure it was baking evenly and perfectly. The smell was mouth-watering. It filled the house, creating a warm, pleasant atmosphere. The crust was browning, and the pie was almost ready.

After the pie had baked to perfection, I let it cool on the windowsill. I could not take my eyes off that perfect pie, fragrant with tendrils of sweet-smelling steam erupting out of the crust vents where it lingered lazily along the edge of the window. Outside, the sun was shining and the birds were singing. This was, indeed, a perfect day for baking. My heart was overjoyed. I felt accomplished. I doted over my confection creation as Pygmalion would have doted over Galatea, his ivory princess.

But no, I could not stop there. I went back to the trees and filled my basket, over and over again, until the trees were bare. All through the night, I baked pie after pie after pie. But no matter how delicious they appeared, I vowed not to taste a single bite of my magnificent creation until after the judging was over. That was our family tradition. The smell was, indeed, alluring, but my need to uphold tradition overwhelmed me, and I continued to refrain from tasting. This marvel could not be left to the judges alone; I knew I had to bake enough pies so that the whole town could bask in my victory. I reveled in unsurpassed joy as I baked through the night.

Before I knew it, it was time for the contest. My housemaid, Sarah, came into the kitchen at her usual time to resume her normal routine. She was confused and taken a back at all the baking I had done. She raised an eyebrow and gave me an astonished look. I had no time to dilly-dally; I instructed her to deliver the majority of the pies to the fair at approximately ten o'clock. I knew the judging would be done by then and I wanted to share my pies with everyone. She called the other house servants to help her. She looked flustered and overwhelmed as I hurriedly prepared to leave. I felt sorry for springing this enormous task on her, but I was sure she was up to the challenge. I had not yet tasted this wonder, but I was certain it would be fantastic. I carefully wrapped the first pie I had baked into a basket, and made my way to the fair on foot.

I joined a group of neighbors who were heading in the same direction. The morning was magnificent. Summer was here, blood-red tulips lined the white picket fences along the dirt road into town. The sky was a radiant blue, just the color of Great Grandmother Queenie's eyes, as if she were looking down upon me with pride. Fallen cherry blossoms littered the road and made it seem as if we were walking on rose petals into town like royalty. The ladies, who were also my competition, were busily discussing their entries.

We came upon the green, manicured lawn of the Wellington County Courthouse, where the competition was just about to get under way. Beneath a red and white canopy, we laid our entries out on our corresponding doilies and place cards. I knew mine would be much sought after for the taste-testing as everyone could smell its alluring fragrance.

The pies were beautifully displayed. Mayor Ryerson, Father Mayhew, and Prissy Vanderbilt, president of the Ladies Welfare League, took their seats at the official judging booth. The first part of the judging was on appearance. My pie was the most beautiful with its golden, glossy brown crust shimmering in the sun, carved and decorated with painstaking perfection. The other pies were almost disastrous in comparison. Their tops were burnt and uneven and sunken in, with poor attempts at decoration. Mrs. Masterson's pie had an awful cut-out of a rooster on top, or, at least, I think it was a rooster; it was a bit charred. The next part of the judging was the taste-test. The judges cut a small piece from each pie. All of the ladies were beside themselves with anticipation as the judges made their rounds. I giggled to myself. Once the judges tasted my creation, nobody else would have a chance. Greta Applegate stared blankly in the direction of her famous huckleberry pie as Father Mayhew took an enormous bite. He looked pleased with the flavor, but when he got to my pie, the very last in the row of entries, he paused. The fragrance wafted toward his wide-open nostrils, which flared in delight. It was plain to see, by the expression of pure ecstasy on his face, that he was absolutely delighted with my pie. I saw Greta Applegate cringe and gasp in astonishment. She had won the ribbon the last three years in a row. Now, she looked nervous. I grew more excited: to beat Greta Applegate would be the icing on the cake. It would also, no doubt, gain the approval of the Ladies Welfare League. Perhaps now, they would seriously consider my application to join.

Soon the Mayor and Prissy Vanderbilt joined Father Mayhew in tasting my pie. They were really digging in. Only when they had finished the entire pie did they gather for a decision. It only took a moment for them to agree. To my absolute delight, I was named the winner! What a day! I was flabbergasted. Finally, I would be able hold my head up high and take my place among our family's cherished line of blue ribbon bakers. Tears welled up in my eyes. I felt proud, and I shook my fist to the sky in victory, acknowledging Great Grandmother Queenie. Surely, she would have been proud.

I was about to make my way to the winner's circle and accept my prize, when Sarah, joined by the rest of the house staff, came charging over the hill, bearing basket upon basket of pies. They had barely unwrapped the pies and set them on the picnic tables before the town's people ran to them curiously.

In the excitement, nobody noticed I had collected my prize. I grabbed the blue ribbon from the judging booth and was looking around for a photo opportunity. The 2nd and 3rd place ribbons were sitting there unclaimed, as well. No matter. I looked around and found everyone now had a piece of pie. I was beaming with pride over my accomplishment. My friends and neighbors really seemed to be enjoying these wonderful pies. My pies. My blue ribbon pies.

It was at this moment that the events turned ugly.

People who were at first timidly and politely consuming their confections, suddenly became ravenous. They buried their snouts in the pie plates, greedily consuming bite after bite. They were behaving like pigs. Prissy Vanderbilt's face was covered in filling, and her eyes darted wildly and hungrily about, looking for more. She seemed like a wolf that had just made a kill and was out for more blood.

The town's people commenced shoving entire fistfuls of pie into their mouths like hungry carnivorous animals, pushing one another out of the way. Fights broke out over bits of crust and crumbs. Picnic tables were turned over. It was as if everyone had become demonic, frighteningly mad, with the craving for these pies. My pies. My blue ribbon pies.

All-out brawls developed, and people started to riot. The proper society women of the Ladies Welfare League tore each other apart, pulling bits of pie out of each other's mouths and shoving them into their own. The Mayor knocked over his elderly mother to get at a piece of pie. The schoolteacher was on her belly licking the grass, trying to absorb any leftover crumbs or filling. Father Mayhew ran off like a wild-eyed savage, hording several half-emptied pie dishes to himself.

I was terrified. What plague had I unleashed onto these poor, honest people? I was confused and stricken with remorse. I had collected a new fruit and fed it to an entire town, turning them into monsters. How could this be? I ate of the fruit. I enjoyed and devoured the queenfruit, yet I wasn't crazed or manic with hunger. Then, it hit me. I recalled the strange, supernatural bonding of the queenfruit to apples like a parasite choosing a host. The hybrid had created something else, something unnatural that was driving these people mad. I realized I was to blame.

When every bit of pie had been devoured, every pie plate licked clean, and every crumb accounted for, the famished and unsatisfied crowd turned on me. "More? More. More!" they groaned and bellowed as they slowly drew toward me.

At a quicker pace, I retreated down the road before me. The white picket fences now seemed like hungry, open jaws. The red flowers along the path were like blurry splotches of gory pie filling. The town's people chased me at top speed. I ran as fast as I could through the town, down the streets, into the country, across the meadows, and at long last to a cliff where the frenzied mob finally cornered me. Still they stalked me, mouths foaming with unsettled hunger, relentlessly demanding "MORE PIE!"

At that moment, one of these starved beasts discovered a bit of pie filling smeared on another's face and dove for it, taking a gigantic bite out of another man's cheek. Driven by uncontrollable hunger, the crowd followed suit, finding other forgotten pieces of filling on collars, shirts and bibs.

They turned on each other even more violently than before. They ripped at each other's faces, exposing muscle and bone. The Mayor tore open stomachs to get at digested bits of pie, shoving piles of gore and entrails into his dislocated jaw. Faces I no longer recognized were smeared with pie and blood. It was the most horrifying spectacle to witness greedy, pie-starved fiends who tore into each other like savage beasts. I recoiled in fear. I stepped back to retreat from this absolute abomination. What I can only describe as half a human torso scooted closer to me on its bloody, bone-exposed arm stumps. Its face, no longer a face, but an animated red skull with eyeballs, was fixed upon me. Its mouth was open, gurgling the unmistakable word "PIE." I remember losing my balance, and then everything went black.

I awoke, wounded. I could barely move. I used every muscle to sit up. The sky told me it was close to twilight. How long had I been there? It had occurred to me that something was very wrong, even more so than waking up alone and hurt amongst the bushes. Something bad had happened. But at the time, I could not remember what.

I looked down, only to realize I was inches from falling to my death. I looked up and found that if I only climbed ten feet I could make it to solid ground. I knew I must have lost my footing and gone over the edge of the cliff. But what had I been doing there?

Lucky for me, I fell onto an under-lip. Some berry bushes on the side of the cliff had broken my fall. Above me, a single-rooted branch of some sort reached out of the cliff like an arm. Something was caught on it, waving in the wind like a flag; it was my blue ribbon turning over and over in the breeze. My heart sank to see it so helpless and…filthy? Was that… blood? I stood up and reached for it just as the wind picked up and blew it away. It twirled as it fell to the rocks below. The earth beneath me crumbled away and rolled down the side of the cliff violently. I caught hold of the branch with one hand just in time to save myself. Somehow, I found the strength needed to survive the burning in my muscles and urged myself onward.

Without thinking, I pulled myself over the top to safety. I buried my face in the cool wet Earth, thanking God I was still alive. But then I began to remember something. No. It could not be true. I lifted my head. My neck was weak and quivering. There laid the carnage of a battle unsurpassed by the bloodiest in history, a red sticky swamp of body parts, gore, and pie.

The entire town was dead. Dead eyes stared at me. Silent, lifeless mouths were crammed full of pie and other unspeakable things. I hung my head in shame. "My pies," I cried. "My blue ribbon pies!" I shouted into nothing, my sorrowful pathetic voice echoing through the hills.

That evening, when I returned home, alone, the mysterious tree that had bloomed so suddenly on my property was now fruitless. It had shriveled up and turned to ash, which blew across the field until it was gone all together. There was silence. The wind blowing through the trees and across the meadow was the only sound. Even the animals were gone. Our fence had been trampled. I was alone, the only soul left in town.

I walked twenty-seven miles that night to the next village. I worried that the town's animals had fallen victim to my pies as well, but as I traveled that night, I wasn't alone. Herds of sheep, pigs, horses, cows and chickens passed me in the darkness, waddling to safety like heartbroken war refugees. It was as if they knew they were abandoned, and, I swear, as each animal passed me, I was greeted with a disapproving stare. None of us were ever to return to our homes again.

I found the outside world beyond county lines going on the same as it always had, except now, there were the gruesome stories and rumors of the Wellington Pie Massacre.

Only I knew the truth.

To this very day, I am unable to even look at a pie without remembering and shuddering. I now turn away from simple pastries in disgust; I put my handkerchief over my nose and mouth while passing by bakeries. The rich aroma luring people in for fresh breads and treats turns my stomach and makes me retch. I am unable to bring myself to bake another pie. This once beloved family tradition is lost to me, for it brought about the destruction of my entire hometown. The only item I brought with me when I left Wellington County was my family's box of recipes. Today, I took the box to the rocky beach near the ocean. I used my dress sash to tie a rock around it before I flung it into the sea. I know I shall forever live in shame.

Masque of the Red Death
by
Edgar Allan Poe

The *Red Death* had long devastated the country. No pestilence had ever been so fatal, or so hideous. Blood was its Avatar and its seal—the redness and the horror of blood. There were sharp pains, and sudden dizziness, and then profuse bleeding at the pores, with dissolution. The scarlet stains upon the body and especially upon the face of the victim, were the pest ban, which shut him out from the aid and from the sympathy of his fellow men. And the whole seizure, progress and termination of the disease, were the incidents of half an hour.

But the Prince Prospero was happy and dauntless and sagacious. When his dominions were half depopulated, he summoned to his presence a thousand hale and light-hearted friends from among the knights and dames of his court, and with these retired to the deep seclusion of one of his castellated abbeys. This was an extensive and magnificent structure, the creation of the prince's own eccentric yet august taste. A strong and lofty wall girdled it in. This wall had gates of iron. The courtiers, having entered, brought furnaces and massy hammers and welded the bolts. They resolved to leave means neither of ingress or egress to the sudden impulses of despair or of frenzy from within. The abbey was amply provisioned. With such precautions the courtiers might bid defiance to contagion. The external world could take care of itself. In the meantime it was folly to grieve, or to think. The prince had provided all the appliances of pleasure. There were buffoons, there were improvisatory, there were ballet-dancers, there were musicians, there was Beauty, there was wine. All these and security were within. Without was the *Red Death.*

It was toward the close of the fifth or sixth month of his seclusion, and while the pestilence raged most furiously abroad, that the Prince Prospero entertained his thousand friends at a masked ball of the most unusual magnificence.

It was a voluptuous scene, that masquerade. But first let me tell of the rooms in which it was held. There were seven -- an imperial suite. In many palaces, however, such suites form a long and straight vista, while the folding doors slide back nearly to the walls on either hand, so that the view of the whole extent is scarcely impeded. Here the case was very different; as might have been expected from the duke's love of the bizarre. The apartments were so irregularly disposed that the vision embraced but little more than one at a time. There was a sharp turn at every twenty or thirty yards, and at each turn a novel effect. To the right and left, in the middle of each wall, a tall and narrow Gothic window looked out upon a closed corridor, which pursued the windings of the suite. These windows were of stained glass whose color varied in accordance with the prevailing hue of the decorations of the chamber into which it opened. That at the eastern extremity was hung, for example, in blue -- and vividly blue were its windows. The second chamber was purple in its ornaments and tapestries, and here the panes were purple. The third was green throughout, and so were the casements. The fourth was furnished and lighted with orange -- the fifth with white -- the sixth with violet. The seventh apartment was closely shrouded in black velvet tapestries that hung all over the ceiling and down the walls, falling in heavy folds upon a carpet of the same material and hue. But in this chamber only, the color of the windows failed to correspond with the decorations. The panes here were scarlet -- a deep blood color. Now in no one of the seven apartments was there any lamp or candelabrum, amid the profusion of golden ornaments that lay scattered to and fro or depended from the roof. There was no light of any kind emanating from lamp or candle within the suite of chambers. But in the corridors that followed the suite, there stood, opposite to each window, a heavy tripod, bearing a brazier of fire that protected its rays through the tinted glass and so glaringly illumined the room. And thus were produced a multitude of gaudy and fantastic appearances. But in the western or black chamber the effect of the fire-light that streamed upon the dark hangings through the blood-tinted panes, was ghastly in the extreme, and produced so wild a look upon the countenances of those who entered, that there were few of the company bold enough to set foot within its precincts at all.

It was in this apartment, also, that there stood against the western wall, a gigantic clock of ebony. Its pendulum swung to and fro with a dull, heavy, monotonous clang; and when the minute-hand made the circuit of the face, and the hour was to be stricken, there came from the brazen lungs of the clock a sound which was clear and loud and deep and exceedingly musical, but of so peculiar a note and emphasis that, at each lapse of an hour, the musicians of the orchestra were constrained to pause, momentarily, in their performance, to hearken to the sound; and thus the waltzers perforce ceased their evolutions; and there was a brief disconcert of the whole gay company; and, while the chimes of the clock yet rang, it was observed that the giddiest grew pale, and the more aged and sedate passed their hands over their brows as if in confused reverie or meditation. But when the echoes had fully ceased, a light laughter at once pervaded the assembly; the musicians looked at each other and smiled as if at their own nervousness and folly, and made whispering vows, each to the other, that the next chiming of the clock should produce in them no similar emotion; and then, after the lapse of sixty minutes, (which embrace three thousand and six hundred seconds of the Time that flies,) there came yet another chiming of the clock, and then were the same disconcert and tremulousness and meditation as before.

But, in spite of these things, it was a gay and magnificent revel. The tastes of the duke were peculiar. He had a fine eye for colors and effects. He disregarded the décor of mere fashion. His plans were bold and fiery, and his conceptions glowed with barbaric luster. There are some who would have thought him mad. His followers felt that he was not. It was necessary to hear and see and touch him to be sure that he was not.

He had directed, in great part, the moveable embellishments of the seven chambers, upon occasion of this great fete; and it was his own guiding taste, which had given character to the masqueraders. Be sure they were grotesque. There were much glare and glitter and piquancy and phantasm -- much of what has been since seen in "Hernani." There were arabesque figures with unsuited limbs and appointments. There were delirious fancies such as the madman fashions. There was much of the beautiful, much of the wanton, much of the bizarre, something of the terrible, and not a little of that which might have excited disgust. To and fro in the seven chambers there stalked, in fact, a multitude of dreams. And these—the dreams—writhed in and about, taking hue from the rooms, and causing the wild music of the orchestra to seem as the echo of their steps. And, anon, there strikes the ebony clock which stands in the hall of the velvet. And then, for a moment, all is still, and all is silent save the voice of the clock. The dreams are stiff-frozen as they stand. But the echoes of the chime die away—they have endured but an instant—and a light, half-subdued laughter floats after them as they depart. And now again the music swells, and the dreams live, and writhe to and fro more merrily than ever, taking hue from the many-tinted windows through which stream the rays from the tripods. But to the chamber which lies most westwardly of the seven, there are now none of the maskers who venture; for the night is waning away; and there flows a ruddier light through the blood-colored panes; and the blackness of the sable drapery appalls; and to him whose foot falls upon the sable carpet, there comes from the near clock of ebony a muffled peal more solemnly emphatic than any which reaches their ears who indulge in the more remote gaieties of the other apartments.

But these other apartments were densely crowded, and in them beat feverishly the heart of life. And the revel went whirling on, until at length there commenced the sounding of midnight upon the clock. And then the music ceased, as I have told; and the evolutions of the waltzers were quieted; and there was an uneasy cessation of all things as before. But now there were twelve strokes to be sounded by the bell of the clock; and thus it happened, perhaps, that more of thought crept, with more of time, into the meditations of the thoughtful among those who reveled. And thus, too, it happened, perhaps, that before the last echoes of the last chime had utterly sunk into silence, there were many individuals in the crowd who had found leisure to become aware of the presence of a masked figure which had arrested the attention of no single individual before. And the rumor of this new presence having spread itself whisperingly around, there arose at length from the whole company a buzz, or murmur, expressive of disapprobation and surprise—then, finally, of terror, of horror, and of disgust.

In an assembly of phantasms such as I have painted, it may well be supposed that no ordinary appearance could have excited such sensation. In truth the masquerade license of the night was nearly unlimited; but the figure in question had out-Heroded Herod, and gone beyond the bounds of even the prince's indefinite decorum. There are chords in the hearts of the most reckless, which cannot be touched without emotion. Even with the utterly lost, to whom life and death are equally jests, there are matters of which no jest can be made. The whole company, indeed, seemed now deeply to feel that in the costume and bearing of the stranger neither wit nor propriety existed. The figure was tall and gaunt, and shrouded from head to foot in the habiliments of the grave. The mask, which concealed the visage, was made so nearly to resemble the countenance of a stiffened corpse that the closest scrutiny must have had difficulty in detecting the cheat. And yet all this might have been endured, if not approved, by the mad revelers around. But the mummer had gone so far as to assume the type of the Red Death. His vesture was dabbled in blood—and his broad brow, with all the features of the face, was besprinkled with the scarlet horror.

When the eyes of Prince Prospero fell upon this spectral image (which with a slow and solemn movement, as if more fully to sustain its role, stalked to and fro among the waltzers) he was seen to be convulsed, in the first moment with a strong shudder either of terror or distaste; but, in the next, his brow reddened with rage.

"Who dares?" he demanded hoarsely of the courtiers who stood near him—"who dares insult us with this blasphemous mockery? Seize him and unmask him -- that we may know whom we have to hang at sunrise, from the battlements!"

It was in the eastern or blue chamber in which stood the Prince Prospero as he uttered these words. They rang throughout the seven rooms loudly and clearly—for the prince was a bold and robust man, and the music had become hushed at the waving of his hand.

It was in the blue room where stood the prince, with a group of pale courtiers by his side. At first, as he spoke, there was a slight rushing movement of this group in the direction of the intruder, who at the moment was also near at hand, and now, with deliberate and stately step, made closer approach to the speaker. But from a certain nameless awe with which the mad assumptions of the mummer had inspired the whole party, there were found none who put forth hand to seize him; so that, unimpeded, he passed within a yard of the prince's person; and, while the vast assembly, as if with one impulse, shrank from the centers of the rooms to the walls, he made his way uninterruptedly, but with the same solemn and measured step which had distinguished him from the first, through the blue chamber to the purple—through the purple to the green—through the green to the orange—through this again to the white— and even thence to the violet, ere a decided movement had been made to arrest him. It was then, however, that the Prince Prospero, maddening with rage and the shame of his own momentary cowardice, rushed hurriedly through the six chambers, while none followed him on account of a deadly terror that had seized upon all. He bore aloft a drawn dagger, and had approached, in rapid impetuosity, to within three or four feet of the retreating figure, when the latter, having attained the extremity of the velvet apartment, turned suddenly and confronted his pursuer. There was a sharp cry— and the dagger dropped gleaming upon the sable carpet, upon which, instantly afterwards, fell prostrate in death the Prince Prospero. Then, summoning the wild courage of despair, a throng of the revelers at once threw themselves into the black apartment, and, seizing the mummer, whose tall figure stood erect and motionless within the shadow of the ebony clock, gasped in unutterable horror at finding the grave-cerements and corpse-like mask which they handled with so violent a rudeness, untenanted by any tangible form.

And now was acknowledged the presence of the Red Death. He had come like a thief in the night. And one by one dropped the revelers in the blood-bedewed halls of their revel, and died each in the despairing posture of his fall. And the life of the ebony clock went out with that of the last of the gay. And the flames of the tripods expired. And Darkness and Decay and the Red Death held illimitable dominion over all.

Finley's Last Chapter
by
Alexandra Wolfe

"Hi, my name is Finley," she writes on the scrap of paper with a broken pencil Georgia gave her earlier. "You can blame Georgia for this, for what I am about to write, it was at her suggestion, well, insistence really that I write it all down, how we came to this moment in time." She pauses and looks out across the ink-black darkness, straining to see anything moving, but sees nothing. It's all gone quiet.

Too quiet, the incessant shelling having stopped a few hours earlier. No one really knows what it means. Was it the proverbial calm before the storm, or maybe the eye of the storm? Did it really matter which? The small pockets of resistance fighters, like her small group, were losing what was left of the war. She isn't even sure what it is they are fighting for anymore.

Survival? That was a joke.

They were, according to Thomas, down to their last few scavenged tinned rations. No one had found anything 'living' for several days. Nothing flew across the skies; no birds sang a morning chorus. No animal, if any still yet lived, scurried or foraged above ground. Not even the rats showed their faces, those hardy creatures that could survive through just about anything were nowhere to be seen.

Finley knows they are living on borrowed time. Georgia knows it too. By the morning, the rest of them will know it as well.

A slight breeze blows and ruffles what is left of her straw-blond hair. It started coming out in clumps days ago. She hides the fact during the day beneath a wool-knit hat that proclaims her a fan of the Ottawa Senators. She has no idea who they were or what team sport they might have played. But she's thankful nonetheless for the warmth and head cover it affords her.

Drawing her attention back to the dirty piece of paper, Finley focuses her thoughts once more, trying to make sense of it all. But instead of writing, she stares at Charlie. Then, she almost laughs out loud at the absurdity of it. Here she is, a petite thirty-five-year-old woman dressed in Army fatigues, sat on a shattered wall, writing her life story on a scrap of paper by torchlight, with a small plush monkey sat on her knee watching the proceedings.

"Do you think I'm going crazy?" She asks the monkey in all seriousness then grins. Charlie simply stares back, his dirty face probably mirroring her own.

Here is her thread, she thinks, the one thing that leads her back through all the years to her childhood. A monkey. Not this particular monkey, which is a tattered remnant that Georgia rescued a couple of days earlier from a heap of abandoned rubbish. A mot amid the wreckage of what was once a children's hospital.

No, the original Charlie, a chimpanzee that had been twice the size of the child Finley, was long since lost. As were the subsequent 'Charlie' monkeys she had owned over the ensuing years. Just like they all would be, so very soon. Not just her little group of bedraggled rag-tag fighters, dug-in amid the ruined skyscrapers of what was once a part of civilizations crowning achievement, but the entire human race.

Extinct.

The ache in her chest threatens to overwhelm her.

"It doesn't bear thinking about, of course, she's right," Finley writes. "The more I look at what possibilities lie in wait with the coming of a fateful morning, the more fear grows in the pit of my stomach. So I'll try, for her, for everyone, but most of all, for myself to remain calm, and focused." Finley looks at the words written in a small, tight scrawl. They seem as alien to her now as do the invaders who have swarmed across the planet obliterating everything in their path. To these invaders, it wasn't simply about destruction; it was nothing less than the complete and utter annihilation of every living thing on planet earth.

Why do I need to know where it is I came from, and what it is I'm fighting for, in order to do what needs doing tomorrow? The million-dollar question.

Because. It's Georgia's favorite word of the moment. Because we need to. Because it has to be done, and it might as well be us. . .because, someone has to stop the invaders.

Because. This is for her mother. This is for her father. This is for all those who have gone before her, who gave so much in order for there to be a future for their children and their children's children.

How could she do anything less than they had when the need arose?

Finley chews her pencil and beseeches Charlie.

"What do you think, should the crazy lady just march up to the ugly alien and shake its hand?" It is all so plausible.

They had at hand maybe the greatest weapon they had to offer against a seemingly un-defeatable enemy.

"That's if it works..." Finley mutters.

"It will do...it has to."

Startled, Finley knocks Charlie from her knee turning to see the owner of the softly spoken words. Georgia, mouth curved with a lingering smile, sits next to her leaning in against her.

"Is that it? Is that all you've written?" The smile stretches.

"My life, in one chapter," Finley says sheepishly, realizing she's managed to while away a couple of hours while Georgia was dealing with their crew, giving her some much-needed downtime alone.

An arm snakes across the back of her shoulders. She leans into the comfort that act offers, her head going to a welcoming shoulder. She feels Georgia press her face into her hair, warm breath caressing the top of her head, as the taller woman consoles her against the coming dawn and what's to come. Time was running out for them both.

"Didn't Charlie give you any pointers," Georgia finally says.

"No, not much, his spelling isn't that much better than mine." Finley sees the monkey lying in the dirt staring face-up at her, as if beseeching her. She moves, scooping him up, clutching him to her chest and leans back in against the warmth of her companion hearing the soft laugh.

"You know a girl could get jealous of that monkey."

"Really? I never thought *you* the jealous type and, after all, it was you who introduced us, remember?"

"Hmm...that was a bum move on my part then?"

"Jealous."

"Am not."

"Are too—" They stare at one another for one long moment.

Opening a button of her shirt, Finley slips the dust-cover monkey half in, half out. He looks as if he's saying to all the world, *'Hey, look where I am!'*

"And do I get to slip inside there too?" The quietly spoken Georgia asks.

Feeling a rise of color to her cheeks, Finley gives the woman, who means so much to her, her answer. A mouth-stretching grin. Taking Georgia's hand, she stands. Charlie safely stowed, she likewise flips off her torch and stows it in her combat pants along with the scraps of paper and pencil. And, with a gentle tug of the rough-skinned hand she holds, takes a step backward thinking that there are far better ways they could be consoling one another, before the dawn's early light.

"I might lead this bunch of reprobates, but in all else, especially matters of the heart, you've always mastered me," Finley says to the woman stood before her.

"Then I'd better lead you to where I've bedded us down for the night, before first light steals what little time we have left."

"You'd better," Finley says, falling in step with her lover, as they move off into a darkness, which swallows them, whole.

* * *

In the fierce light of day, as the overhead sun beats down from a clear blue sky, adding to the heat haze that gives the vista an ethereal quality to it. A lone figure, bathed in the sun's white light, stands atop the rubble of bricks, waiting. In her left hand, she clutches her one and only possession, a small stuffed monkey. In her right, she holds a detonation switch that will end it all. Unleashing what they all hope will be humanity's last chance—tiny engines of destruction—deadly bacteria. Deadly that is to the aliens, as they had found out weeks earlier. How ironic the scientists' bacteria were harmless to humans yet, so deadly to the *'Uglies.'*

Vials and vials of it lay housed in the underground laboratory right beneath the point where she now stood. A laboratory they had rigged with enough explosives to make their own miniature mushroom cloud.

All Finley has to do is flip the switch and it will all end—for her at least—in one cataclysmic explosion. All the while raining down a biological terror from the skies upon the assembled alien invaders now just visible through the haze, in the far distance.

She doesn't turn and look behind, knowing she'll see no one there—the others of her unit, now under Georgia's command, having long since left the ruined city. Georgia had made love to her slowly in those last few hours together, as if memorizing every last piece of skin, every curve and contour of her wrecked body.

Now, with her gaze fixed squarely on the future, the future of mankind, she lifts her right arm to hold it out in front of her. Steady.

"Is it time, Charlie...what say you?" She brings the monkey up and holds him tightly against her chest, the child in her needing the comfort against the dark, as with her right thumb she does one last act of bravery.

Life of a Child
by
Samantha Boyette

I was born on a small farm in Arkansas. My father and mother loved me very much, I have never doubted that. I grew up with woods and fields to play in, I captured butterflies and tadpoles and imagined I was king of my own little world. My family had no friends, but I never felt like we needed any. I had no idea how special I was. It would have been a good life, to grow old not knowing who I was.

Each night, my mother tucked me into bed. She kissed my hair and made sure a nightlight was left on. Looking up into her warm brown eyes, framed by choppy blond hair, I saw love.

"You are my boy," she told me. I can still hear her voice, soft and musical in my mind. "You are a miracle. Every day I spend with you is one more than I had ever hoped to know."

Back then, I didn't understand her words. They warmed me, and I felt her love. I was barely five years old. But I smiled each night and snuggled into bed, happy that she was there. I thought of my father downstairs in his favorite chair, with his pale blue eyes and sandy blond hair. Mother had often told me how much I looked like him. On nights when I couldn't sleep, I crawled into his lap and begged for a story. Safely surrounded by the lingering hints of clove and mint, I would fall asleep to the sound of his voice.

It wasn't long after my sixth birthday that the soldiers arrived. It was a perfect summer day, warm and bright with a light breeze. I was playing on the lawn while my mother hung laundry. I ran back and forth through the damp sheets, pretending I was a bull. I remember we both looked up at the sound of trucks roaring up the road. I was excited to see four trucks at once.

"Trucks," I said, clapping my hands and jumping up and down.

When I looked at my mother, I expected to see her smiling. Instead, her usually tan skin had turned white. She scooped me up in her arms and ran into the house. My father had gone fishing early that morning. Crying, she shoved me into the kitchen cupboard under the sink. It was cramped and dusty, but I was small enough to fit.

"Be as quiet as a little mouse," she said. Her voice was thick. I began to cry. She tucked my stuffed rabbit into my arms and patted its head.

"Where are you going?" I asked. I didn't want to be left alone. She jumped as someone pounded on the front door.

"I'll be right back. Be brave," she said. She smoothed my hair away from my face and kissed my head before shutting the door. I sat in the dark cupboard, trying my best to be brave and quiet as the smell of bleach filled my nostrils.

I heard the door open. Heavy footsteps filled the hall. A pair of them clomped into the kitchen and then back out again.

"Where is he?" boomed a man whose voice was harsh and full of anger. It was so different from my father's.

"Who?" My mother asked. "My husband is away. It's only me here." I heard the crack of a hand against skin. My mom cried out. I hugged my knees closer to my chest, squeezing my fists tight and biting my lip.

"Where is he?" The voice grew louder with each word. "The boy."

I shut my eyes, burying my face in my knees.

"There isn't a boy." My mother cried. "There are no children. No one has children. What makes you think I would have a boy?"

I heard a gunshot, though I didn't know what it was at the time. My mother's crying stopped.

"Find the boy," the voice ordered. "He's here somewhere."

I waited in the dark for what seemed like forever before the cupboard door opened. I didn't lift my head from my knees or open my eyes. I prayed that I would be invisible. Rough hands took me by the shoulders and tugged me out into the light. Only then did I open my eyes.

The man who held me had dark brown hair. He didn't seem to belong in our yellow kitchen where the dough was rising on the counter. We would have had fresh bread with supper that night. The man looked at me with open awe. Carefully, as if I was made of glass, he lifted me into his arms. I wish now that I had fought him, but back then I didn't have the strength. I simply lay limp and frightened against his chest, clinging to my toy rabbit. I kept thinking everything would be all right if only my father would come home.

"I have him," the man called. His voice was high and light. He was not the booming man.

Cradling me, he carried me out of my home. We passed my mother's paintings on the walls, the couch where we had all cuddled up to read, and the marks on the door that measured my height. I saw my mother lying on the floor by the door, her plain dress stained red across the chest. The soldier stepped into the sunshine, which felt warm on my face. Above me, the sky was still blue, and below me, the grass was still green, but my world had come to an end.

The next days were a blur. I remember being taken on a very long ride in one of the trucks, which had to stop often to refuel or cool the engines. I clung to the man who found me, simply because he was less frightening than the rest of the men. At night, we camped along the road, and no one tucked me in to my bed.

I was taken to the home of a man and was later told that he was the President. I had never heard of a president before then. Apparently, he had heard of me. The President was a tall man with gray hair, dark eyes, and a weary smile. His wife had nearly as much gray hair as him and kind blue eyes. He was nice enough. He gave me a bedroom of my own with plenty of toys and a soft bed. I did as I was told, even though it hurt every time I called them by their new names, father and mother.

I lived with the President and his wife for three years. In that time, I learned a great deal about who I was. When they didn't think I was listening, they spoke of a special drug called Fullterm. They said it was supposed to be a miracle.

For twenty-five years, Fullterm was given to every child born. The disease that had been killing so many before they reached adulthood was stopped in its tracks. By the time doctors linked Fullterm to the falling birth rates, it was too late. Because of Fullterm, I shouldn't have been born. I don't know what made my mother different.

On the many nights when the President drank, he came quietly into my bedroom. I never heard him until he sat at the edge of my bed and I awoke to the smell of gin on his breath.

"You are the last, Finnegan," he used to say. "The only child left in this world, and we have done you wrong. It's only that we wanted a child so badly." He put his head in his hands and cried. I thought he would never stop. Eventually, he sat up again and patted my back. "May God grant you the strength to forgive us when you are a man."

Not every night was the same, but the words he said usually added up to the same thing. I thought a lot about being the last child in the world. *Was I really the last child?* I asked the other people in the house what the President meant, but no one ever answered me.

I was almost ten when another man decided he wanted me. This time, the men came in the middle of the night, as I lay in the bed I had come to think of as my safe place. I listened to gunshot after gunshot, as the danger came closer to me. I stared at the ceiling, counting the painted stars that glowed there. When I heard the familiar creak of hinges on my bedroom door, I was almost relieved. A man with glasses and a close-cut-beard stepped into my room.

"Finnegan?" he said quietly. "I need you to come with me."

I didn't answer. I climbed out of bed and put on my shoes. I pulled on a sweatshirt and held my tattered, stuffed rabbit close. The man took me by the hand and led me out of the house. We passed a dozen guards, all dead on the floor. There was no sign of the President or his wife.

Outside the house, we joined a group of others who were with the man. I was put in the back seat of a car and buckled in safely before we started the long journey to the next house. On the way, I learned that my new father was named Jonah. He had been planning to take me away for a very long time.

"Do you know that you are the last of your kind?" Jonah asked.

"There are no other children?" I asked. "Are you sure?"

"None as young as you," Jonah answered. "But we also found a girl, Maria. She is fourteen. When you are older, you'll marry her."

"Is she a mother?" I asked. I had only known mothers in my life, never a young girl.

"She is barely more than a child now," Jonah answered. "But you'll make her a mother." Back then I didn't understand what he was talking about or how important it was.

I never got the chance to make Maria a mother. Within a year, she killed herself. Jonah stomped about the house in a rage for weeks. I hid in the small room that had been made mine, and I cried for Maria. She had been a sweet girl with dark hair past her shoulders and an easy laugh.

When Jonah decided he was going to leave in hopes of finding another girl, the group was divided. Half of them wanted to go with him, believing that there could be another girl, while the rest wanted to stay behind. They had given up hope.

In the end, Jonah convinced them all to follow him. They left two men to watch me. I think it was easier for Jonah's followers to keep moving rather than to wait in the house.

Barely a day later, the front door banged open. I had just settled down to dinner with the two left behind, when a ragged-looking man, unshaven and armed, burst through the door with a rifle. My kidnappers went for their weapons, but they were too late. With two shots, the ragged man left them dead in their chairs. I cringed, wondering where I would be taken next, not looking up from my meal. I hugged my toy rabbit tight and focused on the hard chair beneath me and the smell of cooked meat. I hoped this man wouldn't kill me along with the others. Instead, the unkempt man crouched beside my chair. I studied his torn, flannel shirt from the corner of my eye.

"Finnegan?" There was something familiar about his voice.

I looked up and met his eyes, which were pale blue just like my own.

"Father?" My throat was tight. I could barely begin to hope that it might actually be him.

He pulled me into a tight hug. I felt his rough beard and breathed in his scent. Cloves and mint. It was him. His arms felt the same, strong and safe around me. I pulled back and glanced into his face, so familiar, and yet so much older than I'd remembered.

"How did you find me?" I asked.

"I never stopped looking for you," he answered. "I followed every rumor I heard, I searched every place you could be, until I saw you three days ago. Since then, I've been waiting for my chance."

When we left that house, I took pleasure in leaving the door open, inviting in the vandals and wildlife to do what they wanted. My father led me through the woods to where he had hidden his car. We drove away. I talked all night, telling him everything that had happened since I had been taken. When I was done, Father told me how he had come home to find my mother dead and me gone. He said that he had heard that I was with the President, but the President's house had been too well-guarded to attempt rescuing me.

After three nights of driving, we came to a small house at the top of a hill. The house was very much like the one we had lived in before. Only one floor high, it had large inviting windows and walls painted in cheery colors. Father had even saved some of my mother's paintings and hung them in the tiny home. I sat on a big couch. It was so soft that I sank into it, and smiled to be back where I belonged.

My father showed me the land he farmed. He taught me how to make sure the corn grew in straight lines and how to keep away the birds. Together, we milked the cows, collected eggs, and planted rows of vegetables. We laughed at old memories and ate chocolate cake on Mother's birthday, her favorite. Once a month, we packed up an old cart with produce for trade in the village. My father went alone. I waited on the farm, always with a gun ready, until he returned. For two years, we lived happily, until the sickness came.

Father was the first to get it. It started as a small cough that wouldn't go away. After two days, it turned into a fever. On the third day, I forced him into bed. Father was swaying on his feet so badly he could hardly stand. He didn't eat, and he couldn't sleep. I stayed beside him the whole time.

"Drink this," I said, coaxing some water down his throat. He coughed up most of it. I winced. "You'll be better soon."

"I won't be." He gave me a weak smile. "Leave an old man to die." But he wasn't old, and I wasn't ready to let him go.

"No." I shook my head. "I've only just come home to you."

"Two years," he said. "Two more years than I ever thought I'd have with you. Your mother was right when she said every moment is precious. Now you understand what a miracle you are."

"I hate it," I said with a scowl. "There's no reason for me to dream or hope for my life. I'll never be a father, or live a real life."

"There are always reasons to hope and always reasons to live," he said. "Even if they are hard to find."

This was the last conversation I had with my father. The next morning, he was dead. I cried and cursed as I dug his grave. Standing chest-deep in the hole, I wished for death to come to me as well.

I began to cough that very day.

The next morning, I managed to milk the cows and collect eggs. But in the afternoon, I climbed into my father's bed. The coughing was painful; it pulled at every muscle in my body. After a particularly bad fit, I lay panting on the mattress, trying to catch my breath. At that moment, I knew I had been a fool to wish for death. I didn't want to die, I was afraid to die.

I used to think that I had nothing to live for. But my father was right, there was always something to live for.

I used to worry that I'd never know the kind of love my father and mother had. But now, I wondered. Maybe I could have found another girl like Maria, who was still young enough for children, or maybe I would have grown old knowing nothing but friendship. With death as my shadow now, it seemed like friendship would have been enough.

I pushed myself from the bed and stumbled out into the yard, resting against the fence for a moment. I continued forward and opened all the doors and gates to let the animals free. Someone would find them and take them in. As I struggled for air, I saw a truck on the road from the village.

Adrenaline sparked through me, giving me the strength to run to the house. My father's rifle was just inside the door, where it always stood. I filled my pockets with bullets and spilled more on the floor. Hugging the rifle to my chest, I clattered down the porch stairs and stumbled through the yard in uneven steps to the old stonewall.

My chest heaved, working for every breath, while my shaking hands loaded the gun, just the way my father had taught me. I peered over the wall as the beaten-up truck pulled to a stop at the end of our lane. They were about a hundred feet away, well within rifle range. As the first man climbed out from the truck, I pulled the trigger.

I wasn't ready for the recoil. The butt of the gun slammed into my shoulder. I felt a burst of pain. The shot went wide, but the man ducked anyway. Moaning, I leaned against the rough stones and started to cough. Another man and a woman got out of the car.

"Don't come any closer," I shouted, leveling my gun again. Pain made my vision swim, and it took three tries to get the gun steady on the man.

"Whoa, son," the first man said. He raised his arms. "Just hold on a minute, no need for weapons. I'm Buck, and this here is my daughter, Ellen, and her husband, Georgia. We aren't looking to start something. We come as friends."

I laughed, but the laughter turned to coughing again. When I was able to fill my lungs, there was blood on my hand. I wiped it on my pants and fumbled with the rifle. Even with the gun propped on the wall, the barrel wavered.

"I won't go with you," I said, trying to take aim at the intruders. "I want to stay here with my father. Please, just let me stay with my father." Tears started to fall; I wiped them away but couldn't stop myself from crying.

"We heard about you and your father. We aren't here to take you away," Buck said again. His bulk shimmered, and I tried harder to focus.

"Just go away," I shouted, pulling the trigger again. The shot went wider than the last one, and the force of the recoil flipped the weapon over the wall.

"I'm not even hardly a child any more. Don't take me away from my father." The words sounded thick. I was thirteen, but I felt older than my father. I leaned heavily on the wall, too tired to hold myself up.

"Finnegan," Buck said softly. "We are looking for help." I heard kindness in his voice. It shocked me. I looked over the wall at him, my eyes clear for the moment.

Buck motioned for the woman, Ellen, to step forward. At first, I didn't understand. Then I noticed the bundle of clothing in her arms. I saw it for what it was, a child. No more than two years old and sound asleep despite everything. All the fight left me as I looked at that small face.

I pushed myself to my feet and awkwardly climbed over the wall. A child, one younger than me. A dozen thoughts swam through my head as I lurched toward the family. I wanted to see the child, to touch it and know, first hand, that I wasn't the last. When Buck took a step forward, and the others followed, reality came rushing back.

"No," I shouted. I stopped, and waved them back with my arms. The movement caused me to lose my balance and I fell to the ground hard. I held on to tufts of grass as my head spun. "There is a sickness here. Keep moving. Keep the child safe." I picked up a rock and threw it at them. It missed, but it made them hesitate.

"Take the child away," I yelled, tears coming again. "Don't let anyone have it. A child should grow up with its family. A child should be happy. Don't trust anyone."

Ellen held the child tighter to her body. After a long look at me, Buck nodded to Ellen. She put the child back in the car, and climbed in as well. The other man opened the passenger side door. Only Buck stayed where he was.

"Can I give you anything?" Buck called. "Food? Water?"

"No," I answered. I slumped over. He had already given me more than I could have asked for. I heard the car door slam and the sound of the engine. I watched as the car drove back down the lane, before disappearing over a ridge.

My vision began to blur. I laid back and closed my eyes. Breathing was getting harder as my body shut down. An hour ago, I had been scared. Now, with the sun warm on my face, I thought of the child. I didn't know if it was a boy or a girl, but it didn't matter.

I wasn't the last. The realization hit me like a punch in the stomach. I had been taken from my family, my mother had been killed, and my childhood destroyed, all because of something that was no longer true? Had it ever been true? I thought of Maria, sure that someone had told her she was the last child as well. How different our lives might have been if we had known we were not the last. I laughed, or coughed, I wasn't sure which. Death, which had been washing slowly over me, was now pulling me free of myself.

For the first time, I wasn't afraid. I welcomed whatever was taking me away. With my final breath, I thought of the baby, hoping it wasn't the last.

The End of the World
by
Hillarie Belloc

One day I met a man who was sitting silently near Whitney, in the Thames Valley, in a very large, long, low inn that stands in those parts, or at least stood then, for whether it stands now or not depends upon the Fussiest, whose business it is to Fuss and, in their Fussing, to disturb mankind.

He had nothing to say for himself at all, and he looked not gloomy, but sad. He was tall and thin, with high cheekbones. His face was the color of leather that has been some time in the weather, and he despised us altogether; he would not say a word to us until one of the company said, rising from his meat and drink, "Very well, there's a thing we shall never know 'til the end of the world." He was talking about the discussion that the young men had been holding together. "There's a thing we shall never know 'til the end of the world, about which nobody knows!"

"You will pardon me," said the tall, thin, and elderly man with a face like leather that has been exposed to the weather, "I know about the End of the World, for I have been there."

This was so interesting that we all sat down again to listen.

"I wasn't talking of place, but of time," murmured the young man whom the stranger had answered.

"I cannot help that," said the stranger decisively. "The End of the World is the End of the World, and whether you are talking of space or of time it does not matter, for when you have got to the end, you have got there, as may be proven in several ways."

"How did you get to it?" said one of our companions.

"That is very simply answered," said the elder man. "You get to it by walking straight in front of you."

"Anyone could do that," said the other.

"Anyone could," said the elder man, "but nobody does. I did it when I was a boy in my father's parsonage, having heard so much about the End of the World and seeing that people's descriptions of it differed so much and that everybody was quite sure of his own. I used to take my father's friends and guests aside privately, for I was afraid to speak with my father himself, and I used to ask them how they knew what the End of the World was really like and whether they had seen it. Some laughed, others were silent, and others were angry, but no one gave me any information. At last, I decided that the only way to find out a thing of that sort was to discover it for one's self and not to go by hearsay, so I decided to go straight on without stopping until I got to the End of the World."

"Which way did you walk?" said yet another of my companions.

"Young man," said the stranger, with solemnity, "I walked westward toward the setting Sun. I walked and I walked and I walked, day after day and year after year. Whenever I came to the seacoast, I would take work on board a ship. I went in this way through all known lands and over all known seas, until at last I came to the shore of a sea beyond which -- so the people who lived there told me -- there was no further shore. 'I cannot help that,' I said. 'I have not yet come to the End of the World, and it is common sense that such an expanse of water must have something at the back of it to hold it up. Besides which, there is a strong wind blowing out of the gates of the west and from the sunset. Now, that wind must rise somewhere, and I am going on to see where it rises.' One of them was kind enough to lend me a boat with oars. I thanked him gratefully, and then I set out to row toward the End of the World, taking with me two or three days' provisions."

"When I had rowed a long time I went to sleep, and when I woke up the next morning, I rowed again all day, until I went to sleep the second night. On the third day, I rowed again. A little before sunset on the third day, I saw before me high hills, all in peaks like a great saw. On the very highest of the peaks, there were streaks of snow, and at about six o'clock in the afternoon, I grounded my boat upon that gravelly shore and pulled it up upon the pebbles, though it was evident either that the tide was high or that there was no tide in these silent places."

"I offered up a prayer to the genius of the land and tied the painter of the boat to two great stones so that no wave might move it, and then I went on the land. When I had gone a little way, I saw a signpost on which was written, 'To the End of the World One Mile,' and there was a rough track to which it pointed. I went along this track; everything was completely silent. There were no birds, there was no wind, and there was nothing in the sky. But one thing I did notice was that the Sun was much larger than it used to be, and as I went along this last mile or so, the Sun seemed to get larger still. It may have been my imagination, though, for I must tell you my imagination is pretty strong."

"Well then, gentlemen, when I had walked a mile or so, I saw another signpost, on which there was a large board marked 'Danger,' and a hundred yards beyond the track, between two great, dark rocks, there I was! The road had stopped short; it was broken off, jagged, like a torn bit of paper, and there was the End of the World."

"How do you mean?" said one of the younger men in an awed tone.

"What I say," said the stranger decidedly. "I had come to the end; there was nothing beyond. You looked down over a precipice where there was moss and steep grass, and on the ledges, trees far below, and then more precipice. And then, miles below, a few more trees were clinging to the steep slope, then more precipice, and then darkness. Far away before me was the whole expanse of sky, and in the midst of it, I saw the broad red Sun setting into the brume; it was not yet dark enough to see the stars, and there was no moon in the sky.

"I assure you it was a very wonderful sight, and I was awed, though not afraid. And how glad I was to find that the world had an edge to it and that all the talk about its being round was nonsense!"

"When the sun was set, twilight grew dark, and I returned to find my boat, but I must have missed my way, for the track became broader and better, and at last I came to a gate resembling those of humankind, with an initial on it that showed that it had been put up by some landlord. It was an open gate, and after I had entered it, I came upon a wide highway, beautifully metal led, and when I had gone along this for less than half a mile, I came to this inn where I am now sitting. That was a week ago, and I have been here ever since. They took me in kindly enough, but they would not believe what I had to tell them about the End of the World. It is a great pity, gentlemen, for that wonderful sight is to be discovered somewhere hereabouts, and a mere accident of my losing my way in the darkness makes it difficult for me to find it by daylight."

Having said all this, the stranger was silent.

One of my companions whispered to me that the old man must be mad. The stranger overheard him and said with a thin smile:

"Oh, I know all about that; several have suggested it already, but it is no answer, for if I did not come from the End of the World, where did I come from? No one has seen me hereabouts during the last few days, until I came to this inn. And all the first part of my journey I can very easily explain, for I have notes of it, and it lasted for years. It is only this last part that seems to be so difficult. I tell you I lost my way, and when a man has lost his way at night, he can never find it again in the daytime."

As he spoke, he took a little piece of folded paper, rather dirty, out of his inner pocket, on which a rough map sketch was drawn, and he began touching it with a stub of pencil that he held in his hand. His eyes grew dimmer as he did so, and he leaned his head upon his hand. "I think I have got hold of it, gentlemen," he said.

We did not get up or go too near him, for we thought he might be dangerous.

"I think, gentlemen," he repeated in a more mumbling, lower, and less-certain voice, "I think I have got hold of it. I go backwards again through the gate to the right, just as then I went to the left, and after that it cannot be very far, for I see those two rocks in front of me. Besides which," he muttered less and less coherently, "I ought to have remembered those very high and silent hills with nothing living upon them." And he added, half asleep, as his head dropped upon his hand, "It was westward. I had forgotten that."

Having so spoken, he seemed to fall asleep altogether, and his head fell back upon the corner of the wainscoting behind the bench where he sat. He made no noise in breathing as he slept.

It was the first time that any of us young men had come across this fairly common sight of a man who took things within for things without. Some of us were frightened, and all of us wished to be rid of the place and to get away. As we went out, we told the landlord nothing either of the old fellow's vagaries or of his sleep, but we left and reached the town of Whitney, and when we had stayed there for a couple of hours, we walked southward to the station to wait for the train to take us back to Oxford.

While we were waiting, two farmers were talking together. One said to the other: "Are, if he'd paid them, they wouldn't have minded so much."

To which the other answered: "Are, 'tisn't only the paying. It's always an awkward thing when a man dies in your house, ‘specially if it's licensed. My wife's brother was caught that way."

Then, as they went on talking, we found out that they were talking of the man in the inn, who it seems had not slept very long, but was dead and had died in that same room. It was a shocking thing to hear. The first farmer said to the second when we had all gotten into the railway carriage: "Where'd he come from?"

The other, who was an old man, grinned and said, "Where we all come from, I suppose, and where we all go to." He touched his forehead with his hand. "He said he'd come from the End of the World."

"Ar," said the other gloomily in answer, "like enough!" And after that, they talked no more about the matter.

Arturo
by
M. Sullivan

Twenty-one of us were left when the final sweep for humans was complete. Scattered all across the Earth, I was the last to be collected, picked off my roof like a stray weed in a yard. Amidst the burning and devastation, I would have taken the hand of the devil, himself, to get out. Instead, a dark, green, windowless spaceship with a long, metallic arm gently whisked through the air toward me. Under its belly was a gigantic, clear cargo container filled with my fellow *Homo sapiens.* The arm clasped firmly, but not painfully, around me and dropped me carefully into the box.

"Hey, everybody," I said. A handful muttered something back in English. The rest ignored me, intent on staring at the smoldering world below them.

The ship twirled in the sky, spinning dizzily above my hometown, and then shot upward toward an incalculably large mother-ship that had paused above our planet.

Our planet. Man, that was something. We flew to the height of jets, where we could see whole burning cities through the clear sides. We kept going and going, up and up, faster and faster. I wished at this moment that the view was less spectacular; that these aliens would have put a solid-colored floor or at least a carpet in the box to block the landscape beneath us. Majestic mountaintops? Pluming gusts on the tops of white clouds? My stomach threatened to deposit not just its contents, but a few other organs as well. The back of my throat churned with that flavorful nausea so familiar from childhood visits to theme parks and rides like the Vomit Comet or the Hurl-y Burly. I began to scream.

AAAAAAAA!

AAAAAAAAAAAA!

AAAAAAAAAAAAAAAAAAAAAAAAA!

What can I say? Heights and amusement rides have always made me sick. I never dared to go on a roller coaster, until I discovered at the age of ten that screaming made my stomach less queasy. It worked back then, and it worked now, thirty years later, in the transport. In the sealed, stuffed box, my howls soon drowned out the questions, the whimpers, the crying, and any other sound from my fellow men, and I was comforted.

Moments later, the others started screaming, too. At first, I thought they knew about my remedy, that their stomachs were as knotted and tortured as mine, but then I noticed that they were all glaring at me with a look that made me glad the box had a top.

A guy in a bright yellow Nirvana shirt stuck his nose against mine. "Shut up!" he barked.

I continued to scream.

"Somebody shut him up!" screeched a tall goon behind him.

The others quickly joined in, shouting and yelling in a dozen different languages, shaking their fists. It felt like a Third World bazaar. I covered my ears, kept screaming, and stared at the mother-ship rapidly approaching from above. I decided there must be just one alien spaceship designer in the entire universe, whose creativity when it came to mother-ships was limited to boxes or swollen Frisbees. This ship had no frills, just mechanics—it was a minivan of interstellar travel. The bottom looked like a pot top someone had covered with a bunch of hard drives. Copper veins shot across its underside. Silver towers, circular drums and metallic canyons crisscrossed its surface.

Shaded by the mother-ship's circular body, the container grew dark. The two vessels docked, and then the powerful mother-ship pushed us out to a safer distance to watch our planet be extinguished. I couldn't help but look. God, She burned. My house, my city, my town, my country, and beyond. I watched as the orange, red and black devoured the blues, the greens, and the whites. Would the whole planet explode from the heat, like a giant Jiffy Pop bag ready to burst? Was She getting larger? Was She filling with gas or lava or some other noxious substance boiling up from Her core? We needed to get higher. Much higher. Watching the Earth move farther away, I heard in my mind the clack-clack-clack-clack of the climbing rollercoaster. Why had I looked? My stomach heaved.

I screamed even louder.

AAAAAAA!

AAAAAAAAAAAAAAAA!

AAAAAAAAAAAAAAAAAAAA—WHAM! Something slammed off the top of my head, and I slumped to the container floor, losing consciousness. I'm not sure what it was, but I think it was a shoe with a *really* firm sole.

I woke up in a corner by myself, feeling a small knot on my skull. Four of the twenty-one men glimpsed back at me disapprovingly, then turned around to stare out of the box once more. The eagle had landed.

We were inside the mother-ship, but we had been separated into smaller containers. Like the original, they were clear on all sides, allowing us to see the entire bay where we were being held. The containers were about eight feet high, twenty feet long and fifteen feet wide. I got up unsteadily and walked to where my container-mates whispered among themselves. When they offered no welcome, I looked out of our new home.

Across from us was another container of humans. Next to that, another. Beside us, another. Clear lanes were marked between the units. Far into the bay, other containers, small and large, were visible and filled with various species of animals: elephants, dogs, hippos, sharks, things furry, scaled, and feathered, and also various types of vegetation: shrubs, trees, grasses. I imagined the riotous sound of all of us, humans, animals and vegetation, suddenly being joined in one glorious, sealed box, but that was wishful thinking. The only sound in our container was the breathing and occasional snort of concern of the four other co-inhabitants.

After a moment, I said, jokingly, "Whoever would have thought Noah would turn out to be an alien?"

"It's a lab, idiot, not an ark," the guy next to me said, pointing to a bank of high-tech looking contraptions that flashed in the middle of the bay.

I might have argued my point, but some of our captors floated by at that exact moment and, I have to say, those guys looked smart. As substantive as incense smoke, their seven-foot forms reminded me of upside-down shopping bags. But as they neared us and began to interact with our containers, their hands, tendrils, legs, and any other necessary limbs effortlessly congealed out of the smoke. They worked speedily, without hesitation, zipping back and forth, touching the units and making colorful panels appear. One made a spray of mist gush down upon us and we all screamed, covering our heads. The captor stopped the precipitation immediately and manipulated some other colors.

The container instantly chilled, and our wet clothes began to freeze on our bodies. We screamed.

More manipulations.

The container scorched, and the frozen clothes were now steaming, fogging up the walls.

We screamed.

Finally, the captor got the right temperature. I screamed just to make a joke. I swear, it looked at me amused, watching as the other four went about pulverizing me. Then it left.

"You're a freaking idiot," the tallest man said. "Are you trying to get us killed?" Spittle spattered onto my face.

There's always one idiot in every crowd, isn't there? I wondered how long before our captors figured this out and what they would do about it. Would they assume he was the leader because the other men stood behind him and give him room? Then this moron would get to speak for all of us. One of the other men—the guy in the Nirvana shirt—punched the tall man on the shoulder. "Leave the dork alone. Come on." The three laughed derisively and paid no more attention to me. I listened as they exchanged names, excluding me in the ritual.

Great. They're all idiots.

I got up from the floor and moved to the opposite corner, checking the status of my face in the reflection off the wall. A little bruising on my left cheek, but otherwise I saw the same bland Irish-Italian features that had always been present. I parted my sandy hair to check my knot. Still tender from the shoe experience, it was turning a wickedly dark purple. I touched it gently and winced. Idiots.

I gazed out into the lab area again at the other containers like ours, each filled with four men with the same type of sorting. The majority stood against the wall nearest to the central lab, talking or gesturing among themselves, pointing. Then there was one man like me, sitting far in a corner, watching. I waved to the man in the container next to ours. He was dark-skinned, South American maybe, a José or Borges, I guessed. He waved back. A captor approached his container and conducted the weather experiment. Borges, too, screamed until the temperature was right, laughing to himself. I laughed with him. His mates then beat him up and left him alone, just like mine had. When he saw me staring, he shrugged and mimed a word. It looked like he said, *idiots*, but maybe that meant something different in his language.

The two of us settled into our corners, nursing our bruises.
Below us, far below us, the Earth fell.

My suitemates approached the next morning, having said nothing else to me the previous day. Barry was in the lead, the tallest one. Nirvana-shirt was named Maurice. The third guy, who looked like an actor I'd seen in a bunch of cell phone commercials, was named Andy. The last one, the least verbal of the gorillas, was named Robin. He did actually look like a bird with his pointy face and a beak-like nose.

"Hey, it's the Bee Gees," I said, as they stood in front of me. Apparently, only I thought that being taken away by aliens and placed in a container with four guys whose names matched the falsetto marvels of the 1970's and 80's was funny. I'd gotten thumped for saying something similar yesterday evening, so I flinched and prepared for another whipping. But Barry did nothing; he just gave me a withering stare. I acted like he was looking over my shoulder at something and turned my head to see what it was.

"They grabbed a guy out of the other unit yesterday, and didn't return him," Barry said.

"I know," I responded and started humming "Staying Alive" loud enough to be distracting.

Barry continued. "They took one from another unit this morning, and he hasn't returned either."

The three stooges nodded in agreement behind him.

"I know," I said, adding just audibly, *"Staying alive…ah ah.."* while I did that hand-spinning disco move.

"We're going to FIGHT them," Barry said, pounding a fist into his open palm. His buddies imitated the action.

"Okay," I said and looked out the container for Borges, wanting to make the universal "*They're Crazy*" gesture to him.

Barry kicked my foot. "*WE'RE* going to fight THEM," he repeated, pointing to me. "*WE.*" He drew a circle in the air to include all five of us.

I slid back against the wall to escape being in the circle.

Barry kicked my foot again. "Listen…" He glanced helplessly at his cohorts, realizing instantly from their blank faces that they hadn't thought to ask my name either. He turned back to me and reluctantly waited.

"The name's ... Miranda." I bit back my laughter, enjoying the queer expression on Barry's face. It's actually Michael, but

Michael wouldn't make Barry's face scrunch up like he'd swallowed a lemon.

Barry attempted to soften his tone, forcefully slowing his words. "Listen, ahem, Miranda. We need to stick together in here. We're it. The last of the human race. If we die, then there's no hope for our kind." He drew another circle, but this time included all the containers. "*We* need to survive."

"*We* won't," I said simply, without breaking a smile.

Oh, Barry got mad then. He reached down and pulled me up by my hair, slamming my face against the wall.

"We will. We will. We will," he chanted.

I almost chanted back, We won't, we won't, we won't, but I caught a glimpse of my friend Borges from the other container in the exact same position –his face was up against a wall and his version of Barry had him by the hair. I smiled and tried to wave to him. He did the same. We both got spun around and slapped in the face.

"Miranda!" Barry yelled.

I couldn't help myself, I laughed again.

Barry wound up and slapped me twice…three times…four times more, until my entire face was red and numb, a trickle of blood formed in the corner of my lip. He raised his hand to deliver a final blow, with fist clenched and teeth gritted, but before his hand landed, several of our captors zipped inside the container. They grabbed Barry, and whisked him away struggling.

"HELLLLLP!" he screamed, flailing his arms toward me.

I drew a circle in the air around my remaining container-mates just as the door was closing. "*WE* can't," I said. Barry was gone.

Minus their lead singer, the other Bee Gees remained frozen a moment longer, staring at the door as if there might be an encore. When he failed to reappear, they disbanded and returned to their side of the container.

I fixed my clothes, rubbed the blood away from my mouth, and settled back down on the floor. I could have told the group, prior to Barry's abduction, that I had noticed none of the *corner-dwellers* were taken in the roundups. Meaning, it made no sense for *me* to fight our captors. If the Bee Gees knew what I knew, they'd have gone to the corners, themselves, and there were only four. I knew exactly who would have been left out, not Barry, Robin, or Maurice, or even Andy, who was never part of the real Bee Gees anyway. No, it would have been me. Miranda. I laughed to myself, picturing the agony on Barry's face as he was whisked away.

My container-mates eyed me suspiciously, but they were now a lost bunch, without Barry. I closed my eyes and rested, my head again filling with disco.

"Staying alive...ah ah..." I sang a few lines more.

Those first few days set the tone for the months to follow. Most of the original twenty-one humans struggled like Barry, huddling together, interlocking their arms like protestors. In the beginning, just a few captors would enter, their shapeless forms coalescing into powerful arms and hands as needed, but as the men became more and more desperate, more captors were necessary. When that happened, it was as if the entire container filled with a thick fog. Men punched and kicked at beings that were rarely solid. Occasionally, though, flesh and bone met something soft and pliable. "It's like hitting dough," Nirvana reported.

When the unit finally emptied after each struggle, I would repeat my mantra, "I wonder what they want." No one cared to discuss this. As, one by one, the fighters were all taken, there was no one to discuss it with anyway.

Within half-a-year, or so it felt not having a calendar, there were only five of us left—only the corner-dwellers remained. Quietly we had watched, and quietly we had taken what was offered to us: the meals, the medicine, anything. We went up to the door, and returned to our corner. Up to the door, return to our corner. The routine was simple to follow, perhaps too simple for the others—the non-corner dwellers. Man loves to struggle or, at the least, to think he has something to struggle against. There's never a shortage of enemies, internal or external.

To pass the time, we devised a crude sign language, to communicate from container to container, our new words consisting mostly of describing whatever food was brought to us. We signed the word "again," often, by raising the right hand, palm up toward the ceiling, and lifting our eyebrows.

Green stuff. Thumbs down.

Again. Right hand, palm up, eyebrow boosted.

This sucks was made by acting like you'd just bitten into a piece of dung.

Then one day the captors came for Borges. It was no big production. We both awoke from a night's rest to see his container's door slip open and a captor enter. My friend looked over to me, shrugged, and waved goodbye.

One by one, the other corner-dwellers were taken. Not a single one offered resistance. We all waved to each other.

A few hours later my door opened.

I was led down a long hallway, through a set of massive doors into a type of college auditorium. I thought I might find several hundred captors in there, but only three waited for me, each floating near the floor beside a surgical table.

I tried to imagine horrific human screams coming from the table as limbs and body parts were severed from their victims before being catalogued, but the ambience wasn't there. Rather, there was a general affect of depression hanging over the room. A sadness. Our captors even floated with a lack of enthusiasm, their smoky forms as heavy as storm clouds.

I was escorted to a chair beside the table. I sat and faced the three floating captors.

A conversation started in my head, forced in by the captors. I heard the first one project, *We're sorry.*

For killing the Bee Gees, I thought in return. *No big deal. They were real jerks.*

I did miss Borges and tried to keep my thought hidden, but the captors were intent on conveying something else. Within moments, a type of video played inside my head. They were showing me something. There were sixteen short clips in all. The theme was the same each time: a man was brought into this room struggling, violently kicking, biting, hitting, attacking the captors, injuring some of them. In each scene, I noticed how calm the captors remained when attacked by the human. How gentle their approach was, regardless of the hostility toward them. But the result was the same every time. As they were brought into the room, the men fought and fought, until even I knew that the kindest thing to do was to make them stop. Not one made it to the chair I now sat in. I felt out of place.

The video images stopped, and again, I heard, *We're sorry.*

I see, I thought back.

We only experimented after.

I understand. I nodded.

Again I heard, *We're sorry*, but this time, each captor sunk a bit, heartbroken.

I told them something I'd known from the beginning: *We won't survive. We can't survive. No amount of science can change that.*

That is what the others said, they answered. *But we hoped.*

Hope doesn't make babies, I said.

There are other means, one voice interjected. *We could crossbreed you.*

A picture of some crossbreeding opportunities flashed in my mind. Slimy earthworm species from other planets and humans…. *Yuck, no, thank you.*

But it will mean the end. The end of your race.

Then it's the end, I sighed.

That is what the others said, they repeated and went silent. The tops of their bodies leaned in against each other, forming a soft, undulating pyramid.

What others? I tried to ask, but the connection had been cut. As easily as they had entered, they left. They were done speaking with me.

"What others?" I demanded aloud. An arm extended out of my escort and latched onto my shoulder. "I want to know what others!"

I ran through the videos, recalled this time from my own memory. The sixteen men were fighting and falling, like rabid animals that had to be put down. Twenty-one of us had survived the destruction of the Earth, only to die shortly after. The corner-dwellers—my friends—were gone, not even recorded. I felt my legs weakening, two towers ready to collapse. My mind shifted at that moment, warped, for the first time, unable to bring levity to the truth I knew. I was it. I was the last man. The last human. And now… Now I was to be disposed of or left to ponder out my lonely existence in some glass cubicle in space. Not in a lab or an ark, but in a zoo of sorts. Me and the hippo side-by-side, on display for the plastic bag people.

In my mind, I raced out of the auditorium, down the hallway. I dashed into the bay, and leaped out of the ship, launching myself freefall to wherever the Earth was now, a million miles away, a million billion pieces. I swam in an ocean of things-that-will-never-be-again. My house, my city, my town and country. Everything that was familiar, even the containers. My life. The goddamn Bee Gees!

"WHAT OTHERS?!" I screamed and finding relief again in that howling. I screamed it louder. "WHAT OTHERS?! WHAT OTHERS?! WHAT OTHERS?!"

Easy came a voice, the captor's beside me. It attempted to intrude another short clip into my thoughts.

"No!" I yelled, grabbing my head. I didn't want it. I didn't want *their* talk or *their* images. I didn't want *them* inside me. Not anymore. I wanted people.

Watch, forced the captor. *Watch.*

No, I tried. *No.*

He held me up as the video bore into my conscience.

A brown horse crashed into my sight, jerking and whinnying, its legs kicking and its head shaking. It reminded me of Barry's video, except the horse's handlers were the same as those at any fairgrounds—a set of well-trained humans dancing about the animal, intricately touching, talking, and calming. The picture panned out. It was a scene I'd witnessed dozens of times on television. The animal was not being led to the slaughterhouse or to some distant pasture, but to a derby gate, hurting only itself by struggling.

Easy, the captor thought again. I watched as the horse settled in the gate, preparing to run, focused on what was in front of it. The rider and the handlers soothed it, and brought its terrified body to a level of peace visible in every muscle.

I'm not a damn horse! I sent.

True, the captor thought back. *But horses will survive.*

Horses will?

I snapped around to face the captor, my hand clenching at my side. Like dough, like dough, I seethed, preparing to thrash at the murky form. Its mist rolled in gentle waves across its front, curling up to where a face might be. Sure enough, one began to form. But not just one, an amalgam of many. I recognized in it the features of a hundred people I'd known, some loved, and some not.

Stay out, I begged. *Stay out of my thoughts.*

The faces went through another short series, changing bone structures to become other people I used to know. Was it choosing their expressions? Was it forcing them to look caringly at me?

Stop, I commanded. *Stop.*

Slowly, they dissolved, and with it, too, my anger. I could feel my escort's hand again on my shoulder. My fist was relaxed.

The others, I thought to him. *The others...*

Somehow, after I said this, I sensed that my escort looked off toward its own kind, the three captors remaining in the auditorium, its "others." The form slipped away from me for a moment and melded effortlessly with the pyramid. They shared in some silent meditation together and then my escort nudged me gently onward. Wordlessly, I obeyed, trudging slowly out of the room.

We walked on for several minutes in silence, the only sound the faint, eternal humming of the ship and the slapping of my feet on the floor. Eventually the hallway ended in a set of double doors, easily ten or twelve feet high, as solid and impenetrable as a fortress entrance. An arm formed out of the captor's mist, and it worked another colored panel. The doors opened, and, taking a deep breath, I stepped inside.

There were no containers. There was no lab. The space was outfitted like a college dormitory room on some exotic campus. Five beds stood side by side, along with tables, piles of books, and things to write and draw with, all set on a flat, wood-like surface. Beyond these were grasslands and small hills, a body of water and trees. Yes, bushes and shrubs, too. The contents of the other containers. I listened and heard the faint chirp of birds. I was almost cheered by this.

"They put the rhinos elsewhere," someone suddenly said beside me. The accent was thickly South American. I turned and saw Borges, smiling, jovial. He slapped two hands on my shoulders and kissed both sides of my face in welcome.

"*Hola,*" he baritoned, tapping his chest. "*Me llamo Arturo.*"

I pulled away from him, shocked. "Arturo? Ar-tur-o?"

"Arturo," he repeated. "Same in Spanish or English. Slow or fast. Arturo."

"Not Borges?"

"Who's Borges?" he asked.

Borges was my friend. Borges was the man I knew in the containers before my mind leapt from the ship. Who's Borges? The question is, who's Arturo? I imagined Arturos with mustaches, thin ones that raced out to their cheeks, and maybe sharp, black leather boots or sneakers with really firm soles. I could see an Arturo cutting in front of me in line at the grocery store or waving a cowboy hat atop a mustang. No, Borges fit him better—middle-aged, stocky. Why did he have to be Arturo? Why did he have to be the only Arturo?

Arturo cleared his throat, his face raised in expectation.

"Oh, sorry," I mumbled. "My name is Michael."

His smile sank. "Michael?" he asked.

"Michael," I repeated indignantly. "Mi-chael."

"Not Wilford?"

Wilford! "Who's Wilford?" I asked. Was he serious? Wilfords are slight of build. They wear glasses, and have blonde hair. I didn't look like a Wilford.

When Arturo mumbled something I couldn't hear, I kicked the ground.

We stood there, not looking up, not talking for a minute, lost. Then I remembered something. The Bee Gees. "I made the other guys think my name was Miranda," I said, cracking a smile.

His face brightened slightly. "Miranda?"

"Yes," I nodded.

He tapped his chest again, like he had moments ago, and said proudly, "Evita."

"No!" I cheered. "Evita?"

"Si!" he yelled and launched, off-key, dramatically into the lyrics from the musical.

The final note droned on like a sick crane. We started laughing and the sound was like a fire inside us, bubbling, boiling, breaking apart some resistance we had held. It shook us from our feet to the top of our heads, and at long last, when it felt like the laughter might go on forever, we switched almost imperceptibly to weeping. Both of us. The tears coursed through humor, sadness, regret, and finally subsided into camaraderie. When it did, we dried our eyes on our shirts, looked again at each other, and smiled, relieved.

"Arturo," I said.

"Michael," he beamed. Then he wrapped his arm over my shoulder and led me to the tables. "The others will be here soon. They are out in the preserve."

The others... The last men.

The others, a voice intruded. I turned around to see my captor, my savior, bow graciously out of my new home.

Neigh, I thought to it.

I swear it looked at me amused for a moment before departing.

Going Home
by
Kodilynn Calhoun

We stand in line like zombies, one after the other, waiting for the Cure, a deadly cocktail in a little glass package. The other werewolves actually *want* this. They call it freedom. I call it insanity. They think it will be better on the other side. They want to be Cured. They want to be human again, just like they once were, once upon a time. Before the bite. Before *I* changed them. Don't they know that they're perfect the way they are? *Don't do this.*

But they want it. They chose this, even though it no longer feels like a choice.

Bekka and I are the last in line, which stretches on forever between buildings of steel and glass that blot out the sun. She's holding my hand, her fingers squeezing mine. Anxiety drips from her, a sickly sweet stench. I try not to breathe through my nose. My inner-wolf is pacing below the surface of my skin, wanting out. Wanting to run. I can't help it. This is insanity. I don't want to be like the rest of them—powerless, weak Fleshlings who use guns and knives to protect themselves. Not when I have claws and teeth. Not when I have an army at my command. *But you don't have an army anymore. Do you, Camden? They all want the Cure.*

The line moves quicker than I'd like. Each step forwards makes my heart sink further and further in my chest. Dread is like cotton in my throat. I turn to run, but the soldiers behind me, with their guns probably packed with silver, stop me. The humans want us gone, just like all the other wild ones they've killed off. The Kumazi, a pride of jaguar shifters in the neighboring canyon, are now nearly extinct. We are competition to humans and I hate them. What have I ever done to them?

Bekka squeezes my hand again, pulling me towards her, her wolf-gold eyes pleading for me to stay. *Please stay, please behave, Camden. No more Changing. No more fighting. We'll have a good life together; please listen to me...*

I want to snarl at her. *We'll be mortal. Don't you see that? Can you really imagine a life without hunting, without the feel of the summer wind against your fur? Do you really think becoming human will change anything? You still lost the baby. We lost our son. It's not like the Cure will bring him back.* My mind reels and I jerk away from her touch, angry with myself. How can I be so cold? She is my life-mate, the only female I've ever loved. *It's not cruel unless you say it out loud.*

One by one, werewolves step into a building of steel through black doors that open and shut like the gates of Falla, the Barrenlands—wolf hell. After what seems like an eternity, the doors open again, and the next wolf is escorted inside by two burly guards in black, with guns in holsters at their sides. I watch the soldiers; hatred for the humans balls in my stomach like a rock-hard fist. My brethren will emerge from the building Cured. Human. Bastard traitors. *We had something good. We had Pack. Family. Wasn't that enough?*

Mirra is next in line. She's pregnant and has staved off the Change for three moons in order to keep the wolf child in her womb. *"I want my baby to survive, Camden."* We both knew she couldn't keep from Changing for the rest of her term. She would slip up and lose control, losing the child like Bekka lost hers.

The door slides open with an electronic buzz. Mirra jerks back as if stung, but the men in black drag her in. They treat her like she is an animal, grasping and tugging at her arms. I know she's strong enough to get away. *You just have to want it, Mirra. Please want it. Break away from them. Change—become wolf and run.* She catches my eye; her gaze is filled with panic as she's pulled through those doors. They shut and seal her within. The other soldiers remain on the outside with the rest of us.

"Things will be all right, Camden," Bekka's voice is in my ear, distracting me. She tilts her face up to mine and kisses me on the lips, gentle, chaste. I groan and pull away. "Please. It's our time. Being human won't be so bad. Think of all the new memories we'll be able to create. Together, Camden. We'll still be together."

"And then in forty years or so, we die. The end." I glower. I am immortal. As long as I'm not intentionally killed, I will keep on living. I don't want to die. I'm afraid of death; where do you go when you die? Besides, I want to live as long as the woods, as long as the moon and the rivers and the forests where we make our home. *Please don't do this. Don't take this away from me.* But the humans will. They don't care about what we want. They never have. We are beasts in their eyes. Animals. *I'll show you an animal.*

But I don't.

We stand there, silence lapsing over us.

Then it's Bekka's turn. She reaches for my hand. I take it, squeezing. Reassuring her when all I want to do is turn and run and risk being shot, just to be free. To feel the wind in my fur again, one more time. *Damnit, let me go...* But in freedom, I would be *alone.* Once Bekka goes in there, I will be the last wolf standing. I was alone once. But that was a very long time ago, before magic was recognized or accepted as normal, back when I had to hide what I was from everyone. I never want to be alone again.

I take a deep breath. The doors slide open, agonizingly fast. I can see a long hall of tile floors and empty walls. There's another door at the end. A black door. The Cure is beyond that door; I know this with dread in my heart. There is no longer a line of werewolves, just empty space.

The faint, sickly stench of death is covered up by a medicinal odor. It's probably undetectable to human senses, but my lupine nose picks it up. The wolf inside rebels and I rein it in, but not before glancing between the group of men and their guns. *Can I kill them? Kill them and run? Could we get out of the building, back to the woods? Back home?*

The hair on the back of my neck prickles. *Run. Get away.* Bekka lets out an anguished growl as two soldiers try to hustle her through the doors. I can feel her wolf lurking below the surface as she twists, reaching for me. She's on the verge of Changing; her pupils are mere pinpricks of black against gold, a patch of dark fur sprouts down her nose, which is already elongating into a muzzle. "Camden," she calls.

Even though I'm terrified, scared of what I'll become once I get Cured—if there is such a thing—I can't let this happen. I cling to my wife. I can't let her go inside alone. A group of soldiers crowd around us, so close that I can smell the sweat on their brows. "I will go with her." No turning back now. It's a one-way street.

"You'll have your turn." A soldier jabs my side with the gun stock.

I bare jagged wolf teeth, letting the Change morph my face. A thick wolf snout covered in fur the color of spun gold springs from my nose with a crack of bone. I open my mouth and let loose a low, threatening growl. The soldier jerks back.

I want to go with Bekka, into that room with the black door. She tries to stay with me. I feel the soldiers' hands on my arms, as if Fleshlings like them could hold me back. In this moment, I *feel* animal. I feel trapped. The soldiers exchange a look. "We could always shoot him now."

They chuckle among themselves for a moment before a short guy in a white lab coat hurries down the hall towards us. It's Dr. North—the man who invented the Cure. I recognize the doctor's face from the news. "What's the hold up?"

I step forwards, moving against the soldiers' hold on me, my eyes narrowing at the doctor. I pull the wolf back inside, the Change subsiding. As a human, I've got a baby face and fine, gold hair. Hardly threatening. "I want to come too. She's not going in there alone."

North eyes me over a pair of wire-rimmed glasses, then shrugs. "Hurry up. I don't have all day." He turns away. The big guys in black hustle us after him. The rest of the soldiers go back outside. The doors shut, sealing us in that hallway.

Bekka holds my hand tightly. The smell only gets thicker, making my stomach churn as the black door at the end of the hall swings inwards. One man gives Bekka a shove and she stumbles through the doorway. Anger soars in my gut and I turn on the man with a snarl. The Change overtakes me rapidly, bones crunching and realigning, flesh stretching taught over muscle. In the blink of an eye, I'm covered in thick, blond fur. My fangs sink into his wrist before I can stop and think about what I'm doing.

A shot goes off.

Pain explodes in my thigh and I drop back, cradling my injured limb against the warmth of my stomach. Blood streaks down my leg and drips onto the floor, forming a pool of crimson. I keep waiting for the burn of silver, but it never comes. The men in black have a regular, everyday arsenal of bullets. I wonder how many shots my body could take before I'd die of blood loss. Bekka's at my side, smoothing down my fur. Fury burns inside me and I snap at her without thinking, and lunge my wolf-body at the man with the gun. *I will end this.* She wraps both arms around me, holding me back. She is the only one in the room that can stop me. I don't *want* to be stopped, but I collapse into her lap.

That's when I glance around me.

We're surrounded by corpses, piled high, staring at us with glassy, dead eyes. Familiar eyes—the eyes of my fellow Packmates, my wolves. The only family I've ever known. I see Ulrich, my best friend, and Mack, the man I Changed to heal the cancer killing his human body long ago. Closest to me is Mirra, her belly round with the child she'd tried so hard to keep alive. Now the baby will never be born. How could the humans do this? My heart feels like it's tearing in two.

Bekka lets out a strangled sob. I gaze up, into the face of the man I'd bitten. In a matter of days, he will become one of us, the very thing he hates. A wolf. I want to laugh. Instead I growl and struggle to stand. *You killed them. All of them… They* trusted *you. They believed with all of their hearts that you'd Cure them.*

The bitten man doesn't have a chance to run through the woods or have a taste of freedom. The other guard turns on him. He stares the gun down, but it doesn't change the end result. He lands with a thud on the floor, his blood seeping out to mingle with mine like a long-lost lover. Behind us, Dr. North clears his throat and Bekka spins on him.

"I thought you were going to Cure them." Her voice is fragile, thin like moth-wings. "What happened to *saving* them?"

"The Cure…reacted badly." He pushes his glasses higher up on his nose.

"To all of them?" I'm human once more, reaching for Bekka, holding onto her like she's my lifeline. She's all I have left.

"Unfortunately, yes, a shame," the doctor begins. "A few of them would've made descent humans." He laughs then. "But it has to be done. Come here, wolf." He points at Bekka.

The guard grabs Bekka's wrist, wrenching her away from me and he gives her a shove towards the doctor. She lets out a wild scream. I can feel her wolf pacing the surface, begging to be let out. *No. Not Bekka.*

"I'll give you the same choice I gave all of them," North says. "The Cure or a bullet in your brain. Pick one."

Bekka spits in his face. North jerks back in surprise, wiping it away with a sleeve. The remaining guard is reaching for his walkie-talkie, pressing down a little red button. "We need backup—" Before he can finish, Bekka turns on him, ignoring the gun aimed at her and she Changes in mid-lunge. Her slender body shortens, hands and feet turning into large paws, tailbone lengthening to form a tail. Like a shutter flash, she's covered with a coat of black fur. The guard hits the ground. The gun goes off and fires blindside, spinning across the tile, stopping against the pile of wolf corpses.

I lunge for the gun. So does the doctor. He gets there first, cocking it and shoving the barrel against my forehead. "Back off." His voice is thick, a hint of fear lurking there, but he's otherwise confident. I raise my hands with a growl, turning back for Bekka.

Bekka's black form hovers over the guard, paws on either side of his waist. Her muzzle jerks back and forth, a long trail of intestine hanging from her jaws. She pulls, sending it flying in an arc across the room. It lands at the doctor's feet with a splatter of blood. The guard's hands are flailing weakly, beating at her.

"Bekka." My voice is commanding. She spins on me, the wild in her eyes easing. She eyes the doctor and his gun, no doubt sizing up the situation. She begins to pace; a growl rumbles in her throat. She pauses and locks eyes with the doctor. He turns the gun on her.

The door slams open and seven soldiers hustle in; their guns shine under the fluorescent lights. Seven pinhole red lasers light up Bekka's black fur and there's a series of clicking as they cock their weapons.

Bekka freezes, suddenly wary. I step forwards, a growl on my lips but I bite it off. There's no way out of this. One wrong move and we'll be shot full of silver, our flesh sizzling as the acidic bullets burn us from the inside out. It would be a slow, agonizing death. I turn to Bekka. "Change back."

The Change is quick. Soon, Bekka is stumbling into my arms, her eyes dull from the shift's wear on her body, her dark hair spilling over her shoulders in tangles. I shoot a glare at North, who holds up a little glass bottle. It's filled with a murky, blue liquid. He places the bottle into the top of an injection gun with a needle tip.

Without further delay, the doctor presses the needle against Bekka's arm. She squirms. I can see she doesn't want this. "You were brave to attack them like that," I whisper in her ear. A ghost of a smile touches her lips as the Cure bleeds through her veins.

We wait for many minutes, me holding her, rocking her like I would've rocked our child. Bekka begins to whimper. I feel pain wash through her aura, smell the agony on her skin. Her wolf is writhing. She begins to plead with Fenrir, as if that will do any good. She's so hot, she's burning up. The Cure is burning the wolf out.

"You can do it, baby. You can make it." We ease to the ground. My wounded leg gives a throb of indignance.

"Don't leave me…"

"I'll never leave you." I hold her tightly, kissing her hair. "I'm sorry. I'm sorry I blamed you for our son's death. It wasn't your fault. It was never your fault." She seizes in my grip, once, twice and with one last shudder, falls still. Blood seeps from her nose, smearing on my shirt. The smell of death overtakes her natural, earthy smell. She's dead. It's too late. *My Bekka. No…*

A howl of agony builds and rips from my throat. I cling to her body. *Not Bekka. Please.* The lasers light up my chest as the soldiers shift their weight. They glance between me and North, but the doctor waves them off, and they lower their guns once more. North turns to me, touching my shoulder, but hesitantly, as if he might catch my disease. "You're the last one."

I am. I'm the last werewolf. The last of the Pack. I look up at the guns staring me in the face. No chance of escape. Pain thrums in my chest. It's my turn to pick now, pick my choice of death. My heart twists. My family is gone. Bekka is gone. He's killed them all and for what? The glory of the fact that he created a Cure for the werewolf disease?

Anger boils in my stomach, rising like bile in my throat. I lunge at North with a roar, curved claws sprouting from my fingertips. I'll rip him to shreds! My claws graze the surface of his throat as I'm jerked back. Fingers dig roughly into my skin. I scream and struggle, but the soldiers hold me back. They force my arms to my sides. Why haven't they shot me yet? Then North, his face ashen, quickly reloads the injection gun and forces the poison into my veins.

I'm warm now, getting hotter by the second. As my temperature soars, I wish that the arms holding me down were the arms of my brethren, filling me with love instead of with anger. Pain rockets through me, like I'm being set on fire and stuck with pins and needles all at once. Tears prick in my eyes. I hold them back, fists tight at my sides. Was this how Bekka felt? *Save me. Someone save me.* I feel myself spasm, my muscles twitching and jerking.

It's worse than my first Change, all those years ago. At the time, I never thought anything could be worse.

Nausea grips me and I gag, retching over and over until all that's left is bile and foam. With a moan, I sag against the arms that are holding me. They drop me to the floor, where I land on my side in the mess I've made. What does it matter? I'm as good as dead. I press my eyes closed to ward off the double vision. *Take me away. I'm ready.*

Death is painless. Suddenly, I'm standing in a room, with blinding sunlight peering through the windows. The walls are so white they almost glow. The room radiates a sense of peace and love. The pack is all around me, welcoming me home with hoops and hollers. I see Ulrich with his dark hair and ornery eyes, grinning his trademark grin. Mirra pulls me into a one-armed hug, her baby in the other arm, giggling gently. Then there's Bekka. I run for her. She meets me halfway and we collide into each other's arms. I brush dark hair away from her face, and cup her chin in my hands. "I told you I wouldn't leave you."

"I know." Her smile is tender, sweet.

"Oh Bekka, I love you."

Then my vision goes black.

My eyes flutter open. I find myself staring up into the shocked face of the doctor who thought he had killed me. The soldiers in the doorway look curiously my way. "Bekka?" My voice slurs. I struggle to sit. Pain... No. Something's wrong. *No. I want to go back. Take me* back*!* I collapse against the tile once more. *No. No. No.*

"You survived it?" North leans over, checking my pulse.

Bekka's corpse stares at me with empty gold eyes, taunting me. She's dead and I'm alive.

"Did it work?" I ask.

"What?"

"Did The Cure work? Is the wolf gone?"

The wolf. The wolf's my last chance. Once they see that their Cure failed, they will kill me, just like they killed the others. Closing my eyes, I will the beast to cover me with its fur. I will the wolf to rise, to take my body as its own. *Come to me.*

It never comes.

I sag and keep trying, over and over again. Nothing. No wolf. Frustration blinds me. My hands ball into fists. "No…" The Cure has done its job. But Bekka is dead. *Bekka.* "No!" I am no longer werewolf. I am human. I am all alone.

"It worked... It actually worked. This will make the press. Local Scientist Cures the Werewolf Disease." The doctor is prancing around in a dance and I stare at him, anger rising again, though it's not as fierce without the wolf's force behind it. *This is what you wanted. You wanted to be alive. You wanted to be free.*

This isn't freedom...

"You're a free man." North waves his hand dismissively, slipping his pistol into the waistband of his pants. The soldiers glance at me, wary, as if they don't believe I'm human. Then, one by one, they leave the room. The door shuts behind them, leaving me with the doctor, who is smiling at me, smiling like we're old friends, as if he didn't just kill my family. For a moment, his grin reminds me of Ulrich's. It sends a new rush of anger to the surface, but I keep my face carefully blank.

I drag myself to my feet. My leg threatens to buckle under my weight, the pain reminding me that I'm still wounded—I am human now. No more werewolf speed-healing. I sway where I stand. I glance around at all the corpses, my gaze lingering on Bekka's form before I look to the doctor. North meets my gaze as he packs up what little equipment he brought with him. "You're free to go home," he says.

Home. I don't have a home to return to. We lived in the woods as wolves. Animals. Besides, even if I did go back and build a cottage there, it would never be home. Not without Bekka. Wolves mate for life and even though I'm human now, I'm wolf at heart. I will always have the animal inside of me.

He took my family from me.

Without a word, I step forwards, reaching for his gun before he realizes what I'm doing. The pistol feels heavy, solid in my hand and my fingers wrap around it. I click back the safety, cock it and raise it. North's eyes are wide; his mouth is flapping open to shout a warning—to whom? The soldiers aren't in the room anymore. They won't hear his call through the heavy black door and even if they hear the shot, by the time they get back here, it will be too late.

My lips twist into a cold smile as the gun goes off, the crack making my ears ring. The bullet makes a perfect little hole between North's eyes, which roll up in his head. He drops to his knees slowly, pitches forward, and lands in a puddle of blood.

I could've gone home if I wanted. I could've let North live and walked out of here, down the hall and out those little sliding doors and the soldiers wouldn't have stopped me because now, I'm no different than them. But home is with Bekka.

I look down at the gun in my hand. *I'll be there in a second, Bekka. Wait for me. I'm coming home.*

Life Gaped Open
by
Alan Gann

When suns bleed will you cry
for a skyscraper, a cockroach, a bell,
for a handful of dirt, a weight of wool?
Will you weave hammer, anvil and forge,
pocket watch, vapors, a shallow sea?

When you cannot bathe in the vile creek,
with your swollen eyes, scaly nostrils,
gnarled lips unable to spit or laugh—

when your whole life gapes open
and reveals itself a fraud,
will you unlock the ancient trunk and find
rough-cut remnants of dream and quilt—
will you take needle and thread,
and mend rent cloth grateful
that bulbous eyes cannot see the stitches?

The Scarlet Plague
by
Jack London

I.

The path led along what had once been the embankment of a railroad, but no train had run on it for many years. The forest on either side of the track swelled up the slopes of the embankment and crested across it in a green wave of trees and bushes. The trail was as narrow as a man's body and was no more than a wild-animal runway. Occasionally, a piece of rusty iron, showing through the forest mold, advertised that the rail and the ties still remained. As old as the road was, it was manifest that it had once been of the mono-rail type.

An old man and a boy traveled along the path. They moved slowly, for the old man was very old, a touch of palsy made his movements tremulous, and he leaned heavily upon his staff. A rude skull-cap of goat-skin protected his head from the sun. From beneath this fell a scant fringe of stained and dirty-white hair. A visor, ingeniously made from a large leaf, shielded his eyes. His beard, no longer snow-white, tangled, and reaching nearly to his waist, showed the same weather-wear and camp-stain as his hair. About his chest and shoulders hung a single, mangy garment of goat-skin. His arms and legs, withered and skinny, sunburned, scarred, and scratched, hinted at his extreme age and long years of exposure to the elements.

The boy, who led the way, checking the eagerness of his muscles in comparison to the slow progress of his elder, likewise wore a single garment: a ragged-edged piece of bear-skin, with a hole in the middle for his head. He couldn't have been more than twelve years old. Tucked over one ear was the freshly-severed tail of a pig. In one hand, he carried a medium-sized bow and an arrow. On his back was a quiver full of arrows. From a sheath hanging about his neck on a thong projected the battered handle of a hunting knife. He was as brown as a berry and walked softly, with almost a catlike tread. As he went along, he smelled things, endless messages from the outside world. His hearing was acute and operated automatically, missing none of the sounds of the wind rustling the leaves, of the humming of bees and gnats, of the distant rumble of the sea that drifted to him only in lulls, or of the gopher shoving a clump of earth into the entrance of his hole underfoot.

Suddenly, the boy became alert and tense. Sound, sight, and odor had given him a simultaneous warning. His hand went back to the old man, and the pair stood still. Ahead, at one side of the top of the embankment arose a crackling sound, and the boy's gaze was fixed on the tops of the bushes. Then, a large grizzly bear crashed into view, stopped abruptly at the sight of the humans, and commenced growling.

Slowly, the boy fitted the arrow to the bow and pulled the bowstring taut, never removing his eyes from the bear.

The old man peered out from under his hat at the danger. Then, the bear betrayed a growing irritability, and the boy, with a movement of his head, indicated that the old man must step aside from the trail and go down the embankment. The boy followed, going backward, still holding the bow ready. They waited ‘til a crashing among the bushes from the opposite side of the embankment told them the bear had gone on. The boy grinned and led the man back to the trail.

"A big un, Granser," he chuckled.

The old man shook his head.

"They get thicker every day." the old man complained in a thin, undependable falsetto. "Who'd have thought I'd live to see the time when a man would be afraid of his life on the way to the Cliff House. When I was a boy, Edwin, men and women and little babies used to come out here from San Francisco by tens of thousands on a nice day. And there weren't any bears then. No, sir. They used to pay money to look at them in cages, bears were so rare."

"What is money, Granser?"

Before the old man could answer, the boy recollected something and triumphantly shoved his hand into a pouch under his bearskin to reveal a battered and tarnished silver dollar. The old man's eyes glistened at the sight of it.

"I can't see," he muttered. "Look and see if you can make out the date, Edwin."

The boy laughed.

"You're a great Granser," he cried delightedly, "always making believe them little marks mean something."

The old man manifested an accustomed chagrin as he lifted the coin close to his own eyes.

"2012," he shrilled and then chuckled. "That was the year

Morgan the Fifth was appointed President of the United States by the Board of Magnates. It must've been one of the last coins minted, for the Scarlet Death came in 2013. Lord, think of it! Sixty years ago, and I am the only person alive today that lived in those times. Where did you find it, Edwin?"

The boy answered promptly. "I got it off of Hoo-Hoo. He found it when we was herdin' goats down near San José last spring. Hoo-Hoo said it was *money.* Ain't you hungry, Granser?"

The ancient man caught his staff in a tighter grip and urged himself along the trail, his old eyes shining greedily. "I hope Har-Lip 's found a crab... or two," he mumbled. "They're good eating, crabs, mighty good eating when you've no more teeth and you've got grandsons that love their old grandsire and make a point of catching crabs for him. When I was a boy..."

But Edwin, stopped by what he saw ahead, was drawing the bowstring on a fitted arrow. He had paused on the brink of a crevasse in the embankment. An ancient culvert had washed out, and the stream had cut a passage through the fill. Beyond, crouching by a bush, a rabbit looked across at him in trembling hesitancy. Fifty feet was the distance, but the arrow flashed true, and the transfixed rabbit, crying out in sudden fright and hurt, struggled painfully away into the brush. The boy himself was a flash of brown skin and flying fur as he bounded down the steep wall of the gap and up the other side. A hundred feet beyond, in a tangle of bushes, he overtook the wounded creature, knocked its head on a convenient tree-trunk and turned it over to Granser to carry.

"Why do you say so much that ain't got no sense?" Edwin impatiently interrupted. His speech showed distant kinship with that of the old man, and the latter's speech was approximately an English that had gone through a bath of corrupt usage.

"What I want to know," Edwin continued, "is why you call crab 'toothsome delicacy?' Crab is crab, ain't it? I never heard no one call it such funny things."

The old man sighed and did not answer, and they moved on in silence.

The surf grew louder as they emerged from the forest upon a stretch of sand dunes bordering the sea. A few goats were browsing among the sandy hillocks, and a skin-clad boy, aided by a wolfish-looking dog that was only faintly reminiscent of a collie, was watching them. Mingled with the roar of the surf was a continuous, deep-throated barking or bellowing, which came from a cluster of jagged rocks a hundred yards out from shore. Here, huge sea lions hauled themselves up to lie in the sun or battle with one another. In the immediate foreground arose the smoke of a fire, tended by a third savage-looking boy. Crouched near him were several wolfish dogs similar to the one that guarded the goats.

The old man accelerated his pace, sniffing eagerly as he neared the fire. "Mussels!" he muttered ecstatically. "Mussels! And ain't that a crab, Hoo-Hoo? Ain't that a crab? My, my, you boys are good to your old grandsire."

Hoo-Hoo, who was apparently of the same age as Edwin, grinned.

"All you want, Granser. I got four."

The old man's palsied eagerness was pitiful. Sitting down in the sand, he poked a large rock-mussel from out of the coals. The heat had forced its shells apart, and the meat, salmon-colored, was thoroughly cooked. Between thumb and forefinger, he caught the morsel and carried it to his mouth, but it was too hot and was violently ejected in the next moment. The old man spluttered with the pain, and tears ran out of his eyes and down his cheeks.

The boys were true savages, possessing only the cruel humor of the uncivilized. To them, the incident was excruciatingly funny, and they burst into loud laughter. Hoo-Hoo danced up and down while Edwin rolled gleefully on the ground. The boy with the goats came running to join in the fun.

"Set 'em to cool, Edwin, set 'em to cool," the old man prodded in the midst of his grief, making no attempt to wipe away the tears that flowed from his eyes. "And cool a crab, Edwin, too. You know your grandsire likes crabs."

From the coals arose a great sizzling, which proceeded from the many mussels bursting open their shells and exuding their moisture. They were large shellfish, running from three to six inches in length. The boys raked them out with sticks and placed them on a large piece of driftwood to cool.

"When I was a boy, we did not laugh at our elders, we respected them."

The boys took no notice, and Granser continued to babble an incoherent flow of complaint and censure. This time he was more careful when he selected a mussel and did not burn his mouth. All began to eat, using nothing but their hands and making loud mouth-noises and lip-smackings. The third boy, who was called Hare-Lip, slyly deposited a pinch of sand on the mussel the old man was carrying to his mouth, and when the grit of it hit the old fellow's mucous membrane and gums, the boys' laughter was again uproarious. Granser was unaware that a joke had been played on him, and he spluttered and spat until Edwin, relenting, gave him a gourd of fresh water to wash out his mouth.

"Where's them crabs, Hoo-Hoo?" Edwin demanded. "Granser's set upon having a snack."

Again, Granser's eyes burned with greediness as a large crab was handed to him. It was a shell complete with legs, but the meat had long since departed. With shaky fingers, the old man broke off a leg and found it filled with emptiness.

"The crabs, Hoo-Hoo?" he wailed. "The crabs?"

"I was foolin', Granser. They ain't no crabs. I never found one."

The boys were overwhelmed with delight at the sight of the tears of senile disappointment that dribbled down the old man's cheeks. Then, unnoticed, Hoo-Hoo replaced the empty shell with a fresh-cooked crab.

The change of the old man's mood to one of joy was immediate. He snuffled and muttered and mumbled, making almost a croon of delight, as he began to eat. Of this, the boys took little notice, for it was an accustomed spectacle. Nor did they notice his occasional exclamations and utterances of phrases, which meant nothing to them, as, for instance, when he smacked his lips while muttering: "Mayonnaise! Just think, mayonnaise! And it's sixty years since the last was ever made! Two generations and never a smell of it! Why, in those days it was served crab in every restaurant." When he could eat no more, the old man sighed, wiped his hands on his naked legs, and gazed out over the sea, content with a full stomach.

"To think of it! I've seen this beach alive with men, women, and children on a pleasant Sunday. And there weren't any bears to eat them up, either. And right up there on the cliff was a big restaurant where you could get anything you wanted to eat. Four million people lived in San Francisco then. And now, in the whole city and county, there aren't forty all together. And out there on the sea, there were always ships to be seen going toward the Golden Gate or coming out. And airships in the air, dirigibles and flying machines. They could travel two hundred miles an hour. The mail contracts with the New York and San Francisco Limited lines demanded that for the minimum. There was a chap, a Frenchman, I forget his name, who succeeded in making three hundred, but it was risky, too risky for conservative persons. But he was on the right track, and he would've managed it if it hadn't been for the Great Plague. When I was a boy, there were men alive who remembered the coming of the first airplanes, and now I have lived to see the last of them, and that was sixty years ago."

The old man babbled on, unheeded by the boys, who were long accustomed to his garrulousness and proclamations that lacked the greater portion of the words he was trying to say. It was noticeable that in these rambling soliloquies, his English seemed to recrudesce into better construction and phraseology, but when he talked directly with the boys, it lapsed, largely, into their own uncouth and simpler forms.

"But there weren't many crabs in those days," the old man rambled on. "They were fished out, and they were great delicacies. The open season was only a month long, too. And now crabs are accessible during the whole year. Think of it, catching all the crabs you want, any time you want, in the surf of the Cliff House beach!"

A sudden commotion among the goats brought the boys to their feet. The dogs around the fire rushed to join their snarling fellow guarding the goats, while the goats, themselves, stampeded in the direction of their human protectors. A half-dozen forms, lean and gray, glided on the sand hillocks or faced the bristling dogs. Edwin arched an arrow that fell short, but Hare-Lip hurled a stone through the air, whistling from the speed of its flight. It fell squarely among the wolves and caused them to slink away toward the dark depths of the eucalyptus forest.

The boys laughed and laid down again in the sand while Granser sighed ponderously. He had eaten too much, and, with hands clasped on his paunch, the fingers interlaced, he resumed his maunderings.

"'The fleeting systems lapse like foam,'" he mumbled what was evidently a quotation. "That's it—foam, and fleeting. All man's toil upon the planet was so much foam. He domesticated the serviceable animals, destroyed the hostile ones, and cleared the land of its wild vegetation. And then he passed, and the flood of primordial life rolled back again, sweeping his handiwork away; the weeds and the forest inundated his fields, the beasts of prey swept over his flocks, and now there are wolves on the Cliff House beach." He was appalled by the thought. "Where four million people planted themselves, the wild wolves roam today, and the savage progeny of our loins, with prehistoric weapons, defend themselves against the fanged despoilers. Think of it, and all because of the Scarlet Death."

The adjective had caught Hare-Lip's ear.

"He's always saying that," he said to Edwin. "What is scarlet?"

"'The scarlet of the maples can shake me like the cry of bugles going by,' " the old man quoted.

"It's red." Edwin answered the question. "And you don't know it because you come from the Chauffeur Tribe. They never did know nothing, none of them. Scarlet is red. I know that."

"Red is red, ain't it?" Hare-Lip grumbled. "Then what's the good of gettin' cocky and calling it scarlet?"

"Granser, why do you always say so much about what nobody knows?" he asked. "Scarlet ain't anything, but red is red. Why don't you say red, then?"

"Red is not the right word," was the reply. "The plague was scarlet. The whole face and body turned scarlet in a hour's time. Don't I know? Didn't I see enough of it? I'm telling you it was scarlet because, well, because it was scarlet. There is no other word for it."

"Red is good enough for me," Hare-Lip muttered obstinately. "My dad calls red like it is, and he ought to know. He says everybody died of the Red Death."

"Your dad is a common fellow, descended from a common fellow," Granser retorted heatedly. "Don't I know the beginnings of the Chauffeurs? Your grandsire was a chauffeur, a servant, and without education. He worked for other persons. But your grandmother was of good stock, only the children did not take after her. Don't I remember when I first met them catching fish at Lake Temescal?"

"What is education?" Edwin asked.

"Calling red *scarlet*." Hare-Lip sneered, then returned to the attack on Granser. "My dad told me, an' he got it from his dad afore he croaked, that your wife was a Santa Rosan, an' that she wasn't nothin'. He said she was a hash-slinger before the Red Death, though I don't know what a hash-slinger is. You can tell me, Edwin."

But Edwin shook his head in token of his ignorance.

"It is true, she was a waitress," Granser acknowledged. "But she was a good woman, and your mother was her daughter. Women were very scarce in the days after the Plague. She was the only wife I could find, even if she was a hash-slinger, as your father calls it. But it is not nice to talk about our progenitors that way."

"Dad says that the wife of the first Chauffeur was a *lady*—"

"What's a *lady*?" Hoo-Hoo demanded.

"A *lady's* a Chauffeur squaw," was the quick reply of Hare-Lip.

"The first Chauffeur was Bill, a common fellow, as I said before," the old man expounded. "But his wife was a lady, a great lady. Before the Scarlet Death she was the wife of Van Warden. He was President of the Board of Industrial Magnates and was one of the dozen men who ruled America. He was worth one billion, eight-hundred million dollars—coins like you have there in your pouch, Edwin. And then came the Scarlet Death, and his wife became the wife of Bill, the first Chauffeur. He used to beat her, too. I have seen it myself."

Hoo-Hoo, lying on his stomach and idly digging his toes in the sand, cried out and investigated the small hole he had dug. The other two boys joined him, excavating the sand rapidly with their hands till there lay three skeletons exposed. Two were of adults, the third being that of a part-grown child. The old man nudged himself along the ground and peered at the find.

"Plague victims," he announced. "That's the way they died everywhere in the last days. This must have been a family, running away from the contagion and perishing here on the Cliff House beach. They—what are you doing, Edwin?"

This question was asked in sudden dismay, as Edwin, using the back of his hunting knife, began to knock out the teeth from the jaws of one of the skulls.

"Going to string 'em," was the response.

The three boys were now hard at it, and knocking and hammering arose, during which Granser babbled on unnoticed.

"You are true savages. Already the custom of wearing human teeth has begun. In another generation, you will be perforating your noses and ears and wearing ornaments of bone and shell. I know. The human race is doomed to sink back farther and farther into the primitive night before it again begins its bloody climb upward to civilization. When we mate and feel a lack of room, we will proceed to kill one another. And then, I suppose you will wear human scalp-locks at your waist, as well, as you, Edwin, who are the gentlest of my grandsons, have already begun with that vile pigtail. Throw it away, Edwin, boy. Throw it away."

"What a gabble the old geezer makes," Hare-Lip remarked, when, the teeth all extracted, they began an attempt at equal division.

They were very quick and abrupt in their actions, and their speech, in moments of hot discussion over the allotment of the choicer teeth, was truly a gabble. They spoke in monosyllables and short jerky sentences that were more gibberish than a language. And yet, through it ran hints of grammatical construction vestiges of the conjugation of some superior culture. Even the speech of Granser was so corrupt that were it put down literally on paper, it would be almost too much nonsense for the reader. This, however, was when he talked with the boys. When he got into the full swing of babbling to himself, his language slowly purged itself into pure English. His sentences grew longer and were enunciated with a rhythm and ease that was reminiscent of his days at the lecture platform.

"Tell us about the Red Death, Granser," Hare-Lip demanded, when the teeth affair had been satisfactorily concluded.

"The Scarlet Death," Edwin corrected.

"An' don't work all that funny lingo on us," Hare-Lip went on. "Talk sensible, Granser, like a Santa Rosan ought to talk. Other Santa Rosans don't talk like you."

The Last of Everything
by
Cassandra Consiglio

Last of everything
by
Cassandra Consiglio

I am the last crumb of food.
I am the last tissue to blow in.
I am the last fresh breath of air.
I am the last drop of water.
I am the last man standing.
Goodbye earth,
Goodbye me.

Corridors
by
Barry N. Malzberg

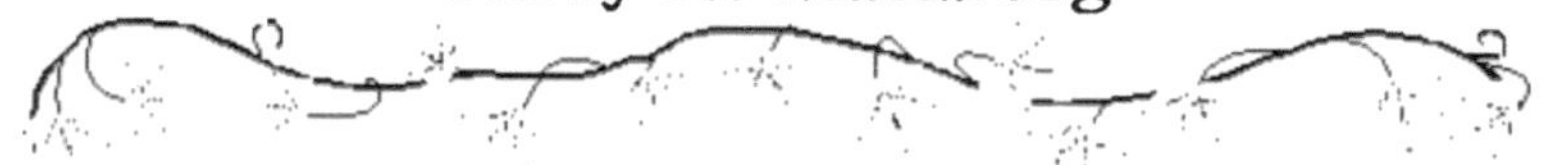

Ruthven used to have plans. Big plans: turn the category around, arrest the decline of science fiction into stereotype and cant, open up the category to new vistas and so on. So forth. Now, however, he is, at fifty-four, merely trying to hold on; he takes this retraction of ambition, understanding of his condition as the only significant change in his inner life over two decades. The rest of it—inner and outer too—has been replication, disaster, pain, recrimination, self-pity and the like: Ruthven thinks of these old partners of the law firm of his life as brothers. At least, thanks to Replication & Disaster, he has a brief for the game. He knows what he is and what has to be done, and most of the time he can sleep through the night, unlike that period in his forties when 4 A.M. more often than not would see him awake and drinking whiskey, staring at his out-of-print editions in many languages.

The series has helped. Ruthven has at last achieved a modicum of fame in science fiction and for the first time—he would not have believed this ever possible—some financial security. Based originally upon a short novel written for *Astounding* in late 1963, which he padded for quick paperback the next year, *The Sorcerer* has proven the capstone of his career. Five or six novels written subsequently at low advances for the same firm went nowhere, but: the editor was fired, the firm collapsed, releasing all rights, the editor got divorced, married a subsidiary rights director, got a consultant job with her firm, divorced her, went to a major paperback house as science fiction chief and through a continuing series of coincidences known to those who (unlike Ruthven) always seemed to come out a little ahead commissioned three new *Sorcerers* from Ruthven on fast deadline to build up cachet with the salesmen. They all had hung out at the Hydra Club together, anyway. Contracts were signed, the first of the three new *Sorcerers* (written, all of them in ten weeks) sold 150,000 copies, the second was picked up as an alternate by a demented Literary Guild and the third was leased to hardcover. Ruthven's new, high-priced agent negotiated a contract for five more *Sorcerers* for $100,000.

Within the recent half decade, Ruthven has at last made money from science fiction. One of the novels was a Hugo finalist, another was filmed. He has been twice final balloted for a Gandalf. Some of his older novels have been reprinted. Ruthven is now one of the ten most successful science fiction writers; he paid taxes on $79,000 last year. In his first two decades of the field, writing frantically and passing through a succession of dead-end jobs, Ruthven did not make $79,000.

It would be easier for him, he thinks, if he could take his success seriously or at least obtain some peace, but of this he has none. Part of it has to do with his recent insight that he is merely hanging on, that the ultimate outcome of the ultimate struggle for any writer in America not hopelessly self-deluded is to hang on; another part has to do with what Ruthven likes to think of as the accumulated damages and injuries sustained by the writing of seventy-three novels. Like a fighter long gone from the ring, the forgotten left hooks taken under the lights in all of the quick-money bouts have caught up with him and stunned his brain.

Ruthven hears the music of combat as he never did when it was going on. He has lost the contents of most of these books and even some of their titles but the pain lingers. This is self-dramatization, of course, and Ruthven has enough ironic distance to know it. No writer was ever killed by a book.

Nonetheless, he hears the music, feels the dull knives in his kidneys and occipital regions at night; Ruthven also knows that he has done nothing of worth in a long time. *The Sorcerer* is a fraud; he is far below the aspirations and intent of his earlier work, no matter how flawed that was. Most of these new books have been written reflexively under the purposeful influence of scotch and none of them possesses real quality. Even literacy. He has never been interested in these books. Ruthven is too far beyond self-delusion to think that the decline of his artistic gifts, the collapse of his promise, means anything *either.* Nothing means anything except holding on as he now knows. Nonetheless, he *used* to feel that the quality of the work made some difference. Didn't he? Like the old damages of the forgotten books he feels the pain at odd hours.

He is not disgraced, of this he is fairly sure, but he is disappointed. If he had known it would end this way, perhaps he would not have expended quite so much on those earlier books. *The Sorcerer* might have had a little more energy; at least he could have put some color in the backgrounds.

Ruthven is married to Sandra, his first and only wife. The marriage has lasted through thirty-one years and two daughters, one divorced, one divorced and remarried, both far from his home in the Southeast. At times Ruthven considers his marriage with astonishment: he does not quite know how he has been able to stay married so long granted the damages of his career, the distractions, the deadening, the slow and terrible resentment which has built within him over almost three decades of commercial writing. At other times, however, he feels that his marriage is the only aspect of his life (aside from science fiction itself), which has a unifying consistency. And only death will end it.

He accepts that now. Ruthven is aware of the lives of all his colleagues: the divorces, multiple marriages, disastrous affairs, two-and three-timing, bed-hopping at conventions; the few continuing marriages seem to be cover or mausoleum...but after considering his few alternatives Ruthven has nonetheless stayed married and the more active outrage of the earlier decades has receded. It all comes back to his insight: nothing matters. Hang on. If nothing makes any difference then it is easier to stay with Sandra by far. Also, she has a position of her own; it cannot have been marriage to a science fiction writer, which enticed her when they met so long ago. She has taken that and its outcome with moderate good cheer and has given him less trouble, he supposes, than she might. He has not shoved the adulteries and recrimination in her face but surely she knows of them; she is not stupid. And she is now married to a $79,000 a year, which is not inconsiderable. At least this is Ruthven's way of rationalizing the fact that he has had (he knows now) so much less from this marriage than he might have, that fact that being a writer has done irreparable damage to both of them. And the children. He dwells on this less than previously. His marriage, Ruthven thinks, is like science fiction writing itself: if there was a time to get out that time is past and now he would be worse off anywhere else. Who would read him? Where would he sell? What else could he do?

Unlike many of his colleagues, Ruthven had never had ambitions outside the field. Most of them had had literary pretentions, at least he had wanted to reach wider audiences, but Ruthven had never wanted anything else. To reproduce, first for his own pleasure and then for money, the stories of the forties *Astounding* which moved him seemed to be a sensible ambition. Later of course he did get serious about the category, wanting to make it anew and etc...but that was later. Much later. It seemed a noble thing in the fifties to want to be a science fiction writer and his career has given him all that he could have hoped for at fourteen. Or twenty-four.

He has seen what their larger hopes have done to so many of his peers who started out with him in the fifties, men of large gifts who in many cases had been blocked in every way in their attempts to leave science fiction, some becoming quite embittered, even dying for grief or spite, others accepting their condition at last only at the cost of self-hatred. Ruthven knows their despair, their self-loathing. The effects of his own seventy-three novels have set in, and of course there was a time when he took science fiction almost as seriously as the most serious...but that was *later*, he keeps on reminding himself, *after* breaking in, after publication in the better magazines, after dealing with the audience directly and learning (as he should of always known) that they were mostly a bunch of kids. His problems had come later but his colleagues, so many of them, had been ambitious from the start, which made matters more difficult for them.

But then, of course, others had come in without any designs at all and had stayed that way. And they too—those who were still checking into *Analog* or the Westercon—were just as miserable and filled with self-hatred as the ambitious, or as Ruthven himself had been a few years back. So perhaps it was the medium of science fiction itself that did this to you. He is not sure.

He thinks about things like this still...the manner in which the field seems to break down almost all of its writers. At one time he had started a book about this, called it *The Lies of Science Fiction*, and in that bad period around his fiftieth birthday had done three or four chapters, but he was more than enough of a professional to know that he could not sell it, was more than ready to put it away when *The Sorcerer* was revived. That had been a bad time to be sure; ten thousand words on *The Lies of Science Fiction* had been his output for almost two full years. If it had not been for a little residual income on his novels, a few anthology sales, the free-lance work he had picked up at the correspondence school and Sandra's occasional substitute teaching, things might have bottomed. At that it was a near thing, and his daughters' lives, although they were already out of the house, gave Sandra anguish.

Ruthven still shudders, thinking of the images of flight, which overcame him, images so palpable that often they would put him in his old Ford Galaxie, which he would drive sometimes almost a hundred miles to the state border before taking the U-turn and heading back. He had, after all, absolutely nowhere to go. He did not think that anyone who had ever known him except Sandra would put him up for more than two nights (Felicia and Carole lived with men in odd arrangements), and he never lived alone in his life. His parents were dead.

Now, however, things are better. He is able to produce a steady two thousand words a day almost without alcohol, his drinking now a ritualized half a pint of scotch before dinner and there are rumors of a larger movie deal pending if the purchaser of the first movie can be bought off a clause stupidly left in his contract giving him series rights. Ruthven will be guest of honor at the Cincinnati convention three years hence if the committee putting together the bid is successful. That would be a nice crown to his career at fifty-seven, he thinks, and if there is some bitterness in this— Ruthven is hardly self deluded—there is satisfaction as well. He has survived three decades as a writer in this country, and a science fiction writer at that, and when he thinks of his colleagues and the condition of so many with whom he started he can find at least a little self-respect. He is writing badly, *The Sorcerer* is hackwork, but he *is* still producing and making pretty big money and (the litany with which he gets up in the morning and goes to bed at night) nothing matters. Nothing at all. Survival is the coin of the realm. Time is a river with banks.

Now and then, usually during the late afternoon naps which are his custom (to pass the time quicker before the drinking, which is the center of his day), Ruthven is assaulted by old possibilities, old ambitions, old dread, visions of what he wanted to be and what science fiction did to him, but these are, as he reminds himself when he takes his first heavy one at five, only characteristic of middle age. Everyone feels this way. Architects shake with regret, doctors flee the reservation, men's hearts could break with desire and the mockery of circumstance. What has happened is not symptomatic of science fiction but of his age, his country. His condition. Ruthven tells that to himself, and on six ounces of scotch he is convinced, *convinced* that it is so, but as Sandra comes into the room to tell him that dinner is seven minutes away he thinks that someday he will have to get *The Lies of Science Fiction* out of his desk and look at it again. Maybe there was something in these pages beyond climacteric. Maybe he had better reconsider.

But for now the smells of roast fill the house, he must drink quickly to get down the half-pint in seven minutes, the fumes of scotch fills his breath, the scents and sounds of home fill all of the corridors and no introspection is worth it. None of it is worth the trouble. Because, Ruthven tells himself for the thirty-second time that day (although it is not he who is doing the counting) that nothing nothing nothing nothing nothing matters.

Back in the period of his depression when he was attempting to write *The Lies of Science Fiction* but mostly trying to space out his days around alcohol, enraged (and unanswerable) letters to his publishers about his out-of-print book and drives in his bald-tired Galaxie...back in that gray period as he drove furiously from supermarket to the state border to the liquor store, Ruthven surmised that he had hit upon some of the central deceptions which had wrecked him and reduced him and so many of his colleagues to this condition. To surmise was not to conquer, of course; he was as helpless as ever but there was a dim liberation in seeing how he had been lied to, and he felt that at least he could take one thing from the terrible years through which he had come: he was free of self-delusion.

Ruthven thought often of the decay of his colleagues, of the psychic and emotional fraying which seemed to set in between their fifth and fifteenth years of professional writing and reduced their personal lives and minds to rubble. Most were drunks, many lived in chaos, all of them in their work and persona seemed to show distress close to panic. One did not have to meet them at the conventions of hand out with them at the SFWA parties in New York to see that these were people whose lives where askew; the work showed it. Those who were not simply reconstructing or revising their old stories were working in new areas in which the old control had gone, the characters were merely filters for events or possessed of a central obsession, the plots lacked motivation or causality and seemed to deal with an ever more elaborate and less comprehended technology. Whether the ideas were old or new, they were half-baked, the novels were padded with irrelevant events and syntax, characters internalized purposelessly, false leads were pursued for thousands of words. The decay seemed to cut across all of the writers and their work; those that had been good seemed to suffer no less than the mediocre of worse, and there was hardly a science fiction writer of experience who was not—at least to Ruthven's antennae—displaying signs of mental illness.

The decay, Ruthven came to think, had to do with the very nature of the genre: the megalomaniacal, expansive visions being generated by writers who increasingly saw the disparity between *Spaceways* and their own hopeless condition. While the characters flourished and the science gleamed, the writers themselves were exposed to all of the abuses known to the litterateurs in America and—intelligent, even the dumbest of them, to a fault—they were no longer able to reconcile their personal lives with their vision: the vision became pale or demented. At a particular bleak time, Ruthven even came to speculate that science fiction writing was a form of illness which, like syphilis, might swim undetected in the blood for years but would eventually, untreated, strike to kill. The only treatment would be retirement, but most science fiction writers were incapable of writing anything else after a while and the form itself was addictive: it was as if every potential sexual partner carried venereal disease. You could stop screwing but only at enormous psychic or emotional cost, and *then* what? Regardless, that virus killed.

Later, as he began to emerge from this, Ruthven felt a little more sanguine about the genre. It might not *necessarily* destroy you to write it if you could find a little personal dignity and, more importantly, satisfaction outside the field. But the counsel of depression seemed to be the real truth: science fiction was aberrant and dangerous, seductive but particularly ill-suited to the maladjusted who were drawn to it, and if you stayed with it long enough, the warpage was permanent.

After all, wasn't science fiction for most of its audience an aspect of childhood they would outgrow?

This disparity between the megalomania and anonymity had been one of the causes of the decay in his colleagues, he decided. Another was the factor of truncation. Science fiction dealt with the sweep of time and space, the enormity of technological consequences in all eras, but as a practical necessity and for the sake of the editors all science fiction writers had to limit the genre and themselves as they wrote it. *True* science fiction as the intelligent editors knew (and the rest followed the smart ones) would not only be dangerous and threatening, it would be incomprehensible. How could twenty-fourth century life in the Antares system be depicted? How could the readership for an escape genre be led to understand what a black hole could be?

The *writers* could not understand any of this, let alone a young and gullible readership interested in the marvels that were to be made accessible. (Malzberg had been into aspects of this in his works but Ruthven felt that the man had missed the point: lurking behind Malzberg's schematics was the conviction that science fiction *should* be able to find a language for its design, but any penny-a-word stable hack for *Amazing* in the fifties knew better and Malzberg would have known better too if he had written science fiction before he went out to smash it.) So twenty-fourth century aliens in the Antares system would speak a colloquial Brooklynese, commanders of the Black Hole Explorer would long for their Ganymede Lady. The terrific would be made manageable, the awesome shaped by the exigencies of pulp fiction into the nearby. The universe would become Brooklyn with remote dangerous sections out in Bushwick or Greenpoint but plenty of familiar stops and safer neighborhoods.

The writers, awash in the market and struggling to live by their skills, would follow the editors and map out a universe to scale...but Ruthven speculated that the knowledge that they had drained their vision, grayed it for the sake of publication, had filled them first with disappointment and finally self-hatred: like Ruthven they had been caught early by the *idea* of science fiction—transcendence and complexity—and however far they had gone from there, they still felt at the base that this was a wondrous and expansive genre. Deliberately setting themselves against all for which the field had once stood could not have been easy for them. Rationalization would take the form of self-abuse: drink, divorce, obesity, sadism, in extreme cases penury, drugs or the outright cultivation of death. (Only H. Beam Piper had actually pulled the trigger on himself but that made him an honest man and a gun collector.) That was your science fiction writer, then, an ecclesiastic who had been first summoned from the high places and then dumped in the mud of Calvary to cast lots with the soldiers. All for a small advance.

That had been some of Ruthven's thinking, but then he had been very depressed. He had done a lot of reading and thinking about the male mid-life crisis. Sandra and he were barely dealing with one another; they lived within the form of marriage but not its substance (didn't everyone long married end that way?). His sexual panic, drinking, terror of death and sense of futility were more characteristic, perhaps, of the climacteric than of science fiction. The poor old field had taken a lot of blame over its lifetime (a lifetime, incidentally, exactly as long as Ruthven's: he had been born on April 12, 1926) for matters not of its own making, and once again was being blamed for pain it had not created. Maybe.

It wasn't science fiction alone which had put him in the ditch at late mid-life, Ruthven thought, any more than science fiction had been responsible for Hiroshima, Sputnik, the collapse of Apollo or the rotten movies of the nineteen-fifties which had first enticed and then driven the public away. The field had been innocent witness to much of these and the target of some but it was unfair to blame the genre for what seemed (at least according to the books he read) an inevitability in middle-class, middle-aged, male America.

It was ambivalence—the inability to fuse his more recondite perspective with the visceral, hateful feeling that science fiction had destroyed all of their lives—which stopped *The Lies of Science Fiction.* Ruthven does not kid himself: even if the contracts for *The Sorcerer* had not come in and his career turned around, he probably would have walked away from the book. Its unsaleability was a problem, but he knew that he might have sold it *somewhere*, an amateur press, and he had enough cachet in the field to place sections here and there in the fan magazines. It wouldn't have been much but it would have been more per diem that what Sandra was making or he from the correspondence school.

But he had not wanted to go on. His commitment, if anything, had been to stop. Ruthven, from the modest perspective of almost four years, can now admit that he was afraid to continue. He could not bear to follow it through to the places it might have taken him. At the worst, it might have demonstrated that his life, that all of their lives in science fiction, had been as the title said: a lie...a lie which would lead to nothing but its replications by younger writers, who in turn would learn the truth. The book might have done more than that: it could have made his personal life impossible. Under no circumstance would he have been able to write that book and live with Sandra...but the drives on the Interstate had made it coldly evident that he had nowhere else to go. If he were not a middle-aged, married science fiction writer, then what was he?

Oh, it was a good thing that *The Sorcerer* had come through and that he had gotten back to fiction. The novels were rotten but that was no problem: he didn't *want* to be good anymore, he just wanted to survive. Now and then Ruthven still drives the Interstate in his new Impala; now and then he is still driven from sleep to stare at the foreign editions...but he no longer stares in anguish or drives in fury; everything seems to have bottomed out. Science fiction can still do many things to him but it no longer has the capacity to deliver exquisite pain, and for this he is grateful.

Eventually someone else, perhaps one of the younger writers, *will* do *The Lies of Science Fiction* or something similar, but of this in his heart is Henry Martin Ruthven convinced: he will never read it. He may be dead. If not, he will stay clear. Science fiction now is only that means by which he is trying to hang on in the pointless universe and that which asks that he make anything more of it (what is there to make of it?) will have to check the next bar because Henry Martin Ruthven is finished. He knows the lies of science fiction, all right. But above all and just in time, he knows the truth of it too.

Ruthven attends the Cincinnati World Convention as guest of honor. At a party the first night in the aseptic and terrifying hotel he is surrounded by fans and committee, editors and colleagues, and it occurs to him that most of the people in these crowded rooms were not born when he sold his first story, "The Hawker," to *Worlds of If* on August 18, 1952. This realization fills him with terror: it is one thing to apprehend in isolation how long he has been around in this field and how far the field in its mad branching and expansion has gone from all of them who started in the fifties, but it is quite another to be confronted in terms that he cannot evade. Because his career has turned around in the decade, he is guest of honor, he is hardly ignored, but still—

Here and there in the packed three-room suite he sees people he knows, editors and writers and fans with whom he has been at conventions for years, but he cannot break out of his curious sense of isolation, and his conversations are distracted. Gossip about the business, congratulations on having survived to be a guest of honor, that sort of thing. Ruthven would almost prefer to be alone in his room or drinking quietly at the bar but that is obviously impossible. How can a guest of honor be alone on the first night of his convention? It would be, among other things, a commentary on science fiction itself and no one, least of all he, wants to face it.

None of his family are here. Felicia is no surprise: she is starting her second year of law school in Virginia and could not possible miss the important early classes; besides, they have had no relationship for years. Maybe never. Carole had said that she might be in from Oakland, would do what she could, but he has heard that kind of thing from Carole before and does not expect her. The second marriage is falling apart, he knows, Sandra will tell him that much, and Carole is hanging on desperately (he surmises) much as Ruthven himself hung on years ago when, however bad it might be, there was nothing else. He wishes that he could share this with Carole but of course it would be the finish of him. There are hundreds of sentences which said to the wrong people would end his marriage on the spot and that is another of them.

Sandra did want to be here but she is not. She has been feeling weak all year and now at last they have a diagnosis: she will have a hysterectomy soon. Knowing what being guest of honor meant to him Sandra had offered to go regardless, stay in the room if she could not socialize, but Ruthven had told her not to. He knew that she did not want to come, was afraid of the crowds and the hysteric pulse and was for the first time in her life truly afraid of dying. She is an innocent. She considers her own death only when she feels very ill.

Not so many years ago, being alone at a large convention, let alone as guest of honor, would have inflamed Ruthven. He would have manipulated his life desperately to get even a night away alone, a Labor Day weekend would have been redemption…but now he feels depressed. He can take no pleasure from the situation and how it occurred. He is afraid for Sandra and misses her a little too, wishes that his daughters, who have never understood him or his work, could have seen him just this once celebrated. But he is alone and he is beginning to feel that it is simply too late for adultery. He has had the opportunity now and then, made his luck, but well past fifty and into what he thinks of as leveling out, Ruthven has become resigned to feeling that what he should have done can be done no more—take the losses, the time is gone. There are women of all ages, appearance and potential here, many are alone, others are in casual attachments, many—even more than he might imagine, he suspects—available. But he will probably sleep alone all the nights of the convention, either sleep alone or end up standing in the hotel bar past four with old friends drinking and remembering the fifties. The desperation and necessity are gone: Sandra is not much, he accepts this, but she has given him all of which she is capable, which makes her flaws in this marriage less serious than Ruthven's because he could have given more. His failure comes from the decision, consciously, to deny. Perhaps it was the science fiction that shut him down. He just does not know.

Ruthven stands in the center of the large welcoming party, sipping scotch and conversing. He feels detached from the situation and from his own condition; he feels that if he were to close his eyes other voices would overwhelm him...the voices of all the other conventions. Increasingly he finds that he has more to hear from—and more to say to—the dead than to the living. Now with his eyes closed, rocking, it is as if Mark Clifton, Edmond Hamilton, Kuttner and Kornbluth are standing by him glasses in hand, looking at one another in commiseration and silence. There is really no need for any of them to speak. For a while none of them do.

Finally, Ruthven says as he has before, "It hurts, doesn't it? It hurts." Kuttner nods, Kornbluth raises a sardonic eyebrow. Mark Clifton shrugs. "It hurts," Clifton says, "oh it hurts all right, Henry. Look at the record." There seems nothing more to say. A woman in red who looks vaguely like Felicia touches his arm. Her eyes are solemn and intense. She has always wanted to meet him, she says; she loves his work. She tells Ruthven her name and that she is a high school English teacher in Boston.

"Thank you," he says. "I'm glad you like the books." Everybody nods. Hamilton smiles. "You might as well," Kornbluth says with a shrug. "I can't anymore and there's really nothing else." Ruthven shrugs. He tells the woman the next scotch is on him and more properly the committee. He walks her over to the bar. Her hand is in his. Quickly, oh so quickly, her hand is in his.

At eight-fifteen the next evening Ruthven delivers his guest-of-honor-speech. There are about three thousand in the large auditorium; convention attendance is just over ten thousand but thirty percent is not bad. Most attendees of modern world conventions are not serious readers now; they are movie fans or television fans or looking for a good time. Ruthven has thought for months about this speech and has worked on it painfully.

Once he thought—this was, of course, years ago—that if he were ever guest of honor at a major convention he would deliver a speech denunciatory of science fiction and what it did to it writers. Later, when he began to feel as implicated as anyone, the speech became less an attack than an elegy for the power and mystery that had been drained by bad writing and editing, debased by a juvenile audience. But after *The Lies of Science Fiction* had been put away and the edge of terror blunted, the very idea of the speech seemed childish. He was never going to be guest of honor and if he were, what right did he have to tell anyone anything? Science fiction was a private circumstance, individually perceived.

Nonetheless he had, when the time came to plan, considered the speech at length. What he decided to do, finally, was review his career in nostalgic terms, dropping in just enough humor to distract the audience from the thrust of his intention because after bringing his career up to date he wanted to share with them his conviction that it did not matter. Nothing mattered except that it had kept him around until the coincidence of *The Sorcerer* and *The Sorcerer* meant nothing except that Ruthven would not worry about money until he was dead. "Can't you see the overwhelming futility of it?" he would ask. "The Lies of Science Fiction" seemed a good title except that it would be printed in the convention book and be taken as a slap at the committee and indeed the very field which was doing him honor. Better to memorialize his book through the speech itself. Anyway, the title would have alerted the audience to the bitterness of his conclusion. He wanted to spring it on them.

So he had called it "Me and the Cosmos of Science Fiction." Harmless enough, and Ruthven delivers the first thirty-two minutes of his thirty-five minute address from the text and pretty much as he had imagined. Laughter is frequent; his anecdotes of Campbell, Gold, and Roger Elwood are much appreciated. There is applause when he speaks of the small triumph of the science fiction writer the day Apollo landed. "*We* did that," he remembers telling a friend, "at three cents a word." The audience applauds. They probably understand. This much, anyway.

Then, to his astonishment and disgust, Ruthven comes off the text and loses control. He has never hated himself so. Just as he is about to lift his head and explain coldly that none of it matters his voice falters and breaks. It has happened in the terrible arguments with Sandra in the old days and in the dreams with Kornbluth, Hamilton, Kuttner and Clifton, but never before in public, and Ruthven delivers the last paragraphs of his speech in a voice and from a mood he has never before known:

"We tried," he says. "I want you to know that, that even the worst of us, the most debased hack, the one-shot writer, the fifty-book series, all the hundreds and thousands of us who ever wrote a line of this stuff for publication: we tried. We tried desperately to say something because we were the only ones who could, and however halting our language, tuneless the song, it was ours.

"We wanted to celebrate, don't you see? We wanted to celebrate the insistent, circumstantial fact of the spirit itself, that wherever and in whatever form the spirit could yet sing amidst the engines of the night, that the engines could extinguish our lives but never our light, and that in the spaces between we could still thread the colors of substantiation. In childhood nights we felt it, later we lost it, but retrieval was always the goal, to get back there, to make it work, to justify ourselves to ourselves, to give the light against the light. We tried and failed; in a billion words we failed and failed again, but throughout was our prayer and somewhere in its center lived something else, the mystery and power of what might have been flickering.

"In these spaces, in all the partitions, hear our song. Let it be known that while given breath we sang until it drew the very breath from us and extinguish out light forever."

And then, in hopeless and helpless fury, Ruthven pushes aside the microphone and cries.

The Last of the Great Coffee Shop Philosophers
by
Koos Kombuis

July 4, 2184
Last lecture delivered from the podium of the Department of Philosophy of the Independent University of San Francisco.

Friends, academics, and fellow mutants, I address you today in my capacity of new Chairman of the Socratic Society, on the first, and probably the last, day of my tenure.

Thank you for electing me. Thank you for placing your trust in me. Thank you for accepting my intellectual credentials in spite of my outer deformities.

As you can see, I am one of the last of the old humans. Those of you who resemble me have become so rare that we are seen as "mutants," though, of course, we are not a new variation of species, but the last representatives on earth of a human life form that has been dominant for more than thirty-thousand years.

From my point of view, and from the point of view of those who resemble me, we, of course, are not mutants at all.

Permit me to explain the world as I see it. At the risk of being controversial, I want to enlighten you; I want to open your eyes to a perspective of our history that is rapidly becoming obsolete. In fact, this perspective has become so utterly unfashionable that this may very well be the last lecture of this sort ever to be delivered from this podium, or from any university podium, ever.

In the presumed words of Thomas Beckett, and with due apology to T.S. Eliot, who so eloquently dramatized the demise of that great man: "Death comes to us all, my lords."

I shall begin my lecture from a position of inaccuracy. I am thus making a declaration of ignorance, however painful it is for me, especially as newly elected Chairman of this prestigious Society, to admit to such a fallacy. Fortunately, I am by no means alone in my uncertainty.

I don't know—and I am not sure if anyone really knows—exactly when and where the change began. Some say it is a recent development; others believe that the evolution of man had already reached its pinnacle with the development of the large-brained, gentle-natured Neanderthals, who were shoved into extinction by the first competitive, patriarchal Cro-Magnons. Be that as it may, we can only now begin to see the bigger picture, in retrospect. We can only see the few of us who escaped the results of the latest massive reversion.

To describe the change as a "reversion" or, even better, a "regression," is an utterly discredited statement, I know. But bear with me for the moment, while I lead up to my central argument.

No one expected such a thing to happen, least of all the so-called *intelligentsia* of this great city—those like us—during those brave days when trade was strong and every quirk of nature could be rectified, more or less, by new technology.

When we ran out of fossil fuels, we created electrical cars, and eventually, we made hovercrafts. When antiquated methods of generating electricity failed, we switched to solar power, wind power, whatever we could lay our hands on. Global warming and climate change? It wasn't as dangerous as it was cracked up to be. It was based on mostly false predictions, like the Y2K scare at the turn of the twenty-first century

There had been solar flares, hurricanes, and earthquakes since the beginning of time, and, sure, the first half of the twenty-first century was a turbulent era in terms of the unexpected moods of Mother Nature, but, alas, the worst doomsday scenarios never came true! The Big San Francisco earthquake simply never arrived; though, God knows, there were enough of those elsewhere on the planet! Life went on, 2012 came and went, and nothing really terrible happened to the world. The Mayans and Nostradamus had been wrong after all.

Or so we thought.

And who could blame us for being at least cautiously optimistic about the future?

Even the one thing that had been our biggest collective headache—the radical Islam threat, the constant skirmishes, the guerrilla warfare, and the fear of the Bomb—sort of began balancing itself out by the latter half of the twenty-first century. After the fall of China and the successful counter-revolution in Iran, the fundamentalists lost steam, exactly as P.J. O'Rourke had predicted! That was more or less the time when Islamic youth discovered Internet pornography, tight-fitting jeans, and hip-hop music. Their conservative elders had no effective weapon against the successful imperialism of Narcissism coming from the West.

By the year 2084, a new World Order had more or less established itself. The Universal Rule of the Individual had arrived, supposedly for the first time in the history of the race called man. Countries were run like private companies; politics had been abolished. Consensus by e-mail and virtual clicks had taken the place of voting. All corporate decisions were based on supply and demand.

True enough, literacy had suffered a heavy blow, and an alarming number of young people could hardly read or write properly. They only understood SMS language and had never heard of Dostoevsky, Shakespeare, or even Nabokov. But hunger had been abolished, many broken cities had been rebuilt, and, as for the many species of animals that had been destroyed by large-scale entrepreneurship and engineering projects, who cared? Generic foods took the place of original products, and, after a while, nobody could remember what real steaks were supposed to taste like.

By the turn of the next century, the beeps and buzzes of electronics had very much replaced the sound of birdsong in the morning, but hardly anyone noticed.

The first time we felt cause for collective alarm was in the year 2112, when the first wave of human babies were born inexplicably covered with full-body fur and sporting short, ape-like tails. This was the first generation of children who were unable to speak in full sentences, who merely grunted and rummaged for free food in the countless malls of the New World.

They could handle remote controls, and most of them had a savant-like grasp of everything relating to IT software, but as for "normal" human interaction, an understanding seemed to be strangely absent. They completely lacked social skills and logical coherence, lived only for the moment's instant gratification, and had the psychological profiles of low-level psychopaths.

The press, oddly enough, downplayed the phenomenon. After all, the diagnosis of "psychopath" had been abandoned decades before as being discriminatory and patronizing. Since the 2050s, when psychiatry had become almost exclusively a field for chemical research and commerce, the concepts of "morality" and "personal responsibility" had been eroded for so long that such ideas were, academically speaking, extinct, and therefore meaningless. There was no concept of "free will." The only real choices left to the individual had mostly to do with what to wear, what channel to watch, or which holographic personality to adopt in the various new 3D simulation games.

Which meant that when the proverbial battery chickens finally came home to roost—pardon my sarcasm—and mankind lost its collective conscience, the intellectuals of the day had no way to aptly label the phenomenon. And, because no word existed to describe the disease, it was not recognized as one.

But more problems were to come. If only we realized, way back then, during the early twenty-second century, how incredibly fast the process of reverse evolution would occur! For those of us who believed, perhaps mistakenly, that twenty-first century urban *homo sapiens* represented the highest rung of the ladder ever reached, the sudden fall from grace was simply too much to comprehend. To think that it had taken mankind millennia to scale the heights of civilization, only to glide back down into the jungle within the scope of a generation or two!

Perhaps it had something to do with inertia, the attraction of chaos, or genes taking the easy way out during the shortest time possible. Whatever the real cause, it was possible that we were guilty of setting off this process ourselves. Then again, it might not have been our own fault at all; it might have been an inevitable decline after evolution had reached its peak. What if evolution was never supposed to go in one direction only, but instead swing back and forth like a giant pendulum?

Oh, we'd always assumed we'd go on forever, getting cleverer and cleverer, smarter and smarter, brainier and brainier. And of course, we'd always been afraid of many things along the way. We were afraid of war and economic meltdown and losing our grip on ecology and all the normal stuff, but never this; not even Darwin had seen this coming, though he had predicted the first cycle of the process quite nicely, thank you.

Now, we are no longer certain of anything, and, in the face of new evidence, Darwinism has become as obsolete as the laws of Newton when faced with the discoveries of Einstein and the paradoxes of quantum physics.

It is now the year 2184, and very few of us are left. By "us," I mean human beings, normal human beings, as the idea was understood in, say, in the year 2000. And, needless to say, we have become outcasts of our race, the vanishing eccentrics, the last true thinkers, the last of the book readers, the last talkers and thinkers, the last of the great San Francisco coffee shop philosophers—ha! Yes, even they are virtually extinct! We are the marginalized few, the ones reduced to standing on the sidelines and watching the rest devour each other and, ultimately, us.

Our cities have been turned into jungles. But not like the jungles in the old sense of the word, with abundantly growing creepers and strange looking carnivores and bug-infested swamps. Ha—there's hardly any greenery left! But oh, look closely, and you will see that these cities are jungles nevertheless.

Though the restaurants might serve edible meals, the hovercraft lines and underground trains all run on time, the hospitals are clean and efficient in the care of well-trained robotic medical staff, and automation takes care of all the day-to-day running of the cogs of this mighty machine called Modernity, the beneficiaries of this vast array of mechanical service delivery are nothing but a bunch of unappreciative, selfish, dumb apes who, if left to their own devices, would be even more helpless than their prehistoric ancestors. At least prehistoric man knew how to make fires and design their own wheels! These modern hairy specimens, with their heavy brows and low skulls, are only adept at pushing buttons and experiencing cheap thrills.

It has come to this. The beast slouching toward Bethlehem to be born has at last been born and is standing in front of us, fully grown, in all his vulgarity and loathsomeness. No longer do the monsters inside our own psyche haunt mankind. The monsters are plain for all to see. With their prominent noses and flared nostrils, vacant eyes, swaggering gait, and wagging tails, these new hairy mammals, these descendants of Adam and Eve and Charlie Chaplin and Hitler and Picasso and Mother Teresa and Mugabe and Jesus and Stalin are the physical embodiment of everything we have already spiritually become.

If one can call it "everything." I prefer the word "nothing," for we have indeed become nothing. We strode into the abyss and the abyss became us. We reached for the voids of outer space, and fell into a greater void. We are the Last Generation. The center cannot hold for much longer.

Once the machines run down, chaos will ensue, and the world will become a dark and random place once again, with shadows skulking in corners and man devouring man for flesh, gratification and brute survival. But this is what they are already doing.

This is the Final Genocide. This is the Collective Suicide of our species.

I know that many of the statements I have made here this afternoon will be seen as some kind of intellectual blasphemy by most—by many—of my fellow philosophers and scientists. Already, some of you have started reporting me, talking in low whispers into your mobile phones. I know that as this lecture is being streamed live onto the World Wide Holographic Web, it is being analyzed and scrutinized by the last corrupt judges in charge of our decadent and crumbling legal system.

During this lecture I have been guilty of hate speech, of inflammatory inter-species sentiments—the modern equivalent of racism—and I have belittled and insulted the apes. This is probably the most politically incorrect lecture ever to be delivered from this lectern, in this or any university. But, God help me, the things I said here today simply had to be said.

It's no use barricading the windows and doors. They are coming. Outside this staid old building, the sea and the rusting, unused Bay Bridge lie glistening as always in the bright midday sun. The last innocent mutant families of holidaymakers may visit the countless confectionary stalls along the proud old beachfront to buy soft drinks and ice cream for their ape-like offspring. Nothing will prevent them from coming. They have no shame, no respect, no dignity, and they are not even aware of the importance of this date to the American people. They are coming, in all their simplicity and one-dimensionality, to destroy me. I am the new enemy. By my statements, I have undermined their freedom. And their freedom is incompatible with my freedom of speech.

I can already hear their grunts and monosyllabic squeals. We are outnumbered. The enemy is stronger than us. I can hear their paws scraping across the tiles of the foyer; I can see the bloodthirsty hunger in their eyes. We are done for, myself, and all of you, my so-called fellow "mutants," who have listened to these arguments without interrupting me.

Here I stand, a lone rebel against the inexplicable follies of evolution, representative of the last of a dying race, personal ambassador of the most ingenious, brave, and resourceful breed in the known universe.

Thank you for listening. I shall have my last drink now, for I am thirsty.

Short pause as the speaker takes a sip of cold Starbucks coffee from a plastic container, and remains standing, gazing upward through the skylight at the clear blue sky.

And now I shall surrender myself to the inevitable.

Into the hands of Socrates, I commend my spirit.

Last Call
by
Mark Edwards

I.

Ginny had woken to a giant vision of her face, sallow, jaundiced about the eyes, lips dried and cracked; a mummified version of her self. One of the nurses must have thrown the wrong switch and called up the camera that monitored her, as they did with her charts from time to time. It had been bad enough to read such things as "cirrhosis" and "expected: terminal outcome" on the wall in letters a foot high. The sight of her ravaged face had brought on a seizure.

Ginny kept her eyes closed most of the time. Even when her lawyers, now just two serious mellifluous voices, told her that they had lost her appeal, and it was unlikely that they would be able to appeal again in time for her to survive. They told her that they still had some of the public on her side, and that the press was turning her demise into a major story so maybe something could be done on that front …

Ginny just nodded and counted down in her head the moments to her next Vicodin patch, as she had for weeks.

II.

"I can't watch the face protests anymore," said Evelyn Mars to her husband Darcy. "The crowds all look alike. It's a horror movie." She hit the touchscreen and the set went blank. "You'd think they would be happy to just be alive."

Darcy just grunted a response, still on his handset, still working, and Evelyn found it strange to watch the new, smaller fingers jump over the keys with the old dexterity. He had opted to port into a new body at forty, ten years and two hundred thousand dollars sooner than was usual, and had gone for the risky, but now trendy, option of changing genders. Dan was now Darcy, and though Evelyn had to admit that Darcy was beautiful – she had helped him choose the body after all—she missed Dan's general Dan-ness. Over the past few months she had missed his penis as well.

"Maybe the protests remind you that you're due for a port," Darcy said.

"I haven't worn out this bod yet," Evelyn said. Since his change, he'd been after her to port as well.

Evelyn was on her second body, a body she had ported into thirty years before when there were few choices and when she couldn't afford the more expensive ones. She refused to call it skinfare as some did—the new body may have been government issue, but the one she had left behind had been growing a tumor the size of a cantaloupe. The mature look became a trademark for her in the PR business; the best hack in the country who was nearly eighty and looked fifty. It actually gave her an edge in meetings with clients and colleagues. Her crow's feet and graying hair were a suggestion of authority in a room filled with smooth, youthful faces.

Her reasons for not jumping to a new body, when even the poor were allowed to at age forty and every two decades after, were unclear even to her. She suspected that she was grateful to the new body for saving her life and somehow owed *it* longevity.

Darcy turned the wall back on. The camera finished another sweep over the crowd in the Mall, the capitol building looming in the background, the tens of thousands of similar bodies and faces milling about. The announcer was winding up, "... and unlike in '56, so far these rallies have been peaceful, and the face protests have not become face riots."

"I swear that a third of them have your bod," Darcy said.

"It's a robust model—they've been using it for decades," Evelyn said, wondering if she sounded defensive.

The screen changed, a familiar shot of the gray, multi-windowed face of Yale Medical Center's Transport-Transplant Hospital. A reporter stood in the rain and intoned seriously at the camera, a crowd behind him, very much like the one at the mall, just smaller and wetter.

"I can't believe that they won't give that poor girl another chance," Darcy said. "They give illegal immigrants new bodies, for Christ's sake. So she likes to party."

Evelyn wondered, not for the first time, if Darcy had also lost some IQ points during his transport. Or perhaps his forty-year-old mind was being taken over by the bod that looked like a twenty-year-old's. "She's destroyed three bodies. Thousands and thousands in free medical treatment each time. Well, not free. We pay for it." Evelyn took the remote and turned off the sound, "I'd rather have immigrants get the chance than someone who wastes it."

Darcy turned to her and Evelyn knew they were in for another fight. Her handset beeped.

III.

"What's going on?" Ginny asked. She had opened her eyes to slits to watch the nurse fuss about. She also saw the short, stocky woman put the packet of Vicodin patches in her left side pocket after applying one to Ginny's hip. There was a sound coming from the window, like a distant chorus.

"You've caused a stir Ginny. They're out there protesting that you lost your appeal. Those people want you to get a new body."

Ginny smiled. "Well, nice to have friends. Think any of them will bring me a bottle of Jack Daniels."

"Might as well kill you now," the nurse said.

Ginny couldn't remember her name. She had stopped trying a few weeks back when she'd been riding the DTs. She grabbed the woman by the wrist. "I want to see. Help me sit up." Ginny pulled herself half upright.

"Easy," the nurse said, holding her down. She was strong like the rest of her tribe. "There's no way we're going to get you over to that window. I can turn on the screen if you want to see it on the news."

Ginny held her for a moment, a near hug, and then settled back. "I bet a bunch of them are face protestors. Trying to get the government to give them sexier bods."

"My two sisters and a cousin all have the same bods," the nurse said. "Makes family picnics confusing for the kids. It would be nice if they had some more variety by the time I'm up for my first port." The nurse stopped talking and looked at Ginny. "Sorry hon, forgot who I was talking to."

Ginny held her eyes for a moment, and then closed her own. "Hell lady, anything they give you will be an improvement over that dumpy ass of yours."

There was a pause and she heard the nurse clatter out of the room. Ginny waited ten minutes, and then took the packet of patches that she'd lifted from the woman's pocket out from under the blankets. Her fingers counted eight of them, and she wondered if she could get them all on her skin before passing out.

IV.

"Mrs. Mars, we'd like to hire you," said the Surgeon General.

Evelyn had retreated to her office, leaving Darcy with the set and the protests. She'd been called by a secretary who had bumped her up to another secretary and then to the SG's personal secretary who had turned her over to the Surgeon General himself.

"This is a tough case for all of us Mrs. Mars. We've got a public that wants changes in our Corporal Replacement policies, and they're latching on to this Ginny Fargo case."

Evelyn had learned that many times when creating spin, it was often best to cut to the simplest solution, "Then my advice would be to give that girl a new body. Now, no matter the cost. I'll text you my bill tonight."

There was a pause on the Washington D.C. side of the line. He must have decided he was kidding, because he laughed.

"We would like to, believe me, we would. This administration is not without compassion. But the law is the law, and to change it would be dangerous precedent. I don't know how well you know history, Mrs. Mars, and not to patronize you, but we can't begin to make a special case for an addict, after doing so much to remove them from society."

Evelyn knew. Centuries of crisis, brought about by those who could not escape chemistry, could not manage to exist without harming others while chemically altered or to feed their need. Tens to hundreds of thousands of murders and rapes each year and thousands left dead on the road by drunk drivers. Spouses and children abused. Addicts in government and the military undermining their duty with the bottle, the pill, the needle.

Some historians had even pointed to addiction's contribution to genocide—Hitler was an Amphetamine addict, Pol Pot a heroine user ... the list went back into history, all the way to the drunken warmonger Alexander.

The U.S. was a better place after the purge. It was best not to think of the time of the camps, the banishments, or the sterilization of any who had shown signs of addiction.

In two centuries addiction had been basically bred out. Except for the rare throwback such as Ginny.

"Sir, I agree, in principle, but in reality, letting this woman die when a new bod can save her is going to look bad no matter what you do."

"Not if she absolves us. On camera."

"How do you expect to get her to do that?"

"You will convince her."

V.

"Remember me, Ginny?"

She felt absolutely awful, worse than she had in months. She suspected they'd used adrenaline or something to pull her back from the Vicodin coma. But she knew the voice. She opened her voice to see the sad gray eyes and the white hair.

"Bill W. the 405th, isn't it?"

"Bill W. the four hundred and eighth actually, my dear," Bill said.

"What's your real name?" Ginny asked. "I always wondered."

"Once a leader assumes the mantel of Bill, his past name no longer matters. Only the steps matter."

"Oh right," she said. I'm dying, and now this. "Let me see what were they? Oh yeah. Imagine me telling you twelve different ways to go screw yourself."

His benign expressing did not change.

"And you know where you can stick your Higher Power too. Isn't it illegal for you to be in the U.S.?" she asked.

"I've come under the protection of the Canadian ambassador. He seems to have convinced your president that I can take you back to the Ottowa A.A. colony. I have hopes as well."

"Even though I checked myself out?"

"Even so," Bill said. He pulled a chair closer to her bed, sat, and took her hand. "If we can get you to promise to come to the colony, and if we can get you back to Canada alive, we'll give you a new bod there. You'd just have to stay in the colony permanently."

"So death, or the rest of my life surrounded by all of you twelve step types? No booze?"

"I'm afraid not. But you could help others. And we're not such bad sorts." He held her hand in both of his. "I know you tried to kill yourself last night. You don't have to do that. There is a good life beyond this disease."

"Do you like holding my hand?"

"What?"

"You did that with all the women at the colony. You know what they called you? A thirteenth stepper. Trying to make all of the people you were supposed to be counseling."

He dropped her hand, and stood up. His face was still composed, but his posture had changed. "If you're willing to listen to silly rumors…"

"Hell, at least you're interesting. The rest of you bastards just want to tell war stories about your drinking and drugging." She closed here eyes again, exhausted. "You're a bunch of sad, sick, bores, you know that?"

"Ginny…"

"Go Bill W the four hundred and sixth, or whatever you are. Try not to cry on the plane about what a great opportunity you missed for the program, what a great public relations coup. Go before I puke on you."

He started to speak again, and then she really did begin vomiting.

VI.

"I actually wasn't trying to kill myself," she told Evelyn. "I was just trying to get well and truly high. This dying thing is boring."

Evelyn nodded. She had opened up the curtain a bit, hoping that the sunlight would get Ginny to open her eyes for more than a moment or two at a time. She regretted it when she saw Ginny's face.

"So what do they want you to do?"

"I'm a Public Relations pro, Ginny. One of the best. They thought I could convince you to say some things that let the government off of the hook."

Ginny laughed, a sad sandpapery sound. "Did they pick you because we have the same bod?"

Evelyn was startled. That was why Ginny's state was so compelling. It was her, in her current bod, but drink ravaged and old before it's time. Ginny at thirty-two looked like she was ninety. Evelyn at seventy looked twenty years younger. "I hadn't thought of that. But yes, probably. Maybe they thought you'd have more empathy."

"Do you know about Mozart?" Ginny asked.

"Yes," Evelyn said.

"And Hemingway and Joyce and Burroughs and Van Gogh and Jimi Hendrix and all the other geniuses who were addicts?

What happened to those sort of people? What are we missing since we kicked and bred them out?"

"We seem to be doing ok without them. Do you have any talent, Ginny?"

"No." The dry laugh again. "Except holding my liquor."

"Well, maybe we're talking about exceptions then."

Ginny's eyes were wide open and wet, "But I never hurt anyone, either."

"I would guess not."

"Are there still protestors outside?"

"There were when I came in," Evelyn said. "So, will you make a statement on camera? Maybe about how you made your own choices. That seems to be the truth."

Ginny nodded. "Tomorrow. I need to rest now. Tomorrow, since it has to be soon. The doctors say that toxins are reaching my brain, because my liver is failing. I may not have long where I can think straight."

Evelyn turned to leave. At the door she turned, "Tell me. You wore out three bodies. Was any of it worth it?"

Ginny sighed. "There were moments. I can definitely say that."

VII.

They had told her at the twelve-step colony that addicts lie. So she'd done it one more time.

Everyone had always wanted something from her, and she'd just wanted be left alone with the bliss of ethanol. Was that so hard to understand?

In the hour after 3:00 a.m. there was only one nurse on in the ward, and she was addicted to some sort of computer solitaire. Ginny had found that if she was really quiet, she could get up and explore the shelves in her room and the next and the supply closet one door down. And the meds weren't locked up, because no one was an addict anymore.

She pulled her stash from her mattress. A bottle with six Oxycontin. Four Vicodin patches. Eight morphine patches. And best of all, some doctor or nurse's private stash, or the leftover from a celebration, a bottle of single malt with at least two shots left in it.

She would start with the drink first, so as not to fade out before the burn hit her stomach and mind. And then the patches and then the pills. One last drink, one last party—she was the last of her kind and she deserved it.

Author Biographies

Visit our website to learn more about the writers, including what their favorite book is, and why SF is important to them.

Mark Brandon Allen, England, his work has appeared in *Demon Minds Anthology, The 5th D, Pedestal Magazine, Sciphi Journal* and *Everyday Weirdness, Matters Most Extraordinary,* and *Sounds of the Night.*

Lane Ashfeldt lives in London, England. Awards for her fiction include the Fish Short Histories Prize, a Hawthornden Fellowship. Her story *Snowmelt* was short listed for the Jane Austen Short Story Award. Her stories have appeared in raucous *Punk Fiction* and *Dancing With Mr. Darcy.* www.ashfeldt.com.

Hilaire Belloc was an English writer during the early twentieth century. A political thinker and historian, he published several novels, including *Mr. Clutterbuck's Election*, 1908, and the *History of England*, 1915.

Ray Bradbury is a veteran writer with numerous award and publications. His novel *Fahrenheit 451* is a classic novel still read in high schools across America. Bradbury used a typewriter at school to compose the book, night after night, and sent it off to a publisher for instant success.

Samantha Boyette lives and works in the Finger Lakes region of New York State. Her novel *Prime* is a finalist in the Textnovel.com book award. This is her first published piece, but she has been writing in her free time for years: samanthaboyette.com

Kodilynn Calhoun lives in Northeastern Indiana, and is an avid reader and writer of sci-fi and fantasy. You can contact her at http://foreverthunder.blogspot.com.

C. J. Cherryh writes both fantasy and sci-fi with over sixty novels to her credit, including *Hammerfall* and *The Chanur Saga*. She holds numerous awards, including the Hugo and Nebula for her novel, *The Faded Sun*. www.cherryh.com.

Jaleta Clegg is the author of *Nexus Point*. She lives in Utah with her husband, a horde of children, and an ancient toothless cat. Her day job involves school children, starship simulators, and an inflatable planetarium. www.jaletac.com.

Liz Coley, Ohio, was hooked on science fiction at an early age thanks to alien Tripods, spacetime warping tesseracts, and a martian maid named, Thuvia. Her credits include Immortals, in *Cosmos #32*, Messiah, in *FlashMe*, and The Final Gift, in *Strange Worlds Anthology*. www.lizcoley.com.

Cassandra Consiglio, attends third grade in Montclaire Heights, New Jersey. She lives with her mother, father, and dog, Yodel. She likes karate, soccer, video games, and writing poems.

Alicia Curtis lives in Atlanta, GA, with a divining cat and a pair of guppies. Alicia will try to convince you she's from the future. She may actually be. You can find more of her work at arthearth.blogspot.com.

Michael D. C. Drout is Professor of English and Chair of the English Department at Wheaton College, Mass., where he teaches Old English, Middle English, medieval literature, fantasy, science fiction and writing. Drout's scholarship is focused on tenth-century English literature and culture, meme-based theories of culture, computational stylistics, and the works of J. R. R. Tolkien. His website is michaeldrout.com.

John Dudek is an English graduate of Univ. of Hartford. He was named one of Connecticut's Student Poets for 2009-2010. He is the recipient of the *Phyllis Abrahm's Award for Poetry*. His poems have been published in *Aerie* and *Connecticut Review*. http://hotlungs.blogspot.com.

Mark Edwards writes stories and plays, directs occasional theatre, and teaches various media studies course at Sacred Heart University in Fairfield, CT. He has an MA in communication arts from New York University and an MFA in creative writing from Lesley University. His play, "Ladies in Hats," was performed at the Boston Theatre Marathon in May of 2010, and his story, "The Man Who Shot Bigfoot," is forthcoming in *Space and Time Magazine.*

Jacquelyn Fedyk resides in the mysterious town of North Bend, Washington. When not writing for her blog or with her writing group, *SnoValley Writes,* she enjoys playing ukulele with her band *The Little Black Bottles* and illustrating her friend's online steampunk serial, *Martius Catalyst.* www.jacquelynfedyk.wordpress.com.

Jack Frey is a Canadian who currently lives in Beijing, China with his wife and two young boys. His work has appeared in *Shelf Life Magazine, Writers' Bloc* (Rutgers), *Fractured West,* and *Anemone Sidecar.* He has published scholarly work as well. He is completing his first novel. jackfrey.wordpress.com.

Robert Frost was an American poet that wrote of the simplicity of New England life and winner of four Pulitzer Prizes of Poetry.

Koos Kombuis is a novelist and folk singer who works from his home base in Cape Town, South Africa. Previously very active in the struggle against apartheid, he is now increasingly turning his attention to science fiction and fantasy.

D. H. Lawrence was an English author, poet, and playwright. He is known for his outspoken angst against industrialization, as well as his novels, "Lady Chatterley's Lover," and "Sons and Lovers."

Murray Leeder is the author of *Plague of Ice* and *Son of Thunder* for Wizards of the Coast and over twenty published short stories. He holds a Ph.D. at Carleton University in Ottawa, and has published in the *Canadian Journal of Film Studies*, and the *Irish Journal of Gothic and Horror Studies.* murray.leeder@nucleus.com.

Jack London is an American author know for his books *The Call of the Wild and White Fang.* His story *The Scarlet Plague* was published in 1915, three years before the Flu Pandemic of 1918-1919 began.

Jeffery Ryan Long graduated from the Univ. of Hawaii and spent two years in Ukraine as a Peace Corps Volunteer. Jeff has purchased a ticket to Venice, Italy, resigned from his office job, and will spend the next three months writing or failing at it.

Barry N. Malzberg is a sci-fi writer with numerous credits and award, including the Hugo and Locus. Many of his novels deal with US space exploration like *The Falling Astronauts, 1971 and Beyond Apollo.* He served as an editor for various publications, including *Amazing Stories,* and is an accomplished violinist.

George Moore teaches literature at the University of Colorado. His poetry has been published in *The Atlantic, Poetry, North American Review, Colorado Review.* He was nominated for the *Rhysling Poetry Prize,* and two Pushcart Prizes. His collections are *Headhunting and All Night Card Game in the Back Room of Time.*

Edgar Allen Poe, in Boston. He lived in Virginia, Baltimore, London, and NYC. He served in US Army, and is best known for his tales of the macabre and horror, like *The Raven, & Pit and the Pendulum.* Poe is also considered a founding father of sci-fi.

André Saglio, also known as Jacques Drésa, (1869-1929), was a French painter, curator, art historian and Minister of Fine Arts.
Michael Shreve is a translator currently living in Paris, France. His publications include works by Jean Meslier, John Antoine Nau and André Laurie among others. He can be found on the web at www.michaelshreve.wordpress.com

Nicholas Samaras won The Yale Series of Younger Poets Award with his first book, *Hands of the Saddlemaker.* He lives in New York and teaches in Westchester County at the Charles Xavier School for Gifted Youngsters.

Caitlin Kenzie Scott is a published poet, and named one of Connecticut's Student Poets for 2009-2010. She is a graduate of Connecticut College and currently pursing an MA in Religion from The Yale Divinity School.

Dr. Janelle A. Schwartz is Assistant Professor of English & Environmental Studies at Loyola University New Orleans. Her forthcoming book is *Worm Work: 18th Century Natural History & Romantic Aesthetic Frontiers* (Univ. Minnesota Press, 2011).
Percy Shelley, England, husband to Mary Shelley, was a poet that suffered a tragic death in a sailing accident in the early 1820s. He's M. Shelley's inspiration as she writes *The Last Man.*

Darryll B. Snyder, Maryland, is a retired United States Navy Veteran, who spends his time writing science fiction. He lives with wife, dog and cat.

M Sullivan is a writer, storyteller, nurse, poppa, and husband based in Richmond, VA. He's fallen in with all sorts of alien crowds and is happy to have found a whole gaggle of corner-dwellers in his travels. www.msullivantales.com.

Mark Taylor is an author of Science Fiction and Dark Fiction. He lives in Kent, in the South East of England, and can be found at filingwords.blogspot.com.

Sara Teasdale published her first poem in 1907. She went on to win the Pulitzer Prize in Poetry in 1918. Her poem, "There Will Come Soft Rains," was the inspiration for Ray Bradbury's story, of the same name.

H. G. Wells, England, the author of such classic science fiction stories as *The Time Machine* and *War of the Worlds.* His novels focused on the future & how it would affect humankind. He was especially concerned with overcrowding, pollution, & the rapid rise of technology & scientific knowledge.

Big Jim Williams, California, is the author of *The Old West* and *Tall Tales of the Old West* books, has written for *Western Horseman, Shoot!, Livestock Weekly, Radio World, Writer's Journal, Cadroom Poker News* and *Snipits.* bigjimwilliams2@cox.net.

Aaron M. Wilson lives in Minnesota where he attempts to understand life, others (including his two cats—one good and one bad), himself, and especially his wife—in that order. He earned his M.F.A in Writing from Hamline University. www.soullessmachine.com.

Alexandra Wolfe, Canada, is the publishing editor of *Kissed by Venus* and the *Wry Writer*, as well as the founding member of the speculative fiction writer's group, the Hive Mind. Her fiction has appeared in numerous venues including, *Odyssey, Flights of Fancy, Quantum Edge,* and *Quark's News.* alexwolfe.ca

William Wood lives with his wife and children in the mountains of Virginia in an old farmhouse turned backwards to the road. His work has appeared in *M-Brane SF/Hadley Rille Books, Library of the Living Dead, Black Matrix Publishing, Northern Frights Publishing,* and more.
writebrane.blogspot.com.

Acknowledgements

The editor would like to thank the following people without whom this collection would not be possible:

Lee Robin for slaying dragons.

Ray Bradbury, Michael D. C. Drout, C. J. Cherryh, Barry N. Malzberg for their contributions and mastery. To each and every writer.

Alexandra Wolfe, graphic designer, for inspiration, community, artistic integrity, and more. (*If you like the cover art for the LMA, please consider Ms. Wolfe for your next project.* alexwolfe.ca)

John Dudek, poetry editor, for his insight into poetry, the road, and for believing in the art of the individual.

Cheri Woods-Edwin for marketing and promotions assistance, as well as consultant work.

To Cheryl Lawtone Malone and Erica Solari, fiction editors and proofreaders, for their steadfast, pointed, and speedy editorial work. They are Wizard's Elves.

To Thomas Cleaves and Pinar Ozturk for additional support. More secret elves.

Proofreaders: Lisa Johnson, Seb Parker, Heidi Parton, Kelly A. McGuire, Candice Peaslee, Caleb J. Schultz.

Readers: Sci-Fi Saturday Night Broadcast team and many Broad Universe members, and many other secret elves.

A special dedication to you—(*yes, you with the book in your hands*)—our community of readers and writers. We welcome you into our guild and thoroughly hope you enjoy our humble efforts.

About the Editor:

Hunter Liguore is the editor of the *Last Man Anthology: Tales of Catastrophe, Disaster, and Woe*. She holds a BA in history and is completing her MFA in creative writing from Lesley University. Her work has appeared most recently in *Bellevue Literary Review* (Katie Ireland) and *The MacGuffin* (The Last Soucouyant). Her short story, "Red Barn People," was nominated for the 2010 Pushcart Prize. She hosts a blog dedicated to her writing odyssey, a journey around the world in thirty countries and thirty genres.
www.theworldinthirtystories.com

About Sword & Saga Press:

At Sword & Saga Press our commitment is to our readers. Besides sourcing works of fiction from across the globe, we offer a place to talk books. We think of our press as the coliseum, the open fire, the desert range, the place to connect you with fiction that resonates a sense of nostalgia for the old days, while at the same time offering a view of the future.

www.ingramcontent.com/pod-product-compliance
Lightning Source LLC
LaVergne TN
LVHW091038080826
845145LV00002B/545

9780615385051